MY SISTER'S KEEPER

Also by Shirley Lord

Golden Hill
One of My Very Best Friends
Faces

MY SISTER'S KEEPER

SHIRLEY LORD

CROWN PUBLISHERS, INC.
NEW YORK

Published by Crown Publishers, Inc., 201 East 50th Street, New York, New York 10022. Member of the Crown Publishing Group.

Random House, Inc. New York, Toronto, London, Sydney, Auckland

CROWN is a trademark of Crown Publishers, Inc.

Manufactured in the U.S.A.

Design by James K. Davis

Library of Congress Cataloging-in-Publication Data
Lord, Shirley
   My sister's keeper / Shirley Lord.
      p.   cm.
   1. Cosmetics industry—New York (N.Y.)—Fiction. 2. Women—New York (N.Y.)—Crimes against—Fiction. 3. Women in business—New York (N.Y.)—Fiction. I. Title.
PR6062.0724M9   1993
823'.914—dc20   93-22939
                                                                                                 CIP

ISBN 0-517-582716

10 9 8 7 6 5 4 3 2 1

First Edition

To
A.M.R.

Acknowledgments

My thanks to James Tregar for corroborating facts from the past in his *People's Chronology* (Holt, Rinehart & Winston); to Tad Szulc for his wise guide to postwar Europe in *Then and Now* (William Morrow), and to the authors Iris Gioia and Clifford Thurlow for their vivid *Brief Spring, A Journey Through Eastern Europe* (Alan Sutton); to the much missed Patrick O'Higgins for memories we shared about Helena Rubinstein in *Madame* (Viking); and to G-3 pilots Chuck Coates and Jack Mullen for checking my aeronautical facts.

My thanks also to my husband, A.M. Rosenthal, for his weekly encouragement and advice; to Cherry and Peter Barker for their constant welcome to their exquisite home in Wiltshire, England, where I wrote so many chapters of this book; to Owen Laster and Betty Prashker for their unerring suggestions; and last, but certainly not least, to Nicole Tysowsky and to Laurice A. Parkin for their help with the word processor in delivering this manuscript.

MY SISTER'S KEEPER

New York, 1990

"THE BEST WAY to explain it is I was never in love with my husband."

She would think it slipped out, but it hadn't. I knew every word I was going to say. I always know what I am going to say—now. When I was young, when my innocence and trust in others was reflected in what I said and how I behaved, I paid for it. Events, people became uncontrollable. But for years, decades, I have known that words, once recorded, can live to haunt you, just as actions eventually tell you the truth about other people's words.

The pause had been long enough. "There is another kind of love, one that is vested in respect, admiration. He taught me everything." A soft laugh. "Well, almost everything. You could say I paid him homage. We were really exceptionally happy together, despite the difference in our ages . . ." I knew when to pause again. ". . . and the jealousy of his children."

Like a child at a treasure hunt, aware that hidden gifts are all around, the important journalist, who was also my godchild, Penelope Davidson eagerly pushed her tape recorder another inch toward me. I watched Penelope, usually called Penny, as I answered her questions—watched her more than she watched me, because although we had been meeting now for nearly three months, there was still something uneasy about her body language. I longed to correct it.

It is both my curse and my blessing that I always long to correct anything and everything that spoils a woman's appearance. Women need all the help they can get—now more than ever—and thank God, they'd been getting a lot from me for years. It was one reason I was so obscenely rich.

Even though Penny had inherited both her mother's and her grand-

1

mother's lengthy, slender arms and legs, she never seemed to know what to do with them. Now the top half of her torso was bent forward awkwardly over her legs, which were crossed at mid-thigh. The whole position cried anxiety. I had to restrain myself from pushing her back against the tapestry cushions, to show her how to look relaxed even when she was not, but today was not the day.

Penny had received a sophisticated upbringing, surrounded by educated, gracious people, one of whom—her grandmother and my oldest friend and first supporter, Alexandra Sanford—was without question a noted leader of New York society. Yet like the rest of her generation Penny seemed to be unable even to sustain eye contact. Understandable, perhaps, in view of what she had been told during this visit, but if she had been my granddaughter I would have taught her by now that direct eye contact in business, as well as in moments of pleasure, is an unfailing way to capture more attention and, most important of all, to be remembered. It is something the Japanese have never needed to be taught. Oh God, it was still Benedict's voice in my head, directing my thoughts as he had always done in the past; I could hardly remember anymore how I used to think for myself.

When Anne Marie came in to remove the coffee tray, I leaned back and briefly closed my eyes. It was a far better signal than allowing a clock to strike or, of course, glancing at a watch to imply that time was up. So obvious and vulgar, as Benedict had often said. It was almost the time I usually left for my weekly bridge game at the club, but I was glad I'd canceled it before Penny arrived. I intended to spend the next few hours much more constructively.

"I've taken up too much of your time today," Penny was saying. "Thank you so much for lunch ... mm ... when do you think we can ..." This stopping in midsentence was, I'd learned, a habit of hers, one that perhaps she had found useful in prompting indiscretions from the unwary and untutored.

Months before, I'd asked her to explain more clearly the request contained in her letter for "an in-depth interview that will never appear in your lifetime."

Perhaps it was because English was not my first language, more likely because Benedict's tutoring had driven me to have the final *i* dotted and the last *t* crossed, but I had to be entirely sure I understood what she meant.

"I know you don't grant personal interviews anymore, Aunt T, but I've been assigned to the ... to the ..." Penny stumbled and stopped, appearing to be unsure of herself when I called for a clear explanation.

It was a lack of self-confidence that her sharp, telling pieces in print never suggested.

I hadn't helped her.

". . . obituary page. It's very important that not only the correct information is in our files, but that in the case of the most important people, such as yourself, the richness and power of their personality is also on record." She gathered momentum. "We thought, my editor and I thought, with your contribution to the economy, with the increasing attention being paid to Louise Towers by Wall Street, with your new appointments, the approaching anniversary, and these persistent rumors of a takeover and you perhaps stepping down, that the files would not contain the true story or . . ."

So that was it.

As Penelope had stopped again, I'd been bored rather than aggravated, and I'd allowed it to show. "So, Penny, you've been drafted to find out the true condition of the patient, eh? I can assure you and your editor that, to use Mark Twain's words, reports of my death have been greatly exaggerated. Despite the formidable number of years I've spent running this company, I've actually never felt better. If it would help you, I would be quite willing to have Dr. Askbury confirm this in writing."

"Oh, oh, of course not, Aunt T. This is nothing to do with death . . . I mean your health or age or anything like that. It's simply a matter of ensuring that your incredible life story is on record, the story only you can vouch for, Aunt T."

I was not her aunt, but she'd been calling me that since she was a child, for over twenty-five years, much to the family's displeasure.

"My editor wants me to become another Alden Whitman. Do you know who I mean? The man who made the obituary page required reading at *The New York Times* because of his . . . his writing ability, but also his knowledge and perception of outstanding personalities."

"You mean he brought his interviews to life?"

I hadn't been able to resist that remark, and as we'd both laughed, I'd been happy to hear Penny's voice brighten, reminding me that I was really fond of the girl. She'd then repeated, "It's nothing to do with death, life or death, or a person's age or health. In fact, if you won't agree, they've asked me to update Madonna's obit in my own way." No wonder they said the child had a future. I'd let Penny think I'd agreed to the many interviews the obituary would require because of my trust in her ability and judgment and my affection for her grandmother and mother, but that wasn't the reason. Of course not.

When Benedict died—hard to believe it was already twelve years ago—I'd given up being interviewed. I'd always hated it, but Benedict had insisted that interviews were "a necessary part of the job." Of course, interviews were only "granted" to a chosen few, but whether it was *The New York Times* or *Vogue* or French *Elle* or British *Harper's Bazaar*, *The Australian* or *Asahi Shimbun*, it all meant the same to me—an hour or so when a stranger was permitted to pry and poke into my past, present, and/or future. No more interviews. It was one of many things I changed about my life when Benedict died. I was still known as a woman you could set your watch by, a woman of her word, a woman of meticulous manners and punctuality; but I knew, although others did not, how since Benedict died I indulged myself, from time to time, with deliberate acts of unpredictability.

The only time I now told the huge, insatiably hungry public anything anymore was on television, on my own carefully scripted four times a year specials, "Ninety Beautiful Minutes with Louise Towers," which always rivaled Barbara Walters in the ratings.

Like most decisions in life, it was a matter of timing. Although she didn't know it, Penny's letter had arrived at a most propitious time. Late last year I'd discovered that another book about my life was being attempted, another irritating "unofficial biography," full of the usual half-truths and whole lies. I was tired of them, but as an army of legal libel experts had informed me at great expense over the years, as a public figure I had no redress. This was a more disturbing attempt. Not only the trash papers, but also the *Times* and the *Washington Post* had confirmed that Steven Holt had received a two-million-dollar advance to write the story of my life.

It wasn't a record sum. In this age of instant trivia incessantly consumed and regurgitated, it was average considering the success of Holt's previous six-hundred-page dissections. One problem with Holt was his own persona. He appeared as an amazing replica of a gentleman; he used words millions of his readers had to look up in the dictionary to receive the full, vicarious cutthroat thrill contained in the tell-all paragraphs. Then, for some reason, every so often the respectable press liked to analyze how and why this attracted more, not fewer, blue-collar readers and these analyses "permitted" others, who considered themselves well read and high up on the social ladder (terrified to be caught on the beach with the wrong sort of book), to gobble him up, too. So Holt was read by everyone, "upstairs and downstairs," so to speak, and was often called the most successful writer alive and well in the Western world.

Alas, people talked to Holt without knowing how much they were saying. Since learning of his planned invasion into my life I had read most of his books, and astonishing indiscretions from people who should have known better showed up throughout.

A few days before my conversation with Penny, I'd received the disquieting news that Fiona, my wayward, foolish little Fiona, had talked to him. It was extremely painful and it was also dangerous.

Until Penny's proposal I'd never thought of attempting a book myself; I had always been too busy and uninterested to find the right biographer—if indeed such a person existed—and I had no inclination to sift through the ashes of my memory as Betty Bacall had done to write *By Myself*. Penny's letter had planted a seed.

I knew from her reputation that she would come well prepared, and she had. The newspaper "morgue" had provided her with a fairly accurate chronological Louise Towers outline, but her editor had been right. There were hundreds of facts in the files about my life and the lives of those who'd affected me and the business, but there were also thousands of conjectures, opinions, and analyses of my triumphs and tragedies, personal and professional. Written and rewritten over and over again, small mistakes had grown into large ones, journalistic opinions had been propagated into facts. Then there were the figures, lots and lots of figures with naughts and dollar signs sometimes added, sometimes subtracted. The files were cold, emotionless, not conveying in any way the truth of how I had become—after the First Lady—the most famous woman in America, and the most successful.

Before I'd given Penny my answer, I'd looked back during several sleepless nights and realized that the treachery I was now combating, from those I thought loved me the most, had been inevitable. Perhaps after all I could save what I had achieved by telling the truth in my own book—or at least in my own way.

As Penny sat there now, so awkwardly twisting and untwisting those long legs of hers, as she recorded me for posterity and a future I hoped was still far off, she didn't know that, during our past interviews and today, I had simultaneously been recording myself for the present, for a story that would not end with the death of Louise Towers. It was for a story of rebirth, a story that would forever sear and torment the minds of those who were betraying me now.

We kissed good-bye in the way women in the upper social strata tend to do, missing flesh, lips brushing the air, and then I went to my bedroom, followed by Powder Blue, my Siamese cat. Anne Marie was waiting there to uncoil my chignon and brush my hair, thinking I was about to have an unusual afternoon nap. In fact, I was looking forward to working in bed. Today I intended to listen to the tapes of the interviews from the beginning and add to the notes I had been making, pages and pages of notes. At our first meeting I'd been happy to discover that Penny was indeed an astute journalist, that her questions were exactly what I had been hoping for to probe and stimulate my memory—as well as my imagination.

As Anne Marie turned down the cool linen sheet, Banks called from the first floor to tell me the revised list of VVIPs, all of whom were to have limos for themselves during the anniversary weekend, would be coming over this afternoon, together with final plans for the opening ceremony of the new wing and yet another version of my speech. He also told me in his wonderfully reassuring way that the wretched Pieter Mahler was under close observation and seemed to be calming down about his inability to see Kristina.

It was two-forty-five. I was so relieved I'd decided to stay home for a change, particularly as I had to go to Marlene's for dinner that night. I told Banks to take the car and deliver four of the new Louise Towers travel kits to the girls at the club with my apologies. "They're on the hall table, already gift-wrapped. Then tell Pebbler to pick up Kristina and take her out to the Hamptons. And, Banks, you needn't come back. You can begin your weekend off now."

When Anne Marie left the room I locked the door and went to my safe to take out the tapes. With today's, I was surprised to see there were already six. Soon I would talk to Penny about the book I wanted her to write from the tapes and my extensive notes. I couldn't delay much longer. Perhaps I'd talk to her about it at our next meeting in ten days' time, just before the anniversary weekend. Yes, almost certainly then.

In the soaring Towers Building, the executive express elevator made its first stop at the fortieth floor, bypassing twenty floors of lowlier Towers employees, who used three other elevator banks.

As Louise Towers' famous pale gray limousine, with its dark gray windows that shut out the world, drove toward the exclusive Bridge Club on the second Friday in June, Marlene Angela Towers was on her way up to the forty-second floor to a review-of-the-anniversary-events meeting. She hadn't been invited, but she considered it essential that she attend. She had to be able to relay to her sister-in-law Louise, who at last had consented to come to dinner and bridge that evening, that everything was being carried out to her satisfaction.

Marlene Angela Towers, who signed her in-house memos "M.A.T.," was known throughout the cosmetics industry as "the doormat." She also talked in clichés and slogans in a little-girl voice, and it was common knowledge that outside the business many people wondered why Louise continued to put up with her after Benedict's death.

Inside, they knew. Behind her back Marlene may have been laughed at, and even despised, for her obsequious fawning around Louise, but no one questioned her value. It wasn't only her "Take This Job and Love It" seminars for finger-weary facialists and masseurs, her "Self-Improvement Win-Win" workshops for footsore in-store beauty consultants; it was her ability to deliver both with infectious energy and enthusiasm only minutes after stepping off a plane from halfway around the world.

Unlike most people in elevators, Marlene never looked up at the floor numbers as the car ascended; she looked down at people's feet, checking that anyone who worked on or above the fortieth floor adhered to her regular M.A.T. dress-code memos, which pointed out, among other things, that sneakers were not appropriate to wear to the executive offices.

As Marlene exited on the forty-second floor, an unfamiliar scent engulfed her. Her nostrils twitched. Tuberose—yes, she could spot the heady tuberose, tropical, sexy—good, good. Like a bloodhound she stood still, inhaling, trying to identify the other notes. Was this the final choice for the new fragrance, created with so much else to commemorate the twenty-fifth anniversary of the first Tower of Health and Beauty Spa, long documented as a major turning point in the company's fortunes? Was this No. 25, the code name for the fragrance that would be given to a select few like the First Lady, Barbara Walters, a slew of top-name Hollywood stars, and even the Queen of Spain, who was flying over with her royal husband for the gala dinner?

Something had been going on without her knowledge or approval. She had been left out again in the decision-making process, and in an area where she was without question, except for Louise, the best qualified. Couldn't anyone in the wretched company remember that Benedict had publicly praised her nose, had said it was of professional caliber, when sales of Bravado reached a million dollars in no time at all, when people had to be put on waiting lists to receive it—all achieved without scent strips and today's kind of multimillion-dollar saturation advertising campaigns? Couldn't anyone remember how much she'd had to do with Bravado's selection from all the submissions, the first time her advice had ever been taken seriously?

Indignantly she headed toward the small boardroom where Bobby, her secretary, had told her the hush-hush meeting was to be held. Bobby had been ferreting out information for her since the day she joined the company, following the demise of her husband, Leonard, younger brother of Benedict, chairman of the board.

"Aunt M., this is a surprise. I thought you were still in Denver, selecting the annual silver-cuppers?" Kick Towers's tone showed what a non-surprise Marlene's appearance was. He brushed a hand over his tanned face as if to stifle a yawn.

To Marlene's relief, her daughter Zoe wasn't there. It was bad enough putting up with her grandnephew Kick's double-crossing, but recently she'd begun to suspect that Zoe was turning into a serpent's tooth. The younger generation thought they knew all the answers, but they hadn't a clue.

"Oh no, no, no, Kick. I told them in March I couldn't stay for the 500 Silver Cup Celebration, but it's going to be wonderful. Four girls made it, so that's . . ."

"One thousand new customers," Kick interjected smoothly. "Well, let's hope they show up at the counters. Denver's showing has been poor. However, if you'll excuse us, Aunt M., we're trying to fathom out some financial problems here."

Marlene glanced around the table. Her grandniece, Kick's sister Fiona, sat stony-faced between two senior financial officers, Craxter and Fromme. Poor girl, when Fiona didn't smile, all the worst traits of the Towers side of the family showed up.

"Oh, oh, Kick, I thought it—this—was a meeting for finalizing the anniversary program. Every little bit helps, I thought . . ." Marlene's voice trailed away as she saw in front of Kick what appeared to be a lengthy letter with a logo that even upside down, she recognized clearly. *Natasha*, a vivid red zigzag scrawl, was a logo she would recognize anywhere! Her heart beat fast. Everyone was looking at her, saying nothing, expecting her to leave. What was going on?

She wanted to curse them all, to scream out her hurt, her suspicions about the fragrance filling the air on the forty-second floor, but instead she allowed Kick to walk her out into the hall, toward the elevator.

"Do you like what you're smelling? Louise isn't sure. You're such a great nose—we were waiting for Rhylls to come in with another version on Monday before we showed it to you, but as usual we can't surprise you, can we, Aunt Marly?"

The warmth of his voice and the name he used for her, the one he'd used as a child, made her blush. So at least Kick realized how valuable her contribution could be. "Well, I was a little surprised, Kick. There are several unusual florentals in there . . . a strange middle note I'm not sure about, but of course without the pulse-point check, how can I know? We're not dealing with potpourri here, are we?" She wanted to make a strong statement, but to her embarrassment, she knew she sounded weak, silly. As the elevator arrived with a discreet ping-ping, Kick kissed her affectionately.

"Absolutely not. Can we discuss with Rhylls on Monday? Is eight-thirty too early for you? It's going to be hellishly busy with less than fourteen days to countdown."

"Of course, eight-thirty's fine. I'm always in by eight, you know that, Kick." They all knew it. She had no one to stay in bed with, nothing to stay home for. Except for the much-looked-forward-to dinner and bridge with Louise, the weekend loomed ahead like a penance.

The appreciated feeling stayed with her until she reached her own office. Then two things hit her, one after the other.

"That child could charm an army into laying down its arms," her husband Leonard had said about Kick. "He's the truest chip off an old block I've ever seen." She'd been charmed by the truest chip all right, out of the boardroom and into the elevator, without even realizing it. She thought about the document with the zigzag Natasha letterhead on the boardroom table, and felt sick. If Louise had been in the office, she'd have gone to see her there and then, but of course she was at her Friday-afternoon bridge game.

Should she mention it to Louise tonight? There had to be a reasonable explanation, probably some petty industrial espionage about a lipstick formula or something similar. There were always disloyal people wanting to make an extra buck. All the companies had to deal with the problem, although not so much as in the old days when Revlon and Lauder were in the same building, the General Odors Building, as it had been called then.

She tried to work, but her heart wasn't in it. At five o'clock she went home. Viola was singing under her breath in the kitchen, which was a good sign. Marlene knew better than to ask if everything was going smoothly, and she saw for herself that the cold salmon had been dressed magnificently by Grace's Marketplace.

Louise was arriving thirty minutes before the others—she'd suggested it so that Louise could tell her privately if there was anything, anything at all in the world, she could do that she wasn't doing already to make the anniversary the greatest event of the year, if not the decade. Would she be able to tell her then what she'd seen? Face-to-face, Marlene knew it would be even more difficult. Louise's huge, dark eyes, the overlong silences Louise believed in between her attempts at conversation, still inhibited her, despite expensive sessions with a shrink and a hypnotist.

In the shower, Marlene thought of a number of ways to bring up the subject of the Natasha letter, but dismissed them all. It wasn't as if Natasha were just a major competitor. There was so much bad blood between the companies that sometimes she found it hard to remember Louise and Natasha were sisters. She realized she'd thought *"had been* sisters," as if, like a married couple, they'd divorced or annulled their relationship. She was one of the few in the company who knew when they'd loved and supported each other like sisters, who remembered when Natasha had been rescued from Prague, how they'd worked together for the good of Louise Towers, Inc. She was also one of the very few who knew what had come between them.

Now, with all the money and influence in the world, Louise could do nothing about a sister the world knew she loathed, a sister whose own business grew more successful every year, partly owned and financed by the K. Avery pharmaceutical giant, who had set out to beat and bury Louise Towers in the marketplace. How galling it had to be for Louise to realize her sister was also . . .

"Ma'am, ma'am . . ." Viola's querulous voice outside the bedroom door broke her train of thought. It was just as well. She was thinking dangerously. "Ma'am, can you come taste the soup?" In her robe she went downstairs. As usual, Viola had to receive a compliment to keep her in a good mood. Marlene knew the soup would be good. It was the only thing Marlene could rely on about her housekeeper's cooking.

She told Viola to put fresh candles in the candelabra, blocking her ears to the bleat that they'd only been used once before, then rushed back to her dressing room to put on the new green-gray Armani that Louise had told her to buy.

Six-forty-five. Louise wouldn't be leaving for at least another twenty minutes to arrive by seven-thirty. Louise was always exactly punctual. With what she had now decided were Kick's deliberately false words of praise emboldening her, Marlene dialed her sister-in-law's number. It would be better if Louise was told before she arrived about the Natasha letter, which had obviously been a subject of discussion among members of the family and other top executives. Then they could talk about it in the thirty minutes before the other guests arrived.

As she heard the phone begin to ring in the Louise Towers mansion, Marlene had her opening sentence ready.

"The Skater's Waltz" . . . da-da-da-da-da, ding-ding-ding-ding, da-da . . . It was a favorite tune, but the music was so off-key it hurt her ears. Anne Marie could feel one of her blinding headaches coming on, the kind that Madame had sent her to her own doctor to diagnose, the headache that boomed *brain tumor, brain tumor* . . . The doctor had told her to stop eating chocolate and drinking so much red wine, diagnosing a food allergy, a diagnosis that had miraculously turned out to be right. No more chocolate, much less wine, and no more head-aches until now. Oh, oh, please, God, make it go away.

It wasn't until the rhythm began again, da-da-da-da-da, ding-ding . . . that Anne Marie realized it wasn't music. It was the incongruous blend of the phone ringing with a stanza from Madame's erratic ancient music box. In a haze, Anne Marie could visualize the battered box that stopped and started for no apparent reason. It was the one Madame said she'd brought with her from Prague in her youth, which contained her favorite jewels, although they were the least valuable. The gold bracelet with her old name engraved on it, and pearl earrings in the shape of miniature perfume bottles with tiny gold stoppers, both presents from Mr. Towers during their early married years, she'd once told her wistfully.

Anne Marie tried to cover her ears, but she couldn't. Nausea filled her as she discovered her hands were tied. Her hands were tied behind her back!

"Madame . . . help . . . help . . ." she tried to scream, but made no discernible sound. Slowly, as though coming out of the anaesthetic she dreaded at the dentist, Anne Marie found she was blindfolded, gagged, and bound. She couldn't cry out or move. There was the taste of salt on her tongue, a result of endless tears soaking through the material tight around her mouth. She twisted, turned, rolled, wrenched, tugged, but she remained helpless, hopeless, drenched in sweat and tears as more consciousness returned and she remembered.

Banks had left with Pebbler, the chauffeur/bodyguard, in Madame's car. He was dropping something off at the Bridge Club, then taking the rest of the weekend off, while Pebbler was taking Kristina someplace in the country to get her away from her father, and both daytime maids had long gone home.

Anne Marie sobbed again as she remembered the young man—boy, really—angelic-looking, with hazel eyes and freckles, who'd rung the back doorbell. Banks had told her to expect a package from the office. "Public relations," he'd said in a cheery voice to match the looks she'd seen on the in-house TV intercom. "I have an envelope for Mrs. Towers."

At the precise moment she'd unlocked and opened the door, the front doorbell had rung. What a nuisance, she remembered thinking. Who on earth could that be? Although everything and everyone had been unexpected for weeks, ever since the arrival of the Czechs and all the people in and out of the house all day, working on this and that for the anniversary.

Freckle-face hadn't minded waiting outside while she dealt with whoever was at the front. She'd shut the back door—she would stake her life on it—but she hadn't locked it.

The phone was still ringing, stabbing her head with pain. Through the blindfold over her eyes she could just see a glimmer of light. Was it from the window at the top of the second-floor staircase or the downstairs library? She couldn't remember where she was, upstairs or downstairs. She was wet with the sweat of terror as she thought she heard a sound. Holding her breath, she strained to listen. No sound, nothing, no sound from Madame, either. What had happened to Madame? Oh God, oh God.

She began to struggle again, strength coming from somewhere, trying to edge her body forward to where the phone kept ringing, but more nausea and dizziness stopped her.

She'd picked up the intercom for the front door. The voice had been strange, foreign, like that of the Czech, Pieter Mahler. She'd made a mistake by not recognizing his voice once before, and Madame, who hadn't been at all pleased, had reprimanded her about her manners. She had wanted to be sure not to make another mistake, and it had sounded a little like him. Oh, God forgive her, she was sure it had, but when the TV intercom showed nobody there, she'd left the kitchen to go into the front hall to make doubly sure, looking through the front-door security peephole. Still no one. Why hadn't she been suspicious . . . why?

Instead, like an innocent child she'd hurried back to the kitchen to the boy outside from "public relations." She moaned through the gag as the terror of the moment came back. There had been no young boy outside. There were two men inside, both in black—black masks, black suits, black boots, black guns. She'd run screaming out to the hall, to the main alarm, but one had caught her skirt and tackled her to the ground, while the other had walked insolently past her to the alarm panel cunningly concealed in the stairwell, opening it as if he had every right to do so, switching off the system that had cost thousands to install. Again she held her breath as she realized the brute had known exactly where it was!

They'd forced her up the stairs, one black-gloved hand around her mouth, another twisting her arms behind her back, the gun held at her temple. Up, up toward Madame's closed door. They hadn't expected anyone to be there. "Fuck! She's still there," one of them had said as, clear as a bell, they'd heard Madame's composed voice on tape. "I helped Natasha escape in 1968. We hadn't seen each other in over twenty years . . . it was my worst mistake . . ." Over the taped voice had come Madame's real voice, hesitant, concerned. "Anne Marie? What is it? Anne Marie, is that you?"

She hadn't been able to answer; the black glove was suffocating her. One brute had tried the door and found it locked. "Open the door or we'll kill your bitch of a maid." The brute hadn't shouted, but the threat had been loud, loud. She would never forget that voice, never, never.

She moved her head back and forth in torment, and a miracle happened, the blindfold slipped down. She could see. She was in the antechamber to Madame's bedroom, half in, half out of the doorway, her head immediately beside the antique cat doorstop. With sight came resolve. She leaned forward, the gag catching on the cat's steel paw, and wrenched her head back, deeply scratching her skin, but tearing the cloth. Again and again she moved forward, sometimes catching the gag, sometimes missing the claw, wounding her cheek, her chin. Blood ran down her face, but she moved like a machine, using all her Pyrenees-bred strength, until bit by bit the gag loosened, and with a final wrench her mouth came free.

"Is it true, Anne Marie? Are you in danger?" Madame's voice had been so calm. Even as the glove had been removed and she'd sobbed, there was a gun at her head, and the other brute had shot a hole in the painting she'd always been so attached to, the Monet from her beloved France, which hung on the second-floor landing.

"The sooner we do what we've come to do, the sooner we'll be gone." The voice had been menacing.

There had been a moment's silence. Madame must have tried to ring the alarm, which went straight through to the Seventieth Street police station, then realized it was dead. Madame had unlocked the door, her beautiful dark hair loose over her shoulders, and she had tried to wrench herself away to rush toward Madame with her arms outstretched. It was the last thing she remembered. One of the *bêtes* must have knocked her out cold.

Anne Marie lay still, trying not to cry, summoning up what remained of her strength to push her body along the floor. The phone stopped ringing as, with enormous effort, she pushed her feet against the wall and propelled herself through into the bedroom.

She screamed. Tables were overturned, drawers emptied out, chairs, lamps smashed, broken china and glass everywhere, and the door of the safe behind the small Picasso wide open. But it wasn't the destruction and chaos that made her scream. Blood soaked the cool linen sheets where Louise Towers, the most successful woman in America, lay still and silent.

She was still screaming when Marlene Towers arrived with the police fifteen minutes later. "Too late . . . too late . . ." she sobbed. "Madame's been murdered . . . that Czech sister of hers, Natasha. Madame said so herself . . . just listen to her tape . . . the Czechs, oh, the Czechs, they've finally murdered Madame."

Ludmilla

Prague, 1946

SITTING ASTRIDE HIM, through the attic window Ludmilla could clearly see the statue of Atlas carrying the world on his shoulders that towered over the gateway of the Vrtha Palace, home of the U.S. Legation in Prague.

"Look at me, look at me, beloved, beloved ..." His groans were imploring, but his fingers, treating her breasts like reins, were commanding, urging her as did his body, in a frenzy of movement, to ride him faster and faster as she'd told him she once, long ago, had ridden a pony in Cesky Raj, the Bohemian Paradise.

It was her wedding night, a night her mother had, in her own shy way, tried to warn her she might not enjoy. She hadn't listened because she never listened to her mother, who would certainly have rushed to confess her daughter's sins as if they were her own, if she'd learned her daughter had already once, no, twice, experienced the delirious feeling of sex produced by Milos's probing thumb and fingers.

"Oh, oh, Milos, no, no, no ..." Ludmilla cried as she felt her body parts splitting inside.

It didn't stop him. This was not the Milos who'd always babied her, giving in to her every whim. This was not the patient man who had entreated her so piteously to be allowed to touch her naked breasts, her thighs, then later had begged for more and more. This was not the man who had told her repeatedly that despite the suffering she was causing him, he respected her resolution to remain a virgin until the day she became his bride. It had been understood between them that this could only happen when she reached the age of consent, at twenty-one. She had been in no hurry, not until she realized that Milos could offer her a chance to escape to a utopia thousands of miles away.

Milos had turned into a stranger, a relentless monster. The more

17

she cried out, the crazier he became, his hands now pressing her shoulders down to lock her more firmly over his giant penis. She was bleeding. There was blood on the sheet. He had to know she was still bleeding from his first thrusts of a couple of hours ago, ones that he'd admittedly warned her, oh, so sweetly in the weeks before their wedding, might hurt as he penetrated her vagina in a way his fingers never could.

"Ludmi . . ." Milos half yelled her name, as his body shuddered to a stop and with closed eyes he released her shoulders to collapse against the pillow. It was a repetition of what had happened before, except now her vagina burned in a scorchingly painful way, as the soles of her feet sometimes burned through threadbare shoes in the rare Prague heat waves. She looked down at him with disgust. He was already asleep, as if with the release of the flood of semen his body had shut down.

The first time it hadn't been so bad. He'd carried her across the threshold of his two-room apartment, and allowed her to go behind a screen in the corner to change into her new nightdress, so beautifully embroidered by her aunt for her trousseau. He had admired the embroidery and, cozily, side by side, sitting up in bed with glasses of plum brandy, they'd toasted each other *Nazdravi* one more time before switching out the light.

At first he'd been his usual gentle self, playing with her until her nipples hardened, arousing her wetness. She had just begun to feel the surge toward "that special feeling" when, without asking her permission, he'd suddenly lunged on top of her body and forced her legs apart with his knee to enter her. Yes, she had felt she was splitting apart then, too, and a sharp pain had stopped her surge of pleasure as effectively as the voices they'd heard one day approaching their usual hiding place in the woods. But because he'd warned her, she'd put up with the pain, had moved her body as he'd instructed her to do, biting her lip when it seemed he would never stop, trying to concentrate on her future with him, the future he'd promised her in America.

Now she mentally apologized to her mother for laughing when she'd told her to shut her eyes and pray to the Holy Mother to help take her mind off "what might happen on your wedding night." The thought of America had helped the agony the first time, but not the second. Could there possibly be a third onslaught in one night? Had she married a sex fiend?

Milos was sleeping deeply now, with the sweet expression she knew so well. Was it all the drink inside him that had unleashed this unspeakable passion? That had to be the answer. Well, it would never happen again.

Ludmilla limped to the sink in the corner. She was about to run the water when Milos stirred. She couldn't risk waking him, and yet there was no way she could sleep, feeling so defiled. Furiously she wiped herself with the towel stamped U.S. PROPERTY. Now she was property herself, but surely it was going to be worth it.

Milos was her passport out of grayness and poverty, away from the sickening smells of perming and coloring solutions and, worse, chemicals for removing hair, which permeated every inch of the house where she'd been born and still lived. He was the lifeline to pull her out of a life of drudgery in the family "beauty salon," which in every other house on their street was the front parlor. He was her ticket to the United States of America, where he'd told her Helena Rubinstein and Elizabeth Arden had salons that were like palaces, where every family had a bathroom and a car, where nylon stockings and lipsticks and matching nail enamels in dozens of colors were piled high on shop shelves, where coupons and ration books to buy food and clothing were unheard of.

When Milos had first described to her the things on sale in the American post exchange in Prague—the PX, as those attached to the legation called it—Ludmilla hadn't believed him until he'd been allowed to shop there himself. The evening he'd brought her parents the present of the Virginia ham in an American can was, Ludmilla was sure, the turning point in their halfhearted acceptance of him. The frog of a car mechanic who was not good enough for their beautiful daughter had suddenly turned into the prince who was "the American colonel's chauffeur, our future son-in-law." She'd heard her father use that description with pride even to Father Kusy, the family priest who, six hours ago, had performed the wedding ceremony.

Ludmilla pressed her head against the cool windowpane, looking beyond the gates to the brilliantly lit palace where Colonel Benedict Towers, commander of the U.S. legation and her husband's employer, lay sleeping. He didn't know his chauffeur, mechanic, guide, and sometime interpreter had just married his childhood sweetheart with only a few members of their families present. He didn't know, nor, they hoped, would he ever know that the marriage had just taken place secretly because of one of the few conversations he'd had with Milos months back, when he'd told him he was not only the best driver he'd ever had, he was a genius of a mechanic. "I might even get you sent back to the States with me, Milos. Keep up the good work and I'll think about it."

If Milos hadn't given it much credence, telling her about the compliment as he told her pretty much everything, Ludmilla had thought of little else. Then Milos had told her with a stupid long face that perhaps Colonel Towers did mean it, because he had mentioned it again, now even talking about sometime in the spring of '47. He'd almost cried, as he'd said, "How can I leave you behind, when I can't live without seeing you every week, every day, if only I could?" It hadn't taken her a minute to give him the simple solution.

She wasn't quite twenty, but surely the colonel wouldn't—couldn't—separate a man from his wife, so why wait? And after discussing the situation with her parents, they had finally agreed, her father bringing home cherry tree branches before Saint Barbara's Day to decorate the salon and the front hall, hoping to force them to bloom indoors with heat from the stove. And they had bloomed, making everyone happy, including herself, because it fulfilled the Czech tradition that cherry blossoms before Christmas ensured that any daughter at home would find a good husband, and that went for her sister, Natasha, too, although she was still only a little girl.

Her parents had been surprisingly understanding—probably even relieved, in view of their lack of money, with no sign of business improving—that the wedding had to take place so quietly. At least it was better than during the German occupation, when permission to marry had to be obtained from the authorities and could take months, if it was granted at all. Her father especially agreed that if the colonel learned about their wedding before it took place, and before he'd firmly made his mind up about giving Milos such an incredible opportunity in the States, it would be a good reason for him to change his mind.

For that reason, of course, she couldn't move in with Milos to share the rooms provided by the United States government; before tonight it had been the only thing she'd been unhappy about, knowing that after the wedding night she'd be returning home, where Milos would join her only on his nights off. How relieved she was about that now! Wherever she lived, she was now Milos's wife, who legally could refuse him nothing.

Ludmilla felt tears at the back of her eyes. It was a huge gamble. She had staked her life on the hope that when Milos confessed he had a wife he wanted to take with him to America, a wife who was just as good a housemaid (or hairdresser, if the colonel had a wife) as he was a chauffeur and mechanic, the colonel would be kind and understanding and not cold and uncaring as Milos had often described him.

Although Ludmilla had never met Colonel Towers, she had seen him once and told herself now that in his photographs, which occasionally appeared in *Narodni Politika*, Prague's daily paper, he looked kind.

She had been with her parents among the jubilant crowds on the Charles Bridge that day in mid-May the year before, when Towers had arrived in an American jeep. His arrival, as the first American officer in uniform to appear in the capital since Germany's formal surrender the week before, had created a sensation, and along with everyone else Ludmilla had struggled to get near him, longing to touch or kiss the victor's stern, handsome face. She'd cheered herself hoarse, at the same time wondering, as everyone did, "Where are the American tanks?"

It had taken a few weeks to learn that Towers, along with a couple of Czech-born U.S. intelligence officers, had been sent to Prague from General Patton's advance army headquarters in Pilsen on a specific official mission: to reopen the U.S. Embassy, not to act as a pathfinder for occupying American troops.

Ludmilla had cried because her parents had cried, fearful on discovering the truth that because Russian troops had arrived in Prague from the northeast first, to "liberate" them before General Patton crossed the Czech border in the south, it would be Russians who would occupy their country in the months after the war. The Russian troops were still there, and according to her parents and their friends, it seemed likely they could be there for years, their unsmiling heavy faces everywhere, adding to the gloom of the shortages, the endless long lines even for a loaf of bread. No wonder her parents so selflessly wanted better things for her.

"Ludmilla, what are you doing there? Come to bed, my little cherub . . ." Before she could answer, Milos had turned over and, with a deep grunt of what she took to be satisfaction, fallen asleep once more. How long would she have to wait before she could be sure he wouldn't attack her again? When she crept over to the bed and positioned herself gingerly at the very edge, one foot still on the mat, she realized she was following her mother's advice after all. "Holy Mary, Mother of God, pray for us sinners now and at the hour of our death. Holy Mary, please, I beg you, intercede for your miserable daughter, Ludmilla Sukova, and soften the heart of Colonel Towers to allow her to accompany her husband to the United States of America one day soon . . . soon."

"Architecturally, Prague is a jewel box of treasures from Romanesque to Cubist to art nouveau, most in remarkably good order, considering the country's present state of economic despair. Some buildings are girded in scaffolding that has become virtually integral to the structure, an emblem of the half feckless, half grittily enduring aspect of Czech nature, like the good soldier in Hasek's quixotic tale."

The phone rang, and Colonel Benedict Towers stopped typing on his battered Olivetti. He hadn't been speaking for more than a minute when he was cut off. He jiggled the cradle up and down, only to get a high-pitched buzz in his ear.

Goddamn it, for weeks he'd been putting off writing the piece for Honey to deliver to her women's group at the Everglades Club, and now this, the third interruption in an hour, had ruined his train of thought for the rest of the day, probably forever. He'd been up since six-thirty, banging out the six badly typed pages beside him. He was sure it wasn't what the spoon-fed Palm Beach audience of phony intellectuals wanted from Honey anyway, although she seemed to think it was.

Well, it would have to do. He'd kept his promise, and perhaps Milos could forage out some postcards to go along with the text to improve their minds, if there was such a thing as a postcard left in this beautiful city of the damned. He suppressed a shiver. There was something about Prague that made him shiver a lot these days, something that came from glimpses of the recent and distant past that strained at his memory, while the Russians he was dealing with every day triggered his imagination into nightmares about the future of the Czechs.

If only the Czechs weren't so goddamned obsessive about the past. Every so often, even Milos wasn't deterred by his unresponsive face and blurted out some dog-eared piece of information about his blessed Czech heritage; at least it was more entertaining than listening to his moans about the latest outrage perpetrated by the Russians, adding to the continued deterioration of life in the capital.

Towers stood up and stretched. God, how he wished he was in Palm Beach right now, looking out over the ocean with a very dry martini at his elbow, waiting as he had always had to wait for Honey to rush in, pink and white, a petite Dresden doll, dressed in the latest, perfumed with the latest. When he'd first gone overseas, she'd scented her writing paper until he'd told her to stop. "Too painful," he'd written. In fact, it had been too sickening, sometimes making him gag.

If she'd ever irritated him to the point when he'd invented a business reason to get away for a few days, he wasn't prepared to remember it now. He didn't miss her the way he knew so many of his men missed their women, but, oh, he suddenly, achingly, missed everything Honey represented, especially, oh God, especially the children, his exasperatingly spoiled, adorable daughter, so like her mother in looks and disposition, and his amiable, adorable, but so far untalented son. Perhaps that was how his own father had regarded him at sixteen, but he didn't think so. By sixteen, having spent every school vacation in a different department, he had already shown he had a head and a nose for the business; he'd shown it at six, some of his father's old sycophants had told him.

He knew why this morning his mind was unusually full of thoughts of home. It had started the day before, when Norris's weekly report arrived in the diplomatic pouch with news that Procter & Gamble's breakthrough washing detergent, Tide, was sweeping the market and Westinghouse was bringing out a front-loading washing machine that seemed to have Tide totally in mind. All his own competitive instincts had come alive. If he'd ever wasted a minute over Truman's offer to join him in Washington, Norris's update had made him realize he had never really seriously considered it. He wasn't interested in the political arena, except insofar as the Food and Drug Administration could affect his business.

Towers Pharmaceuticals was in terrific financial shape—God knew, it should be, after the millions of drugs they'd been supplying during the past terrible years—but the world he was returning to back home was not the world he'd left behind in 1942, and it never would be again. Now that the company was so enormously cash-rich, he had another battle to fight, one he was much more equipped to deal with than the one he'd just fought. Norris's update had made him realize how eager he was to get started on the diversification and expansion plans he'd been thinking about for the past six or seven months, ever since he'd begun to get the legation in some sort of running order.

Funny how in '44, after the exhilaration of being with Patton during the liberation of Paris, he'd actually thought of selling the company when the war was over. He could remember the exact moment. Norris had just told him on the Third Army's private phone link to the States that P&G had been forced to pay Lever Brothers ten million dollars in damages in an out-of-court settlement, for stealing Lever's soap lathering formula, which they'd used to improve their Ivory soap. It was one of the biggest industrial-espionage settlements ever, but it had left him cold, indifferent, in a peculiar way even ashamed that he'd accepted Norris's urgent call about a case of espionage so far removed from the espionage that was at that time responsible for both saving and losing so many lives.

His grandfather had started the business with a horse, some test tubes, and a couple of hundred dollars; his father had brought it into the twentieth century and "died with his boots on" in 1937, making it into one of the largest pharmaceutical companies in the United States. By the time Benedict had joined the army, he had been well on the way to expanding the company into a worldwide operation, adding a couple of soap divisions that had become thorns in P&G's side.

He'd been called "the boy wonder" by *The Wall Street Journal,* but on that day in Paris in '44, he guessed he'd wanted to do more for mankind than just make more and more millions of dollars supplying the needy with drugs and soap products. He'd even noted down the names of the international brokerage firms he might ask to form a consortium to underwrite the huge stock issue it would inevitably have to be, and daydreamed about the price they'd have to come up with. The next day Patton had sent the unit under his command to help an airborne division under heavy fire in the southeast, and by the time he'd arrived in Prague eight months later, weary in mind and body, he'd changed his mind entirely.

After he showered and dressed, he went down to his office to read the communiqués before his usual 8:00 A.M. meeting with the deputy chief of mission and the legation's number-three man, the political counselor. The less efficient of his two secretaries—and the one who unfortunately thought she didn't need to wear a bra—was waiting for him in the hall outside with a cable marked TOP SECRET—FOR YOUR EYES ONLY.

"Irina has the influenza; she must stay in bed today," she mumbled. He nodded curtly and gestured for her to leave. As he read the cable, he flushed as he'd once flushed on receiving a rare compliment from his father.

YOU'VE DONE A GREAT JOB, BEN. GEORGE MARSHALL AND I ACCEPT WITH RELUCTANCE YOUR DECISION TO RETURN TO MANAGE YOUR OWN AFFAIRS; GIVE US UNTIL THE END OF MARCH, WHEN WE CAN NAME YOUR REPLACEMENT. AGAIN, WELL DONE.
   HARRY TRUMAN

It was very cold in his office as it always was in the middle of the month when the oil supply for the heaters ran out, but today he didn't notice. The end of March! Three and a half months away. It was exactly the kind of time frame he'd hoped for. It meant Honey would already have supervised the closing of the Palm Beach house, so he wouldn't have to waste any time there, and their reunion would take place in New York, where Honey always loved to be in April and May, and where he loved to be at any time. New York was the headquarters of Towers Pharmaceuticals. After a couple of days devoted to Honey and the children, he wouldn't waste a moment getting together with

Norris and, thank God, two of his top marketing men who'd survived the war, to map out the campaign of the century.

There was a discreet knock on the door. "Come in, come in," he called out warmly. The DCM came in, looking like Banquo's ghost. Poor guy, underpaid, overworked, shuffling along—you could hardly describe it as "up"—the diplomatic ladder, waiting to fill a dead man's shoes. Would he be happy to hear the news!

Towers knew he was scared shitless he was going to get the official appointment and stay on as ambassador. It was a pity he couldn't put him out of his misery yet, not before he had officially confirmed with State his exact date of departure, but there it was, he'd tell him as soon as he could.

He worked like a demon for the rest of the day, acknowledging to himself, because he didn't cough once, that maybe his asthma, worsened, as he often bitterly complained, by Prague's winter air, thick with the smell of soft coal, was psychosomatic after all.

He looked at himself in the old-fashioned wardrobe mirror after he put on his dress uniform. Not bad, in fact, for a man of thirty-eight, not bad at all. He was pleased that so far, unlike his father, there wasn't a trace of gray in his dark brown hair, and the uniform, made when he'd been at his thinnest, even felt a little loose at the waist. No wonder, with the lack of edible cooking in the house. He'd given up trying to educate the kitchen on how to respect an American prime rib.

For a second he was tempted to call the bewitching wife of the French consul, to tell her he would come to dinner the next night after all. She'd made sure he knew her husband was once again going to be away for a week, but that was the problem. Towers sighed. It was the memory of the delicious soufflé she'd served last time that was tempting him, just as much as, if not more than, the thought of the perfectly shaped pert little breasts with the extra large dark nipples she would also have ready for him to suck before they moved on to more imaginative things. If only she weren't so insatiable . . . well . . .

He picked up the phone, then put it down again. No, it wasn't worth the complication. He'd do without the soufflé and hope that tonight Jan Masaryk, the Czech foreign minister, might have *zverina*—venison—on the menu, one of the few Czech dishes he'd grown to like. He was in a good mood as he ran downstairs, although he knew the evening ahead would be stiff and formal. Now, though, because like a schoolboy longing for the vacation, he could check off the days on the calendar until his departure, he was determined to enjoy every single moment left.

His mood was obviously contagious because he noticed that Milos was beaming from ear to ear as they drove beside the river toward Hradcany Castle and the seat of government.

"At the first sign of spring I want to go and visit more of your beautiful country, Milos. I'd like to go to Piestany, to the Carpathians, for instance. Isn't that where the famous cures are, handed down from that bloodthirsty countess of yours, who stayed young forever taking baths in the blood of young virgins?"

"Yes, sir. In Cachtice, in the Little Carpathians, sir." Milos's response was leaden, and Benedict saw that his request had also wiped the smile off his young driver's face.

He leaned back against the dark leather, wondering why, after all the lyrical descriptions of the countryside that the young Czech had subjected him to, he was now so unenthusiastic about the idea of a tour. Then he remembered. Of course, he knew why. He'd mentioned to Milos that in the spring he might consider taking him back with him to the States, and in fact he was still considering it. He certainly had never come across anyone so knowledgeable about the inner work- ings of an automobile; Milos seemed to have magic fingers. There was also no question that he was the kind of driver he could totally trust with Honey and the children. On the other hand, it was just another headache, arranging his papers, fitting him into his household. He had enough to arrange in the coming weeks. He'd make a decision in the next couple of months, whether Milos drove with a long face from now on or not.

As it was, a letter from Honey made his mind up earlier.

"Suzanne called to say she was going with Maisie to the first night of Arthur Miller's *All My Sons* at the Coronet, so I said Mercer could take her. Can you believe it, he never turned up after the performance and they had to walk in the rain halfway home before they could get a cab. So embarrassing, because Maisie's such a snob. It quite ruined Suzanne's evening. It certainly would have ruined mine if I'd known our daughter was walking late at night through New York streets. Mercer, of course, swears Suzanne said she didn't need him, that she was going off with somebody else to a first-night party but the truth is he's old and deaf and doesn't like to stay up past ten o'clock. As soon as you get home I hope you'll put him out to pasture and we'll find another bright young man like Jeffers who's looking after me reasonably well here in P.B. although he makes a face when he's asked to help out in the garden.

I only wish Suzanne would go out with some other young men, now that so many have returned home. I keep telling her she's not engaged, and as far as I know Dudley hasn't even intimated he'd like to marry her, but she's so stubborn, says she's not interested in seeing anyone else, is just waiting for Dudley to return from the Pacific or wherever he is now. The war's been over for nearly eighteen months, so why his ship isn't back I'll never understand, but I suppose you do, not that you ever explain those kind of things to me."

Now that Honey knew when he was coming home, her letters were beginning to have a familiar, querulous tone. It depressed him, but he told himself she had been running three homes for the past five years with, in the main, an aging staff, so he shouldn't criticize her. Well, luckily in this instance he could quickly please her with a good replacement for Mercer.

"Irina, tell Milos I want to see him now in my office."

When Milos came in ten minutes later, Benedict was looking out at the gray, desolate street. "Sir, you wanted to see me, sir?" His voice cracked with nervousness, and he twisted an oily rag that in his haste to come he'd obviously forgotten to put down.

Benedict smiled. "Relax, Milos. I think I have good news for you. As I told you last year, I will be returning to the States this spring—the first week of April, in fact. I would like you to continue to work for me over there, and if everything works out satisfactorily, eventually I'll find a position for you in my private household. How does that sound?"

Expecting a grateful, excited acceptance, Benedict had already risen to see Miles out, his mind on his first scheduled appointment of the day. Instead, to his horror he saw that without making a sound, Milos was crying. "For God's sake, what is it, man? No one's forcing you to go. I thought . . ."

Milos went down on his knees. He didn't know what he was doing. He'd been waiting for this moment; he knew Ludmilla had been praying it would come every day. Not that she had ever nagged or even asked him, but he sensed her anxiety every time he came in the door. Now that the colonel had uttered the words he'd been longing to hear, the confession about his marriage that he had so carefully prepared, and rehearsed in front of the mirror, vanished. He felt like a dying man, knowing this was the most important moment of his life.

Benedict came over to him, pulling him up, irritated that as he did so some of Milos's grease was transferred to his hand. "For God's sake," he repeated, "pull yourself together. What's wrong with you?"

"I'll work night and day, sir. I won't take a day off. Please take us with you . . ."

Had the young man lost his marbles? "But that's what I'm suggesting . . ." Benedict stopped, frowning. " 'Us'?"

"I'm married, sir, to the most wonderful girl, Ludmilla. I've known her nearly all my life. She's from a good family. She can . . ."

"Be quiet." Benedict's voice was thunderous. "You have never mentioned a wife. Why did you never tell me you were married? Do you have children, too?"

Milos was sobbing loudly now. "No, no, no children. We don't want children. We want to work for you in America. Ludmilla is a wonderful girl, a hardworking girl who can clean, sew . . ." As Benedict remained silent, Milos went on hysterically, "She is a hairdresser, too. Her parents, the Sukovas, they have a beauty parlor . . . for years and years . . . Ludmilla is . . ."

"Be quiet," Benedict commanded again, then asked, "How long have you been married?"

It was the one question Ludmilla and Milos had prayed would not be asked, the reason the wedding had been so secret, the reason he was not even sleeping with his wife every night, to his sorrow, the reason he had, of course, told nobody at the legation, not that he had any friends there to tell.

"What, sir?"

"You heard me."

To Benedict's increasing anger, Milos went down on his knees again. "I've loved her for ten years, sir. I've wanted to marry her for ten years. We were waiting for her . . ." Benedict's face was stony. Milos gave up hope. "When you mentioned you liked my work last year, when you mentioned a possible job with you in America, we knew we couldn't be apart."

"So you got married?"

"Yes, sir."

"When?"

"Six weeks ago tomorrow, sir."

Benedict went back to the window, his back stiff, unyielding. A light snow was falling, and down the street he could see two Russian soldiers watching an old woman almost bent in two, carrying a heavy load of wood. Poor devils, no matter what Masaryk said, he had to know what lay in store for the Czech people. Churchill was right. An Iron Curtain was descending from Stettin in the Baltic to Trieste in the Adriatic, and it was moving fast in the direction of Czechoslovakia. So Milos had married his Ludmilla, hoping the colonel would provide a magic carpet to fly them both away to the land of the free.

"Get on your feet," he barked, without turning around. Out in the street he saw the old woman stumble, dropping her load, the wood spilling out. Neither soldier moved. Still without turning around, Benedict said, "Milos, there's a poor old creature out in the road who needs some help with her wood. Go and help her, then come back here and give Irina your marriage certificate. We will also need the birth certificates of all members of Ludmilla's family, including grandparents, whether they're alive or dead. We must run the same security check on all of them as we did on you. Once that is complete, we'll discuss this situation—this problem—further."

"Oh, sir, problem? You mean . . ."

"Get out of here and help that old woman." As Milos scrambled to his feet, Benedict turned to look at him. "Is Ludmilla—your wife—is she pretty?"

Milos blushed. "Oh yes, sir, she's the most beautiful girl you ever saw."

Palm Beach, 1948

EVEN WEARING HER new three-inch spike-heeled "naked" sandals and elaborate feathered toque, Honey Towers was pleased to see she still only came up to her husband's shoulder. Her diminutive height was something she continued to believe brought out his protective instinct for her, although he didn't show it much now. All the same, she felt like a young girl in her first "New Look" dress by the French designer everyone was talking about, Christian Dior.

Benedict was on the phone as usual, with a "Do Not Disturb" notice all over him, but she twirled around the room, loving the feel of the pale violet silk mousseline around her ankles, the exactly matching long feathers softly brushing her cheeks as a light breeze came in from the terrace.

Thank heavens for the darling little Dior toque. Alberto did his best, but his best didn't approach the way her hair always looked in New York. One day she would have to tell Elizabeth Arden to her face that she should send her first string of hairdressers to her Palm Beach salon in the season. It was amazing the old girl didn't understand herself that during the winter season from New Year's to March the wives of many of America's most influential men were in their Palm Beach homes, and required the same standard of coiffing they were used to receiving in New York, Texas, or California the rest of the year.

As she often did, Honey started to quick-step to the tune in her head. "I'm all yours in buttons and bows . . ." Slow, slow, quick, quick, slow; slow, slow, quick, quick, slow. She'd got into the habit when Benedict was overseas. Nowadays, as she frequently complained to her closest girlfriends, he was away so much on business, she sometimes had a hard time remembering he'd ever come home.

"Honey!" He only had to use that tone with her once, and as she'd told him several times in the last few months, he took all the fun out of her and turned her into a little wallflower, a Cinderella from Tennessee, who was too old to find another Prince Charming.

She went out onto the terrace. Far out on the horizon she could see a line of small, dark dots slowly moving along, a convoy of ships sailing toward Cuba. Oh, how she wished she were on her way there—cha, cha, cha—to dance all night in Havana as she had before the wretched old war came along to ruin everything and change her fun-loving, tall, dark, and handsome lover into a boring husband who now seemed to show passion only for a balance sheet.

"He adores you, Honey," all her friends consoled her when she told them he couldn't get down until Saturday and wasn't even staying for Mary Sanford's big party the following Friday, so she had to rustle up someone to take her—not that she ever had any problem with that.

"Consider yourself lucky, Honey, that it's his business he's crazy about," all her friends reassured her, "and not some money-hungry blonde. After all, you only have to read the papers to know he's building an empire. Someone has to run it."

As she heard Ben put down the receiver, she twirled back inside. Would he notice the most daring thing about her just-arrived-from-Paris, to-die-for new Christian Dior evening dress? And if he did notice, would he be angry and insist she have it taken out? Honey glanced down quickly at the plunging neckline, which revealed more of her breasts than she'd ever revealed in public before, more than she actually had to reveal, because every ounce of her flesh was pushed up with the help of an ingeniously constructed built-in padded bra.

"Very pretty." Benedict Towers sounded about as excited as if he were looking at some new curtain material.

"Benedict . . ." He was pouring himself a martini, but he didn't need to look at Honey to know there would be a hurt pout on her face.

There were a couple of time-honored ways to get rid of the pout now and for the rest of the evening. As she was made up and ready to go, all he had to do was lift her off her feet into the air, and kiss whatever part of her anatomy was bare, on the way up or the way down . . . or he could take her in his arms and dance close once or twice around the terrace, whispering some kind of rubbish in her ear.

The problem was, tonight he couldn't be bothered. If she wanted to pout, she could go alone to the Spencer Loves' anniversary dance. It would be a pity, because Spencer Love was one of the few self-made millionaires in Palm Beach he didn't mind spending an evening with. He knew he could depend on Spencer to take time out of the evening ahead to talk business and politics in his library, smoking a good

Havana, while the women danced their feet off with all the gigolos who now seemed to be spending the winters in Florida.

"What's wrong, darling? You've only just arrived and you've been on the phone all day and now it's as if I don't even exist." Honey stood before him like a crushed, crestfallen little girl, as he leaned back against the bar, looking down at her coolly, not touching her.

She was still very attractive and the body he knew so thoroughly looked very good tonight in the dress he supposed was the one he'd had to hear so much about, the dress that had taken such an interminable time to come through customs. If it made his wife look like that, it was worth waiting for, but although he would normally have done his duty and pretended he found her so desirable he couldn't wait for the party to be over, his mind was too full of other things.

He had to get the synthesized-cortisone deal sewn up before Squibb or Lilly caught on. He had to be sure Norris finalized on the California land for the next plant complex. He had to get the television pilot down to Palm Beach, but he was in no hurry to buy into television—not after buying the twenty radio stations in the Northeast. He would probably go personally to Switzerland to learn about the new antibiotic development, and yes, he would agree to sit down with Royal Little, who was diversifying in such an amazing way into fields unrelated to his textile group.

Since Spencer Love had founded Burlington Textile Mills, Benedict made a mental note to ask him at the party what he thought about Little's latest maneuvers.

Honey's nails were sharp. He took her hand away from his wrist and perfunctorily kissed it. "Very pretty," he repeated. "You will knock everyone's eyes out. Is that the dress from Paris? From that Christian Scientist?" To his relief, Honey started to laugh.

"Oh, Ben, you know that's not right. It's from Christian Dior, the designer who created the New Look last year. You know his name very well; the papers have been full of him. Do you really think it's a knockout? I'm sure there's never been a dress like this in Palm Beach. I can't wait to see Marjorie Merriweather Post's stuffy face!" Again she twirled around to show him how the new long skirt billowed out to show glimpses of her shapely legs.

"It's a little low, a little risqué, *ma cherie, n'est-ce pas?*"

"Oh, do you think so?" Honey prettily covered her décolletage with her hands as there was a knock on the door and Jeffers came in, now promoted to butler. He looks so pleased with himself, Benedict thought irritably, not for the first time, intending to point out yet again to Honey that the severe cut-away jacket and conservative striped pants she liked Jeffers to wear still couldn't hide the fact the man was a fairy, although Honey continued to refuse to accept it.

Again he decided that one of these days he would ask Jeffers himself how a strapping thirty-year-old six-footer had managed to stay out of the war. "Asthma," Honey had told him once in a reproving, self-pitying kind of voice that effectively shut him up before she could move on to the familiar subject of why he had been so eager to join up. Luckily for Towers Pharmaceuticals chronic asthma had kept his right hand man, Norris out, too.

"The car is ready, madame, sir."

Benedict nodded. "Well, I suppose a Christian Scientist wouldn't rustle up a dress that would put you behind bars, Honey, my dear, but be careful, please, when you shake your shoulders in the samba. I don't want you shaking out anything that belongs to me."

There was still laughter in her voice when she said, "Good evening, Milos," and carefully climbed into the dark green Rolls that Milos's livery exactly matched.

On the train coming down, Ben had read a piece about the problems servicemen were experiencing, readjusting to the demands of family life, often bitterly disappointed that the dreams they'd carried with them throughout the war, about their loved ones left behind, were now so often turning into nightmares.

Honey wasn't a nightmare. Far from it. It was her easy laughter, he reflected now, and willingness to react to his poor jokes that usually reminded him of how fond he really was of her.

The major problem between them was that she had no understanding of the demands the business made on his time and would continue to make for years to come. More exasperating was the fact that she wasn't willing to take the time to understand, either. When he'd first come back, he'd been eager to share with her his plans for Towers Pharmaceuticals, diversifying into areas that, to the outside world and business press, were not immediately going to seem related, but actually interlocked like a brilliant jigsaw puzzle.

Like the servicemen he'd just read about, his dreams of home had included a Honey who would be as dedicated as he was to bringing his grandiose visions to life. But he'd forgotten the length of Honey's attention span, or perhaps when he'd left for the war he'd been a different man himself, and hadn't been aware of Honey's preoccupation with trivia and the endless social rounds.

One thing he'd come to terms with during the past year: there wasn't a woman alive who could compete with the business for his attention;

he had never met one, and he was sure he never would, who could capture his interest and continue to enthrall him the way his business could. For him, women had never presented a challenge; they were too easy, and once taken, they became a drag.

Sexually, Honey gave him no problems; she was a pleasant, easily satisfied duty, and there was always someone who could give him the sexual stimulation he occasionally felt he had to have. He'd been delighted to read this was perfectly normal, according to the Indiana University zoologist, Alfred Charles Kinsey, whose book *Sexual Behavior in the Human Male* was already causing such a furor.

Honey had been quite upset to find him reading a confidential proof copy of the *Report*, sent to him by the Rockefeller Foundation, which had put up some of the research funds for the project, but as usual she hadn't stayed upset; she knew he was always content to come home to her, provided he didn't have to stay too long.

As they joined the line of cars arriving at the Loves' palatial oceanfront spread, Honey's foot started tapping to the beat of the music they could hear coming from the gigantic tent that covered the front lawn. "It's my favorite from *High Button Shoes!* Oh, this is going to be a divine night. Please be in a dancing mood, darling. Nobody quick-steps like you."

He patted her knee absentmindedly. "Don't worry, I'll quick-step your feet off, Honey." As they inched toward the specially erected, flower-covered walkway, where about a dozen valets were waiting to park cars without chauffeurs, Ben caught sight of their chauffeur's miserable profile.

"Is everything all right, Milos?"

"Yes, sir."

"You don't convince me." What a yawn the man was becoming. He really didn't care.

Ever since Milos's wife had finally arrived, after months of waiting for her mother to recover from a heart attack, he couldn't remember seeing a smile on Milos's face. How long had the woman been here? Two months? Three months? He still hadn't really met her face-to-face, although when Irina had given Milos the good news that his wife had received security clearance and that Colonel Towers was prepared to give them a six-month trial in the states, he vaguely remembered Milos bringing her to the legation to thank him.

It had been one of his busiest days, only a week or two before he left, and the last thing he'd wanted was to spend any time dealing with their tearful appreciation, particularly since Milos was one of the few people ever to have pulled a fast one on him. He didn't forget the relief he'd felt that Milos's wife didn't look like a hooker. In fact, he'd stopped being irritated, pleased for a passing minute or two that he was able to give the young couple such a break. The wife, unlike Milos, looked like a refugee, with huge, dark eyes. A cloud of dark hair obscured most of the "beautiful face" with which the young double-crosser Milos was so enraptured that he hadn't been able to leave her behind.

Perhaps after seeing the gorgeous, blue-eyed, blond all-American girls striding along the Palm Beach oceanfront, their firm breasts and tight buttocks outlined by trim beach and tennis clothes, Milos was enraptured no more, or at least not so much.

Well, thank God, Milos's miserable manner was no longer any concern of his. Servant problems were dealt with efficiently by Honey, who'd told him Milos's wife, Loretta or Ludmilla or whatever her name was, after working as hard as any maid she'd ever had in the house, had slipped on the marble floor in the entrance hall and broken a bone in her foot, and hadn't been able to work since. She was probably giving Milos hell at home, poor fella, missing those peculiar, particularly Czech delicacies like *veprova pecene*, *knedlik*, and *zeli*—roast pork, dumplings, and cabbage. God, he'd once thought he'd never get the smell of that cabbage out of his nostrils.

Benedict gave an exasperated sigh. Thank heaven, at least his decision to bring Milos with him had been inspired. No one had ever looked after the cars as Milos did, and Honey had taken quite a fancy to him, as he'd expected she would.

He looked out of the window, marveling at the beauty of the scene. Everything sparkled in the setting sun; everything was so pristine, so perfect, from the immaculate, raked golden beaches to their spectacular royal palms, dipping and shaking their proud heads like Lippizaners, to the glorious mansions of white stone and coral all the way along South Ocean Boulevard. It was hard for him even to recall the true horror of Prague, sunless, grimy, and gray for all its national treasures.

Milos was an ungrateful bastard. What right did he have to look and sound so miserable, when he'd been given not only an exit from hell, but an entrance to a paradise like this?

Benedict didn't respond when, as he left the car, Milos whispered, "Could I have a word with you tomorrow, sir?" He wasn't interested in hearing one word of complaint, and he didn't have time for conversations with ungrateful servants with long faces, however much they knew about cylinders and crankshafts.

Ludmilla was asleep, as Milos had expected her to be at 1:15 A.M. when he wearily let himself into the apartment above the garage for the Rolls. Even with her eyes closed and a peaceful expression on her lovely face, he knew she'd spent the evening crying. No one cried like Ludmilla, silently, no part of her face moving, just tears streaming down as steadily as water from an efficient American faucet. It frightened him because when she cried, she absolutely refused to speak until he began to believe she couldn't speak and perhaps never would speak to him again.

Once she goes back to work, she'll be all right. He told himself that over and over again, because she'd certainly seemed happy when she'd learned on her arrival in New York on an icy, below-zero day that Mrs. Towers did need her in the Palm Beach house after all, so they were not going to be separated, as he'd feared, for the two and one-half months he was going to be spending with Mrs. Towers in Florida. Ludmilla hadn't objected at all to going on the train with the other servants, although he was driving the Rolls down.

"It needs to be let off the leash, to have a good run."

Milos had been startled that Colonel Towers referred to the Rolls as if it were a family pet; he just adored this particular car, one of a fleet of seven, and by now so did Milos.

Ludmilla moaned in her sleep and turned to lie on her belly. Tired though he was, his penis stiffened. He wondered if he dared plunge it into her behind. Now, he moaned out loud with longing. If he did, he would have to put up with weeks, perhaps months, of silence. It wasn't worth it. His wife was frigid and refused to go to a doctor. They'd been reunited for nearly nine weeks, and she'd only allowed him to put it in twice, obviously without any enjoyment. He'd been better off playing with her in the Prague Woods, when at least they'd enjoyed masturbation together. Anything was better than this.

"Have I written you any lies? Isn't everything I've written to you true? Isn't this paradise?" he'd boasted that first evening in their bright and cheerful garage apartment with their own radio and even an icebox and, down below, an orchard full of trees where grapefruits and oranges as large as footballs were actually growing, fruit he'd been told he could pick whenever he felt like it; there was more than enough for everyone in the huge Towers household.

Even then, on that wonderful evening of reunion in their first real home together, after all the months of being apart through her mother's grave illness and then complication after complication with her papers, there had been a strange, almost cold reserve about her. She'd always had a mysterious quality. It was one of the many things about her that fascinated him.

"Yes, it's a paradise for the rich people," she'd said with that half-amused, half-sad smile of hers.

"What a strange remark," he'd said, forgetting it almost immediately as he popped open a bottle of champagne sent with such thoughtfulness by Mrs. Towers and, after gulping down a couple of glasses, forcing her back on the bed to receive him.

Milos shook his head groggily. He'd better get some sleep. It was going to be a very busy week with Suzanne, the Towers' daughter, arriving in Palm Beach the next morning after six or seven months spent polishing up her languages in Europe. According to Jeffers, she was a handful who could do no wrong in her parents' eyes. Milos understood that, all right. That was how he was sure he would feel about any child conceived with his seed in Ludmilla's womb. Again he started to throb with yearning for her.

"Ludmilla, Ludmilla, my cherub ..." he whispered.

There was no response. He sighed heavily, checked that the alarm clock was set for 7:00 A.M., and climbed into bed, where he fell immediately to sleep.

As soon as she heard the key in the door, Ludmilla had been fully awake, aware of Milos's every movement, every sound in the room, willing herself to lie motionless at first, acting out deep sleep, not sure which way to lie in the bed to ensure that he came nowhere near her. Only when his breathing turned into a faint snore did she relax and let out her own breath.

Sometimes she felt that when she looked in the mirror in the morning she would see that her raven black hair had turned snow white, as her poor mother's hair had begun to turn during her illness. She knew it could happen overnight from shock, too; she'd seen it happen to poor old Madame Ffurbringer, when her son was taken away for questioning and never came back.

Now, as she lay staring up at the ceiling, she grimaced bitterly remembering how hard she had prayed for all this, never doubting for a moment that America would take care of all her problems, that as soon as she stepped off the ship, her life with Milos would be "happy ever after."

But it really wasn't her fault. It was natural, after the terrible disappointment of not being able to leave Prague with Milos, that her every waking moment had been directed to the day when she would be able to leave with a clear conscience, certain she wasn't deserting her father, leaving him to run the business, look after a sick wife, and bring up her little seven-year-old sister, Natasha. When she wasn't working in the salon, cooking and looking after her mother, she'd studied English endlessly, so much so that she'd been able to write to Milos quite a few long letters in the language, without making many mistakes.

The day she had received her visa, it was Father Kusy who finally convinced her that her father meant it when he said she was their only hope for any kind of a future, their only hope of one day getting them all out. And like an act of God, her mother had suddenly found new strength, so much so that the day before she left for Hamburg to board the ship, her mother had even given their oldest client a three-hour perm without any signs of it being too much for her.

Ludmilla gulped hard to stop more tears wetting the pillowcase. She had to vow never to cry again. She was ruining her looks. It was bad enough that the doctor had told her it would be another four weeks before she could take up her duties in the house! When Mrs. Towers saw her again, she didn't want to see a wrinkled old crone. In the morning she would put away the music box her parents had given her as a farewell present, and not lift the lid to hear her favorite "Skaters' Waltz" again until she was well on the way to realizing her ambitions and could smile and laugh because she was really happy, not pretending to be for Milos's sake.

In her anxiety to get to America, she'd forgotten the extent of her hatred of housework. Even using hair remover on Mrs. Winkkler's hirsute calves was better than cleaning toilets, even the marble kind that looked like thrones in the downstairs his-and-hers powder rooms of the Palm Beach house.

She had come to realize, during her days trapped in the tiny apartment, that hairdressing, something she also loathed, was actually going to be as much of a lifeline out of Milos's clutches as he had been her lifeline out of Czechoslovakia.

Madame Towers's hair looked like a badly cooked soufflé, rising up when this creature called Alberto finished his "creation," but collapsing before she even got zipped into one of her multi-thousand-dollar dresses. How much did Mrs. Towers pay this poor excuse for a stylist? Ludmilla had no idea, but she was sure it was an exorbitant amount.

How long would it be before she had saved enough of her own to set out into this free world of so many enterprises and start a small hairdressing salon, or at least join the staff of a big one and live on her own somewhere? How was she going to persuade Milos to give her a savings account in her own name? He would surely be suspicious that she wanted it in order to leave him. She had to act like a loving wife, but since her foolish accident she'd found it more and more difficult to act anything.

The tears had congealed into a stinging lump behind her eyes. There was so much money in this paradise. She had never realized there could be so much money in one place, spent on so many unimportant things. It made her sick to hear from Milos about the nonstop, mindless parade of parties and dances and bridge games and fashion shows, going on around the clock in this never-never land. Did Colonel Towers ever mention what was going on in Czechoslovakia? No! He was apparently as indifferent to the suffering back home as was everyone else in this golden place of plenty, despite having seen for himself the Russian machine at work.

As Milos emitted a loud snore and turned over, dragging half of the bedclothes with him, Ludmilla went to look out the window, where, through the tall trees, she could see a sliver of the ocean. Of course, she was sick with envy, nothing else, sick that she was wasting so much time living with a man whose touch she now could hardly bear.

The radio that Milos had pointed to with such pride when she'd seen their "new home in Florida" for the first time had become both a torture and a drug. If she hadn't had to stay off her feet, she would never have known what chaos was happening in the world, listening day after day to the news of the Communist menace creeping over everything like a slimy bog. And the world news was so often followed by programs that emphasized her loneliness and sadness for her struggling family, because the audiences showed how happy and carefree they were by laughing all the time at words that weren't at all funny to her. Milos had tried to explain that these were comedy programs where signs were held up directing the audiences to laugh, but she didn't believe it. There was no reason for Americans not to laugh; they had everything, while back home her family had nothing, not even their liberty.

The last months she'd spent at home had been the worst. Friends spying on friends, simple actions questioned, old clients not turning up and never seen again. She had only received one letter from her parents since her arrival in early December, and now it was the middle of February.

"Did you speak to Colonel Towers about not receiving any letters from home?" she asked. Milos had overslept and was hurriedly getting into his dark green uniform, hunting under the bed for the socks he'd worn the night before.

"I asked if I could see him today. He didn't answer. He wasn't in a good mood. I'll try again." Even though he didn't have a second to waste, he stood at the door watching Ludmilla braid her beautiful, almost waist-length hair, hoping for at least a smile before he drove to the railway station to pick up Miss Suzanne. "What are you going to do today? I should be able to come home early. I believe they have a dinner at home tonight."

She didn't smile. "I am practicing my English. I shall go through all the records and practice my accent. What do you want for dinner? The cook has given me two hens."

"Chickens," Milos corrected her automatically. "So we'll have roast chicken."

The sunlight blinded him as he opened the door to the yard, but he took no pleasure from it. He had kissed the top of his young wife's head as she'd sat braiding her hair so expertly, because she had refused to get up to give him a good-bye kiss. What on earth could he do if Florida sunshine couldn't bring a smile to her face? Absolutely nothing, unless perhaps miraculously there was a letter from home, but he had an ominous feeling there weren't going to be any letters for quite a while. Although he knew he'd led Ludmilla to think that Colonel Towers had no interest in how their families were faring back home and in Czech affairs in general, it wasn't entirely true.

The problem was that, on the rare occasions Colonel Towers mentioned Prague or Czechoslovakia, the news was so bad that there was no point in telling her. As he backed the Rolls out, he looked up as he always did, hoping she might have relented and would be at the window waving him good-bye.

His heart leapt. She was there. He sounded the horn and waved, and to his joy she waved back, brushing a tendril away from her face, before moving inside. Perhaps this was going to be his lucky day. Perhaps this was the day he would find at last the old beloved Ludmilla waiting for him when he returned.

As he headed toward the house, he suddenly had a daring idea, one that at least might take her mind off the lack of news from her parents, one that could break the monotony of her days.

It was her gesture of brushing the tendril away that made him think of it. He'd heard Mrs. Towers complaining to the colonel all the way home the evening before about the impossibility of looking the way she wanted to look for one whole evening. Certainly he'd seen for himself that she'd looked like a different person leaving the party from the one who'd arrived, holding her funny hat in her hand with the feathers trailing behind her, her hair half up, half down, brushing it out of her eyes before attempting to step into the car. Before locking up for the night, he'd had to spend at least fifteen minutes getting rid of all the hairpins strewn over the backseat.

Even Ludmilla had commented during the short time she'd been in Florida how amateurish Mrs. Towers's hairstyling seemed to be. He hadn't taken any notice, because certainly Ludmilla hadn't been trying to push herself. She didn't even like hairdressing, although she was very good at it, but it was something she could do sitting down! And if Mrs. Towers was satisfied, perhaps she wouldn't have to go back to housework, which, of course, she loathed even more than hairdressing. Who wouldn't? It hurt him to think of his princess using her white hands on so many demeaning jobs.

He'd been told to be at the front door by 8:00 A.M. although he also knew from Jeffers that the train didn't get in until 9:35, if it was on time, which it often wasn't.

Who would be going with him to greet Miss Suzanne? Milos was sure that after such a late night it would only be the colonel, and he'd hoped this would give him the opportunity to ask if there was a way the colonel could find out how Ludmilla's family was. Now, with this brand-new idea, he hoped against hope that Mrs. Towers might accompany her husband. It would be easier to broach the idea to the two of them, because Mrs. Towers liked him, he was sure she did, and, more important, after working for her for nine months, she trusted him not to say or do anything he hadn't thoroughly checked out.

But as he'd feared, only the colonel came out, at around eight-forty-five. "They say it's running late, but I don't trust the railroad. Let's go, Milos, and tell me what's on your mind."

"It's my wife, sir . . ." Milos hadn't expected the colonel to be so receptive after his attitude the night before, but seeing in the rearview mirror how relaxed his employer looked, he took a chance. "She's very worried because she hasn't heard anything from her family in Prague for over two months; then, because of her accident, she hears every day on the radio how difficult everything is over there. Is there any way you could find out if her family's safe? She tells me the Russian Communists are becoming stronger and stronger, and our elected government weaker and weaker." Before the colonel could answer, Milos went on, more animated than he'd been in weeks.

"Also, if you'll permit me, sir, I have a suggestion I would like to propose to help . . . help . . ."

"I don't need any help contacting the American embassy in Prague, young fella."

"Oh, no, sir, of course not, sir. This is another idea." By now Milos knew that whenever his boss gave him an opportunity to ask him something, he had to take it at once, or weeks could go by before there would be another chance. "If you'll forgive me, sir, I heard

Madame complaining about the poor standard of coiffure here in comparison to New York." Milos carefully watched his employer's reaction in the mirror, but he was inscrutable. "You may remember that when I first told you about my wife, I mentioned that her family own the very respected Sukova beauty salon in Prague. My wife, Ludmilla, is a highly trained hairdresser, sir. Do you think Madame Towers would give her a chance to do her hair to show her what she can do? I think she could do it soon, even before her foot is out of the cast."

The colonel hadn't been paying attention. As soon as Milos had started in with his "forgive me, sir," his thoughts had drifted to the twenty-year-old daughter he would soon be greeting. He was apprehensive. He didn't know her—how could he know her? He'd scarcely had a chance after four years away when, soon after his homecoming, Honey had persuaded him to send Suzanne off to Europe. Preposterous though it had seemed to him at the time, Honey had forced him to accept that it was all for Suzanne's good, that she had to get away because she was moping so much over the fact that the incredibly tedious, acne-scarred Dudley Hitchingforth had returned from the Pacific and become engaged to someone equally tedious and pimply.

It had seemed impossible, but, looking back, he now had to accept Honey had been right. Suzanne, the cutest, curviest little package any man could hope for, even without the couple of million dollars she had in her trust fund, had been moping and when the Hitchingforth wedding invitation came in the mail, she'd jumped at the chance to go and live in Paris for six or seven months under the watchful eye of his old friend, the American ambassador.

From all accounts she'd had a ball, and now there was this rich Swiss fish who had the hots for her. Well, the Swiss fish would have to cool his fins in the Lake of Geneva, because now he was going to show his daughter, the light of his life, how important she was, that she was far too young to think of getting hooked, and when she did, there were plenty of American fish around.

"So would you consider, sir, mentioning it to Madame?"

"What?" They were stopped at a traffic light, and Milos had turned around to look at him, something that was sufficiently unusual for the colonel to note. "What, Milos?" he repeated, a note of exasperation in his voice.

"Ludmilla, sir, she is a talented hairdresser, sir. Would you ask Mrs. Towers to give her a chance?"

"Yes, yes, why not, and I'll try to find out something for you about her family and yours, too."

*   *   *

As it was, although Milos tried to find a way to remind him every day before he left for New York, Benedict never gave the subject of Ludmilla's hairdressing expertise another thought—not until he returned to Palm Beach on the twenty fifth of February for Suzanne's welcome-home party. This time it was to be a very short visit, as he had to leave from Miami over the weekend on a business trip to Switzerland.

Suzanne met him in the hall with a wry expression. "*Mon Dieu*, Papa, thank heaven you've returned. Mama is in a state of *crise* upstairs. Alberto, the maestro hairdresser, who she has been cursing every day since you left, has had the gall to go to Miami Beach to answer an SOS from Judy Garland, who's appearing for one night in cabaret there. Ooh-la-la, *tant pis*."

Benedict shrugged. "So isn't there anyone else? I thought Alberto was the cause of her hair problems, not the solution."

"Yesterday, yes, Papa. *Aujourd'hui*, she thinks he's a star."

When Benedict went into Honey's dressing room, to his disgust she was sobbing. "Honey, for God's sake, what's all this about? I've come down here at considerable inconvenience for Suzanne's party, and here you are, acting like an idiot over a hairdresser I thought you despised. It's time you learned how to do your own hair."

Instead of pulling her to her senses, his obvious irritation made her sob all the louder. Oh God, how he wished he was a thousand miles away.

The intercom buzzed, and he picked up the phone. "Yes? Okay, put him on." Benedict put his hand over the receiver. "Honey, pull yourself together. I'm ashamed of you—don't act like such a fool in front of your daughter. Anyway, be quiet, someone's calling me from the State Department."

Honey rushed into her bathroom and slammed the door, as Benedict waited to be connected.

"Good God!" He slumped down on a chaise longue. "So that's that. No hope, eh? All right, keep me posted." He leaned back as he put the phone down. So what he had expected had finally happened: a Communist coup d'etat in Czechoslovakia. The freely elected government was out, the Russian tanks were in, and Churchill's prediction of an iron curtain had now shut down tight in Czechoslovakia.

Milos. He'd have to break the news to Milos before he learned about it on the radio or before his wife did.

As he heard Honey splashing next door, he suddenly remembered what Milos had told him. His wife was a hairdresser! Well, there was no time like the present. "Honey!" He raised his voice. "Honey, put on whatever you usually put on for your hairdressing sessions. I may have a surprise for you. At least it's better than nothing."

His wife opened the door an inch. "I hate you," she said. "I thought you, of all people, would understand why I'm so upset. This is the first big party we've given all season, and the first chance to introduce Suzanne to all sorts of attractive young men. You know the Oliphants are bringing the crown prince of . . . well, I forget which country, but I'm told he's madly eligible and good looking! Of course, I wanted to look my best, not my worst. I told Alberto the date at least a month ago. He says I . . ."

"I'm not interested in your fag hairdresser. He can drown himself in Miami Beach for all I care. Listen, I forgot to tell you—it seems Milos's wife, Loretta, is a hairdresser. He asked me if I'd ask you to give her a chance to show you what she can do."

"Loretta? Oh, you mean Ludmilla? But she's a downstairs maid. How on earth can I let her touch my hair?"

Benedict threw up his hands in anger. "I'm really not that interested. Do whatever you have to do. Milos seemed to know what he was talking about. God knows, you've been moaning about having a personal maid who can do your hair. Perhaps, without knowing it, you've already got one on the premises."

"Where's Suzanne? Oh, I don't know. Where's Suzanne . . ." He'd had enough. It was bad enough to have to think about hairdressers, let alone have a family conference about it. He started to walk out.

"Ben, don't go. I'm sorry, but what do you think . . ."

"Suit yourself." He ran down to his study, locked the door, and started to make calls to Washington.

"Daddy, Daddy, it's six-fifteen, aren't you going to get dressed up for your favorite date?" How right she was. Suzanne certainly was his favorite date. He couldn't believe it was so late.

"I'm coming, darling." He shook his head. The last couple of hours had depressed him utterly. He had to get his head clear, to smile, to make small talk, to be the utterly charming father he really wanted to be, but with the news from Prague, it wasn't going to be easy.

As he began to climb the stairs, a tall, slender young woman was limping down, holding on to the banister. This had to be Milos's wife, Ludmilla, the housemaid-turned-hairdresser. So Honey had decided to take the risk after all. He only hoped he wasn't going to have to pay for it with more mindless yapping. "Let me help you," he offered.

He held out his hand, but the young woman didn't take it. "Thank you, I am able to manage for myself, Colonel Towers." The look on the face was as cool as the tone of the voice. All the same, he descended back to the hall to be sure she didn't slip and fall on her ass again.

"Thank you, I imagine you have saved the day. Milos tells me you are a very talented stylist."

"Yes."

She had the darkest eyes he had ever seen. She looked directly at him as if expecting him to say something more, something different. Had she heard the radio?

"I'm afraid the Communist coup we have been expecting in your country has taken place."

"I know, Colonel Towers." He felt awkward, wanting to say something to console her, yet strangely at a loss.

Honey's voice came from above. "Darling, I don't know how to thank you. Wait until you see how Ludmilla has done my hair—and Suzanne's, too. It's never looked so good in Palm Beach. We have found ourselves another treasure. Why Milos never told me before, I'll never know, the naughty boy. Hurry now, you've got less than an hour before everyone arrives."

"Thank you, Ludmilla," he said.

She was not disrespectful, but she continued to look at him directly, without speaking, without any sign of embarrassment or uneasiness. She was tall, at least five-eight or -nine, he reckoned, and yes, he had to admit Milos hadn't exaggerated. Unmade-up and dowdily dressed, she was nevertheless undoubtedly beautiful.

New York, 1949

"THERE'LL BE A good bonus in this for you, Norris. Your advice on the soybean front has been invaluable. With your belief in Boyer and his remarkable process, you were right on target to fund that research. I have to tell you I still can hardly believe soybeans can actually be used to produce a flour that can deliver ninety percent protein! It's incredible! Get the patent stuff started. I agree with you, we can do something for Europe's starving hordes, which will give us brownie points with Washington and make a fair amount of profit, too."

"I don't want a bonus, Ben." Norris was always quiet—some said inaudible—when he was at his most dangerous in a negotiation.

Benedict had been expecting something like this, but he said nothing as his most valuable lieutenant continued, "I'd like some stock and a place on your board of directors." Norris had earned it, they both knew that. They both also knew that as the company was presently set up, it was impossible.

"I'm sorry, Norris. I can't change the rules right now, even for you. My grandfather set up Towers Pharmaceuticals as a privately held company. No one outside the family can sit on the board or hold stock, as you well know. We've discussed this before."

It was the second time Norris had raised the issue. The first time, a few weeks after he'd returned from Prague, more than two years before, it had been easier to deal with. Then, although Norris had undoubtedly shown that he knew how to hold the fort, having built up the profit picture during Benedict's absence, he had been startled and then eager to get involved in the huge expansion plans Benedict had immediately begun to set in motion.

A monumental bonus had shut Norris up then, without even a snide reference to what a dead weight Benedict's younger brother, Leonard, had turned out to be. Benedict didn't blame Norris for still trying to get the rules changed. It had to be galling to know that Leonard, not up to scratch for the army because of a middle-ear problem and not up to scratch for Towers Pharmaceuticals because of a lack of brains, owned Towers stock and was on the board simply because of the blood running through his veins. Even now Leonard didn't seem to understand totally his brother's global objectives; but nobody really understood their massive reach, not even Norris, and he'd given up trying to explain them to Honey. Sometimes, though not often, he became very aware of his solitary planning. It was a strange, lonely feeling that he shrugged off as fatigue from overwork.

If only his children were older! He was in such a hurry to have them by his side in every endeavor, but they hadn't yet reached the mandatory age of twenty-five to become board members, and none of the first or second cousins on the board were of Norris's caliber. Few people were.

Well, it was just too bad. That was the way it was with dynasties and the few royal families still fortunate enough to reign, if not rule. While he was reigning and ruling on the Towers throne, he had no intention of changing anything. He'd heard his father say too often, "Once you let outsiders in, mistakes multiply. In business, blood is definitely thicker than water, and don't you ever forget it." He didn't intend to. It was the reason, he knew, why his own mother had never been elected to the board, although she had been an intelligent, fast-thinking, energetic woman. It was certainly the reason Honey never would be.

Provided he didn't expect more than any board member could deliver, everything worked well, very well. He'd made sure that every member, even Leonard, headed up a committee composed of the brightest talent money could buy, and Norris attended most board meetings. Some of those meetings could hardly take place without him, but he was nevertheless an outsider, and Benedict intended never to lose sight of the fact.

Why had he chosen today to voice his frustration? Benedict showed no sign of his concern, as he swiveled around in his father's beloved old chair, wondering whether Norris was already being wooed by Merck or Upjohn, although his contract wasn't up for another year. He decided to take a different tack.

"Be patient, Norris. Things can change. I'm the only one who can change the rules, as you know, but now isn't the moment. I promise you I'll think about it as soon as I decide whether Charlie will ever have it in him to carry on my battles."

Norris smiled a thin, tight smile. "When you were nineteen, your father knew. I think you know about Charlie now, too. Don't you, Ben?"

Benedict frowned. True, he did, but he wasn't going to let Norris get away with any cheap innuendo. Charles Benedict Towers was his son, and nobody, not even Norris, could get away with a crack about his son. "Charles is doing well at the London office. So far I'm not worried about him. We'll see." His curt tone showed that the subject was dismissed. Norris would accept the bonus when he heard the size of it. For one thing, his greedy wife wouldn't allow him to turn it down.

Anxious to move on, Benedict pushed a large, double-spread color advertisement across the ebony desk. "It's interesting what this guy Revson's doing, eh? Fire and Ice—shade names for fairly ordinary lipsticks and nail enamels, but promoted in this new sexy, enticing way. Enticing to me, anyway, but will it attract women? I think so. I like it. I'm sure it's a winner. Still, rather him than me."

Norris snapped acerbically, "Analysts like Greydon and Finstein call the cosmetics industry inflation-proof and recession-resiliant, but I don't buy it. Women are too fickle. They'll always need soap and soap powders, but the way they change their minds about the stuff they put on their faces never ceases to amaze me."

"Me too," Benedict agreed, relieved to see that Norris looked more relaxed. "One of these days they're going to stop believing the rubbish they're promised, and the powder and paint business won't amount to a hill of beans."

"Well, not soybeans, anyway." Norris retorted sardonically, and picking up a thick file marked BOYER: CONFIDENTIAL, sauntered out, not looking too unhappy. Benedict made a mental note to find out if Norris had been receiving any overtures from the competition. There wasn't much he couldn't find out once he put his mind and money behind it.

Although it was time to leave for lunch with his father's old friend, Conrad Hilton, who wanted to show off his latest acquisition, the Waldorf-Astoria Hotel, Benedict sat staring at the ad that featured the top model of the moment, Dorian Leigh, but he wasn't seeing her face on the page.

As soon as he'd read the words earlier that morning, another face had come into his mind, the face of Ludmilla, the wife of his chauffeur, the ice maiden Honey could now never travel anywhere without, the ice maiden who in one brief moment the week before had shown him a fire was blazing inside her.

He was puzzled that he was thinking about Ludmilla, about her long, pale hands combing, twisting, curling, arranging his wife's hair so beautifully in much the same way, fast and imperious, he'd occasionally seen her arranging flowers.

Fire and ice. Until the week before, Ludmilla had only permitted the ice to show as, with cool, inscrutable expression, she painted his wife's toenails or altered his wife's clothes, taking in, letting out, or massaged Honey's skin, always described by Honey as "terribly, terribly dry."

As his secretary buzzed to say Milos was downstairs with the car, Benedict leaned back and closed his eyes to concentrate on how many different personal services he'd seen Ludmilla perform for Honey, and how many times during the past year and a half he'd seen her, without really seeing her. How was that possible? He still remembered looking into her eyes that first day on the staircase in Palm Beach. He even remembered thinking at the time, *Milos is right; his wife is beautiful.* But then? How could he not have been aware of her until the week before, when Honey had insisted he allow Ludmilla to massage his neck and scalp when he'd come home from the office with a headache that was pounding every rational thought out of his head.

He'd felt too weak to argue, had just wanted to be left alone, to swallow down the new migraine drug they were testing and sleep for a week, but Honey had insisted and insisted. Ludmilla had been summoned, and her long, pale hands had ministered to him, until to his surprise and gratitude the pounding had lessened, and across the room, in the long mirror, he had watched her graceful body moving as her hands stroked away the pain.

Even now he didn't know why what he'd said had made her temper flash out, like a meteor streaking across a still, dark sky.

As he went down in the elevator, he was still thinking about it. He'd been trying to give her a compliment, and yes, for some reason he'd wanted to get a smile out of her. What had he said? Something like "Between you and Milos, your hands are worth a fortune. No one I've ever known can put life back into a car like your husband, and now I find you can put life back into me. Your children will probably all be little Mozarts—or should I say Dvoraks?" She had removed her hands from his neck so quickly he'd turned to look at her. He couldn't remember many people in his life who'd looked at him with such fury. In fact, he could remember only one, a woman he'd spurned years ago.

"I am much more than a pair of hands, Colonel Towers. One day, in your great United States of America, I hope I will be known because of my brain."

The words had been spat out, her huge, dark eyes flashing as though cymbals and gongs and drums were crashing about behind them. He hadn't known whether to laugh or apologize, and because he'd felt fragile, only just released from a day of tormenting pain, he had simply closed his eyes and told her, "Don't stop using your hands now, please, Ludmilla. We'll get around to what your brain can do later."

He'd intended to tell Honey about her precious Ludmilla's show of temper, but then he'd decided not to. Why he was thinking about it again today, as he had a few times during the past week, he really didn't know.

"Your wife is a good masseuse, Milos," he found himself saying as the Cadillac approached Fifth Avenue.

"Oh, I am so pleased you think so, sir. Ludmilla told me about your headache."

"She detonated it."

"Yes, sir." Milos sounded uncomfortable.

"Does she want to receive training—as a beautician or something similar? I am sure Mrs. Towers would be happy to arrange it."

"Oh, thank you, sir, but no, sir, I don't . . . well, perhaps I should discuss . . ." Milos made no attempt to hide the doubt in his voice.

"What does she want to do?" There was a long pause. "Well?"

"I don't really know, sir. She is very interested in business . . . business school . . . well, perhaps shorthand, typing, or college."

"They are scarcely the same thing."

"She is taking different correspondence courses, sir. She never stops studying in her time off, sir." Milos didn't attempt to hide the unhappiness in his voice, either. Interesting.

They were drawing up to the huge hotel on Park Avenue, now in the Hilton group. "Ask her what she wants to do with her brain, Milos."

Benedict expected his question to sound like a joke, but when Milos said in a heavy voice, "Yes, sir, I would like to know that myself, sir," he realized he'd sounded as if he really wanted to know the answer.

For the past year Benedict had been home less and less, and because his trips, however far-flung around the globe, were counted in days and not weeks, Honey had never, expressed a wish to go with him.

Now, with new plants and research centers opening in England, Switzerland, and France, he told her the following Sunday it made the most sense for him to spend from a month to six weeks in Europe. It would be the longest time he had been away since his return from the war.

When she learned the date, Honey made a face as he'd expected she would. "You'll miss the opening night of *South Pacific*. It's going to be the most fantastic night Broadway has seen since before the war. The Rodgerses are counting on us to be there."

"I hardly think my absence will spoil Dick Rodgers's evening. From what I hear, it's been sold out for months." Benedict tried to disappear behind the pages of *The New York Times*, but Honey came over to perch on the arm of the chair.

"Darling . . ."

Suddenly she was purring. She was obviously after something.

"Yep?" Benedict kept his eyes on the paper, as Honey traced a finger down his cheek. "I've just had a wonderful idea. I'll forgive you for *South Pacific* if . . ." She hesitated, not sure of his mood. "Well, the Fords and the Lucius Clays are going over on the *Queen Elizabeth* on the third or fourth, I think. We haven't had a real vacation since you came home, except that week in Virginia. Cynthia mentioned to me that if there was any chance at all of our meeting up with them in Paris . . . but I never gave it a thought till now. To be with you in Paris . . . oh, darling, wouldn't it be wonderful, and I know how much you admire Lucius. I'd simply adore crossing with them on the *Queen*. It's only five or six days . . ."

He didn't answer at first. It was true they hadn't had a vacation, or, rather, *he* hadn't had one. Honey's life was in many ways one long vacation, except he had to admit she was always running houses, supervising servants. The London office, he knew, had rustled up Princess Margaret to do the ribbon-cutting at the plant, which would thrill Honey, and yes, he liked and admired Clay, the major force behind Radio Free Europe, now beginning to beam world news to listeners behind the Iron Curtain, to Warsaw and Budapest—and Prague.

"Let me look at the itinerary. It's not a bad idea, not a bad idea at all," he said slowly. "And, of course, we could spend some time with Charlie in London." He went into his study, followed by Honey, who was bubbling with excitement. He handed her the neatly typed travel plan. As she read it, seeing the one- and two-night stopovers, he anticipated what she was also going to request, and it wasn't long in coming.

"It's very important that as the chairman's wife I took my best, darling, isn't it? Some of these plans don't give me any time to do anything." He waited, hoping he was right. "Could I possibly bring Ludmilla along? Of course, in steerage class on the ship, or whatever it's called. Then I wouldn't have to worry about anything—my clothes, my hair, anything." She looked at him challengingly. "It would save a fortune on beauty salons and"—now there was a triumphant note in her voice—"you've often said that since I found Ludmilla, I've never kept you waiting. Well, hardly ever."

"Of course you can bring her along. It might even make her smile once or twice."

Honey was amazed and looked it. Was Ben turning into a pussycat? It had all been so easy. "Oh, you are such a darling. I can't wait to tell the Fords and the Clays and Charlie. And yes, of course, Ludmilla, too. She won't be able to believe it. What a treat for her. Oh, what a wonderful idea. I can meet Christian Dior and go to the shows and buy French perfume. Oh, darling, thank you so much. I'll make you so proud everywhere we go, you'll see."

"You don't have to go," Milos said miserably. "Mrs. Towers would never be able to replace you, even if you refused to go."

"Perhaps Colonel Towers will ask you, too." They were in the huge servants' kitchen of their employers' Park Avenue triplex. Milos sat at the table watching his wife as she prepared the tisane Mrs. Towers now drank, at Ludmilla's direction, for the sake of her complexion.

"No, he won't," Milos growled. "Rolls-Royce wants to sell him another car in England, and he's already told me they are giving him their best chauffeur for the duration of his stay." He buried his head in his hands, his voice muffled. "He doesn't even realize what he's doing to me, letting you go with Madame."

Ludmilla sat down facing him. "Don't be a big silly." Her voice was unusually gentle. "It will be good for you not to have to put up with me for a short while. I'll bring you a present back from Paris."

"You really want to go, don't you?"

"Why are you surprised? Doesn't every girl want to see Paris once in her life? And just think . . ." She looked at him dreamily. "For the first time in months and months, no ocean water will separate me from Mama and Papa and little Natasha . . ." There were tears brimming in her eyes, but as he reached out for her, she recoiled as always. "Don't comfort me. I don't want to cry. I want to be happy. I long to be happy. In Paris I know I will be."

Milos fidgeted. He hadn't seen her excited like this in years. The kettle started to sing. As she poured the boiling water over the herbs, he came up behind her. When she put the kettle down, before she could move, he put his arms around her, pinioning her arms to her sides. He pushed into her soft behind. "I am your husband. Before I give you permission to go, we must make love." Although she was rigid, like a pole, he continued to rub against her until his penis grew hard and big. There were footsteps approaching the kitchen. "Milos!" she protested angrily.

"Promise, or I'll tell Colonel Towers you're pregnant and cannot go; I will not allow it."

"That is disgusting. I am not pregnant and I don't intend to be, you know it."

"Promise!" He raised his voice, although they could hear the voices of the two upstairs maids just outside.

Her voice was low and cold. "I promise," she said. "Now let me go, you pig."

"God damn it, Norris, if we invented aspirin tomorrow, the government would probably never okay it. I'm tired of the procrastinators at the FDA; when I come back, we've got to get a conversation going with the commissioner. This latest turndown of perfectly ethical testing procedures is too much." Benedict slammed down the phone and returned to sit in front of the Louis Quatorze dressing table in the dressing room of his luxurious Ritz Hotel suite.

Ludmilla carefully put a towel over his white dress shirt and began to trim his hair. Again it was Honey who had brought this about. "My hair's too long. I wish I'd brought Burke, my barber, along," he'd joked at breakfast that morning.

Intent on showing him how much money Ludmilla was saving them on the trip, Honey had immediately extolled the girl's cutting ability, and so far, Benedict thought, so good. Their eyes met in the mirror, and knowing she must have overheard the heated conversation he had just had with Norris back in New York, Benedict didn't want to mislead her into thinking Towers Pharmaceuticals was about to invent aspirin! Honey had misinterpreted him more than once.

"Do you know, Ludmilla, how long aspirin has been with us?"

He was about to tell her, when, without stopping her snipping, she said, "Since Hippocrates discovered salicin in the bark of the willow tree. Since 400 B.C."

As he frowned, she suddenly smiled, a breathtaking, vivid smile that brought dimples to her cheeks and a disconcertingly mischievous sparkle to her eyes. "All right, young lady," he said grudgingly. "I am prepared to be impressed now with your brain." They stared at each other in the mirror for a second too long, the second that makes a difference in a relationship, the second that imperceptibly, without saying a word, gives the impression there is interest in the other person.

It was at that moment, as Benedict later reflected, that he decided he would get to know this strange person with the long, pale hands, the aloof, reserved demeanor, this young woman with so much hidden beauty and brains.

"Ludmilla, I have a surprise for you." Honey sounded self-important as she swished into the dressing room in a dramatic black taffeta evening dress she'd bought in London from a new designer named Norman Hartnell.

"Yes, Madame?"

"You've worked so hard ever since we left New York, and now here is my husband putting you to work," she twittered happily. "Please don't give him too good a haircut, or Burke will never see him again and my hair will suffer."

"So what's the surprise?" Benedict interrupted irritably. If only Honey had come in five minutes later . . . he had a surprise to propose to Ludmilla himself.

"It's on the bed. Don't peek, Ludmilla, until we've gone—which, incidentally, my dear husband, should be in a matter of minutes. Don't tell me Mr. Punctuality is going to keep Mrs. Unpunctuality waiting tonight?" As she bent down to kiss Benedict on his brow, a strong wave of perfume came with her, making him sneeze.

"Good God, Honey, whatever is that foul concoction?" He sneezed again and again.

"It's a new perfume—from Dior. It isn't even out yet, isn't that exciting? He wants me to test it."

"You can tell him from me, it's guaranteed to make men run a mile. A mile *away* from whoever's wearing it."

"Oh, darling, don't be such a tease. I probably sprayed on too much." The phone rang in the bedroom, and Honey ran to answer it, humming under her breath, in heaven to be in Paris wearing a new dress from one hot designer and a new perfume from another.

Again they looked at each other in the mirror, but before Benedict could tell Ludmilla his idea, Honey was back. "The car is *en bas*," she sang out. "Ludmilla, are you sure this chignon is safe? I've never worn one so high before."

As Ludmilla turned to inspect her earlier work, Benedict stood up, throwing the towel on the floor. "That's enough interruption for one haircut." He brushed his hand through his thick, dark hair. Still, he was happy to see, there was no trace of gray. "It looks fine anyway. I can't sit there with you two blabbering over me." As Ludmilla gave him a quick sidelong glance of reproach, he winked at her. It wasn't his style to wink; it happened as naturally as his sneeze.

Ludmilla began to brush up the hair from the bathroom floor as Benedict went inside to put on his dinner jacket, and hear Honey repeat, "The surprise is in the bedroom. When we've gone, you can take it to your room to try on. If it doesn't fit, bring it back in the morning, but I'm sure it will fit. What time do you want me on parade tomorrow, darling?" she called out. "Is there anything before lunch with the Minister of Trade?" He came in, the tall, dark, and handsome husband whose arm she was so proud to be on.

"Nothing before lunch, Honey. Be ready by noon."

When the door closed behind them, Ludmilla went slowly into their bedroom. A dress was on the bed, a delicate silk dress. She picked it up. It looked like moonbeams and was as light as cobwebs. It was a mixture of yellows, as pale as the moon in Palm Beach, as deep as the buttercups that grew in the Prague woods. It was the most beautiful dress that Ludmilla had ever seen, and when she looked at the label she gasped. Christian Dior Boutique. She could hardly believe it. She held the dress up against her, bringing the thin silk to her cheek. It was an irrisistible dress, one she had never believed she could ever own. Even if it didn't fit, she wouldn't—couldn't—give it back. She would take it to pieces to find out its magic and make it fit. She would never part with it, never.

She was seized by a compulsion to put it on immediately. She hated every single piece of clothing she owned. She stepped out of her plain navy skirt and unbuttoned her white shirt so hurriedly that one button went spinning into the corner.

It was impossible to step into the dress. It had to go over her head, and the feel of the silk slipping down her body reminded her of the one time she'd taken a bubble bath in bubbles "borrowed" from a bottle of Mrs. Towers' when she had gone to spend a day with Suzanne cruising along Florida's inland waterway.

It didn't only fit. The dress transformed her. It was simply cut, but the thin silk clung to her body, in some miraculous way appearing to lengthen her torso, sculpturing her firm, lean upper body, curving and rounding her breasts, emphasizing her tiny waist, stroking the shapeliness of her buttocks and thighs. She knew she was beautiful in the dress. The medley of gold tones brought out the rich black of her hair, threw warm notes onto her white skin, reflected the topaz in her eyes. She threw her hands up into the air as if to hold the moment forever, a moment when she had never in her whole life been so happy.

As she moved, her hair, hurriedly pinned up in a twist, unraveled down her back. She didn't attempt to catch it, but just stood looking at herself in the dress that would always stand for so many memories of Paris, for the grand sweep of the Champs Elysées, seen from the limousine window on their arrival, for the Sacré Coeur, looking like a magical wedding cake up in the hills of Montmartre that first day when she'd walked her feet off for hours, the only time she'd had to herself in the seven days they'd been in the city.

She was lost in a dream of happiness. She didn't hear the sitting room door open. She didn't know her employer had come into the bedroom to see her standing so still, with arms stretched high before the mirror.

His body leapt. He knew now why he wanted to know her. He wanted to possess her, to use his mind and body to make her face move with emotion, to see pain and pleasure there. He held on to the door to steady himself. He was going mad.

As he turned to leave, the door creaked and Ludmilla whirled around. "I'm sorry, sir, I . . . I thought you had . . ."

"What are you sorry about?" He still held on to the door. If he went near her, he would have to touch her, and that would be the end. He would never know her.

"I forgot my cigars." He didn't need to explain to a servant why he'd returned, and it wasn't true. He had deliberately left his favorite cigars on the side table. He'd hoped she would still be in the bedroom or the dressing room. Did she know that? No, she was looking her usual somber self—or trying to look somber—in the dress that, all the way through the Ritz lobby to the car, Honey had explained to him was from Christian Dior's less expensive Boutique line. Ludmilla looked like three trillion dollars to him.

It was a modest dress—no décolletage, or side slits through which her long limbs could emerge, but its very simplicity heightened her sexuality. The silk, he decided, looked as if it had been poured over her. He wanted to drink her, to—

The phone rang. He didn't answer it, and neither did she, her cool composure now firmly back in place.

He longed to snatch that mask somehow from her face, to keep her in a state of confusion, wonderment, anxiety, reacting to his every mood, instead of making people react to hers. To cover his own confusion, he barked at her, "It's time you paid some attention to the way you dress. You're certainly paid enough to have a few decent things, yet you seem to delight in going around in drab rags, like some kind of refugee."

She said nothing, but looked so vulnerable in the beautiful dress that he felt at that instant it would change forever the way he regarded women.

The phone rang again, summoning him away from temptation. As he went to the door he said gravely, "I have a surprise for you, too. Or perhaps once again you will surprise me with what you know.

When we arrive in Switzerland, I think you will be surprised by our new plant. I intend to take you there myself."

He was pleased with himself because for a second she looked startled, but she quickly recovered. "What shall I wear, sir?"

"That dress, of course."

As Benedict had hoped and expected, it was relatively easy to take Ludmilla on a tour of the company's new Swiss complex. The day before, Honey had accompanied him to the official opening, which he'd known would bore her out of her tiny mind.

Although he hadn't subjected her to the walking tour of the new facilities in England, or even the much shorter tour of the new research laboratories outside Paris, he insisted that Honey cover every inch of the marvelous new Swiss operation, which took an arduous three and a half hours.

He'd had a hard time persuading her she also had to accompany him to the formal celebration dinner that followed, given by the mayor of Geneva. By the time she limped into bed, Honey was pleading not to have to attend the lunch party he was giving the following day for his European managers, many of whom had yet to see the new facilities, which Benedict was eager to show them himself.

Before he switched out the light he said casually, "I think I'll give Ludmilla a break and take her to the plant. It will be interesting for her to see how Towers Pharmaceuticals actually produces some of its products. Is that all right with you? I can send her back in time for your evening hairdo. We don't have to be at the banquet until seven-thirty."

Honey groaned. "Do I have to go to another banquet? The Swiss are so deadly dull, and I ache all over. I'm sure I've got a chill. Are you sure it will be a break for Ludmilla? I don't want to make her more miserable. She's been so moody since we left Paris."

"Don't worry. It's not a bad idea for the people we depend on personally to see how we earn the money to pay their exorbitant salaries."

Honey was asleep, as he had also hoped she would be when he left at seven-thirty the next morning, leaving her a note to say he was leaving the chauffeur behind at the hotel, in case she had any errands for him to run.

He told himself he was looking forward to driving the new dark red Rolls himself, and talking to Ludmilla to find out whether she really had the capability one day to be known for her brain, as she'd told him so acerbically. He told himself he was arriving at the plant two hours earlier than the European group because he wanted some time to catch up on certain problems. He knew, however, that all he really wanted was to be alone with Ludmilla for a few hours.

It was raining, and he was disappointed to see Ludmilla wearing her usual drab brown raincoat, but as he directed her to climb into the front seat with him, he smiled to see a flash of yellow skirt as she sat down.

If he wanted to find out about her brain, he didn't give her much opportunity to exhibit it as they drove along side the Lake of Geneva and out of the city.

Perhaps it was her stillness, perhaps it was the sense of an intelligence at work, absorbing, understanding, making the right comment from time to time, but Benedict found himself pouring out a stream of information and statistics about the pharmaceutical business. "The public buys pharmaceutical products—drugs—because they trust the company that makes them. Once that trust is lost, the customers that we've taught to trust us over many years are lost.

"It's a hugely competitive business. If there's a report that a patient has died from a competitor's medication or drug, within minutes telephone calls are placed around the world to spread the news. Yet on the surface all of us seem to be on the best of terms.

"One of our biggest problems comes from industrial espionage, copycat companies that steal formulas of successful products, change the names, and rush them onto the market. It costs us hundreds of millions of dollars a year. Italy, for instance, has no patent regulations protecting new drugs. For a bribe of a few hundred thousand lire, anyone can buy formulas and pirate them under other names."

"Is it just Italy that behaves that way?"

"Unfortunately, not. Spain is just as bad, France and West Germany not much better."

"And Switzerland? This must be an honest country, yes? That is why you have invested so much in a new plant here?"

He briefly touched her knee. "Yes, Switzerland and the United Kingdom are honest countries, Ludmilla. How old are you?"

She hesitated, and he knew why. The girl had to know—had to sense and smell, like an animal, his sudden sick hunger for her. "Twenty-three, nearly twenty-four."

He sighed. Only a couple of years older than his own daughter, although it was hard to believe. Suzanne could still act like a bobby-soxer. Ludmilla was as old—or as young—as the Mona Lisa. He shut his mind down like a steel trap. He wouldn't think of Suzanne again today. He already felt carefree and years younger, just talking his head off to this enigma beside him. He was going to enjoy just this day, and that would be the end of it.

He had planned to give Ludmilla an abbreviated tour and then, with her waiting for him, safely ensconced in the car, he intended to deliver a short speech to the managers before driving off to have lunch somewhere. Because of her excitement at what she saw—the manufacturing plant, the toxicology laboratories, the molecular biology area, and the tablet compression rooms where the tablets stamped TOWERS were formed from hundreds of different powders—nearly three hours had passed before he realized it.

Twice he'd been told the managers were assembled in the new boardroom to hear his address. He looked down at her flushed face. She was enthralled, intoxicated with all the things that enthralled and intoxicated him. Should he let her hear him speak? Why not, although it would then be difficult to leave together. They were passing through his greatest pride and joy—the area that housed the most modern sterile room in the world; there was nothing else like it yet, even in the States.

"One more surprise." He knew he sounded like an excited kid. They entered a long, low building through a door marked in French and English RESTRICTED: DO NOT ENTER. Benedict went ahead of Ludmilla and pushed open a heavy inner door. He was waiting to see her face as she came into an enormous, dimly lit room filled with hundreds of cages containing animals. It was hot, humid. She opened her raincoat, and he could see the silk dress clinging to her body. As her eyes grew accustomed to the light, she saw the animals—monkeys, hamsters, rabbits, white mice, some with their heads shaven, crowned with electrodes, others with ugly growths protruding from various parts of their bodies.

"Oh no . . ." Involuntarily she started to back away, turning to him horror-struck. For a second he put his arms around her. Was it his imagination that she moved closer? Mercifully, he saw the heavy door behind her begin to open, and he moved away quickly, striding to a cage where a rabbit's head was attached to a monitor. Benedict read the card on the cage. "We're testing a new pill for hypertension," he said briefly.

She looked around helplessly. "Is all this really necessary?"

"Yes." He touched her fingers. They were trembling. He yearned to put them in his mouth. "These are the experiments that save human lives. Modern drugs are lifesavers, lifegivers, and this is just the beginning of a great new era."

His motivating speech went well. He was good at making speeches, but he felt ten feet tall today, adrenaline pouring through his body as, at the back of the boardroom, he glimpsed the slender girl in the drab raincoat. "Quality control is one of the promises we make to our Towers family of customers. Here, in this complex alone, we have nearly one hundred people working on quality control. You all know it takes between five and ten years to market a new drug, and out of every thousand compounds tested, we will be satisfied with only two or at the most three products . . ."

Ludmilla went, as he told her, to sit in the car as he led the group through some of the facilities, leaving them to enjoy a huge buffet at about one-thirty. It was two o'clock when he drove into the courtyard of an old inn outside Prangins, twenty-five kilometers from Geneva, yet a thousand miles away in atmosphere from the luxurious hotel where Mrs. Towers awaited his return with her personal hairdresser.

Benedict watched with rueful astonishment the natural, graceful way in which Ludmilla accepted everything. She hadn't asked him why he was taking her to a tiny country inn. She read the handwritten menu as if she had been reading French menus for years, and then, when he asked if she would like him to order for her, she gave him the menu with a soft smile.

At first he faced her across the dining table, answering her questions, which now came nonstop, about what she had just seen and heard. After a delicious country pâté, he ordered the local fish, grilled with the sweet corn they'd just seen growing in the fields.

Was she overwhelmed? She had to be, yet something about her—bravado, perhaps—would not allow her to reveal it.

When the fish finally came, she pushed it aside to eat the corn first. There was a trace of butter on her fingers. He took them and, one by one, his eyes never leaving hers, sucked the butter away. At the place where the yellow silk touched her throat, he saw her pulse begin to beat faster. He moved to sit beside her. Now he was as silent as she. When he touched her cheek, it was like an electric charge between them. They stared into each other's eyes. Finally he said her name. "Ludmilla, Ludmilla, will you?"

Her eyes gave him the answer. He went out to the dark reception desk and booked a room, returning to command, "Come with me." He didn't recognize his own voice.

They followed an elderly clerk up rickety stairs into a small, over-stuffed room with a patchwork quilt covering a lumpy-looking bed.

There was no strangeness. It was something he would never forget.

He locked the door. She threw her raincoat over a chair and stretched her arms high above her head in the same way he'd seen her stretch a week ago in the bedroom in Paris.

This time he was going to touch her and touch her and touch her until the madness went out of him.

Jamaica, 1950

DOWN BELOW, SUZANNE could hear an excited murmur of voices, a cackle of high laughter, singing, humming, dogs barking, cocks crowing, the special morning sounds of the tropics.

Yesterday, opening the slatted shutters to hear the old plantation house come alive to a new day, her own spirits had risen. She had felt exhilarated, sharing a new experience, about to celebrate her birthday with her parents, away from Palm Beach in a strange and intriguing environment. Soon she would be leaving home to spend a year away, working as an intern at French *Vogue*, a job arranged through the influence of her mother's favorite designer and now close friend, Monsieur Dior. Ostensibly the idea was that she would perfect her business and colloquial French before working in Towers Pharmaceuticals' Paris office. The truth was, she hoped that while she was away she would be able to make a decision about what to do with her life.

Her father was disappointed, she knew, that so far she hadn't shown much interest in the business. Her brother, Charlie, had no alternative—his future had been mapped out from birth—but luckily, because of her sex, her father reluctantly accepted that she wasn't yet ready to join the company, and of course, even if she was ready, she couldn't join the board until her twenty-fifth birthday, still three years away. What he didn't accept was that the whole idea of plants and research labs depressed her unutterably. Thank heaven, her mother had always been on her side. What neither of her parents knew was that she was going to spend this one more year in Europe in order to make up her mind once and for all whether or not to accept Alex Fiestler's proposal. More important, she was going to decide whether she could face living in Europe, and mostly in Switzerland, for a good part of every year.

Yesterday she'd been able to put all thoughts of Alex and Switzerland out of her head. Like Scarlett O'Hara, she'd been able to say to herself, "I'll think about it tomorrow."

She'd cantered along the Ochos Rios beach with Ludmilla, "picnicked" with the other houseguests and her mother in the shade of a huge saman tree, with everything served on silver salvers, while plantation workers fanned them with huge cocoa leaves, and had managed to persuade her mother later to plunge into the surf, reminding her that for the formal dinner later that night at the just-opened Tower Isle Hotel, they would still be able to look stunning with Ludmilla dressing their hair elaborately with hibiscus and other exotic tropical flowers.

Despite the fact Ludmilla obviously—stupidly—disapproved of their deepening tans, so quickly achieved lying prone under the fierce Jamaican sun, she surely had to admit that nothing complemented a white strapless evening dress better! The evening before, her mother and she had both worn strapless white sharkskin, and neither of them could remember ever having received more compliments.

All the same, her mother's complaints had spoiled yesterday and the days before, complaints that Ludmilla and she had had to put up with ever since they'd arrived—about the heat and about the lizards perched on the canopy above her mother's bed, which apparently watched her every night, as she tossed and turned beneath her mosquito net.

For once she'd shown little sympathy. "All right, Mother. You'll soon be back in boring Palm Beach. Can't you try to enjoy yourself?" She'd been certain her mother would forget all her problems once her father arrived from Kingston with the Governor General, but she'd been wrong. Even when he'd been in the house for only an hour the evening before, she knew they must have quarreled, not in the quick, snippety, soon-forgotten way she was used to back home, but in the way that was becoming all too frequent, leaving a downturn to her mother's mouth for days, even a heaviness in the way she walked and talked.

No wonder her father was away from home so often, arranging trips and treats for them like a travel agent, joining them, leaving them— never, it seemed, spending more than three or four days with them at one time. Even on this trip, at the invitation of the Governor General of Jamaica, conveniently coinciding with a birthday she'd told her father she'd just as soon forget, she knew the "unique celebration" being planned for her tonight was tied in with Towers Pharmaceuticals' interest in Jamaican bauxite and the possibility of the company investing in some of the developments just beginning on the Caribbean island.

From her window Suzanne could see the top of the tent erected for her birthday party, decorated with British and American flags. Beyond lay the northern slopes of the great plantation. She'd been told by an aide of the Governor General that it had thousands of cocoa trees, all perfectly shaded by row after row of immortelles, dazzling with golden red flowers even in the early morning sun.

Only eight-fifteen. How she hated being awake at this hour, and in a vast, antiquated bed that emphasized her feeling of being alone and lonely on her birthday. Her mother was right about one thing: the slatted shutters so loved by the British colonials did not adequately block out the fierce early-morning light. For insomniacs like Suzanne and her mother, it was an impossible situation.

She closed her eyes, thinking about the upcoming party. The best Jamaican band was coming out from Kingston, and in true British style there were going to be quaint dance cards with, she'd been told by His Excellency himself, no shortage of dashing young Englishmen to act as dance partners. There was even going to be a demonstration of fire-dancing, and she was going to be taught a native dance, something called the limbo, so why did she feel so jaded and depressed?

Was she missing Alex? No, and that was probably reason enough to be depressed. In one way she longed to be missing somebody, but there was no one in her life to miss, except Alex.

There was a sharp rapping on the door. "Suzanne, darling Suzanne, are you up?"

"Yes, Daddy, wait a minute." She slipped on her housecoat and ran to open the door.

"Happy birthday, angel. I couldn't wait another minute in this paradise to wish you the happiest, happiest birthday ever." Benedict lifted her off her feet and swung her around. "Wasn't it a wonderful idea to celebrate your birthday here? The Brits are going to treat you like a royal princess. D'you want to have a swim with me before breakfast? I can't wait to wash off civilization. Can you wait for your present?"

"Give me ten minutes. Of course I can wait."

Their feet fell soundlessly on a thick carpet of leaves as they walked toward the beach, the air heady and sweet with the scent of banks of cocoa lilies, whose petals fell like long satin streamers along the trail.

Suzanne looked timorously at her father. Should she ask his advice about Alex? It was a rare moment of togetherness. She tugged his hand, urging him to stop for a second, looking anxiously up into his face.

"Dad, I know you're not too happy about my going to Europe, working for *Vogue* and not for you, and I know . . ." Her voice trailed away as she saw her father's expression change from a relaxed, happy-go-lucky smile to the tense, furrowed look she was much more used to. Why?

She turned to see what he was looking at. Coming toward them was Ludmilla, a dark green towel tied around her like a sarong, her long hair, soaked with sea water, streaming over her alabaster-pale shoulders. She looks more like a mermaid than a maid, Suzanne thought irritably, like a strange, mystical sea creature washed up on the shore. She felt resentful that for some unfathomable reason, their maid's appearance had so totally changed her father's mood and interrupted their time alone together. She was amazed when, instead of passing Ludmilla with a brief good morning, her father said, "That had to be the fastest swim on record, Lu. Why don't you swim some more with us?"

Lu?

Suzanne was about to protest when, to her relief, Ludmilla shook her head. "No, sir, I have to go back. They are expecting me in the flower room. There is a lot to do today." Suzanne stared at her unsmiling, even when she said, "Happy birthday, Suzanne."

"Thank you, Ludmilla. Please see if my mother needs anything before you go to the kitchen." To her continuing surprise, her father turned to watch Ludmilla as she walked quickly back toward the old house.

"Did you know she was swimming?"

"What?" her father seemed lost in thought.

"Ludmilla? How did you know she—"

Benedict threw an arm around her shoulder, interrupting her. "Strange young woman. I saw her go down to the beach no more than twenty minutes ago. I suddenly had this godawful thought, 'What if she gets swept out to sea? Who will be able to cope with your mother's hair tonight, with all this h'aristocracy present, assembled to honor our little princess?' "

Suzanne laughed obediently as she knew he expected her to do, but the strange, ridiculous sense of depression she'd awakened with hovered over her for most of the day, only lightened when her brother, Charlie, called from London as she was getting ready for the party.

"I've had this call booked for two days, sis. It's the middle of the night here now. Happy birthday two hours late. How are you doing in such high and mighty company? Mom wrote to say she was making the sacrifice and leaving the civilized society of Palm Beach for the Jamaican jungle just for you! I hear they've rustled up an eligible young duke or something similar for you tonight. Watch out if he's got a cleft in his chin; it means he's got a cleft somewhere else . . ."

"Oh, Charlie, stop it! How wonderful to hear your voice!" It was!

Her brother sounded so sunny, so uncomplicated, the way he always sounded. The connection broke before she could find out how he was enjoying the London School of Economics, but his call made all the difference to her mood.

When Ludmilla came in to dress her hair in the early evening with seed pearls and ribbons dyed to match the aquamarines in the necklace her parents had given her, she felt much warmer toward her.

Her father was right. Ludmilla was a strange young woman who often irritated her enormously, although she never seemed to get on her mother's nerves. Probably her mother would never allow herself to be irritated because there was no doubt about it, Ludmilla was a treasure who could do anything they asked her to do better than anyone else.

Suzanne set out to be charming. It couldn't be easy, she decided, for Ludmilla, probably not much older than she was herself, to be separated from her husband, who, working back in freezing New York, probably thought his wife was having the time of her life in the sunshine.

"You must miss Milos," she said in what she considered a thoughtful, concerned voice.

"Yes, Suzanne," as usual, Ludmilla's expression showed nothing.

"Well, I'm sure he misses you too, but at least you don't have to put up with the cold." Suzanne moved her painful shoulders, determined not to let Ludmilla know they were on fire from the afternoon spent sailing and sunning. She wasn't going to give Miss Prim and Priggish White Skin the satisfaction of even thinking *I told you so.*

Had her mother invited her to the party? She supposed so, and of course Ludmilla should be there. It wasn't as if she were exactly on the same level as the servants in this house, all as black as the ace of spades.

Ludmilla was attaching the delicate aquamarine and pearl necklace around Suzanne's neck when her mother came in, bringing a gust of French perfume with her. "Oh, my pet, you look ab-so-lute-ly di-vine! I've never seen you look so beautiful. Your dance card will be filled before we even go into dinner."

Honey turned to look with mock severity at Ludmilla. "Now, what are we going to do about you, Miss Ludmilla? What the eye doesn't see, the heart doesn't grieve over. You, miss, are going to the ball. We'll never tell Milos, even if you dance the night away with a tall, dark, and handsome stranger. You are not going to sit with all those black people in the servants' hall like one of them. You are one of us!"

Ludmilla laughed. It was something Suzanne saw so rarely that she registered fleetingly, as her father had done the year before, how a smile could transform Ludmilla's face. "I am not going to sit in the servants' hall, Madame. I'm going to rest, relax in my room. You know I've been on my feet all day. I want to go to bed early."

"That's not permitted—not tonight, not on Suzanne's birthday." Benedict had followed his wife into the room. "Whew!" He let out a whistle of approval as he saw Suzanne. "You are indeed a princess. May I have the honor of the first dance?"

As her father wrote his name on the first line of Suzanne's dance card, her mother commanded Ludmilla to go and change. "I've only once seen you wear the yellow dress I gave you last year. I know you have it with you. I've seen it hanging in your wardrobe." Honey clapped her hands together as she had another thought. "You know, Ludmilla, I've never seen what you can do with your own hair. Why don't you surprise us all? After dinner, join us in the tent for the dancing."

"No, no, I really can't, Madame. Please excuse me."

"We insist, Ludmilla. That's an order." Benedict sounded so harsh that both Suzanne and Honey remonstrated with him.

"Benedict, you're not in the army now," said his wife.

"Dad, really!" said his daughter.

"As you wish, sir," said Ludmilla.

It was well after midnight, Suzanne and Honey had danced their feet off, and still the intoxicating rhythm enticed them back on the floor in the arms of young army officers and Government House aides expertly trained to be charming.

As hundreds of tiny candles on small tables around the tent burned down to their wicks and the tent darkened, Benedict saw Ludmilla dancing. He wanted to kill her and her partner, some weak-chinned English idiot he'd been introduced to before dinner. His anger was so intense, so painful, that he went to the bar and tried to douse it, downing two glasses of neat rum with one gulp after the other.

He hadn't dared dance with her, but he hadn't expected her to dance with anyone else. He had gone over to tell her so when she'd first entered the tent about an hour ago, when he'd given up all hope of seeing her there. She looked like Cleopatra, with her hair coiled into black snakes high on her head, a gardenia at the back, her eyes rimmed with some smoky stuff he longed to scrub away, her pale, slender body shining through the delicate yellow silk.

As the tempo quickened to a mambo beat, Benedict tortured himself by turning to look at her dancing again, just in time to see her excuse herself and slip out of the tent. He looked quickly around the crowded dance floor. Honey and Suzanne were deeply involved in the intricac-

ies of the mambo steps. Their host and hostess had bade their good-
nights at the stroke of midnight.

It was a risk he had to take. He ached for her in a way he had never
imagined was possible. It wasn't mental. It was a physical ache that
he'd carried with him for the past three months, forcing himself to
stay away from her, although he'd made sure her husband stayed away
from her, too, keeping Milos occupied in New York to separate the
couple when Honey left with Ludmilla for her annual winter stay in
the Palm Beach house.

The sensuous scent of jasmine and tuberose in the tropical night
outside made him feel worse; unless he found her, he knew he'd have
to stay out all night. He didn't know what he would do, but it would
be impossible for him to spend the night in the same bedroom, let
alone the same bed, with Honey.

As his eyes adjusted to the velvet night sky, ablaze with stars, he saw a
flash of yellow. She was walking slowly toward the beach. "Ludmilla . . ."
He came closer, close enough to smell her fresh sweat, undisguised by
any perfume. "Ludmilla." Her name was a poem. They moved together
behind a grove of bamboo trees. He pressed her down to her knees,
looking down at her, not saying another word. In the distance the
insistent beat of the mambo went on as he knelt beside her and held
her beautiful head in his hands, slowly releasing her heavy coils of
hair.

It was no use; he couldn't stop now. From the beginning, in Prangins,
he'd been careful. Before, on the few times when it had been safe
enough for him to command her to come to him, he'd been careful.

Now, as he lifted the yellow silk over her head and made her naked,
the ache for her devoured him and he could be careful no longer.

Yogurt, wheat germ, brewers' yeast, blackstrap molasses, and what
was this new addition on the shelf? Powdered skim milk! Milos felt
like sweeping the lot onto the floor with a massive swipe of his powerful
arm, but instead, to satisfy the anger eating away at him, he picked up
only the packet of powdered milk to hurl at the kitchen wall. It broke
in two, and he watched with sullen satisfaction as the contents, like
fine white snowflakes, slowly descended to settle on the corner armchair, where Ludmilla usually sat to read *The New York Times*.

No wonder Ludmilla felt sick, eating this American glop. She deserved to feel sick, following the Towers family's new American food
fad, picked up in Palm Beach, where this maniac Hauser's book, *Look
Younger, Live Longer,* had apparently become the Colonel's bible.

Milos sighed deeply, opened another can of beer, and looked at his watch for the third time in as many minutes. Where was she? She knew the colonel had been called to Washington for twenty-four hours, so he had this unexpected time off, and Mrs. Towers was visiting her sister in Philadelphia, so she didn't need her.

Anger, suspicion, worry—his head swirled with the three emotions that consumed him, emotions that had been building in intensity since his wife had returned with the Towers family to New York.

He paced nervously around their two rooms, part of the servants' quarters in the Park Avenue triplex. Ludmilla had sounded strange, not at all like herself, when he'd called her from the garage earlier that afternoon on being given the good news of his extra time off. He'd put it down to the fact she'd been sick the day before, too, and still looked sickly when he'd left at 7:20 A.M. to collect the Cadillac.

He downed another can of beer. If absence made the heart grow fonder, he had yet to experience it from his wife. Because of the promotion Colonel Towers had given him—he was now vice-president of transport, in charge of virtually a fleet of Towers Pharmaceuticals cars—he'd been prevented from spending the winter working with Ludmilla for Mrs. Towers in Palm Beach this year, but being separated from his wife hadn't, as he'd hoped, improved their relationship. In fact, it was a thousand times worse. Her frigidity had now frozen solid any response she might once have shown him.

In the last month, for the first time since their reunion in America, almost two and a half years ago, Milos had stopped blaming himself, had stopped feeling sorry for the two of them, had stopped making excuses for Ludmilla. One devastating discovery had changed his attitude, no matter how much he tried to talk himself out of it.

Ludmilla had been back in New York for only a few days—days of misery as far as he was concerned, with her lack of interest in him and everything to do with him never more apparent—when he'd surprised her in the bathroom, washing her hair in the sink.

On the nape of her neck, usually covered by her braided chignon, he'd seen a vivid red mark. He'd been so startled that he'd cried out. "Ludmilla! What is that?"

She'd tossed her long, wet hair back so quickly it had whipped him across the face, but without a trace of embarrassment, unease, or regret, she'd looked him brazenly and said, "What? Oh, you mean the mark? My brush caught in my hair; it must have bruised me."

He hadn't been able to say anything then. He'd been too shocked, too confused, too sick at heart, and he'd lain awake all night wondering if in any way she could be telling the truth, again and again coming to the conclusion that her explanation was implausible. He was forced to accept the fact that the mark on his wife's neck could only have come from a love bite.

She had a lover. Ludmilla Sukova, his childhood sweetheart, had a lover. The more he thought about it, the more it explained everything, except for one thing. When would she have had the time? He knew she was on call to Mrs. Towers day and night in Palm Beach, much more than in New York, and their two-week side trip to Jamaica had been over in late January. How long could a love bite stay on the skin? Her skin was so white, so sensitive, perhaps for weeks? That had to mean the lover was in Florida. Or had she rushed into another man's arms immediately when she returned to the city? Around and around his suspicions went, causing sleepless nights and agonizing days, suspicions aroused by everything she now did and didn't do. And where was she now?

He went into their bedroom. He opened her dressing-table drawer. He didn't know what he was looking for. A man's name? An address? A photograph? Fury drove him. He emptied the contents on the floor, and some papers went under the bed. He bent down to pick them up. Receipts for household things; a faded newspaper clipping about the mysterious death of the Czech foreign minister Masaryk, who'd fallen from his apartment window in Prague.

Far under the bed he saw a box. It was Ludmilla's music box. He stretched his arm to pull it out, his eyes filling with tears at the happy memories it brought back of their time together in their native land. He opened the lid to hear the familiar stanza from "The Skater's Waltz." There was a pressed flower inside, its white petals brown at the edges. He didn't know what kind it was, but it still retained a heady, sickly, tropical aroma. He slammed the lid shut, and the box slid from his lap onto the floor, the bottom section coming loose.

There was a card fitted neatly inside. DR. VICTOR MAZNER, GYNECOLOGIST, BY APPOINTMENT, 2792 PARK AVENUE, HOBOKEN, NEW JERSEY. On the back, in handwriting he didn't recognize, was a time, 2:00 P.M., and a date, April 22. He sat looking at the card, dazed. He sat there for fifteen minutes, staring into space, then went to write everything down in his diary before carefully fitting the card back, pressing the box firmly together again and pushing it far under the bed, where he'd found it.

By the time Ludmilla returned, he was calm, as icy calm as he'd learned to be, growing up during the Nazi occupation. "Where have you been?" he asked casually.

"Getting you some *kolacek.*" She emptied a bag of sweet tea cakes onto the table, the kind his mother used to make in Prague.

"Where did you find them?" Before the love bite, before the doctor's card hidden away so secretly, before, before ... oh, how he would have rejoiced at this sign of her thoughtfulness for him. Now he felt sure nothing she could ever do would return the lover's blindness to his eyes.

"Giselle, the new housemaid, told me about this Czech baker on the West Side. I went over there to see for myself, and it's true. His family comes from Moravia ..." She was unusually talkative, but he said nothing, hardly hearing her, instead studying her body, dreading to see what he was sure he was going to see, a slight swelling of her stomach, a rounding of her breasts, the way he remembered his sister had rounded and swelled in the first months of her pregnancy, when, like Ludmilla, she had also suffered from morning sickness.

If she was pregnant, it could not possibly be his child. They had not had intercourse since her return; she had fought him as if he were a rapist. If he had managed to enter her, he would have been a rapist, and for the first time in their unsatisfactory marriage, he had been too desolate to proceed.

If she was pregnant, when was she going to tell him? On April 22? Did she think he was such a fool that he would let her get away with it? That he would allow her to remain his wife and bring up her bastard child?

She was cleaning up the powdered milk in the corner, not saying a word. He wanted to smash her against the wall as he'd smashed the package of powdered milk. He longed to hurt her as he now realized she had been hurting him almost since the day she'd arrived in America. She owed everything to him. Everything!

April 22 fell on the day Ludmilla always had off, and sometimes, if he could manage it, he had the day off too. Whatever happened, he was going to be at 2792 Park Avenue in Hoboken at 2:00 P.M. that day. If his worst fears were realized and he discovered she was seeing a doctor about her fears of being pregnant, he would make sure Colonel and Mrs. Towers knew the truth, that she was nothing better than a harlot. He would do everything in his power to have her thrown into the gutter where she belonged.

It was pouring rain on the twenty-second of April. Milos would have been offended with God if it hadn't been. This was no time for the sun to shine. With the rain, he estimated it would take him well over an hour to get to New Jersey, which, until the week before, when he'd made a test run, had been like a foreign country to him. He'd made a mistake, using the George Washington Bridge instead of the Lincoln Tunnel.

He wouldn't make a mistake today. He had everything planned except what to say to Ludmilla when she emerged from the doctor's office to see him sitting in the waiting room. He even had his wedding certificate ready to show the nurse, in case he needed to prove he had a right to be there.

How was she going to get there? *If* she was going to go there! Perhaps she wasn't. Perhaps the card was for one of her few friends.

During the past two weeks, waiting for the twenty-second to arrive, he'd had moments when he'd seriously questioned his sanity. The moments had soon passed. There had been other late arrivals home, conversations broken off on the telephone when he'd come into the kitchen, and he'd discovered that the gynecologist's card was no longer hidden in the bottom section of the music box.

If he was wasting his time and his employer's gasoline, at least he might be able to regain his peace of mind. He doubted it. If today's expedition was for nothing, he knew his vigil would continue until he discovered what he was now sure existed. Ludmilla's secret life. He had to discover it and destroy it, before it or she destroyed him.

God hadn't only sent the rain. He'd thoughtfully arranged for the colonel's return from Switzerland to be delayed for two days, so although Colonel Towers had sent a message asking him to take Mr. Norris to Philadelphia today instead of picking him up at Idlewild Airport, he'd easily been able to give that chore to his bright young assistant. Mr. Norris didn't care who drove him; he was always buried under piles of paper and never spoke to any of the drivers, not even to him.

As Milos had already discovered the week before, Hoboken's Park Avenue had nothing in common with its gracious New York namesake across the Hudson River. The week before, Milos's sense of despair had deepened as he'd driven along the dreary avenue in Hoboken. Now, arriving much sooner than he'd expected, forty minutes before the mysterious, 2:00 P.M. appointment, he sat slumped at the wheel half a block away from 2792, biting his nails, praying he was making the biggest mistake of his life.

At one-fifty a black Cadillac coming from the opposite direction drew up across the street from 2792. Milos's breath quickened as he saw his wife get out of the car, then lean back inside to talk to the driver. In an agony of indecision, Milos watched her put up an umbrella before crossing the street. He was about to go after her when the driver got out of the Cadillac and called after her.

The shock of seeing who it was turned Milos ashen; he gripped the steering wheel, sure he was about to pass out.

He started to retch as, through unbelieving eyes, he saw Colonel Benedict Towers, his employer supposed to still be in Geneva, take his wife in his arms and hold her close to him, kissing her upturned face as if she were the woman he adored. He was paralyzed. While his brain told him to rush up to them, to separate them, to put his huge fist into Towers's filthy, treacherous mouth, he was unable to move, and he sat numb, sick, as his wife climbed the steps and entered the nondescript house at 2792, while the Cadillac drove away.

He lost track of time as he buried his head in his hands and wept as he had not wept since the Nazis took away his father in 1943. How could it be? What did it mean? Where had Towers gone? Why had he brought her there if he was not going to stay?

Every plan in his head had gone. He felt once again that he was insane, that he must have dreamed what he had just seen. He looked at his watch. Almost thirty-five minutes had passed. He got out of the car, not sure he would even be able to walk. He had no plans, but he had to find out what was happening, even if he fell dead at Ludmilla's feet.

Like a sleepwalker he climbed the steps and entered a small hall smelling strongly of new paint. A brass plaque listed four names, all doctors; Dr. Mazner was on the third floor. There was only room in the elevator for two or at the most three people—only one if the occupant was very pregnant, Milos found himself thinking.

His thumbnail was bleeding. He must have pulled the skin, and the blood had seeped onto his marriage certificate, but he still held it in his hand as he pressed the bell outside Mazner's office and a noisy buzz indicated he could enter. There was no one sitting in the small waiting room, but Milos recognized Ludmilla's raincoat and an umbrella hanging on a coat rack. A white-coated nurse sat at a desk behind a half opened glass partition. She was smiling into the phone, saying, "Yes, everything is proceeding well. I should think another half an hour, Mr. Gates."

Gates? More likely Towers, Milos thought grimly. So that was it. He was calling to find out when Ludmilla could be collected, so that he could hear the news of the tests first. Well, Mr. Gates was about to get the shock of his life.

"Yes? Can I help you?" The nurse was frowning now.

"My wife, she is with the doctor, Dr. Mazner. I want to see the doctor, too. I want to be with her." He realized he was rambling; he brushed his wet hair out of his eyes and gripped the windowsill, preventing the nurse from closing the glass partition as she was trying to do.

"Your wife?" Her tone was frosty, disbelieving.

"Yes, Ludmilla Sukova." He pushed the marriage certificate through the partition to fall on to her desk. "I want to see the doctor now. Is she pregnant or not?" His voice had risen. He saw fear in the nurse's face.

"Just one moment." She got up and turned to go through a door at the back. When the door closed behind her, he didn't hesitate. He opened the door, which led to her tiny reception area, and followed her into what he thought would be the doctor's office. Instead he found himself in a narrow passageway. He could hear low moans coming from the room at the end. The nurse emerged from another doorway, shouting, "You have no right, stop . . ." but he pushed her violently out of his way. The door at the end opened. He could see it was an operating room. A man in a green surgeon's gown was pulling a mask from his face, while behind him stood another nurse, masked. He charged the doctor, bending his bullet head as if he was rushing to the goal in football. "Ludmilla!" he screamed.

For one second, all he needed for the scene to be imprinted on his memory forever, the doctor buckled with pain from the impact, and Milos saw Ludmilla. She was on her back, her narrow hips resting on the edge of an operating table, her knees high and wide apart, with her feet in steel surgical stirrups. Blood was pouring out of her. She was moaning, but her eyes were closed and she wasn't moving.

"Murder, mur—" As he went toward her, a hand clamped a cloth over his mouth. He smelled ether. As the doctor and the nurse began to drag him out of the operating room, twisting his arms brutally behind his back, he lost consciousness.

He came to in a darkened room, his head throbbing with the worst headache of his life. He opened his eyes and then closed them again hurriedly. He could hardly believe it, but he appeared to be back in his own bedroom. Yes, he was. There was the uniform he wore on special occasions, hanging on the door, just back from the dry cleaners, where he'd left it that morning.

As he sat on the edge of the bed, his head swam and he rushed to the bathroom, where he was violently sick. Later he saw that it was eight-fifteen by the clock over the mantelpiece in the kitchen. Was it still the twenty-second of April? Where was Ludmilla? Was the company car still parked on Park Avenue in Hoboken? Who had brought him back? Towers himself? Or the abortionist doctor who had just murdered Towers and Ludmilla's unborn child? He went to look in the pocket of his jacket, where he'd left the key to the Towers car he was allowed to use when he had to, the car he'd twice driven over to Hoboken. It wasn't there. Someone must have used it to drive him back to New York.

Tears welled up. How could he ever look at Ludmilla's evil, treacherous face again? How could he go on working for a monster who had stolen his wife with his power and riches? Now he realized Towers had always been a monster. When his uncontrollable lust had impregnated his wife, he'd taken her to an abortionist to get rid of his responsibility as easily as Milos well knew he got rid of anything or anyone he grew tired of or was displeased with.

"All in a day's work." He'd heard Towers say that often enough to Mr. Norris and other Towers executives, when they'd returned in the car, gloatingly congratulating each other on the successful outcome of some bloody business deal.

This time, though, Colonel High and Mighty Towers wasn't going to be able to shrug off what he had perpetrated. He had to pay. Abortion was murder, a crime. Milos would go to the police if Towers didn't make restitution, and Ludmilla would go to jail, where she belonged. One day he would explain everything to her parents and her little sister, Natasha. He'd make sure, too, that the newspapers knew the identity of the man who'd ruined her.

Ludmilla hadn't returned to the apartment by seven the next morning, when Milos found that his courage had evaporated so much his whole body seemed to be trembling. When he tried to shave, he cut his chin badly.

As again he paced between their two rooms, he realized there was only one person he could turn to: Mrs. Towers. She had been betrayed, too. She would know what to do. Did she know already what had happened? Had his employer dumped him like garbage in the servants' quarters and then returned to the fourteenth floor to announce his return from Switzerland on the day he'd originally been expected? Had he confessed to his long-suffering wife his terrible betrayal with her personal maid? Milos doubted it. He'd always known how clever his boss was; now he realized it was his Machiavellian cleverness that had ensnared Ludmilla in a web of deceit, too. She had betrayed the woman who had been so good to her. Mrs. Towers would never forgive her.

The enormity of what had been going on engulfed Milos again, and he went like an old man to the medicine cabinet, where he kept a bottle of brandy for emergencies. By the time he'd finished a second glass, he'd regained some of his strength, and with it a sense of logic. There was obviously no way Colonel Towers would want his marriage to end, no way he could ever contemplate living with, let alone marrying, a servant girl; therefore, despite the ardor he had seen the colonel display on the dreary Hoboken street, it was quite likely, that now he'd been found out, he would want to end the affair as quickly and quietly as possible.

Ludmilla would be fired, and he would perhaps be able to walk away from Towers Pharaceuticals with a severance pay he could use to buy a small garage somewhere. Slowly, like someone getting out of bed for the first time after a serious illness. Milos began to get ready for what he knew would be a meeting that would affect his whole life.

Honey had never been more miserable. It was beginning to show. Even her sister in Philadelphia had commented on the little lines around her mouth and eyes. She'd hoped to confide in her, but she had too much pride.

How could she tell her own sister that she didn't know how to please her husband anymore? That something was going on she didn't understand? That whatever she did and said was wrong all the time, that he leapt at any idea to send her away? "Why don't you spend a few months with Suzanne in Paris?" "Why don't you go to see Charles in London?" Would he be there to spend those "few months" with her? Of course not. He would fly in, and then fly out again as soon as he possibly could, and there would be no joyful reunions, either. There hadn't been for some time now.

As she lay in her king-sized four-poster bed, she heard the rain beat against the walls. It had rained all day yesterday, but she hadn't cared. Benedict was delayed coming home from Geneva, and she'd made no plans because it was Ludmilla's day off. She'd spent most of the day in bed.

Today was different. She had to switch off her depression somehow. She had a matinee to go to of *The Member of the Wedding*, and then Dorothy Kilgallen's cocktail party. Perhaps she would ask Ludmilla to give her a facial before lunch.

As she leaned across to get her engagement book out of the bedside table drawer, someone switched on the overhead bedroom light. She screamed in terror and then collapsed back on the pillows as Benedict came over quickly to sit on the edge of the bed.

"My God, you scared me half to death. Whatever did you do that for? My God, what's happened? You're soaked to the skin? Why aren't you in Geneva? Mary B. told me you weren't coming home until tomorrow. What is it? Stop staring at me. You're frightening me. What time is it?"

"About seven, seven-thirty . . . I don't know." She had never seen Benedict look so stricken, not even on the day he had learned his father had died.

"What is it?" Honey put her hand to her mouth. "Not . . . not Suzanne . . . Charles . . . oh, Benedict." She began to sob.

"No, no, no. Nothing like that." Her husband got up and went to the window, not pulling the heavy curtains open, but just standing there, his shoulders heaving, trying to control himself. She ran over to him, putting her arms around him.

"Benedict, tell me. Whatever it is, I'm here, I'm here . . ."

He turned to look down at her, his mouth taut, tense. "I don't deserve you, Honey. I've wronged you so terribly."

For weeks she had been expecting to hear Benedict was having an affair. Every time a girlfriend had rung up or she'd met one for lunch, she'd been waiting to hear a name, a story, a rumor that had to be passed on "for her sake." Hadn't she herself been put in a similar situation with her girlfriends from time to time? She had never expected her husband to confess.

She moved her body away from him, but she kept her hands on his arms. "Yes, Benedict, I've suspected something for a long time now. What are you trying to tell me? Do you want a divorce?" Now that it had come, she felt curiously remote, as if she were hearing it from a stranger, as if it had nothing really to do with her.

To her astonishment, he pulled her fiercely back toward him. "Good God, no, never, never. I've been walking all night. I've just come to my senses. I've been crazy—crazy."

She tried to interrupt. "Who, then? What do you—" Before she could say any more, he interrupted her, his voice breaking with emotion.

"Ludmilla, Milos's wife." Again he repeated, "I've been crazy, unforgivably, incredible insane. Yesterday Ludmilla had an abortion. I arranged it. It was my . . . our . . . child. Milos found out. He must have seen us together. He came there to confront her, to kill her. He probably would have killed me if he'd been given the opportunity."

He tried to keep holding her, but she fought to break free, screaming out her pain, her disbelief, her hatred. She ran to the window on the other side of the room and ripped the curtains apart, trying to open the window, to jump to her death rather than live for a minute with what she had just been told.

He overpowered her, trying to kiss her, to carry her to the bed, but she scratched and clawed and screamed out of his arms. "Stay away from me, stay away. How could you, how could you, with a wretched servant . . . stay away, stay away . . . oh, the shame of it . . . the shame . . ."

"Forgive me, oh, please, Honey, forgive me. If it means anything to you, I'll never be able to forgive myself . . ." For over an hour she screamed and cried, trying again and again to go to the window, while he begged for her forgiveness and another chance.

At nine-thirty, while she lay quietly sobbing into her pillow, there was a knock on the door. Her breakfast tray. Benedict opened the door. Giselle jumped on seeing him and his grim expression. "Sorry, sir, I didn't know you were back. Does Madame want her breakfast now, or shall I come back?"

"I'll take the tray."

Giselle looked uncomfortable. "Sir, there's a note from Milos, sir, in with the newspapers. He says he would like to see Madame as soon as possible this morning, something about Ludmilla, sir. He seems very upset about something."

"I'll look after it, Giselle. Tell Milos I'll see him in my office some-time this morning."

"Yes, sir."

When the door closed, Honey sat upright in bed, her face swollen and blotched with grief. "Give me the note," she said coldly.

He handed it to her. She read it silently, then tore it into pieces and crawled back under the covers.

After a few minutes she spoke, her voice muffled. "So he didn't manage to kill the bitch. Where is she now?"

"In a boardinghouse owned by the doctor, over in New Jersey."

"I never want to see either of them again. I want them out of my house now, this minute, this second. Do you understand? I want them fired. Out in the street with every one of their possessions. I never want to hear their names mentioned again in my presence. Pay them what you have to for as long as you have to, but get them out . . . out . . . out into the gutter."

"Yes, Honey, oh, darling Honey, will you ever be able to forgive me?" He tried to uncover her face, but she resisted.

"I don't know. I don't know. Leave me alone, I'm in too much pain, leave me alone. Tell Mary B. to cancel everything, everything. Tell her I've died."

"Oh, Honey . . ." She heard the tears in his voice. It didn't help; she was sure that however long he suffered over what he had done to her, she would suffer more.

In a way, what she had just said was true. The old, optimistic, fun-loving Honey Towers had died. Perhaps another Mrs. Towers, a stronger, better-loved Mrs. Towers, would emerge, but it was going to take a long, long time, if ever.

There was another discreet knock on the door. A very nervous Giselle stood outside. "Sorry, sir, but Milos says he wants to speak to Mrs. Towers first, sir. He says he won't leave the house until he sees her, sir. I don't know what's come over him, sir." Giselle was about to cry herself.

Honey threw back the covers and ran to the door to scream so loudly that down in the front hall Milos didn't need Giselle to repeat the message.

"Get out, you and your whore, you're fired. Get out of my house and never let me set eyes on either of you again." There was a pause, and then Honey screamed again, "Take your whore's things with you now. I don't want her coming near this house, or I'll call the police. Out. Out. Out!"

London, 1951

ON THE BUS to the Grafton Street salon, Ludmilla read first *The Times*'s and then the *Daily Telegraph*'s stories about the Communist riots in Paris, carefully planned to coincide with General Eisenhower's arrival as the first Supreme Commander of SHAPE, "the offspring of the North Atlantic Treaty, the shield protecting Europe," wrote *The Times*. "It doesn't matter about three thousand Communists demonstrating against me," the *Daily Telegraph* quoted Eisenhower. "What is serious is that there shouldn't have been three thousand or even three hundred Frenchmen to demonstrate for me."

She was reading the foreign news to take her mind off the important interview ahead. It was a habit she'd used during the past terrible year, a way to force herself to compare the horrors and hardships, the murders and maimings, going on all over the world with what had befallen her.

"I'm taking stock," she'd written about a month ago in the diary she'd started upon her arrival in London, in an endeavor to make plans, to try to get on with her life. She always wrote in Czech, fearful now that someone, somehow, might one day find out what she had been through. "I'm nearly twenty-five, in good health, with a job that has possibilities. I'm financially secure, provided I live on my income and don't begin to spend the capital put aside for my future. I live in a free, democratic country with a simple but pleasant roof over my head, and above all, I've proved I can live alone. Happily? Certainly far, far more happily than when I shared an impossible relationship with a husband I obviously never loved."

It was still too soon, the wound still too deep, for her to put on paper her thoughts about Benedict Towers. Just as she had steadfastly refused to see him, during the time he was making the arrangements for her move back to Europe, so she concentrated on trying never to think about him. She hadn't answered the one long letter he'd sent on her arrival in London. What was the point? She didn't need an explanation for his decision. She'd lived in his household; she knew better than anyone else what it was he felt he couldn't leave. It helped build her contempt and anger, as much for her own stupidity in believing in "love," as for his unforgivable weakness.

She had resisted getting a telephone (difficult to come by in still-wartorn London anyway), in case one day she'd hear his voice at the other end and would be entrapped all over again.

It had been impossible at first; now, little by little, although her recovery was slow, she felt it was getting slightly easier. She no longer lived with anguish, but it could return unexpectedly to strike her physically, summoned up by a chance remark, the back of a stranger's head, in dreams, or when she saw the Towers Pharmaceuticals name in the papers or on a product.

One day, she promised herself—and not too far off, she hoped—Benedict would no longer know where to find her and she would stop expecting every ring of the doorbell to come from him. She'd taken the first step by quitting the job he'd arranged for her in London's most prestigious drugstore, or "chemist shop," as the English referred to the stylish emporium on Wigmore Street known as John Bell and Croydon.

If she obtained the promotion at Helena Rubinstein, where she'd been working in the salon for the past six months, she would start looking around for somewhere else to live.

As the bus neared her stop in Piccadilly, Ludmilla hastily took out her powder compact. As she'd feared, newspaper ink had made a smudge on her face, and in five minutes she would be meeting for the first time the great Madame herself, whose skin, untouched by the sun, was still flawless, the skin of a woman forty years younger, or so she'd been told.

With her powder puff she rubbed the smudge away and applied a touch more bright red lipstick, Rubinstein's Gala Rose. That would have to do. Jan Feiner, her Polish neighbor in the Mews off King's Road, and the man who had originally let her know about the opening in Helena Rubinstein's Mayfair Salon, had told her what to wear and how to behave. It was mainly because of Feiner that this further opportunity had cropped up. As one of Madame's favorites, Feiner obviously knew what he was talking about. He was a bright chemist, and there were always rumors he might be transferred to Rubinstein's New York headquarters.

She had followed his advice about her dress today, not that it was difficult to choose a sober, dark suit from her wardrobe; both of her two suits were "sober and dark." She wouldn't, however, have added the yellow polka-dot scarf, a gift from Feiner, reluctantly accepted as a "good-luck present." She hated yellow, but she'd learned from the studious, slight man that it was unfortunately one of Madame's favorite colors. "She believes it adds a natural glow to the skin, a sunbeam reflection, when worn near the face," Feiner had said. "Madame is going to love your skin; it will take you halfway toward getting the job. It was what I first noticed about you myself."

"What shall I call her?" she'd asked him nervously the night before, as he'd rehearsed her over gin and tonics at the corner pub. "I know she's a princess in private life. Do I call her Princess Gourielli?"

"No, in the office it's 'Madame' to her face, 'Madame Rubinstein' behind her back. Only if you ever met socially would it be Princess Gourielli; her husband—he's Russian—Georgian—he insists on her title being used, even at the parties they occasionally give for some of the English staff at Claridge's." He'd paused, then laughed. "It's the first time I've ever seen you excited about anything."

How right he was. Later, laying awake, she'd realized it was the first time in months and months that she was looking forward to something and not just going through the motions of living. She was apprehensive, but, as Jan had reassured her, that was totally natural for anyone about to be interviewed for a creative job, not with Ceska Cooper, Madame's younger sister, who ran the English business with Boris Forter, a wily financial genius, but with the formidable Helena herself.

It was the first stroke of luck to come her way. Every few years, she'd learned, Madame Rubinstein descended on Europe to see if any of her foreign subsidiaries, run by various members of her family, contained talent that was not being fully utilized. They all knew they had to produce someone. It was essential for Madame Rubinstein to return to America believing she and only she could improve the business. Both Forter and Feiner had put forward her name as a beautician who used the Rubinstein products, not only with skill but with imagination.

Ludmilla climbed the sweeping staircase to the executive floor. Her hands were trembling, but otherwise she felt sure there was no sign of her anxiety. Mrs. Cooper's secretary was on the phone. She looked at her watch on seeing Ludmilla, then indicated the chair where she should sit. From behind grand double doors Ludmilla could hear angry outbursts and a series of thumps. The secretary paid no attention, not even when Mrs. Cooper rushed out, followed by a harried-looking woman who Ludmilla believed was from the advertising agency.

Mr. Forter, distinguished, calm, came to the door smiling, and beckoned Ludmilla inside. Beside an elaborately carved desk, one heavily bejeweled hand on her hip, stood Madame Rubinstein in a deep crimson brocade suit. She pursed her matching crimson mouth and studied Ludmilla for a second before turning away to pick up something from the desktop. It was a sausage. She bit into it and waved toward a sofa. Still smiling the same serene smile, Forter nodded and exited as Ludmilla went to sit down, noticing that on the toes of Madame's shoes were stamped two golden crowns.

"So you vish to vork viv the product development, eh?" There was no preamble, no "good morning," only a questioning grunt at the end of the sentence. The empress of beauty, barely five feet tall, plumped down beside her like a jewel-encrusted Buddha, several strands of carved and polished rubies covering her ample bosom, her wrists caged in heavy gold, two large emeralds glittering on the second finger of each of her small, perfectly shaped hands, another one pinned to the strange magenta bowler hat she wore.

She crossed her arms, her dark eyes, as deep and as impenetrable as Ludmilla's own, fixed on her. Before Ludmilla could speak, she continued. "Vot makes you think you can do zis, zis very com-pli-cat-ed vork, eh?"

With Feiner's words in her ears, Ludmilla started to praise effusively the new face powder that Rubinstein had just launched. "Its fine particles are so different from other powders. I've sold so much of it in the past week at the salon, and already, with word of mouth, women are coming back to order more."

"I hope you are vorking to give them the facial before you sell them ze powder? Ve make more money from the skin products. My cleanser, it is the best in the vorld," Madame interrupted crossly. Feiner had told her to expect a crusty personality, particularly since her appointment was in the morning. "Her personality's much warmer after lunch."

"Oh, of course, Madame." How easily that word came to mind. How different, by 180 degrees, was the brilliant, self-made multimillionairess sitting beside her from the self-indulged, do-nothing, think-nothing Madame Towers she'd pandered to for almost three wasted years.

"You are Czech?"

Ludmilla nodded. "Yes, Madame."

"Vild people, ze Czech. Poles and Czech, not so good together." Madame laughed throatily, obviously pleased, as Ludmilla flushed. "So Mr. Feiner, he tells me you are a bright girl. Are you sleeping with him?"

What a terrible old woman. Despite her fierce countenance, Ludmilla had begun to think she would like her, but now this! "Certainly not. We are acquaintances, neighbors with a common interest in the beauty business. My parents own a fine salon in Prague," she added defiantly.

Rings and bracelets flashing as she moved her tiny white hands, Madame Rubinstein took a slender gold compact out of her voluminous crocodile handbag. "Look at zis, girl."

Ludmilla obediently took the compact and opened it. It contained pale powder, not loose as she was accustomed to, but set hard in a mold. Madame motioned for her to take a cotton ball from the Venetian glass holder on the desk. "Try it."

"Why, it's wonderful!" Ludmilla proclaimed. "No flying particles, smooth, yet it covers shine." She was genuinely impressed, and it showed.

"It is powder that is pressed—a new development, a very clever development, exclusive to us."

Ludmilla forgot that Jan Feiner had told her not to try out any new ideas, but to concentrate only on all she knew that Madame Rubinstein had introduced and accomplished. "Drown her in compliments," he'd urged.

"This is really wonderful. This pressed idea, surely it could be used for eye colors, too—the delivery is so smooth, so easy."

Madame Rubinstein belched loudly and then yawned. It seemed to Ludmilla that it might be a secret signal, because the secretary bustled in, reminding her she was making a personal appearance at Harrods.

"Come viv me," she commanded Ludmilla, who found herself swept up in a small entourage of fawning assistants, including the manager of the salon, who glared when she saw her following Madame Rubinstein down the stairs. Ludmilla hung back, but *"Vite, vite,* here," cried Madame over her shoulder, beckoning Ludmilla to follow her to the huge pale gray Daimler waiting outside the salon, tapping the seat impatiently for Ludmilla to sit beside her.

No sooner had the car moved away from the curb then, putting her feet up on a footstool carved in the shape of a turtle, Madame Rubinstein closed her eyes and, with her chin on her chest, seemed to fall into a deep sleep. Ludmilla looked at her anxiously all the way to Knightsbridge. She moved slightly nearer, not even sure the amazing old woman was still breathing, she was so totally still.

As the Daimler slowed to draw up exactly beside a bright red carpet streaming out from Harrods's main entrance, Madame Rubinstein came immediately, vibrantly alive, her coal black eyes sparkling. "Ve vill do something viv you. Talk to Mrs. Cooper ven you go back. I zink ve vill find you useful, *ja,* in product development, or, viv that skin of yours, in ze public relations, too."

* * *

"I can't thank you enough, Jan," Ludmilla told the young chemist in the corner pub where they'd gone to celebrate later that evening.

"Did you get a raise?"

Ludmilla smiled, and he had to turn away. Her few smiles affected him too much. He was far too busy and too ambitious, he told himself, to become involved with a young woman, even one as fascinating and extraordinary as Ludmilla.

"Yes, I got a raise, Jan. I can't believe it, but they're paying me a thousand pounds a year! That's more than my wildest dreams, and I owe it all to you."

"No, you don't. I could only open the door, as my brother opened the door for me. You did the rest."

Jan rarely mentioned his brother, but whenever he did, his face lit up with pride. Ludmilla had never met Victor Feiner, a chemist, too, but "so much more brilliant than me," Jan had told her. He was so brilliant, he had apparently been snapped up by a huge Swiss pharmaceutical company, leaving London for Zurich a few weeks before Jan had knocked her down, coming around a corner too fast on his bicycle.

They'd discovered they were neighbors and "both displaced persons," Ludmilla had noted in her diary. "He's from Poland, Jewish, and very, very earnest, but not dull."

When she'd learned he was a chemist in the cosmetics business, he'd seemed heaven-sent. Here was somebody who could help her find a future on the business side of beauty, not as a practitioner, but on the creative, development, or marketing side. It was something that she'd realized, from listening to Benedict, held a great fascination for her.

Before Madame swept out of England and across the Channel to visit her French subsidary, headed up by another sister, Stella Oscestowitcz, she summoned Ludmilla to her Claridge's suite for a lesson in public relations. She was already being viewed coldly by the English staff as "another of Madame's protégés." Jan told her not to worry. "Her 'protégés' don't last, but her 'ideas people' do. If you keep your mind on product marketing, you'll succeed. I know you will."

There was another protégé at Claridge's—Patrick O'Higgins, who'd been on the staff for about a year and was on his first overseas trip as Madame Rubinstein's traveling companion. He turned out to be a delightful, humorous Irishman, whom Ludmilla immediately relaxed with. He winked at her as a black-coated waiter arrived with a silver tray of Polish sausage and presented it to the beauty empress as decorously and formally as if it were the finest pâté de fois gras.

Munching away, she said between bites, "Patrick, he knows about

the publicity. He knows it is just blah-blah-blah vich has to be mer-
chandized. A good free write-up is vorth ten ads. You must make
friends vith the press. Write a clever press release and you save them
vork. They vill use it. All you told me about the powder the other day,
tell Patrick."

Ludmilla hesitated, feeling uncomfortable, not knowing what the old
witch wanted from her. O'Higgins came to her rescue. "It's very different here from the States." He looked with a winsome smile at Madame
Rubinstein, who was perched on the edge of her chair like an expectant
bird waiting to be fed. "In the States they're masters of publicity. May
I tell Ludmilla about the stunts?" Madame nodded abruptly, but as he
began to speak, she interrupted him.

"There's nothing like a clever stunt to get a product off the ground.
Tell her about Heaven Sent."

O'Higgins lifted his hands to the ceiling and, using fluttering movements, brought them down to his sides, explaining, "When the Heaven
Sent perfume was launched a few years ago, hundreds of pale blue
balloons floated down on Fifth Avenue with a sample of the fragrance
attached, and a note saying 'A gift for you from Heaven! Helena
Rubinstein's new Heaven Sent.'"

Madame nodded approvingly back and forth. "It vas a vonderful
stunt! Ve received millions of dollars of free publicity. It sold millions
of bottles. It is *still* selling millions. So? Tell Patrick vot you said about
the powder."

While Patrick had been acting out the pale blue balloons raining
down, Ludmilla had been frantically working out a script. "'Madame
Rubinstein is the world's leading beauty authority,'" she began in a
shaky voice. "'She cares about women and their appearance. She uses
the finest ingredients. The Rubinstein face powder cares for the skin,
even as it transforms it.'"

"Good, good! More!" Madame heaved herself up, breathing heavily,
and came to whack Ludmilla across the shoulder blades.

With more confidence, Ludmilla went on, "'Members of the
English nobility unanimously agree this finest of powders delivers a
Dresden glow to their skin—'"

"Too German," Madame growled. "Make it English."

"Wedgwood, Chelsea—"

"No, no, no. Ve are not talking about cups, plates, pottery . . ."

"Porcelain. A porcelain glow," O'Higgins volunteered.

"Nice!" Madame beamed. "Patrick, give Miss . . . Miss . . . this girl
here the literature. I vant her to learn vot ve are doing here viv the
business."

Two days later, with a suitcase full of "literature"—booklets, package-stuffers, flyers, and other detailed instructions on the use of Rubinstein products—Ludmilla arrived in her new office on the executive floor in Grafton Street. It was more a cubbyhole than a proper office, but it was space she could call her own. Now, she felt, her career in the cosmetics industry could really begin.

Early on Saturday morning, when Benedict went to play squash at the River Club, Honey began what had become an obsessive weekly ritual, going through the contents of his briefcase, the drawers of his desk in the study, his suit and overcoat pockets. The psychiatrist she was now seeing twice a week had pointed out to her that if she continued to behave in this manner, she had to know what she was going to do if she discovered evidence that the suspicions that consumed her were justified.

The psychiatrist was right, of course, and she was wrong to go on searching. She had no idea what she would do if she found what she was looking for—a letter, a phone number, a photograph, a hotel matchbook, a ticket stub, anything that proved her husband was still unfaithful, or even that he was still thinking of and lusting after the Czech whore.

There was nothing incriminating in the pockets of the suit Benedict had been wearing the night before, carefully hung on the clothes stand for the valet to press; there was nothing in any of his pockets.

As Honey went downstairs to Benedict's study, she saw herself in the huge Chippendale mirror in the hallway. It was ironic. She had never looked better. She must have lost ten pounds in the last year, ten pounds that no amount of pummeling at Elizabeth Arden's or Gayelord Hauser diets had ever been able to budge in the past. Her friends begged her for the secret. It was simple. Most days she was so choked up inside that she hardly ate at all. She was sure her whole metabolism had changed, although the doctor didn't think it was possible.

Once or twice she'd come close to revealing everything to Betsy, her oldest and closest friend, but the shame of it all was too deep, too degrading. An affair was bad enough, but an affair with one of their own servants? How could she possibly explain something like that? She would rather die, which some days she thought she would. Could life ever really be worth living again?

Only Suzanne, her own darling Suzanne, had guessed something was terribly wrong. Honey hadn't, of course, told her the truth, but she knew that in some way Suzanne had put two and two together. Perhaps it wasn't surprising, learning on her first visit home from Paris that the two members of the household the family depended on most had left under mysterious circumstances, plus her mother's own obvious unhappiness.

"It's something to do with Ludmilla, isn't it, Mom?" Every time Suzanne came home, she continued probing, but Honey's adamant refusal to discuss it hadn't irritated Suzanne as Honey had thought it would, knowing how much her daughter loathed not knowing everything. On the contrary, the "mystery," as Suzanne still referred to it, had somehow brought them closer together. She was much more solicitous, so much so that Honey sometimes felt their roles were reversed, that she was the daughter and Suzanne the mother. She missed her terribly.

Nine-forty-five in the morning in New York, three-forty-five in the afternoon in Paris. On impulse she picked up the phone to place a call. It would probably take a few hours to go through, so there was a good chance Suzanne would be home, getting ready for a date. Thank God she seemed happy. There was a man in her life, a Swiss banker, that much she knew. Whether Suzanne really cared for him was hard to say. Better she didn't love him too much, Honey told herself fiercely, far better that he cared more; it was the only way to avoid being hurt by a man, in or out of marriage.

Benedict didn't know she knew the combination on his briefcase lock. It was the one he used on hotel safes overseas, a mixture of Suzanne's birthdate and her own. For a brilliant man, he could still behave naively, or perhaps he thought, with typical male arrogance, that she still trusted him blindly. Well, he was wrong, and thank heaven he hadn't changed the combination.

Inside, there were the usual company reports and balance sheets, and, tucked in the sleeve, the file marked Confidential that was there every week, usually full of boring formulas or accounts that meant nothing to her. This morning there still wasn't anything very interesting, although Honey read through one long memo because it was headed "Helena Rubinstein," and said the cosmetics queen was "currently grossing around twenty-two million dollars annually in the United States." She wasn't surprised. She'd heard how good Rubinstein skin-care products were, although she was faithful to Elizabeth Arden.

Was Benedict at last thinking of diversifying into the cosmetics business? He hadn't mentioned it to her. She would have to think of a way to bring the subject up without arousing his suspicions that she'd been reading the contents of his briefcase.

She quickly scanned the rest of the memo. The company was publicly owned, though Helena Rubinstein personally held fifty-two percent of the outstanding shares, worth about thirty million dollars, as well as all of the foreign subsidiaries with the exception of the business in Australia. To Honey's surprise, this, said the detailed report, was the country where Rubinstein had started her company, giving it to two sons and one sister as the business grew. The English business and its subsidiaries in South Africa and the Far East were the property of a Helena Rubinstein foundation set up to avoid inheritance taxes. Bretwell, one of Towers Pharmaceuticals' financial officers who'd prepared the report, had written "murderous" after "inheritance taxes," and Benedict had underlined the whole British reference.

Why, she wondered? Could it have anything to do with the whore? She'd once demanded to know if he knew where she'd gone. "Back to Europe," he'd admitted, while Milos, the cuckolded oaf of a husband, had moved to Detroit and taken a job, probably found for him by Benedict, with the Ford Motor Company.

Over lunch, Honey waited for an opportunity to bring up the subject of Helena Rubinstein. It was easier than she thought.

"You're looking very pretty today," he said. He'd been saying it frequently in the past year. Usually she paid no attention, attributing every compliment, every unexpected hug or kiss, to guilt.

"Oh, I'm glad you noticed. I'm using a new makeup from Helena Rubinstein," she lied.

There was no reaction. None. Benedict simply nodded absentmindedly and went on eating his salad. There was a long silence, the kind she had come to dread, wondering what he was thinking about, wondering if he knew she was still wearing the same Arden pale base she always wore.

He broke the silence with an abrupt question. "Would you like to go on a cruise again this winter?"

"I don't know." It was true, she didn't know. Last winter, doing everything he could to prove to her that he wanted to preserve their marriage and make amends, he'd arranged a romantic cruise to the Caribbean. It had been a disaster. He'd been alternately impossibly moody and irritable, then overly contrite. The beauty of the scenery, the heady scents and sounds of the tropics, had only emphasized their estrangement and her sense of helplessness, as night after night he hadn't been capable of making love to her. It wasn't much better now.

"Well, make up your mind. I thought we might try Hawaii—sail out of there." He sounded as if he were proposing a trip to Antarctica.

Familiar tears began to well up. The fact that he hadn't mentioned the Rubinstein report in his briefcase meant it had some hidden meaning. It would have been the most natural thing in the world for him to say he was studying the company when she'd told him she was now using the products.

"What's wrong now, Honey?" If she thought she'd never looked better, *he* looked like a wreck, gray, tense, anxious.

To what had become a regular question, she gave the answer he expected. "Oh, nothing, nothing at all."

How he was going to get through the weekend, he didn't know. There was bridge tonight, a game he never enjoyed, and a fancy lunch out in Glen Cove tomorrow that Honey wanted to go to. The whole idea filled him with an ennui that was suddenly intolerable. He got up abruptly, his fork falling to the floor.

"Where are you going? Don't you want cheese? Fruit?" If the phone hadn't rung at that moment, he might have told her the truth. It wasn't working. He had to get away, not to see Ludmilla, not to see anyone, but to be alone, to find out if he was ever going to be able to share his life with Honey in a normal way again. He was sick of pretending every damned emotion, of doing things he didn't enjoy in hopes of seeing the old sunny smile back on his wife's face. He'd already messed up too many lives, including his own, but the phone rang and Giselle came in to say Honey's call to Paris was coming through. Honey rushed to her dressing room to take it.

It was one of those rare calls when Suzanne could have been in the next room, every syllable, every intonation was so clear. "What's wrong, Mom? You sound awful."

The concern in Suzanne's voice brought the pent-up tears into her voice. She couldn't help it, but still she said, "Nothing, darling, nothing. I'm just missing you a lot. What are you up to?"

"Frantically busy, Mom. Alex is arriving soon, and I'm taking him to a new nightclub, just opened in a coal cellar off the Champs Elysées. Something called—can you believe it—the Crazy Horse Saloon." She giggled like a schoolgirl. "It's very risqué. I'm probably out of my mind, taking him there. It's a striptease show that is causing a sensation. Everyone's talking about it. The girls are supposedly so beautiful, Vogue has already taken pictures."

Suzanne was being much more communicative than usual; Honey knew she was doing it for her sake. She took a deep breath, trying to control her voice, but it sounded wobbly even to her when she said, "It all sounds like such fun, darling."

"Mom, why don't you come over for a week or so? I could arrange some wonderful things for us to do, and Monsieur Dior would be so thrilled to see you."

"I can't, Suzanne." It was an automatic response, one she'd been making for months, certain she wouldn't be able to endure the worry of leaving Benedict alone, not knowing where he might go or whom he might be seeing. During the past year, Benedict had even curtailed his own business travel, and on the two occasions when he'd had to go to Europe, she'd gone with him. Even as Suzanne tried to persuade her, a premonition of something dire about to happen settled over her. And yet how could anything be worse than what she had already gone through?

"Mom? Mom? Are you still there?"

She hadn't heard a word Suzanne had been saying. She felt she was on the verge of a breakdown. "Sorry, darling, the connection's fading. I'd better hang up before we get cut off."

"You're worrying me, Mom. Are things worse at home? Shall I come home to see you?"

"No, no, no. Don't worry so much. I'll be perfectly all right. I'm just a little under the weather, the flu or something. Do you want to talk to your father?"

Honey looked around to see if Benedict had followed her, but no one was there. In any case, there was no mistaking the anger in Suzanne's voice when she replied, "No, I don't want to talk to him, not until I hear you sounding like your old self. I still think I should come over and find out what's at the bottom of all this. I'm tired of hearing you so miserable. I think it's time I had it out with both of you!"

Honey tried to reassure her that there was nothing to worry about, but the call ended on a low note, and when she put down the receiver, a sense of desolation overwhelmed her. She locked the door and lay on her chaise longue, allowing the tears to flow.

When Benedict knocked on the door, about an hour later, she'd made up her mind they should have a trial separation. Perhaps that was what she should have insisted upon a year ago, instead of watching his every move, his every word. He had encouraged her to cling to him, but it hadn't brought either of them any happiness or peace of mind.

"Honey? What's going on? What did Suzanne have to say? Why have you locked the door? Let me in."

She was calmer now. "Just a minute, Benedict. I'll be out soon." She would go to spend a week with her older sister in Philadelphia. She'd heard there was a new fast train. Her psychiatrist had been telling her to enjoy the comfort and love of family and friends. Talking to Suzanne had made her realize how much she was loved. Perhaps she'd even tell her sister Joyce something. Then, after spending a week spoiled and cosseted as she always was in Philadelphia, she'd think about going to Paris to see Suzanne, and perhaps even London to see

Charles. For some reason the good cry had done her good. She should have given in to it before.

She wouldn't tell Benedict where she was going. When he came home from the office one day next week, she'd be gone. Let him worry. Let him miss her. And if he didn't? Bitterness and anger filled her as she sat before her dressing table, combing her mussed hair, seeing her reddened eyes. Then there would be no more point in keeping up appearances. The separation that in her mind would be a trial would become permanent. Other people got divorced and managed to make new lives. She popped a tranquilizer in her mouth. She would find another man, one who had integrity, someone she could look up to as she had once been able to look up to Benedict Towers.

The apartment seemed much too big, empty without Honey. Benedict hadn't grown used to it. She'd been away for almost a week, and although her absence was mostly a relief, in the apartment where they'd lived and raised their children, there was no question her presence was missed. But then, "something missing" summed up what his life had been about for the past year. The loss of Ludmilla was like the loss of a part of his body. The yearning hadn't gone away, but now it was buried deep under the tons of minutiae he used at home to placate Honey and keep up the appearance of a normal married life, and under a work load at the office that few men would have been able to sustain.

It was strange that without saying a word, Honey had given him the breathing space he'd been craving. It hadn't taken long to establish that she had gone to visit Joyce. Whether she was still there, he didn't know. Probably she was. He guessed Suzanne's call might have had something to do with it, and although her passport was still in the safe, he half expected that her next disappearance would take her across the Atlantic to Paris or London, perhaps to both.

London. How often he took that trip in his mind, turning right from King's Road into the Mews, using the brass knocker on Number 88 to summon Ludmilla to open the door, seeing her standing there, looking up at him with the same strange mixture of obedience and defiance, looking and drowning in her deep, dark eyes. Oh God! He groaned as his body came alive.

After dining alone, he went to the library to study the reports Norris wanted him to read on the success of the cyclamates now being used commercially as artificial sweeteners. He found it so absorbing, he didn't listen to the evening news as he usually did, and it was nearing twelve-thirty before he realized it. If only he could sleep! He poured himself a large brandy. That ought to do it, and in any case he had an important 7:00 A.M. breakfast meeting out of the office. He asked Thorpe, the butler, to call him at six. He still had about thirty minutes of reading to do. He would do it in the car going downtown in the morning.

It seemed he hadn't closed his eyes for more than a minute, when he was being shaken awake by Thorpe.

He looked up at him groggily. "What . . . what on earth is it, Thorpe? What's up?" He rubbed the sleep out of his eyes.

"Sir, I tried to rouse you on the intercom, sir. I am so sorry, but, sir, two police officers are downstairs. There's been an accident, sir."

Benedict was downstairs in five minutes, noticing even in blind panic that the clock's hands stood at ten to four.

They looked like actors playing police officers. He had no sense of reality as he led the two large men in identical drab tan raincoats into the library, where his empty brandy glass was still where he'd left it.

"Lieutenant Potter, sir."

"Sergeant Crawley, sir. I'm sorry to tell you there has been a serious train crash, Mr. Towers. A Pennsylvania Railroad derailment at Woodbridge, New Jersey, sir. We have reason to believe your wife was among the passengers who—" He cleared his throat. "We have reason to believe she may have been one of the victims, sir."

He was shouting, "No, no, no," even as they spoke. It couldn't be true. Not Honey. Not petite, pretty Honey, dancing in her Dior dresses to the quick-step in her head. Not Honey. It couldn't be true. The phone was ringing. Thorpe, his face as white as his starched shirt, was blurting out, "Mr. Towers, Mrs. Erthrington, sir, Madame's sister, is calling you . . . oh, sir."

It was headline news in the morning papers. Benedict didn't see them until the evening, when he returned from identifying Honey's broken body.

EIGHTY-FIVE DEAD, HUNDREDS INJURED . . . PENNSYLVANIA RAILROAD SPOKESMAN ANNOUNCES INQUIRY . . . SUSPICION THAT TEMPORARY TRACK WAS INADEQUATE FOR TRAIN'S SPEED . . . MRS. BENEDICT TOWERS, SOCIALITE WIFE OF TOWERS PHARMACEUTICALS CHAIRMAN, AMONG THE DEAD.

Honey was buried in the Towers family plot, next to his father and mother. The funeral was private, but *The New York Times* reported there would be a memorial service later, when it was expected that friends would come from all over the world. Mrs. Towers was much loved.

Dry-eyed and tight-mouthed, Suzanne stood looking down at her father as he sat slumped at his desk. "I want to talk to you. I want to know what was going on. I have a right to know." Although she appeared to be in control, as she spoke her voice grew louder and he heard a note of hysteria.

Although Benedict had been dreading the confrontation he was sure was going to come, at this precise moment he found he was looking at his daughter—the daughter he'd wronged just as much as he'd wronged her mother—as if she were a stranger. She might have been any one of the many hundreds of anonymous young women who worked for him somewhere around the world in one of Towers's many plants or offices.

"I know something was wrong, terribly wrong. Mom was like a different woman when I came home last time for Charlie's twenty-first. Charlie noticed it, too. It wasn't just my imagination." The bitterness in Suzanne's voice should have scalded him, but as her words poured out, all he felt was relief, a huge outpouring of relief. Suzanne didn't know. Honey hadn't told her.

He'd thought about it often during the past terrible days. He'd waited, like a man about to face a firing squad, for Suzanne to accuse him of bringing about her mother's death. He'd expected it on the day he'd had to break the news to her on the telephone. He'd been expecting it every minute they'd been together since he'd flown over to Paris to bring her back for the funeral. She hadn't said a word until now, the day after the funeral, but her silence and stares of reproach had convinced him she would soon expose him for the miserable bastard he was.

He stood up and went over to her, trying to draw her close, ignoring her attempts to push him away. When he managed to control her, he forced her chin up, making her look up at him. "You're right, your mother and I weren't getting along, but nothing 'happened.' I don't know what you're trying to imply. You're old enough and sophisticated enough, you've been out in the world enough, to know that it sometimes happens that a man and a woman can love each other, but they get out of step. I realized last year I was spending too much time away, I was too wrapped up in the business, and—"

"Why did Milos and Ludmilla leave? Why did they split up? I know they got divorced. Jeffers told me that Milos told him . . ." Suzanne hesitated, flushing, obviously not sure whether to go on.

"Yes? What did he tell you?"

"Milos was half-crazy early last year. Jeffers said he was sure Milos had found out there was another man . . ."

"Yes, I think there probably was," Benedict said calmly. "You ask me why they left. You asked me and your mother the same question at Christmas, but you've just answered it yourself. They left because they split up and went their separate ways."

"Where did Ludmilla go? You called her 'Lu' once, I heard you."

"I believe she went to Europe, to Paris, London, I'm not sure. 'Lu'? Did I? Well, what of it? It's a better name than Ludmilla. Every time I heard the name, I thought of the krauts."

Suzanne wrinkled her nose as if there were suddenly a bad smell in the room. It was a mannerism of Honey's; Benedict had seen her do the same thing a thousand times. It brought unexpected tears to his eyes. Suzanne saw them, and in the next second she was crying like a child, his child. He carried her to the sofa and sat rocking her back and forth.

"Oh, Dad, it's so unfair. Mom was so full of life. I loved her so much. She was my best friend, I realize that now. I'll never get over it, and I hate myself for thinking such awful, stupid thoughts about you and . . ." She stopped. "I must have been crazy. It's living in Paris where everything is so bizarre and anything goes . . . but, oh, Dad, what are we going to do without Mom?"

"I don't know, Suze. I just don't know." He didn't. He tried to rationalize the guilt that tormented him. It had been Honey's decision to visit her sister Joyce, to try to jolt him into missing her, loving her, being able to make love to her again. He hadn't said one word to Honey about the "space" he'd been craving. She'd wanted it too, and it had ended in tragedy, without either of them learning whether they had a future together.

He was fooling himself. The marriage had been over, but who would have had the guts to end it? Honey? Himself? Perhaps neither of them. He didn't know.

Before Suzanne went back to Paris, he told her, after a good bit of thinking, that he'd decided Charles should stay behind and not return to Europe. He'd been learning the ropes in various departments and countries. His performance hadn't been inspired, but it hadn't been a disaster either. It was time he gave his son more personal time; it was time he joined the staff at campaign headquarters in New York.

"I hope I'll hear that *you're* ready soon," he said wistfully to Suzanne over lunch at "21."

"Yes, Dad, you'll be hearing," she said dutifully. She still felt ashamed that she'd cooked up so many scenarios about her parents' relationship, involving, among others, Ludmilla, their own live-in comb-out artist. She felt guilty leaving her father alone, but in another way she couldn't wait to get away from the New York apartment, which without her mother's presence was so depressing and gloomy.

She didn't feel at ease with her father anymore, either. It wasn't that she mistrusted him; there was the same strange empty look about him she'd noticed at Christmas, and now, of course, it was worse. He looked . . . what was the word? Haunted. Yes, that was it.

He'd explained why her mother had sounded and looked so depressed. What woman wouldn't be depressed, knowing there was something wrong with her marriage? She hadn't stopped thinking about her mother, putting herself in her shoes, worrying about growing old, while her husband, with every line on his strong face and every faint trace of gray, just looked more distinguished. No wonder her mother had sounded so desperate that Saturday before the accident.

All the same, it was no more her father's fault than it had been her mother's. People didn't stay the same. Being madly in love didn't last. Her problem was that she'd never been madly in love, either. She'd spent more time worrying about her parents' sad marriage, during what turned out to be her mother's last year of life, than about her own on-again, off-again relationship with Alex. And in the last few weeks she'd hardly missed him at all, but she did miss her freedom and her life in Paris.

"When are you going to get the fashion bug out of you? When are you going to join the company?" Now Benedict's question was sharp. "You're twenty-three, going on twenty-four. You're a good influence on Charlie, and you could be a big help to me here . . . entertaining, traveling on business trips together. It wouldn't be such a hard life. Knowing your quick little mind, you'd pick up things about the business immediately. Any time after you're twenty-five I can invite you on the board. But I'm not going to do it until you've shown some interest and spent at least a couple of years working in the company."

Suzanne kissed her father quickly on the cheek. "Dad, I promise you I'll give you an answer soon." She knew she had to. There would be an ultimatum next, one she wouldn't be able to ignore. The only explanation her father would accept—albeit reluctantly—for her not joining the company was if she decided to marry Alex. Oh, what a bore life was turning out to be.

Across the room, Suzanne saw her brother Charles arriving to join them for coffee. He was looking somber, shaking his head sadly as he obviously received the condolences of the maître d', who'd known them both since they were small children. Despite the absence of his usual laughing, carefree smile, Suzanne's spirits rose. What a catch he was going to be for some lucky girl. He'd inherited their father's tall, dark, and handsome looks, even if, as she had to acknowledge, he didn't have their father's financial genius. As their mother had always said, he'd been compensated with "the sweetest, kindest nature in the whole wide world." She could hear her mother saying it.

With a lump in her throat, Suzanne prayed her father wouldn't be too hard on her brother in New York. Now there was no one left at home to watch out for him.

New York, 1952

PALE WINTER MORNING sunlight created a strange halo effect around his father's head. Although Charles had started out at the 8:00 A.M. meeting concentrating fiercely, as so often happened, he'd begun to daydream. The halo made him think about a religious painting he'd almost bought from a girl he'd met on the ski slopes at St. Moritz. He looked down unseeingly at the lengthy schedule in front of him. Where was she now, he wondered. She'd had a wonderful body, but she'd skied better than she'd painted. He hadn't bought the painting, and she'd rejected his attempt to get her into bed. It had to be almost two years ago, his first but not his last rejection.

"Charles!" He looked up to see his father glaring at him.

"Yes, sir." Oh God, he hadn't heard a word his father had been saying.

"I repeat, what are Hoffman–La Roche's plans for isonicotinic acid hydrozide? Please give the benefit of your attention to Mr. Norris, Dr. Porletti, and the other gentlemen who have taken the trouble to assemble here at this unusually early hour for you. What did you establish from Furger's latest report?"

Charles knew he was blushing. He always colored up when his father embarrassed him in front of members of the staff, whether they were senior, as they were today, or junior.

He deserved it, but it didn't make it any easier to summon up any enthusiasm for the drug business.

He cleared his throat and began to stumble through a summary of what one of Towers Pharmaceuticals' best snoops had managed to dredge up about a major competitor's new coup. "Hoffman–La Roche is about to introduce it—"

"It?" Benedict asked testily.

"Isonicotinic acid hydro . . . drozide as Isoniazid, based on work by the organic chemist Herbert Fox."

"Foxy Fox," Leonardo Porletti growled.

Charles waited politely in case Porletti, one of Towers's leading research chemists, wanted to say more. His father irritably waved a pencil at him to proceed.

"It—I mean, isonicotinic acid hydrozide—will be introduced as a prophylactic against tuberculosis under the brand name of Isoniazid. Mr. Furger has discovered a confidential report that seems to suggest Isoniazid can produce tumors in test mice, but from what I understand, this has not been deemed sufficiently important to delay the introduction of the new brand-name drug."

Charles's shirt was wet through when the meeting broke up about four hours later. His father had invited him to lunch, which wasn't unusual, but he'd said it was to discuss an interesting business idea, which *was* unusual. Usually they ate in silence, after routine inquiries about Charles's work load, his apartment, his love life. Only occasionally was there any evidence that his father cared about his answers, which in any case he had to admit were monosyllabic.

Charles agreed with his sister. They were what she called "Dad-doing-his-duty lunches." Suzanne, he knew, asked questions back, but he couldn't. He had never felt relaxed with his father, and now he worked in such close proximity to him, it was worse than ever.

For the past few months he felt he'd been living in the eye of a hurricane. Papers flowed across his desk in a never-ending stream from factories, laboratories, and offices in Europe, and from franchise holders from all corners of the globe. He was expected to study new product recommendations, sales, and sales projections. He was a member of various committees, which meant that the advertising department, for example, was now waiting for his comments on a number of new campaigns, and the marketing department was waiting for his okay on a number of test markets before submitting the list to Norris, who would then send it with his comments to Benedict for the final approval.

How his father worked at the pace he did never ceased to amaze Charles. Right at this moment, emerging from the meeting called to assess the pharmaceutical competition, he felt he'd just sat for the bar, or taken end-of-term exams. God, how tired he was of being grilled about things that didn't come naturally to him. He was tired of even having to practice the pronunciation of chemical substances, let alone understand how they worked, on their own or synergistically, in complicated formulas.

From the first day, arriving at the head office to join his father's inner circle of advisers, he'd been conscious of a horrifying, inescapable fact: he hated the drug business and everything that went with it.

Thank God, Suzanne was back home in New York, helping to make Dad's life more comfortable, hiring and firing the servants, opening and closing the houses, entertaining for him, enabling him to give not just the ninety-five percent of time they reckoned he'd devoted to Towers while their mother was alive, but pretty much one hundred percent. Certainly, as far as Suzanne and he could see, their father never did anything that wasn't business-driven.

He wasn't interested in sports; he never seemed to put his feet up with a good novel, although his face was often buried in something horribly technical. Even Charles could see that his father still deserved the adjectives regularly used to describe him in the press—"attractive," "vital," "dynamic"—but there was no sign of any women in his life. Weird!

Suzanne, he knew, didn't find that weird at all. In fact she'd blown up when he'd mentioned it. "Mom hasn't been dead a year yet! How can you even think of such a thing, Charlie!" she'd screamed at him.

Perhaps she was right, but seeing his father's age mentioned in the paper one day and realizing he wasn't yet forty-four—he'd thought he was nearer fifty—it had struck him that Dad was still too young to go through life alone, without a companion, and perhaps one day even a wife.

If there was someone his own age to come home to, perhaps he'd learn to ease up a little and realize there were other things in life than empire building. Suzanne would think he was betraying their mother's memory, and perhaps she was right. Well, at least for the moment, until Dad got used to having her around, Suzanne seemed to be off the hook as far as the business was concerned. She didn't have to roll words like "isonicotinic acid hydrozide" smoothly off her tongue.

As long as the champagne was chilled to the right temperature and she kept up with current affairs to discuss at dinner parties, where she seemed to enjoy playing the hostess, she had a temporary reprieve. They were both sure that was all it was, however, a reprieve.

One day she'd have to do her stint at the office, too. Towers Pharmaceuticals was his father's whole life. No wonder, as Suzanne had told him, Mom had been so depressed before she was killed. He hadn't really noticed it, but then he hadn't been home much in the past three years since college. Now he wished he had been, to cheer Mom up. Life was so unfair.

As Charles went to his office, he wished Suzanne could see him now. He'd told her only the night before that he lived in a perpetual state of mental exhaustion. He hadn't told her he was often too tired even to get an erection. He was sure Suzanne, as his big sister, never thought of him as a man who, just before his return to live in New York, had begun to realize he was at last becoming attractive to women and could enjoy the company of more than one at a time.

Charles changed into the spare shirt he kept in a drawer in his desk, and in the men's-room mirror he saw dark shadows beneath his eyes. It wasn't overwork; it was the *wrong* work, and there was no way to get out of it. He was in prison for life. How he longed to go to the club right now for a massage or a game of squash.

He used water to flatten his unruly dark brown hair and fixed his Brooks Club tie. He looked the way his father wanted him to look, like a dedicated, nose-to-the-grindstone young executive, with a seamless life in which work was never entirely separate from play, where ideas about marketing or new products or improvements on staff could, as his father had once told him, spring to mind when you least expect it, even during an orgasm.

He was sure his father was talking from experience. Ideas had probably "sprung" into his father's mind while making love to his mother, but he'd be damned if he was going to think about Towers Pharmaceuticals when making love to a girl.

As Charles went to the Towers executive dining room, he was surprised to see Norris there, looking unusually downcast, talking fast to his father.

Norris stopped short and scowled as Charles approached, but he didn't leave, and in typical fashion Benedict didn't waste a minute in coming straight to the reason for having invited Charles to lunch.

As Charles hastily checked off "grilled sole with mustard sauce" on the menu, handed it to the hovering, black-suited waiter, and swallowed down some ice water, his father was saying, "We've been buying stock in a cosmetics company, Helena Rubinstein. The founder, an extraordinary old bird—she's in her eighties or thereabouts—is intrigued with us. She'll do anything to make more millions, and she has a poor opinion of 'the bankers,' as she calls anyone working on Wall Street, so I've been using our bankers to whet her greedy appetite."

For the next thirty minutes, Benedict directed all his conversation to Charles, hardly paying attention to Norris, who occasionally jotted something down on the small Cartier notepad he always carried with him.

Charles learned that just before the Wall Street crash of 1929, Helena Rubinstein had sold her American business to the investment bankers Lehmann Brothers for eight million dollars. They had tried to widen her distribution drastically, selling the upscale beauty products to drugstores and even grocery stores all over the country. After a year the business was already in trouble and, unknown to the bankers, Madame Rubinstein had been buying back shares whenever they came on the market, as well as collecting proxies from other small shareholders, mostly her women customers.

"With the crash, the stock plummeted, and a little over a year after the sale, she was able to force the bankers to sell the business back to her for under two million dollars. She made an easy six-million-dollar profit, Charlie," his father laughingly told him, although Charles couldn't see why that fact put him in such good humor. "She obviously thinks she can do something similar with us schmucks. I'm meeting her in Paris in a couple of weeks. I want you to come with me. You've been working hard. It will do you good to get away, and it will give me an opportunity to see your famous charm, which I've heard so much about, charm the pants off the empress of beauty." He paused and then added casually, "I know how much you've missed your friends in London. If all goes well, we'll spend a few days there on the way back."

Charles was stunned. "You've been working hard," his father had said. His father had noticed, after all. It made him feel warm all over. It made him realize how much he wanted to please his father and do well for the company. He wanted to get up and hug him, but he never had done so before, and he couldn't start now.

Paris! He was going to Paris with his father on an important business trip, and then London! He couldn't wait to spread the news to a number of young women who would be waiting for him with open arms.

For the rest of lunch he sat forward on his chair, hardly able to eat, terrified not to appear totally attentive, terrified that in some way, by word or gesture, his father might not realize how much he appreciated this first sign that he counted for something. He had never worshiped his father more.

When lunch was over, Benedict invited Norris to follow him into his inner sanctum, off the main executive suite. "Are you sure that's what you want to do, old friend?" Benedict asked gravely.

Norris had given him a shock. Full of resolution and a game plan he'd been mulling over for months, Benedict had been deep in thought, waiting for Charles to join him, when, uninvited, Norris had suddenly pulled up a chair and sat down. It had been out of character, but the desperate look on Norris's face had, thank God, kept him quiet.

"Ben, I'm sorry, but I've got to tell you something. Now. I've been waiting for the right moment, but after looking at our calendars, I realize there's no such thing. I've made up my mind. I'm in love. I'm going to divorce Audrey. It's going to be tough, she'll take me to the cleaners, but I'm thirty-five. Five years from forty. What's life all about?" At that point Charles had arrived, and Norris had shut up like a clam, but out of sympathy, Benedict had gestured to him to stay. Norris knew all about his interest in Helena Rubinstein. The only thing nobody knew was *why* he was so interested.

"Do you want to talk about it now, Norris?" Benedict looked searchingly at the man he relied on more than anyone else in the company. Norris looked white, shaken. It was about one-forty-five, but to hell with it—Benedict went to the bar and poured two glasses of brandy.

Did he ever want to talk about it! For the next hour, Norris seemed to be releasing years of pent-up frustration. He'd never uttered one word of criticism of Audrey before. Now, as Benedict listened to a litany of misery, he reflected that Honey had never liked Norris's wife. He had been indifferent to the little poulter pigeon, whose dresses always seemed a shade too tight, but he'd never dreamed Norris had so much anger stored up. Well, poor devil, he was right. Audrey would take him to the cleaners and then some, but Towers would help him through it financially as well as in the morale department. Nobody could understand better than he.

As Norris talked about the new woman in his life, his face softened in a way Benedict had never seen. A familiar ache started up in him. He had to cut this short. Norris was touching the wound he lived with. Worse, he was making him doubt the effectiveness of his game plan, which, an hour or so before, had seemed so perfect. It was a plan that would once again put him in a commanding position with the wild slip of a woman he'd never stopped wanting, the only woman who'd gone out of his life without a word of complaint or a backward glance, the woman who now appeared to want nothing whatsoever to do with him.

He didn't blame her. She had no reason to believe anything he had to tell her or offer her. She was growing in importance in the Rubinstein empire, too, even traveling among the different European branches, building a small but steady reputation for herself, without once treading on the touchy toes of her Machiavellian employer. "I am much more than a pair of hands, Colonel Towers. One day I hope I will be known because of my brain." He could still remember the look of fury and disdain on Ludmilla's face that day, a lifetime ago.

There wasn't anything Benedict didn't know about Ludmilla's professional life and growing position in the Rubinstein company. There was little he had been able to find out about her private life, except for this Jew, this slimy Polish chemist who apparently had spirited her away in the first place from her trainee dispensing job at John Bell and Croyden.

Luckily for him, Benedict had learned he'd recently been promoted to Rubinstein's top research job and was planning to move to New York. The retired Scotland Yard detective he'd employed to report on Ludmilla since her arrival in London had been unable to find any evidence of Ludmilla going out with any other man—but what, if anything, did this chemist, Jan Feiner, mean to her?

Benedict pressed his heel down on the button hidden just beneath the sofa where he was sitting with Norris. It was the signal for him to be interrupted.

After Norris had gone, smiling with relief to know he had the full support of the boss, Benedict leaned back and closed his eyes. The brandy had been a mistake. He couldn't stop thinking about Ludmilla, a luxury he rarely allowed himself. He imagined at his fingertips her full, aroused nipples; he pictured the soft curve of her chin, her deep brown, sometimes almost black eyes opening so wide as if taken by surprise, although, of course, she knew he was going to kiss her and go on kissing her; he remembered exactly when and where they had been when he first lifted her wonderful fall of hair to place his mouth on the nape of her neck, the white skin of her thighs, his fingers parting her soft, dark pubic hair for his tongue.

Benedict took a deep breath to try to shake away the memories and return to reality, then another one to calm himself to return to his desk. If he had to pay an exorbitant price to the old cow to control his nymph once more, to have her in his power again, so be it. He would make Ludmilla a queen in Europe with a small palace to live in, and he would spend a good part of his life with her across the Atlantic, where relationships of the kind he had in mind were viewed as perfectly natural.

Despite Norris's warnings that the cosmetics business did not deserve its "inflation-proof, recession-resiliant" reputation, that it was still an untested, untried cottage industry where even clever entrepreneurs like Charles Revson could come unstuck, he had always been fascinated by it. More and more it seemed to him to be a natural fit for a drug company, better than some of their other acquisitions. Well, he would see. He wouldn't make the mistake of alienating the founder. Unlike Lehmann Brothers, Towers Pharmaceuticals would make the old girl still feel very much wanted; she would remain as a valued, revered consultant until her death, which couldn't be far off.

*　　*　　*

That night Benedict dreamed he was running fast down an unfamiliar street to stop something terrible from happening; he arrived at a church where Norris was about to marry Ludmilla. "No, no, no," he screamed. "No, she can't marry you. She's mine, she's mine . . ."

When he woke, at about five-thirty, he began to think he'd made a mistake taking Charles with him to Europe to witness the maneuvering usually necessary in a business negotiation. He knew why the idea had come to him. It was because of Suzanne. She was as quick as Charles was slow. No matter how he reacted, with anger, sorrow, or even resignation, on occasion she still brought up the subject of his relationship with Honey with a whole list of questions, whys, hows, and wherefores. He'd suddenly thought that in case there was the remotest possibility Suzanne might somehow connect his visit to Paris and Madame Rubinstein with Ludmilla, he would talk to Charles about the business proposal early on and take him along, to allay any possible suspicions Charles's sister might have.

Now he faced the fact for the first time. He was using his own son as some kind of beard! Was he insane? Paranoid?

Norris's outpouring and the stupid dream had unnerved him. The appointment, at the beginning of March, had been set up in great secrecy to meet Madame Rubinstein with his and her legal and financial advisers in her fabled Quai de Bethune house on the Ile Saint-Louis in Paris. Now Benedict felt panicky, as if he had no time to lose. Why was he waiting so long to see Ludmilla? He couldn't risk changing the appointment with the great Helena—it had been hard enough to set up—but today he felt he could no longer wait to confront Ludmilla.

Whether he told her of his grand plan would depend upon her reaction on seeing him again after nearly two years. She had returned unopened the letter he'd sent telling her about Honey's accident. On the two occasions he'd tried to reach her at her London office, he'd been told she was "unavailable to come to the phone." For all he knew, she might still be unaware of Honey's death.

By the time he reached the office, just before eight, he still hadn't made up his mind how to proceed. As he passed Charles's office, he saw to his surprise through the half-opened door his son studying a sheaf of papers.

"Good morning, Charles."

Charles looked up beaming. Benedict had never seen him look so happy in the office. "Morning, Dad. After our meeting yesterday, Uncle Len got together some reports on Rubinstein's main competitor worldwide. It's Elizabeth Arden. Before we leave, I'll have a thorough report worked up for you on all the players, Coty, Dorothy Gray, Germaine Monteil, Max Factor, Charles Antell, and now Rev—"

"Okay, okay. Sounds good, sounds good." Benedict hurried away, frowning. He'd forgotten to tell Charlie not to talk about the trip with his uncle, not that it mattered. Whatever Leonard thought or didn't think was of no importance, but how could he disappoint the boy now? He'd have to take Charlie along. If only he always showed that kind of industry and initiative. Perhaps something worthwhile would come out of his scheming after all.

As he'd done so many times in the past, Benedict vowed to put his feelings of guilt behind him. "Forward," he murmured to himself as he approached the private elevator that went only one level up to his floor. His secretary, Mary B., was waiting for him. "Mr. Dennon just called from the State Department. He asked you to call him today if possible."

Dennon was on the Czech desk at State. Benedict felt a second's giddiness. He'd even forgotten he'd asked the Eastern European desk months ago if they could forward any news regarding the Sukovas, Ludmilla's parents and sister. The timing was extraordinary. "Get him right away."

He shut his door. When the phone rang, his hands trembled as he picked up the receiver.

"We received word late last night. Vaclav Sukova, father of Ludmilla and Natasha Sukova, died of natural causes, cancer of the pancreas, January tenth."

It was over a month ago. "Anything else?"

"It looks as if Rudolf Slansky, the party secretary, and Clementis are for the high jump." Benedict hardly paid attention. "Any other news about the family?" he interrupted. "I thought the mother was the sick one. Is she still running the salon?" He realized he was acting like a fool, asking such trivial questions, and the pause before the answer was, he felt, justly censorious.

"No more news. It was a surprise to receive this. I imagine the Sukovas are living the same difficult, impoverished lives as all those poor wretches trapped in Eastern Europe. If anyone else dies, I imagine I will be able to let you know that one day." Dennon's cold tone was a rebuke, and Benedict hastened to bring the conversation around to the latest political happenings in Prague.

After he'd hung up, he sat staring into space, ignoring a couple of buzzes on his intercom. Finally he shook his head and buzzed for Mary B. to come in.

"Give me a list of flights through Shannon into Heathrow Airport from next Sunday on," he said hoarsely. "I'm changing my European itinerary. It's London first, then Paris."

In the candy shop on Piccadilly, even the caramels were wrapped in black paper, while next door the window of the lingerie shop was full of black brassieres and girdles. How truly bizarre the English are, Ludmilla thought as she turned into Grafton Street. Even after a week, they were still so devastated by the loss of their gallant king, dead from lung cancer at fifty-six, that there probably wasn't a shop or shopkeeper in the British Isles who wasn't still in mourning.

How much longer would it go on? After listening to the dirgelike music on the radio that morning, she'd belatedly tried to tie a black ribbon around the neck of Shadow, the Siamese kitten Jan had given her for Christmas. Better late than never. Now she had a vivid scratch to show for it, but if Shadow didn't want to wear a sign of respect, at least she'd had the good sense to wear black again to the office, and she'd go on wearing it until she got the signal that it was proper to wear some color again.

Mrs. Cooper would certainly expect it of her. Mrs. Cooper knew now she could be relied on to set a good example. It was ironic, she'd attempted to tell Mrs. Cooper yesterday, that because of what had happened to her family in her native land of Czechoslovakia, suffering behind the Iron Curtain year after year, she should surely wear black every day. She wrote to her family every month, she'd told Ceska, but since her arrival in London she'd had only one reply, and that letter, which had painted a picture of gloom and doom, had taken six weeks to reach her.

Ceska Cooper, however, had not been interested in her problems. With her sister, Madame Rubinstein, in town, she had too much on her mind to listen to anything not related to the business. Until she left for Paris, which she was expected to do any day now, Madame was much too near for Ceska's comfort. The whole salon was depressed over the king and jumpy because of the empress.

Not her. Madame still made her quake and feel uncertain, but as far as Ludmilla was concerned, her rare meetings with the great Helena always left her exhilarated, stimulated, eager to think up more marketing ideas, more "stunts," as the great old lady liked to call publicity events.

She was supposed to be meeting Jan for lunch today, where she would meet his illustrious brother Victor for the first time, passing through London on his way to the United States on business. Ludmilla had been looking forward to it after Jan's great buildup. That anyone could be more brilliant or faster on his feet than Jan, however, she found hard to believe.

It was excessive brotherly love, surely, that made Jan describe him in such an awestruck way. Jan felt he owed his life to Victor, Ludmilla knew that now. He was the one who'd found a way to escape from the Nazis and had practically carried Jan, who'd broken his ankle, halfway across Europe. Well, she hoped soon to find out for herself how brilliant he was, although with Madame Rubinstein's unexpected arrival two days before, everything had to be put on hold.

She was going to miss Jan—a lot. Not only had he become a dear friend; he was her diplomatic guide through the often choppy seas of Helena Rubinstein politics. Ludmilla consoled herself with the thought that at least her friend was moving up and would still be her friend, even when operating at the top from the Rubinstein headquarters in New York. Perhaps one day she'd have the courage to go back to New York herself and work in the city, where the real success stories in the cosmetic business were being made. Perhaps, but not very likely.

Ludmilla's secretary, Poppy, was relieved to see her. "Madame wants you to meet her at Cartier in Bond Street, on the double." She looked at her watch. "In twenty minutes, at nine-thirty."

Ludmilla pulled a face. "Did the samples of the unusual colors come from the lab?"

"Any time now." Poppy grinned in the encouraging way Ludmilla liked so much. "I'll make sure they're here for your return. I'm sure Madame will love them."

Ludmilla ran most of the way to Bond Street, just around the corner from the salon, but by the time she arrived at the famous store, a coterie of unctuous men in frock coats were already hovering around Madame Rubinstein, seated in a private room, a huge sable stole flung over the back of her chair, which was pulled up to a table covered in small red leather boxes.

"Ahh, there you are. I vondered vot you vere up to."

It was 9:25, but Ludmilla knew better than to say anything. Today Madame Rubinstein was without the usual torrent of jewelry around her neck, although on her trademark bowler hat, trimmed in sable, was a large enamel parrot with enormous ruby eyes. The old lady tapped the floor imperiously with a cane topped by a golden eagle, also with ruby eyes. "A chair, a chair for my assistant, Miss . . . Miss . . . a chair." She often forgot or appeared to forget Ludmilla's name, but it didn't upset her. Madame forgot the name of everyone, even those who were related to her.

"What more can we do for the Princess?" one of the men said as a chair was produced, rubbing his hands together, more in nervousness, Ludmilla thought, than in anticipation of a sale.

Ludmilla stared in wonder at the jewels spilling out of the boxes. There were fat black pearls and satin-smooth white pearls, a sparkling daisy chain of diamonds with yellow diamond centers, several amethysts of varying sizes. It was a breathtaking display.

"Rubies!"

"But certainly, Madame." The same man who was obviously the manager clicked his fingers and a younger version of himself went to a wall safe to take out another red leather box, which was decorously presented and opened up to reveal a brilliant blood-red cabochon the size of a gull's egg.

Madame held it up to the light, her lips pursed, her face a mask of stony indifference. "Viv diamonds!" she snapped.

For the next fifteen minutes what appeared to Ludmilla to be an Aladdin's cave of gems was produced and dismissed with either grunts or more requests. When Ludmilla tried to take the agonized look off the manager's face by murmuring "How exquisite" about one dazzling offering, her employer turned and gave her a look of disgust, hissing, "Second rate, second rate." She shut up and waited, wondering what on earth it was all about.

Finally an antique ring of pearls and rubies seemed to please Madame Rubinstein. She opened her usual huge crocodile bag and rummaged around abstractedly. "I can't find my lipstick. I also need a lipstick case I can easily find . . ." She seemed to be talking to herself, her bowler hat bent low over the table.

Apologizing for the inconvenience, the manager suggested they follow him into another room, where, under glass-topped tables, a multitude of gold objects glittered. Madame pointed fast, left, right, left, but Ludmilla, remembering something Jan had once told her, now began to guess what the shopping expedition was really all about.

As different gold pieces were lined up for Madame Rubinstein's approval, she idly picked up a gold case with a black pearl at one end and a white one at the other. As she held it absentmindedly, she leaned forward to look at the other objects, letting the case in her hand fall to the floor.

Accidentally? Ludmilla didn't think so. It was the most perfect choreography. As one of the underlings scrambled to retrieve the case, panting and puffing as it eluded him under the table, Madame said, without looking at him, "I'll take it. How much?"

The manager was obviously taken aback. He was about to lead them back to the other room, where the pearl-and-ruby ring was waiting on a black velvet cushion, but something in Madame's expression stopped him. He fluttered his hands disparagingly, as if to dismiss the importance of such a trivial item. "Eight hundred pounds, Madame."

"I'll give you seven."

To Ludmilla's astonishment, the manager coughed and then said serenely, "Whatever Madame says. Would you like me to send the unique ring you thought you might also like to your home for further appraisal?"

"I'll let you know."

On the way back to the office, Madame Rubinstein examined the lipstick case carefully. "You see, girl, a place for a lipstick at each end. I saw it at lunch yesterday. Some duchess at a lunch party had it. It vill vork vell in the States, too. Vot do you say? I should — shall — have it copied."

Ludmilla looked at the old lady with stunned admiration. "Yes, yes, of course." She thought quickly, knowing something was expected of her. "One lipstick for day, one for night. A.M. and P.M."

She felt the power of those brown-black eyes turn to stare fixedly at her. Madame didn't speak for few minutes, and Ludmilla knew not to fill the silence. She cleared her throat noisily, then said grudgingly, "You think like me. Ya, a double sale, ve can sell smaller lipsticks, one at each end, and charge double. Night and day, like that silly song."

Madame looked out the window as the car approached the salon. "Vot do you hear from your boyfriend?"

Ludmilla paled. "Boyfriend? I don't have any boyfriends."

"Jan . . . Jan vot's-his-name, is he happy to go to New York, or does he have other plans? Vot is he telling you? Is he happy viv the new promotion? Does he vant to go to the States?"

Along with relief came a sense of foreboding. Ludmilla tried to laugh. "Jan Feiner is my friend, not my boyfriend. I think he is honored by the promotion. I don't . . . don't really know what you mean, Madame Rubinstein."

Again Madame stared at her, but this time she only grunted and continued to study her new lipstick case until the car drew to the curb.

By noon that day, Ludmilla learned that Madame Rubinstein had left the office and was now planning to catch the boat train to Paris. She was so relieved; it meant lunch with the Feiner brothers could be on after all.

She hoped to have an opportunity to tell Jan of Madame Rubinstein's strange remark, but it wasn't necessary. After introductions were made,

Jan, looking nervously at his older brother as if to ask permission to speak, began, "Victor and I have something to tell you . . ."

Again Ludmilla felt a sense of foreboding. Victor, a taller, even thinner version of Jan, looked coolly at her through unattractive steel-rimmed spectacles. He doesn't like me on sight, she thought. He probably had to have his arm twisted to meet me. Before Jan could continue, the waiter arrived and she was astonished to hear Victor tell Jan not to order fish, explaining, "It may be contaminated."

English fish! What a ridiculous thought, it was always the best thing on the menu, but obediently Jan ordered a mushroom omelette, which they all knew was going to be made with powdered eggs, because real eggs were still rationed. There was plaice on the menu, but Ludmilla knew that to order it would be seen as a challenge to Victor's knowledge. She ordered shepherd's pie, sure it would be three-quarters potato and one-quarter meat, if that, but she wasn't going to be able to eat much anyway.

"Ludmilla, I wanted to tell you before somebody else did. I am leaving the company. I am leaving Helena Rubinstein."

A heavy stone settled in her stomach. Now she wouldn't be able to eat a thing. She tried not to show how the news distressed her. She waited as only she knew how to wait, looking at her friend without emotion.

"Victor has been asked . . ."

Victor interrupted testily. "Miss Sukova, I have been asked to help build the American subsidary of my company, the Swiss pharmaceutical company, K. Averbach, which is known in the United States as K. Avery. In the course of negotiating my contract and coming to such a big decision, Miss Sukova, I learned of another important vacancy in the United States."

He doesn't talk, he lectures, Ludmilla thought. Although she had been introduced as Ludmilla, Victor continued to pepper his sentences with "Miss Sukova." Jan didn't seem to notice. She was irritated to see he was looking at Victor with adoration.

Victor stopped for a second to inspect his omelette, which Ludmilla was happy to see looked disgusting. He started to eat and talk with his mouth full. "Jan has always been interested in the essential-oil business. This company"—Ludmilla couldn't understand the German-sounding name, which came through a large portion of omelette in his mouth—"is a subsidary of . . ." Again the name was impossible for her to catch. "My brother will have an opportunity to run the company if all goes well, and be correctly compensated for his endeavors with share options. Above all, he will no longer have to cater to the whims and wiles of such a monstrous, unethical old demon as Helena Rubinstein!"

By the time what the English persisted in calling coffee was on the table, Jan had only spoken two or three sentences, and those only in answer to Ludmilla's attempts to understand more about essential oils.

Victor hadn't missed the warm smile of affection that accompanied Jan's answer. "Essential oils from plants and flowers are used in fragrances and flavors. I used to study it in my spare time; I've always been interested in the anatomy of smells. I have an interesting book at home I'll show you."

As Jan talked, Victor watched his brother carefully. It was just as well Jan was leaving London and this Ludmilla woman, whom he instinctively distrusted. She was like so many women from Eastern Europe, "hangers-on," he called them, hanging on and often dragging their men down with them.

This one, as Jan had told him, had an unusual beauty all right, but that made her more dangerous. She certainly wasn't the kind of woman Jan needed, someone who'd stay home and wash and cook for him and raise kids. Thank God, Jan had seen at once the opportunity the new position offered him, despite the promotion offered by Rubinstein, which Jan believed had come coincidentally at the same time. Coincidence? Victor didn't believe it for one moment. The old witch had learned something. Well, he'd outwitted her at last. Once again he would be able to keep a close watch on his naive, trusting brother and make sure he didn't make any wrong decisions.

Again Ludmilla saw Jan turn to Victor, as if waiting for permission to speak. It didn't come, and Jan said haltingly, "Ludmilla, I've told Victor how impressed I am with your ability, your flair for cosmetics. One day, perhaps sooner than later, there may be a place for you with me in New Jersey."

New Jersey! It hit a nerve. She bit her lip as if in pain, which she was. Her baby would have been ... She bent her head down, forcing back the unexpected tears that began to fill her eyes.

"Is anything wrong?"

"No, no, the coffee burned my tongue."

Victor was furious to see how concerned Jan looked. There was something mysterious about this woman. He didn't like it; he didn't like *her*, he decided. Well, Jan would soon be too busy to think about her. A job for Ludmilla with Jan in America? Never! He would make sure that never happened. Victor beckoned the waiter for the bill.

As they walked back to the salon, Ludmilla asked, "Does Madame know?"

Jan looked sad. "No, not yet. I had planned to tell her this afternoon. Ceska told me she was leaving tomorrow, and I didn't want to give her too much time to try to persuade me out of it. Now I'll have to do the cowardly thing and send my resignation in by letter."

"When will you leave?"

Jan smiled ruefully. "You never know with Rubinstein. I am quite prepared to give them whatever notice they want and wait until they find my replacement, but once Madame Rubinstein knows I'm serious, she's quite likely to have me out in twenty-four hours."

"I hope so," Victor snapped. A cold wind was blowing. Ludmilla turned up the collar of her coat. Now the black-draped windows were totally appropriate. She was in mourning, too; she was about to lose her only real friend, and there would be no one at the top of the Rubinstein empire to help her climb up there herself.

At the end of the day, Jan stopped by her office as he occasionally did, and suggested they have a drink at the pub before going home.

"I meant what I said," he told her over their usual gin and tonics. "I admire you. You have a big future in the beauty business. Vreinsdrof"—he spelled it out for her so she could copy it down—"they intend to be the biggest supplier of oils to the cosmetics industry in the world. One day American companies will be making fragrances, just like the French, you'll see. It's an almost unexplored market over there. The potential is enormous."

Jan took her hands in his, surprised to find them ice cold, although they were seated near the pub's coal fire. "Once I'm there, I'm going to keep my ears and eyes open for the right position for you. I don't want to lose touch with you, Loulou."

He misunderstood the sad, downcast look on her face. He'd never called her Loulou before. It was the nearest he had come to showing what he felt for her, because he hadn't known how he felt. Suddenly he knew. He'd fallen in love without even knowing it. Despite Victor's misgivings—and he'd spent thirty minutes that afternoon on the telephone, trying to point out how unfair it was to judge anyone at just one lunch—he'd only that moment realized what a perfect partner Ludmilla would make for him.

"Loulou . . ." he said again, loving the sound of it. He went to put his arm around her, but she moved back, startled. Well, no wonder. Here they were, in a public place, and he, clumsy fool, was showing her what he'd only just realized himself, expecting her to respond immediately.

"Can we go back to your place or my place?"

The tone of his voice and his look of ardor were unmistakable.

Ludmilla felt panic choking her. Not him, not her trusted, beloved friend Jan. She didn't know how to cope with his advances. She couldn't hurt him. In many ways she did love him, as she imagined a sister loved a brother. She didn't want to lose his friendship or his interest in her.

"Jan . . ." she squeezed his hand tightly, knowing her fear showed. She began to speak hastily to cover it up. "I meant to tell you this earlier. Today, this morning, Madame Rubinstein summoned me to meet her at Cartier." She quickly recounted what had happened. "On the way back to the salon she asked me how you felt about your promotion. I had the strangest feeling she knew something, but I didn't understand at the time."

Jan sat back, his face flushed. So Victor had been right after all. The old witch had found out something. Well, so what, she couldn't hurt him now. He had a beautiful future ahead, one he was sure Ludmilla would one day share.

As they approached Ludmilla's tiny house, Shadow was outside on the fence, licking herself. "She's a magician," Ludmilla laughed. "How did she get out?" Jan lunged for her, but the kitten easily ran away.

"Oh, what a nuisance. Shadow, Shadow, come here, come here." It was a familiar pantomime, ending with Shadow springing into her arms.

"Can I come in?" Jan persisted.

"Not tonight, Jan. I feel as if I have the flu. Perhaps it's the shock of today's news." For the first time when he kissed her good night, instead of a hasty peck on the cheek, he turned her face to his. With Shadow in her arms, she couldn't stop him. He kissed her full on the mouth. She shut her eyes, trying to feel something. She did. It was pleasant, warming, but above all it made her think longingly of being kissed by Benedict.

The next day, Ludmilla had to make her usual monthly visit to the two most important Helena Rubinstein accounts, both in London department stores, one at Harrods, the other at Debenham and Freebody. After dealing with problems and complaints and trying to stimulate sales with a number of incentives for the beauty consultants, she didn't get to the office until early afternoon.

"There's been a man, a foreign gentleman called Mr. Kusy, trying to reach you."

"Who?" Ludmilla was reading a memo on her desk, frowning, not paying much attention.

Poppy said again, "Kusy," pronouncing it "quoosie."

"Spell it."

As Poppy spoke, she handed Ludmilla a list of her calls.

Ludmilla gasped when she saw the name written down.

"What time did he call? Where is his number? I told you always to get call-back numbers. Are you sure this is the name? Not *Father* Kusy? What did he say?"

Ludmilla's tone was unusually sharp, and Poppy felt browbeaten. She'd already had Mrs. Cooper shouting at her once today. What was going wrong with the place?

Sulkily, Poppy replied, "I've been trying to tell you. He said he'll call back because . . ."

"When?"

"He's called twice. I told him to call back after three. He says he has some news about your family."

Ludmilla slumped down at her desk. "And you didn't get his number? I can't believe it."

"No, I keep trying to tell you. He was calling from . . . well, I don't know, but somewhere up north. The line was terrible. I think he said Manchester or someplace like that. He's not in London yet, but he will be."

At five minutes before five, when Ludmilla had given up trying to concentrate on catchy names for a new range of nail enamels and, depressed, was thinking of going home, the phone rang and Poppy reported happily it sounded like Mr. Kusy was calling again.

It was still a poor line, and Ludmilla had to shout to ask him to speak up.

"Yes, yes . . ." To Poppy's amazement, although her boss didn't sound as if she were crying, tears began to stream down the face of the usually unemotional Miss Sukova—"the ice maiden," as many people at the company called her—jealous people, Poppy reckoned. To her disappointment, Ludmilla began to speak in Czech, then frantically gestured to her for a pencil.

When she put the phone down, she looked drained. "That was a relation of my family priest, Father Kusy. As you know, I haven't heard anything from my family for months and months. It was a very bad line, but this gentleman is coming to London—yes, you were right, he was calling from Manchester. He has asked me to meet him for lunch at this Czech restaurant owned by a friend of his family in Soho, next Friday at twelve-thirty. Whatever I'm doing, cancel it. This is a lunch appointment I cannot miss."

As Poppy wrote down the name of the restaurant in the business diary, she asked hesitantly, "Did . . . did he give you any news?"

"Not really." The tears were gone. Ludmilla seemed to be in a trance. "I haven't seen my family since November 1947, almost five years ago. He says he has something to give me, that because the line was so bad, it would be better to talk when we met in person." She seemed to be talking to herself. She gave a strange, curt little laugh. "He probably doesn't trust the telephone. I remember I used to feel the same about it myself—always thinking someone was listening, checking up on me. I can't believe that at long last I'm going to be able to talk to someone who has recent news of my family. It's too good to be true."

London, 1952

CHARLES HAD NEVER traveled with his father by plane before. On the day Benedict had arrived in Paris to bring Suzanne back to New York for their mother's funeral, he had flown home alone from London. It had been a somber journey.

Now, as the lights dimmed and it was announced the plane was landing in Shannon to refuel, Charles felt after almost ten hours in the air that he had been attending not only the most lavish banquet—seven courses had been served and devoured, along with numerous cocktails and wines—but the happiest occasion of his life. His father had been incredibly warm, friendly, telling him jokes and anecdotes from his past, "man to man." If his father had said it once, he'd said it half a dozen times. "This isn't anything to tell your sister, Charlie. This is man to man."

Man to man! Charles felt he'd died and gone to heaven. For the first time in his life his father was treating him like a buddy, his best buddy.

It was a bitterly cold, starlit night as they walked to the terminal. His father had already reminded him that it was a free port, as if he could have forgotten. Steeped in misery though he had been a year ago, he hadn't been able to resist buying a fine old brandy for a dollar a bottle.

Now, he was struck again by how incredibly cheap everything was, from the banks of fine Irish woolens, linens, and Scottish cashmeres to the dozens and dozens of bottles of the finest French perfumes lining a wall, all a fraction of the prices charged in New York. Charles, remembering an elegant redhead who lived near Curzon Street in London, was sheepishly asking the price of Chanel No. 5 when his father wandered over.

"We'll take three of the largest size." Benedict smiled broadly at the salesgirl, as he murmured in an aside to a startled Charles, "Some say it's an aphrodisiac. It certainly smells a hell of a lot better on bare skin than in the bottle."

After an hour, when the flight was called, Charles saw his father at a jewelry counter, examining a delicate pair of earrings that looked like small bottles with pearl-and-diamond stoppers. "Very unusual," his father said, but he put them back on the counter and tucked his arm through Charles's to saunter out into the cold night.

Charles was awestruck by his father's obvious VIP status on landing in London. The plane was packed, so he'd envisioned at least a couple of hours' tiring wait in the immigration and customs hall, something he was well used to. Instead, a few minutes after the plane shut off its engines and the steward issued a directive for the passengers to remain seated, the huge front door was creaked open and shortly afterwards a message came over the loudspeaker: "Will Colonel Towers and Mr. Charles Towers please come forward."

Charles looked at his father anxiously, thinking it must be some emergency, but his father was smiling, moving forward to shake hands with a pompous-looking man with a bright red face. The perfect caricature of Colonel Blimp of the British Army, was Charles's first thought. Colonel Blimp, however, escorted them down the steep plane steps and into a limousine waiting on the tarmac. In the car a customs officer welcomed them to London and apologized for the rainstorm, which, he said, would soon blow over. He hardly looked at either of their customs declaration forms, and alighting at the door to the customs hall, Benedict walked ahead with Colonel Blimp, waving to the bored-looking officers waiting for the other passengers to disembark.

Outside the airport, Tim Nolan, head of Towers's British subsidiary, was waiting to greet them, and they were on the way into London in a luxurious company car before Charles realized he was still clutching his passport, which no one had shown the slightest interest in perusing.

He was sitting beside the driver, while his father was already engaged in a business discussion with Nolan in the backseat. Nevertheless, Charles felt he had to ask, "What about our luggage, Dad?"

"It's in the car behind us, son. You don't need to worry about a thing."

And it was true. At Claridge's, a hotel that had always intimidated him, a regal-looking man was waiting in the marble hallway to welcome them, and for a second, struck by the warmth of his father's "My dear Van Thuyne, how good it is to see you!" Charles thought it was an old friend he'd run into by accident. "You know my son, don't you?"

As Van Thuyne extended an impeccably manicured hand, Charles realized he had to be the manager of the hotel, who, without appearing to give any directions, was marshaling a small force of minions to bow and scrape and carry anything they happened to have in their hands as they were led to a paneled elevator with brocade seats.

Charles had lost all track of time. The gold clock in the elevator told him it was four-forty-five, but was that A.M. or P.M.? He couldn't work it out with the time difference, and as usual in London's winter, it was pitch black outside, day and night. He usually felt exhausted and slept for twenty-four hours after arriving on either side of the Atlantic. Now Charles wasn't sure he could sleep at all. He didn't want to miss a second of being treated like the heir apparent! As he followed his father through a huge suite filled with flowers and baskets of fruit, he beamed incessantly, relishing the respect and the good life his father obviously enjoyed wherever he went in the world, not only at home.

He knew for himself how hard his father worked for it all, but it was the first time he'd really appreciated what the rewards could be. Perhaps it was because his father had been drumming into his head ever since he was a child that life was "no free lunch," that one had to earn the good things. And he, much more than Suzanne, had been given so many miserable lessons about the value of money.

As he showered in his bathroom—a room he estimated to be as large as the sitting room in his New York apartment—Charles vowed that one day he'd tell his father this trip was the trip that had really motivated him and changed his mind about the business. From now on his father would not have to complain about his short attention span.

When the phone woke him, it took Charles a few minutes to remember where he was. "I'm going to be busy most of the day. Let's plan to meet for a drink before an early dinner." His father sounded as he did in New York, full of energy and zip, epitomizing *The Wall Street Journal*'s name for him, "Mr. Get-Up-and-Go."

Charles tried to put some semblance of life into his own voice. "Great, Dad, right, I'll call—"

His father interrupted him. "It's about ten-fifteen Friday morning. We'll both be in need of an early night after so few hours' sleep. Tim Nolan's expecting to hear from you, but take it easy. Go over to the Strand and see how our British troops are doing later this morning."

So it had been 4:45 A.M. Charles stumbled groggily to the bathroom. He calculated he'd collapsed into bed about an hour after their arrival, so if it was ten-thirty now, he'd had less than five hours' sleep! He wasn't like his father, who he knew could get by on three or four. It had been one of the many complaints he'd heard his mother make about his father, but he couldn't function, let alone report on a visit to the British Towers's HQ in the Strand without more sleep. He asked the operator to call him at one o'clock and climbed back into bed, praying his father wouldn't call again.

Almost two hours later, though light snow was beginning to fall, Benedict wasn't aware of it as he walked briskly from his lawyer's office off Pall Mall, up Lower Regent Street, crossing Piccadilly and Shaftsbury Avenue to arrive at the cozy, intimate Czech restaurant recommended to him in Soho. There he had reserved a table for two in the name of Kusy.

He'd wanted to walk. He had to clear his head and prepare for the meeting ahead with all the cunning and charm he possessed. It had been easy to arrange—too easy, perhaps. But Benedict never doubted that Ludmilla would come. It had been easy to find a name in the Sukova file that he could be sure Ludmilla would respond to. What better name than that of her family priest, the priest who'd married her to the pathetic Milos.

The Czech whom the detective had used as bait had reported that Ludmilla had needed no persuasion. On the contrary, Detective Brittan said, even before the Czech implied he had some news from Prague, Ludmilla had been the one who was anxious to set up a meeting— "overanxious" was the word the detective had used.

It was twelve-fifteen. Ludmilla would be on time, if not early. It was another characteristic Benedict admired, accustomed as he was to women's unpunctuality in general and Honey's in particular.

Benedict didn't like the table he was given. Without fuss, he indicated and was given the one he wanted, with a good view of the entrance but situated in the corner so that, although he could see Ludmilla arrive, she would not be able to see him until the last minute. It was the kind of restaurant he generally loathed, gloomy as opposed to dark and romantic, with heavy tapestry wall hangings and chandeliers made from deer antlers. But the tablecloths were pristine and white and the glasses thin and tall. He ordered a slivovitz because he recognized that he was nervous.

At 12:25 she came in, taller than he remembered her in his daydreams and much more elegant in a stylish, heavy black coat with some kind of black knitted collar pulled up high around her chin. But then, of course, she was a career girl now, a successful, brainy career girl. Her beautiful hair—he ached as he saw the black, glossy hair he'd caressed so often—was piled high on her head. He was glad she hadn't cut it. She was giving her coat and umbrella to the checkroom girl. Thank God it was winter. She wouldn't run straight out into the snow, even if she felt like running once she saw him.

As she followed the maitre d' down the middle of the restaurant, Benedict could see she looked tense, worried, her chest heaving with . . . what? Anxiety? Anticipation? It couldn't be the same nervous anticipation she had exhibited before their illicit meetings in the past, because she didn't know she was meeting him. That nervousness had always heightened the sensuality of their coming together. Now there would be no more reason for their meetings to be illicit. He wasn't likely to marry again. There would be no wife he would have to lie to when he went to visit her in Europe, where it would be accepted that she was his most cherished mistress.

These thoughts rushed through his mind as she approached. He felt a flood of relief as the man at the next table got up, blocking for a second her view as the maitre d' indicated where Mr. Kusy was waiting. He stood up. When the man moved away, he was waiting, with arms outstretched.

She turned so pale he thought she was going to faint, but her eyes never left his face and his never left hers.

She still loves me, he thought, exulting. He can't forget me, but he still lies to achieve his purpose, she thought with a mixture of excitement and resignation.

Later, when he was able to think straight, he wondered how long they'd stood there, he pulling her to him, she not resisting at first. Probably no longer than one or two minutes, although it seemed endless.

As usual, her first words were straight to the point. "So you are Mr. Kusy."

They stared into each other's eyes. Something she saw there made her sit down heavily. She looked up at him, eyes brimming. She said, "But you do have news? News of my family?"

Fool! He'd forgotten how deeply she cared for her family. To think up a plot to bring her to him, he'd concentrated only on her probing, her pushing for him to find out all he could about her family's fate— the only thing, in fact, she had ever asked of him—overlooking the very deep feelings that had prompted her questions.

Now, after all the agonizing months apart, fool that he was, the first thing he had to give her was bad news, very bad news. Now, when the first thing she wanted to know was if there was any truth in the ruse he'd used to bring about their meeting, he had to tell her her father was dead.

She wouldn't make a scene. She had never made a scene, not before at the worst of times, not now, when at first things would not seem any better. He was the one who had made the scenes.

Benedict waved the hovering waiter away with a scowl and took her hands in his.

How natural it felt, Ludmilla thought, so different from the night over a week ago when Jan had held her hands, wanting for the first time to express his love for her.

Along with the exhilaration of seeing Benedict again, so overwhelming it almost made her nauseous, now came a weariness. She wanted to leave her hands in his forever. She wanted to put her head on his shoulder, to stop fighting and to accept whatever he now wanted. As quickly as that feeling came, it went.

She tried to take her hands away, but he held on as he always had, used to getting what he wanted, when he wanted it, not even recognizing that there could ever be any opposition to his demands.

"There are many reasons I went to the trouble to arrange this meeting today." Benedict spoke carefully, as if he'd rehearsed every word. "When I use the word 'trouble,' I am trying to justify what I know must appear to you to be more proof of my duplicity, but I had to find a way to make sure you would meet me."

Ludmilla remained still, silent, listening to him as no other woman had ever listened. "My darling, yes, I do have news of your family." He hesitated, then said, "Sad news, your father died last month." She jerked her hand away so violently she knocked the water glass over, soaking the tablecloth.

"How?" It was a low moan. "How did he die? Was he murdered?"

"Cancer. It was fast. He didn't suffer," he lied, not knowing any more than the bare facts Dennon had passed on.

Her eyes were brimming, but no tears fell. It was inexplicable, but she'd had a premonition that the news from "Mr. Kusy" was going to be bad. She'd arrived expecting to hear that her mother was gone. It was hard to believe that her tall, strong father, who'd taught her how to ride a pony, who'd made all the ladies in the beauty shop blush when he praised their new haircuts and haircolors, was the parent she would never see again.

She didn't realize how pale she was. Benedict summoned the waiter. "Two slivovitzes and some more water, please."

She started to talk about her father, haltingly at first and then with more feeling. He paid little attention to what she was saying. He felt heady, listening to the cadence of her voice, seeing the way the white, slender stem of her neck was emphasized by the black turtleneck of her sweater, watching the quick rise and fall of her breasts as her grief burst out in increasingly agitated sentences.

The waiter brought some peculiar appetizer that he told them was a speciality of the house, called "devil's toast," which Ludmilla murmured was a typical Prague dish of ground meat on toast with cheese and horseradish. She didn't eat. He ordered whatever the waiter recommended, and plates came and went almost untouched.

As coffee came and he paid the check, she sighed and turned her deep, dark eyes on him. "You were good to go to the trouble. I am grateful you came to tell me. It would have been harder learning this from anybody else."

"I love you, Ludmilla." It was the last thing he'd expected to say. He had never said those words to her. She had once told herself she didn't need to hear them.

She lowered her face. "Thank you."

"You returned my letter; you refused to speak to me."

"What was the use? It has taken me a long time, but I have accepted what you felt was the right thing to do. We agreed not to see each other again. We must make the same decision again."

He felt panic, the panic he'd awakened with after the dream. He forgot what he'd planned to say. He hardly knew what he was saying. "But it's no longer necessary. If you had read my letter, you would know that I am alone. Honey was killed in a terrible train accident last year, one that took many lives."

Her expression didn't change, but her body stiffened. "Last year?" she repeated slowly.

"Yes, I wrote to you. I tried to phone you. It was a terrible time for the children, especially for Suzanne. She knew—she suspected—something was wrong with our marriage."

Again she repeated his words. "Suzanne suspected?"

He couldn't stop himself. He cupped her beautiful, grieving face in his hands and kissed her long and deeply on the mouth, tasting the sweetness of her, sensing the immediate response, knowing her body was as ready for his as it had been that first time in the little inn in Switzerland, when she'd admitted she'd thought she was frigid, that she hadn't known the meaning of enjoyment in sex.

But even as he went to encircle her shoulders, his hands longing to feel again her full breasts, she withdrew. "It's no good," she said weakly. "Your children, your family will never accept me."

He didn't know what she meant. Children? What had his children to do with their relationship? "My family?" He looked puzzled, then began to speak eagerly, like a young swain, an ardent lover. "I didn't know how you would feel about me. I have been watching your success . . ." He told her how much he knew about her growing importance at Helena Rubinstein and, because of it, his own interest in the cosmetics business. He was so carried away he forgot his doubts. She didn't need to say anything; her body had already said it for her.

He started to tell her of his plans for her, and about his meeting with the great Madame the following week. "I think it's best if you move to Paris. I'm going to find you the apartment of your dreams. If you want to stay with the business—which I hope you will—you will run Europe from Paris. You may not know that your remarkable boss cannot benefit from one penny made by the English company, although it grosses several million pounds a year, because she had the foresight—or was advised—to transfer its ownership to a foundation. This is because the British tax system is so onerous; taxes are prohibitive, but also there is the specter of incredible death duties levied on private estates here."

As he drew in broad strokes the way he saw her future life, using the words "as my partner" over and over again, Ludmilla grew chilled. No wonder he had looked so surprised when she'd mentioned his children and family. He wasn't proposing that she become his partner in marriage; he was proposing, or rather taking for granted, that she would become his mistress.

It would all be so easy, so wonderfully easy, to acquiesce to everything he was saying, to accept the dream of an apartment in Paris and the luxuries he would shower on her, but how long would it last? Even as he was saying with lovesick eyes how he ached for her, how at last their relationship needn't be illicit, he was lying to himself. With every word and every promise, he was also telling her, although she was sure he didn't even comprehend it, that she didn't belong in his everyday world. She was outside, not inside; downstairs, not upstairs, whether or not he managed to buy the company from Madame Rubinstein—something she doubted even Benedict Towers could pull off.

Yes, she thought bitterly, he probably does love me, or thinks he does. All these months she had certainly been trying to stop herself from loving him, if love was the word for the wanting and needing she carried deep inside for him, the man who had taught her everything about sex, who had even made her understand Milos's hunger for her.

She sat up very tall and looked at him, steeling herself. She knew what she had to say and what she had to do. "It's no good," she repeated, but this time firmly.

He looked at her with amazement. "What do you mean?"

"I told you once—we often laughed about it—that I wanted to be known for my brain. Well, I am beginning to be known for my ideas. I am ambitious. A relationship . . ." She was trembling, stumbling, but she forced herself to go on. "The relationship you are describing would never work—it would arouse too much jealousy. You can't get the best out of people if they think you have an unfair advantage."

He interrupted brusquely. "Darling little Lu, I don't care whether you work or not. I thought you would want to."

"But of course I want to. I am going to work. I am going to be someone." Her anger began to rise. How could he take her for granted so quickly, after spending only a couple of hours with her, as if all the months away from him had counted for nothing. Two pink spots appeared on her cheeks. He was forcing her to say things she didn't intend to say. "I have already been offered an important job in America. I have my own plans for my future. I don't need your . . . your patronage, your . . ." She couldn't think of the right English word. "Your charity," she said.

She stood up, putting out her hand. "It's best we say good-bye now."

For a moment he sat stunned, his mind racing, unable to believe she was walking away from everything he was offering her, out of his life. "Don't go," he cried, but she was already walking fast to the checkroom to collect her coat.

He followed her out into the street, where the sky was darkening and snow was now pouring down. Thank God he'd told the car to meet him at the restaurant. As she pulled up the collar of her coat, he clutched her arm. "Let me take you back to work, to the salon."

"It's better if you don't. I'll get a taxi."

He took no notice, pushing her into the backseat as the chauffeur held the door open. "Take a long time to get to Grafton Street," he said gruffly, then shut the dark glass partition dividing the driver from the passengers.

They both began to speak at once, he aware of impending loss, she suffering from a sense of unworthiness, a lack of pride, familiar feelings that she'd thought she'd overcome with hard work and the realization that she could achieve something on her own. There was pain in both their faces.

The car swerved to miss someone running across the street. She was in his arms and he was opening her coat and they were devouring each other, his hands beneath her sweater, her bra, searching for her beautiful breasts, his mouth on her neck, her body beneath his.

She was the one who forced him to stop, even as her face told him she needed him as much as he needed her. "You're ashamed of me," she cried, as a flurry of snow obscured the world outside the car windows.

"Ashamed?" He was stung. "I don't understand you," he cried angrily. "And who is offering you a job in America The dirty Pole? I'll ruin him!"

"How dare y—" He put his hand over her mouth, angrily forcing her back against the plush seat, lifting her sweater, her bra, his mouth on her breast. "No, no, no . . ." she moaned, but she made no attempt to stop him beneath her skirt, her woolen underwear, longing for him to come nearer, nearer, to feel again inside her his fingers, his tongue, himself. She fought herself, winning, losing, crying out, as the car edged slowly forward.

He was saying all the things he didn't believe in, the crazy, mad words of being in love that he'd never said to a woman before. "I can't live without you . . . I love you . . . I need you."

"But not enough. Your children . . ." there was no mistaking her bitterness. "You aren't prepared for me to meet your children, your friends. You want to hide me away like some . . . some whore, as your wife called me. You want to turn me into a whore!"

He suddenly pushed her away. How could she speak to him like this? This little nobody from Czechoslovakia, who had known nothing until he'd taken her into his arms? How dare she? He couldn't believe what he was hearing from her.

As the car turned down Bond Street, he sat glowering in the corner, watching as Ludmilla carefully buttoned her coat and took a mirror from her handbag to inspect her makeup. Once more she looked like the Ludmilla of old—unapproachable, mysterious, a goddess of fire and ice with whom, God help him, he was totally infatuated—or did he actually, really love the girl?

Now she was as phlegmatic as ever, except for her smudged lipstick, showing no trace of the wildness that had only minutes ago possessed her as it had possessed him. She stared out at the snow, determined, Benedict was sure, to prove to him she could go on without him, as she had indeed proved she could during the past two years.

"I don't want to see you again," she said in a low voice. "You've already told me, even though you don't realize it, that I don't belong in your life."

Benedict dug his nails into his palm. She meant it; he knew it. Ludmilla wasn't like the playacting women he'd been used to all his life, who said one thing and meant another. She was prepared to go out of his life as she had two years before, without a backward glance, and this time it would be forever.

He was slumped in despondency as the car approached the Helena Rubinstein salon on Grafton Street, a salon he'd looked forward to Ludmilla showing him in the not-too-distant future. Now all interest he'd had in the Rubinstein company was gone, dead, as he felt he was himself.

There was a familiar figure standing in the lofty doorway, forlornly looking out for a nonexistent taxi. It was Charles, his son. He'd obviously been doing some homework. Before the car reached the curb, he saw Charles go back inside the building.

To Ludmilla's astonishment, Benedict started to laugh. Instead of fear and guilt, what emotion had swept over him as he'd seen his son standing there? He couldn't believe it. It was relief—fresh, unpolluted, joyous relief—and in that second he knew exactly what he was going to do, no matter what anyone, including his beloved daughter Suzanne, thought or said.

How could he have been such a fool? As Norris went through his travail with Audrey, he would keep him company if he had to put up with some cold-shouldering from Suzanne and society. He didn't care a damn about society, and Suzanne would soon get over it. He could hardly wait to tell Norris that they would be rebuilding their lives with new sexual partners at more or less the same time.

When the car stopped, he sat with his arms crossed, smiling as Ludmilla looked at him icily and said, "I don't know what is amusing you so much, Colonel Towers, but whatever it is, I want to say good-bye. I mean it. It's the end."

How wonderful it was going to be to melt the ice, to ignite the fire, to rein in the turbulent spirit of this wild and wonderful young woman. How satisfying it was going to be to nurture and guide her talent, to teach her how to be a hostess, to see her blossom, to father her children. Benedict felt lightheaded with joy at the thought of her youth, her animal energy. She would keep him young forever.

Although the chauffeur was getting out with an umbrella, when Benedict didn't move, Ludmilla tried to lean across him to open the door. He pushed her back in the seat, saying, "Not so quickly, young lady. You will have to learn to let others do menial tasks for you." He put his hand over hers, pleased to find she was trembling. He would make her tremble forever, with joy, with fear, with passion.

"Please, Benedict, let me go. Let me say good-bye."

"But it isn't good-bye, my sweet Lu. This is not the end. This is, in fact, the beginning for both of us." He smiled as she flushed with anger once more. "Did you ever meet my son, Charles?"

Had he gone mad? Ludmilla shook her head as she replied curtly, "Yes, once, twice, a few times in New York, very briefly. Now please let me go." Her voice was breaking. He knew her heart was breaking. She was thinking he didn't care.

"Charles is based in the New York office now, but I brought him with me on this trip to meet you properly." In the last few minutes the lie had become the truth.

She looked at him wide-eyed. "To meet me? I don't understand."

The chauffeur opened the door. "Are we getting out here, sir?"

"Yes, yes, but give me a few minutes, Pat. Tell my son—he's inside the salon—that I'm coming in with someone I want him to meet. Then I'll give him a ride back to the hotel and you can take Miss Sukova home."

The snow was coming down now with ferocity. Soon it would be too dangerous to drive. "I can't go home yet," Ludmilla said uncertainly. "I have work to do."

"I'm not allowing that. I want to be sure you get home safely in this weather but first we'll go inside for you to meet Charles."

"I don't understand," Ludmilla said tremulously again. A few tears streaked her cheeks.

"At last I do," Benedict said gravely. "You are going to be my wife."

Was that what all the "man to man" business had been about? Had Dad been preparing him for the shock of his life? Charles had promised him he wouldn't call Suzanne, yet he felt so guilty not doing so. Surely he had to warn her that her suspicions had been right on target; Dad did seem to be infatuated with someone who'd once worked for them.

Charles didn't know how he felt. He didn't know what to do. He'd sat at the dinner table, trying to make intelligent conversation about their British subsidiary, aware he was still half asleep with the time difference and the journey, until his father had opened the bomb doors and dropped his own atom bomb, letting it out one, two, three.

"Charles, I have to tell you, one of the reasons I came to London was to see the beautiful girl you met this afternoon."

It was funny how no amount of pharmaceutical or cosmetics business talk had been able to prop his eyes fully open, yet immediately with this admission from his father, he'd become wide awake, as if he'd been injected with something.

"You mean Ludmilla? The girl at Rubinstein's who used to do Mom's hair?" He hadn't recognized her. Once they reached the hotel and she'd gone home, somewhere in Chelsea, in the company car, it was his father who'd reminded him that she'd once worked for Mom. It was only then that he'd remembered Suzanne's mysterious hints and allusions to some kind of funny business with the hairdresser that had depressed Mom, although Suzanne had had to admit she didn't really know anything. Well, she soon would know she'd been right about the "funny business," whatever it had been.

Dad wanted him to get to know Ludmilla! Dad knew he was going to like her very much. Those had been his parting words the night

before, and now here he was, getting dressed to meet her for lunch
with his father acting like some crazed idiot, telling him what to wear,
pacing up and down the suite as if they were going to Buckingham
Palace instead of to some kind of café in Chelsea, the kind of place
his father usually shunned like the plague. He wished he could get
out of the lunch, but at least his father hadn't raised any objections to
his date with the Curzon Street redhead that evening.

An hour later he had to admit Ludmilla Sukova or Sukorina or
whatever she called herself was one gorgeous piece of woman. He
wasn't surprised his father had come to see her, although exactly what
he had in mind, Charles still wasn't entirely sure. How old was she,
he wondered. Certainly much nearer his age than his father's.

"Charles."

He jumped, wondering if she had read his mind. He loved the way
she said his name with a slight *sh*, like "Sharles." In fact he liked the
way she said most things, although he could have done without the
proprietary look on his father's face every time she opened her mouth,
as if he'd invented her.

She encouraged him to talk about sports, skiing in particular, something he usually never dared do in his father's presence.

"We could take a side trip to St. Moritz after Paris. Would you like
that, Lu?"

Charles was pleased to see that Lu, as his father persisted in calling
her, had the grace to look embarrassed.

"Well, I don't know if I can take the time off then."

Charles looked away, not knowing what else to do, as his father put
his arm around Ludmilla's shoulders and said, "You'll be making those
decisions for yourself soon. I asked if you'd like to go to St. Moritz,
not whether you can take the time off or not."

Charles was relieved in one way when the lunch came to an end,
although his father was right. He did think he would like Ludmilla,
or Lu, as he was beginning to think of her. It was difficult to see how
there could be anything not to like, though he doubted Suzanne would
agree with him.

Later that evening Benedict returned to Chelsea to see Ludmilla's
little house for the first time. She would cook dinner, she told him.
He had already sent her two dozen red roses and arrived carrying a
dozen more. He had dreamed of the moment when she would open
the door. What would she be wearing? What expression would be on
her lovely face?

"Benedict!" Her face told him everything. They had been apart for only
a few hours. For both it felt like days, although she had spent the time

preparing the best meal she could with the ingredients available, spending a week's salary on champagne and liquor at the off-license nearby.

He threw off his overcoat. The roses fell to the floor as he lifted her high in his arms. She was wearing a yellow angora cardigan with a black velvet skirt. That was all. No stockings, no underwear, nothing. She had bought the cardigan in a weak moment a few months before, dreaming of the yellow dress. She had never been able to wear it.

His hands slid under the skirt. He felt her warm, bare skin. "Oh my God, oh my God, you are so unbelievably beautiful, my Lu, my Lu." He buried his face in the soft wool.

"Quickly, quickly," she whispered. He carried her upstairs to her all-white bedroom with her music box and his red roses on the side table. On the bed, Shadow was asleep.

"Where did that come from?"

She wasn't thinking. She was delirious with happiness. "Shoo, Shadow, shoo . . ." As the kitten quickly ran under the bed, she was laughing. "Jan gave her to me for Christmas."

"Jan!" He threw her down on the bed. "Jan!" He wanted to kill. She still laughed up at him, at the anger and jealousy on his face.

"Oh, darling, he's just a friend, a dear, dear . . ." He went crazy. He ripped the cardigan open; buttons scattered in all directions. His mouth bruised her breasts, her neck, her mouth. There was no waiting, no gentle lovemaking. He forced her apart, wanting to hear the velvet skirt split, entering her, leaving her, entering and leaving, each time thrusting deeper, wanting to make her marked, scarred with him, so that she would carry the memory of him inside her with very step she took.

There was no dinner, and little sleep that night and all through the weekend. She wanted his savagery. She was as savage and demanding as he.

Early on Monday morning, hearing hail and snow beat against the window, Benedict kissed her awake. "You're not going to work today. Perhaps you're never going there again. What does this Jan"—he could hardly bring himself to say the name—"this Jew mean to you?"

Sleepily she asked, "What time is it?"

He gathered her hair up from her shoulders and breasts and buried his face in it. "I'll ask you one more time before whipping the truth out of you. What does this man mean to you? Do you work with him? Do you see him every day?"

As he grew large against her, incredibly her own desire grew again. He was pulling her hair; it hurt, but she didn't care. Every sign of his wild jealousy thrilled her. He was the only man in the world who knew how to arouse her, but she would never let him know it. All the same, she had to speak the truth for Jan's sake. Benedict was a dangerous enemy. Who knew what lengths he would go to if he believed Jan had been more than a friend to her? "He means absolutely nothing. He has been kind to me, that's all. He's leaving the company, as well as the country. He has an important new job, and although they've tried to tempt him to stay, now that they know they can't, this is his last week."

"Is he the one who offered you a job in the States?" As she began to laugh, Benedict wrapped her hair around her throat, tighter, tighter.

"No, no, no. I only said that because you were making me so unhappy." Over his back, she saw the time on her bedside clock. "I must get up. It's late. I have to go to . . ."

"You're not going anywhere." He pulled her down beside him. "Turn over."

She started to protest weakly, but soon she was moaning as he slowly caressed her behind, opening her, preparing her.

She didn't go to work that day or the next. Benedict told her to stay in bed when he went himself around noon on Monday to the nearest telephone to ask his secretary to call the Rubinstein office and explain that Ludmilla was home with a bad cold. He next called Charles, but didn't explain his absence, or attempt to pretend he'd been away on business. There would be no more pretense, no more excuses.

He told Charles to make the most of his time off. "Enjoy yourself, as I'm doing," he said, unaware that he sounded so unlike himself, hardly making sense, adding to Charles's worry and confusion.

"When am I going to see you, Dad?"

There was a pause, then, "Perhaps tomorrow son." There was another pause. "Well, no, let's say Wednesday. I'll check in tomorrow and let you know what time." He bought a razor and some shaving cream before he went back to Ludmilla's house, already aching for her.

It was the most complete lovemaking of his life. By the time he left Ludmilla early on Wednesday morning, he told her he hoped they'd made another child. "Please stay home again today in the little nest I bought for you. While I'm working, I want to think of you all day, naked, waiting, wet for me." He knelt down and tenderly kissed her belly. "I'm going to keep this full of my seed. You're mine forever now, Ludmilla. Neither of us must think of the past and the terrible decision I made for both of us. Now we have only happiness to look forward to."

As he ran down the stairs, he saw the wretched cat in the hallway. His anger rising, he tried to grab it to throw it out into the street, but it ran beneath the hall table. Well, he'd make sure he got rid of it on his return.

When he reached the office, there were several phone messages waiting for him from his French lawyers. To their surprise, Benedict took the news calmly that the old beauty empress had evidently changed her mind about meeting him. "She says there really would be no point in meeting at this time."

Benedict's *"Sans faire rien"* irritated the lawyer.

"Madame Rubinstein is having a problem that necessitates her having to return to the United States earlier than she anticipated. However, I would like to pursue this further—that is, if you are still interested."

Benedict found he really wasn't. "I'll let you know," he said casually, later explaining to Charles, "I haven't given up, but there's more than one apple on the cosmetics tree. From what I know about this particular old fruit, the best way to pique her interest is not to seem too eager."

They sat before a roaring fire in the Claridge's suite, roasting chestnuts. Benedict had spent most of the day at the office, except for an hour at the leading diamond merchant in London's Hatton Garden. He tried to appear relaxed, but, aware of time passing, his anxiety to be back with Ludmilla was growing. It was as if he had to make up for every second of the two years he had lost with her. He felt like a man released from a hunger strike. He'd sent the chauffeur over to her house with a note telling her to be ready for him at six. Now, at 4:50, he wished he'd said five.

As Benedict looked at his watch for the third time in just a few minutes, Charles asked nervously, "Are we going home, then?"

"Yes, yes, of course we are." He hadn't meant to snap. He wanted to tell Charles what was going to happen, but, seeing his son's strained face, he didn't know how to begin. Well, perhaps it could wait until they were home.

Only the crackling of the fire broke the silence. Finally, his heart thumping, dreading the answer, Charles asked, "Is . . . is Ludmilla . . ." He stopped as his father threw up his hands as if to say "I can't help myself." They looked at each other warily. There was another long silence, but now Charles knew what his father was going to say. He was right.

"Ludmilla is going to join me—us. Yes, she's coming back to New York."

He had to ask the question for Suzanne's sake, if not for his own. "Why, Dad?"

"I'm going to marry her, son."

*   *   *

As Benedict was breaking the news to Charles, there was a knock on Ludmilla's door. The chauffeur had left an hour before, and hoping that Benedict had been able to come earlier, Ludmilla, just out of the bath, powdered and perfumed, wrapped a towel around her and ran downstairs. "Who is it?"

"It's Jan. I've been worried about you."

"Jan, I can't see you," she said quickly. "I've been sick, but I'll be back in the office tomorrow."

"I've brought you some soup, and some cat food for Shadow. I won't be in the office anymore. Ceska called me in and said it was better I didn't come back." He laughed the self-deprecating laugh she knew so well. "She said it was making the staff restless, that my 'betrayal' could be infectious." Jan shook the doorknob. "Please open the door, Ludmilla, just for a minute."

Ludmilla thought quickly. Benedict would be leaving for Paris this weekend for his meeting with Madame Rubinstein. "Jan, I'm not dressed. Look, I know, let's meet on Sunday at the pub for a farewell drink."

"Will you come back to my place for dinner afterwards?"

Ludmilla had no intention of showing up, but she said warmly, "Of course, Jan, of course."

"I'll leave everything outside, then. I'll call you at the office tomorrow to fix the time. Take care of yourself."

When she was sure he had gone, Ludmilla opened the door and collected the soup and cat food. Dear Jan, it was a pity, but it was probably better that they didn't meet again. She couldn't risk Benedict finding out. He would never believe how innocent their relationship had been. She would write to Jan to explain. What would she say? That she was going to be married, of course.

Ludmilla Katrina Sukova, until recently an executive with the Helena Rubinstein cosmetics organization in London, England, was married yesterday to Benedict Charles Towers, Chairman of the Board and Chief Executive Officer of Towers Pharmaceuticals.

Justice Terence Applegate of the Appellate Division of the State Supreme Court performed the ceremony at the Manhattan home of Mr. and Mrs. Mellon Sanford III. A blessing was given by Monsignor Oldham, S.J., who is dean of Fordham College, New York. Alexandra Sanford attended the bride. The best men were the groom's brother, Leonard Towers, executive vice-president of Towers Pharmaceuticals, and the groom's son, Charles Towers, vice-president of Towers Pharmaceuticals.

Mrs. Towers was born in Prague, Czechoslovakia, and, until her immigration to the United States in 1947, helped run the well-known Sukova beauty establishment, founded in the capital by her father in the 1920s. She joined Helena Rubinstein in London in 1950.

Mr. Towers, grandson of Charles Towers, the founder of Towers Pharmaceuticals, graduated magna cum laude from Harvard University and has a master's degree in international studies from Johns Hopkins University. During World War II, Mr. Towers served on General Patton's staff, where he rose to the rank of colonel, receiving the military cross for bravery in action in Bastogne in 1944. At the end of the war, Colonel Towers was appointed by President Truman to head the American legation in Prague. He resigned this post to return to private life in March 1946.

Mr. Towers was widowed in 1951. The previous marriage of Mrs. Towers ended in divorce.

Of course, there was no mention in *The New York Times* of the nonappearance of Miss Suzanne Towers at the simple ceremony, held in the home of Benedict's Harvard roommate. Suzanne's own marriage in Geneva, Switzerland, to the textile manufacturer Mr. Alexander Fiestler, was duly recorded a month later, while Mr. and Mrs. Benedict Towers were still on their honeymoon.

Faithful Norris cabled the news to Benedict, but he already knew. Charles had phoned to tell him it was going to take place. Charles had behaved magnificently—everyone said so—even though he'd been caught in the middle, between his sister and his father. Few people knew that was where he'd been since that March afternoon by the fire at Claridge's, when his father had taken him into his confidence about his plan to marry Ludmilla.

It had been a terrible shock, not so much because of Ludmilla herself—in her company it was easy to see why even someone like his father could become intrigued with her—but because of what he knew they were all going to have to face with Suzanne.

It had been terrible, all right. Dad had asked him to be there when he told her, but he hadn't had the courage. Suzanne had cried for a week, had had hysterics, threatened to tell the papers "the truth about Ludmilla," whatever that meant. This was followed by threats of suicide, then elopement, and finally—to Charles, the most dangerous attitude of all—she seemed to accept things, waiting with icy calm for Ludmilla's arrival after she'd resigned from Helena Rubinstein and packed up her affairs in London.

Charles had warned her not to try any of her tricks and risk alienating herself from the family.

"Family!" Suzanne had exploded, using language he didn't know his sister knew, let alone ever used. "What family? Do you think in a million years I want to be part of any family"—she'd made the word sound like a curse—"that contains that fucking housemaid whore! I'd rather be dead."

"Or married to Mr. Starched-shirt Fiestler," Charles had said under his breath.

Since Ludmilla's arrival a month before the wedding, Charles had known there was no way Suzanne was going to give her a chance. No way. No matter how Dad connived, entreated, threatened, and sulked, in Suzanne's mind Ludmilla was little short of a murderer. He hadn't been able to stop her from sending Ludmilla a photograph of their parents, obviously taken when they were still in love, with his father looking down adoringly at Honey, his diminutive wife. Suzanne hadn't shown him the letter that went with it, but, knowing his sister, he'd known it had to be lethal.

He only saw Ludmilla and Suzanne together once, at the horrible cocktail party Dad had thrown in the executive dining room for some of the Towers Pharmaceuticals staff to meet Ludmilla. The first thing he'd noticed was that Ludmilla was wearing the earrings he'd seen his father study at Shannon Airport, the ones that looked like little perfume bottles with diamond-and-pearl stoppers. So Dad's trip to Europe had involved her from the start. Charles often wondered why he'd wanted him along. He could only suppose it was for mental support, which in some weird way made him feel proud.

His heart had gone out to Ludmilla at the party, which must have been an ordeal for her anyway, even if Suzanne hadn't behaved like a pig. Ludmilla had behaved with such courage and dignity when Suzanne, supposedly accidentally, had spilled cocktail sauce all over her pale lace dress and then had totally burned her bridges with Dad when she'd said in a voice loud enough for everyone to hear, "Well, no one knows better than you, Ludmilla, how to remove stains. You were known for it in Palm Beach, when you first worked for us as a housemaid."

There were moments on the honeymoon when Ludmilla thought back to that night, which had ended with Benedict telling his daughter that until she apologized, he didn't want to see her again. She thought about Suzanne's letter to her, too, which she'd never shown to Benedict, knowing that if he ever read it, the rift would quite likely be impossible to mend.

She'd remembered the letter on the first night out on the maiden transatlantic voyage of the SS *United States*. She'd been late dressing for dinner and had met Benedict in the bar, wearing the most elaborate evening dress of her trousseau, only to learn that "one never dresses for dinner the first night out." She'd thought of it again when, in front of the wine waiter, she'd asked for red wine, not white, with her lobster, and when, at the captain's table, she'd caused barely disguised titters from a couple of blue-haired matrons when she'd thought Mark Twain was the name of a Hollywood actor.

Each time Benedict had frowned, that was all; nothing and no one could spoil one second of the passion that existed between them. He only had to touch her, or she to brush by him, to generate the electricity between them, but when, exhausted and sated, he slept beside her, she thought about him frowning and that made her think of Suzanne's cruel words. "What makes you think you could possibly be a fitting wife for my father, one of the most accomplished, most brilliant men in America? How long do you think his middle-aged lust for a cheap, ignorant peasant like you is going to last? When he realizes what he has done to our family name and honor, then and only then will he try to make amends and throw you out on the garbage heap where you belong. If only it were in my power to make you suffer now for the death of my mother, which you caused to come about. My only consolation is that you will suffer for it one day, and probably sooner than later, when my father's eyes open and he sees you for what you really are, a worthless, gold-digging tramp."

Louise

New York, 1954

"BENEDICT DOESN'T LIKE me to smoke. He says the *Reader's Digest* warning is true."

Ludmilla hoped she didn't sound as wistful as she felt as she shook her head, and Alexandra Sanford slipped her onyx cigarette case back inside her purse. She watched with undisguised admiration the graceful tilt of Alexandra's chin as she received a light from the maître d' and inhaled through her trademark ivory-and-diamond cigarette holder. "I only smoke filter tips. Tell your darling husband not to be so bossy."

Her tone was light but reproving, reminding Ludmilla that it wasn't the first time during the lunch when she had referred to Benedict's likes and dislikes.

"Benedict likes me to support American fashion."

"Benedict doesn't like short hair."

"Benedict dislikes upheaval; he likes his apartment more than any other in New York. He still doesn't want to move."

Probably Alexandra Sanford, one of the most important names in the social register, thought she was totally under Benedict's thumb. In a way it was true. She was, but that was where she wanted to be. For the moment. Soon, with the small step she was about to take—albeit with Benedict's full permission—she hoped she would be able to show the world, Benedict's world, something of her true, fierce, independent spirit.

"I admire you for wanting to work," Alexandra said as their coffee arrived. "For some reason, all the best skin-care people seem to come from Rumania and Russia, like you. I think your shop—or should I say salon—is going to be a raving success. To think you're going to be almost next door! If I come every day, is there a chance my skin will ever look like yours?"

"Of course! Even if you come every other day."

Ludmilla had told Alexandra more than once that she came from Czechoslovakia, but she didn't correct her. She owed her so much. Unlike most of the women Benedict had encouraged her to meet, Ludmilla liked and was beginning to trust Alexandra, although she had been a friend of Honey's and was certainly nearer Benedict's age than her own, with teenage twin daughters, Harriet and Penelope.

"What does that wretched contractor say now? Has he fixed the heating system? Have you an opening date in mind?"

"I'm aiming for two weeks after Labor Day. One of Benedict's public-relations advisers tells me that's when most women come back to New York. Do you agree?" Without realizing it, she blushed slightly as she added, "As you know, Benedict doesn't like me to go to the Long Island house in the summer, when he has to be in the city."

How charming she can be, Alexandra thought. Charming, probably deliberately inscrutable, and far more intelligent than most people, women especially, give her credit for.

From the beginning, most of the invitations Benedict wanted Ludmilla to accept, she knew now, came from women who viewed her as a curiosity or some kind of sexual freak. She was still a cause of gossip, not so much in the columns—that had died down because they went so rarely to public events—but among the idle rich society women, who discussed and dissected her inch by inch, longing to discover just what had prompted such an outstandingly eligible man like Benedict actually to marry her! Benedict, who could buy and sell "a hundred just like you," as Suzanne had once told her icily.

Today, as at other lunches and teas during the past two years, Ludmilla felt that Alexandra genuinely wanted to help and befriend her. She had already helped her considerably, finding the best new staff for the Park Avenue apartment, when, except for faithful Thorpe, the butler, the rest had walked out when she became Mrs. Towers. But this lunch was to celebrate something far more significant. She had already said it; she felt she had to say it again.

"Alexandra, I can never thank you enough for telling me about the shop—and I owe you even more for helping me persuade Benedict to let me have it." To her surprise, her voice broke as she said the last few words.

Alexandra blew a perfect smoke ring and looked at Ludmilla carefully. Was the "sexy savage," as many of her friends called Ben's young wife, having a tougher time than any of them knew? "I know what it's like to go mad with boredom, my dear," she said conspiratorially. "You're a new bride. I've been married for more years than I care to tell you. For Benedict to keep you on too tight a leash would be a big mistake. I told him so. You're far too young, beautiful, and talented to spend your time lunching and shopping and bitching. I asked Paunch to give me the flower shop five years ago because I knew I was heading into a potentially dangerous affair. I never dreamed I'd end up loving it so much I can hardly tear myself away to go to Santa Barbara in the winter. I can tell you, if the weather in New York wasn't so foul, I'd never leave my little Petals."

Under Alexandra's direction, Petals had become one of the most fashionable florists in New York. Paunch, her amiable, easygoing husband, from a lineage as illustrious as her own, was one of Benedict's oldest friends, although they seemed to have almost nothing in common.

"Paunch hasn't worked a day in his life," she'd heard Benedict laugh without the trace of censure he usually displayed toward those he called "the underemployed, brainless set." Benedict had also explained that his friend was only called "Paunch" by those closest to him, although Mellon Sanford III had long since lost the adolescent blubber that had earned him the nickname.

She would never understand the American sense of humor, the explanation given for so much of their outlandish childish behavior. By now no one expected her to join in the shrieking laughter which accompanied some of their antics. One of the things about her, which in the early days had attracted and fascinated Benedict the most, was, she knew, her natural reserve, her ability to remain, as he called it, "regally silent" when everyone expected some response. He'd admitted her coldness had originally attracted him because "I sensed it wasn't a coverup for shyness. You were trying not to let anyone see you felt goddamned superior, weren't you, little Lu?"

It wasn't true, but he had insisted she never try to change. "If you don't understand something, stay silent. No one knows how to stay silent better than you. Ask me later. I'll explain."

In the beginning she'd felt it was more because he was anxious, as she was herself, that she didn't embarrass him with gaffes that showed the enormous gaps in her education, not only about America but about the world. Last year he'd told her over and over again that she exuded "mystery, never stupidity." But what did he think she really was? Mysterious or stupid? It was a question she'd tormented herself with after dinner parties where she'd desperately tried to pick up threads of conversations to make at least one intelligent remark. Like the one that had involved who was fighting to buy Francis Bacon's *Study After Velazquez: Pope Innocent X*, a Bacon who turned out to be a controversial modern English painter and not, as she'd thought, at first proud of herself, the man who might have written the works of William Shakespeare.

All this had begun to change after one miserable evening she would never forget, when Benedict and she had had their first row. It had happened after they saw *The Crucible,* a play in which Benedict had invested, about the seventeenth-century Salem witch trials (which she'd never heard of either), intended by the playwright Arthur Miller as a parallel to the persecution of alleged Communists in the United States. Her support for McCarthy attempting to stem the evil of Communism had been received in stony silence, at the supper party they'd hosted after the performance, which had ended embarrassingly abruptly.

"Don't you ever read the papers?" Benedict had stormed. "There's no excuse for you not to be totally informed about current affairs, even if you were being taught how to use some damned curling tongs when you should have been in school! Don't you know that Joseph McCarthy is crucifying innocent people, people who give about as much support to Communism as I do?"

He had lashed out at her in the same demoralizing way she'd heard him lash out at Suzanne in the month before their wedding, and at Charles before he'd granted his request to return to London to take over the vacant number-two spot in the English subsidiary.

Ludmilla had expected Benedict to follow her to bed, to show her in seconds with his body how sorry he was, but he hadn't come. She'd finally fallen asleep without him, waking at about six to find he'd gone to an early meeting out of town, leaving her a brief note instructing her to read the pieces he'd marked during the night in a pile of magazines and back issues of *The New York Times.* He'd never apologized, and neither of them had ever referred to it again, but they'd fallen into each other's arms as if they'd been apart for days, not hours, when he'd returned that evening.

It had been a terrible warning that Benedict Towers wasn't like other men, that however much power she appeared to have over him in bed, there was a part of him that would always be able to view her critically, dispassionately. She remembered how he had once told her shame-facedly that he'd never realized until she came into his life how thoroughly boring his life with Honey had been.

From then on, Ludmilla had vowed never to let Benedict down again. She had filled the time she had available—when she wasn't traveling on business trips with him—with study, taking course after course in foreign affairs, American history, and French and English literature, as well as interior design, gourmet cooking, and table settings. She had never stopped trying to please Benedict, who checked her homework as thoroughly as any teacher, rewarding her with expensive gifts placed beneath her pillow when he saw and heard results.

It had paid off. He had begun to respect her opinions, to ask her occasionally to sit in on business meetings at home and afterwards give him her impressions of certain participants or ask her what she thought of the decisions that had been made.

"Why do you really think Benedict is allowing you to start your own business?" Ludmilla was startled by Alexandra's question, but she gave her the honest answer.

"To humor me. He knows I love the beauty business. When I first told him about the shop, he said I looked as if I'd fallen in love again." Ludmilla smiled shyly, remembering what had happened afterwards. "He asked for my business proposal, and when I gave it to him the next day, he gave the lease to me for my birthday."

"How many facialists did you say you'll have?"

"Two to begin with, although if everything goes well, I can take over the floor upstairs in a year."

"And you're introducing your own family's botanical cream, I forget the name, the one you say really can take wrinkles away?"

Ludmilla suppressed the temptation to laugh. Helena Rubinstein, who had refused the invitation to their wedding, had given her a much more valuable present than the hideous enamel vase she'd sent to Benedict's office with a formal note of congratulations.

She had gathered up every one of Madame's invaluable pearls of wisdom, and she would never forget them. She could hear Madame's voice now. "Only neglect is aging. Use zis cream regularly to take zose crow's feet avay. Do I believe in it? Of course I believe in it. It is a secret family recipe. No one in the vorld can make anything that comes near it. Here, let me rub a little into your wrist. Have you ever felt anything so velvety, so vonderful? Zis is how your skin is going to feel from now on if you use zis cream regularly."

What else had Jan told her the old witch had once told him when he'd asked her the secret of her success? "You've got to be lucky first. Then take advantage of the situation and every situation that follows, and vork harder than everybody else."

Well, she had taken advantage of the situation, all right. One of the most important and richest men in the world had fallen in love with her. She had gambled on that situation. She had refused, despite her poverty and terrible predicament, to give in to his demands to move into an apartment and become his mistress; she had insisted, after her abortion, that he provide for her in a location as far away from him as possible and never try to contact her again. Unused to being thwarted, he had followed her across the world, where again she had refused him. Now she had been his wife for two years and she was about to take advantage of another situation, embarking on a business career in which she was prepared to work harder than everybody else, although Benedict didn't yet know it.

Ludmilla slowly opened her bag and rummaged through it in the way she had seen Madame Rubinstein do a dozen times.

"Ah, here is a tiny sample." She took out a small tube and squeezed out some of the cream onto the back of Alexandra's extended hand. "Isn't it velvety? See how immediately the skin absorbs it . . ."

Alexandra touched her skin with her forefinger. "Yes," she said thoughtfully. "It does feel like velvet. What is it called? I want to order a ton!"

Ludmilla smiled, knowing now how effective her infrequent vivid smile could be. "In my family it was called Hanacke Dozinky, which means 'harvest festival,' an important celebration in the villages of the Hana region in Moravia, where my father came from. Sometimes the cream was simply called 'wedding cream,' because it was so special we kept it for very important occasions." Not one word of what she was saying was true, but it wasn't spur-of-the-moment either. She was practicing what she would soon be telling the press. She had carefully prepared every word. Again, without knowing it—how infuriated she would have been—her benefactor, Madame Rubinstein, had taught her some of the secrets of skin-care public relations.

"How perfectly darling," Alexandra enthused. " 'Wedding cream' is absolutely darling, although let me think . . ." She leaned her head back against the banquette. "Don't you think it may put off some old maids most in need of it? Why don't you just name the shop and the cream after yourself? Use Ludmilla! It's an unusual name. After all, if Benedict has anything to do with it, you're going to be another Helena Rubinstein or Elizabeth Arden!" She paused, then added wryly, "I'll bet he'll want to use your full name, my dear, Ludmilla Towers, with 'Towers' in the biggest, boldest letters."

Later that night—soft and balmy, with a full moon—when Benedict came home from the office, Ludmilla asked Thorpe to set up a table for two on the terrace outside their bedroom. Below, the city sparkled with thousands of lights all the way to the horizon.

"Leave everything, Thorpe. I'll ring when we've finished." It was the kind of meal Benedict liked best, a simple yet spicy cold soup, perfect cold salmon and salad, a good Brie, and a bottle of Pommery on ice.

As Benedict showered, Ludmilla changed out of the suit she'd been wearing for lunch into one of his favorite negligees, pale gray chiffon through which her skin glowed like alabaster.

He looked tired, and as she often did when he came home from the office, she slowly caressed his neck and shoulders as he sat at the table. After a few minutes he said, "Come here."

He pulled her onto his lap, moving the chiffon away to run his hands over her skin, cupping her bare breasts. "They seem fuller . . . yes, fuller." He brought first one, then the other nipple to his mouth. "Is this romantic rendezvous to tell me what I'm dying to hear? Are you pregnant at last, my darling?"

She stiffened. Although he'd continually asked that question in the first year of their marriage, he hadn't mentioned it now for some time. "No, no, I don't think so."

He crushed her to him. "I want your baby. Let's skip dinner and go to bed now. I have a feeling this is the night."

For once she forgot her role of total acquiescence to whatever her husband said or did. Still crushed against his jacket, she said, "Later, can it be later? I'm longing to tell you about my lunch today with Alexandra."

Benedict pushed her an arm's length away to look at her in the way she was now so used to, somewhat bemused, somewhat irritated, as if to say, "What on earth are you going to surprise me with now?"

"How details of a lunch with the estimable Mrs. Sanford can possibly compare with what I have in mind for you beats me, but all right. Sit over there, far out of my reach, and feed me. Then I'll listen."

As they ate, Ludmilla repeated what Alexandra had said, almost verbatim, including the remark about the filter-tipped cigarettes. "She suggested I might call the salon and the major treatment cream 'Ludmilla.' It's not a bad idea. What do you think?"

Benedict frowned. "I think it's godawful."

Ludmilla shivered, inexplicably nervous. "Why? I thought . . . I thought you liked my name."

"Like it?" He seemed to be considering it for the first time. "I like *you*. I adore you, in fact, but your name . . ." He paused. "When I think about it, I've never liked it. That's why I call you Lu." He swallowed down half a glass of wine.

Ludmilla looked at him with, he was glad to see, a downcast, sad expression. He didn't like his wife suggesting they delay going to bed. He would make her pay for that later.

He poured himself another glass of wine and drank it without either of them saying anything. He stood up and walked to the edge of the terrace to stare out at the glittering city. With his back turned, he finally said, " 'Lu' can be short for something other than Ludmilla. That's a Kraut name. It's too Germanic for any successful business in this country, even now. As I said to Norris today, it may be almost ten years after the war, but I don't see many Americans buying the new Mercedes, even though it's going to employ the first fuel-injection system for cars." He turned, leaning against the balustrade. "I'd certainly never buy one, and that goes for buying anything Japanese, too— if they were ever fool enough to start making cars."

Ludmilla seethed, though outwardly she looked impassive, patient, waiting for Benedict's lecture to end. Germanic! How could he insult her like that, knowing the life her family had endured under the German occupation? As Benedict talked on about postwar relationships, Ludmilla's thoughts went to her poor mother and darling little Natasha. How terrible it was that her young sister was growing up under another equally evil conquering power. Natasha. She wanted to sob. Her little sister was fourteen now, and had never known what it was like to live in freedom.

Thank God, she was receiving mail from Prague more regularly. With Benedict's contacts, she was even able to send them things occasionally, including a ballerina doll for Natasha, who'd written that she wanted to be a ballerina when she grew up. In a recent photograph she looked like a ballerina doll herself, her tiny body emphasized by a tutu, which Ludmilla knew must have been made by her mother, who'd probably bartered a perm or a haircut to get the necessary material.

Ludmilla was aware of silence. Benedict was staring at her. She'd been lost in thought for too long. She was still too hurt to speak, but she forced herself to smile, throwing back her head, lifting her throat, knowing from practice that it was one way to fake a happy expression.

He came over and put his arms around her. Without speaking, he pulled the gray chiffon off her shoulders, down to well below her waist, to expose her belly button. He clumsily unfastened her hair to cascade over her shoulders and naked breasts. As he leaned over and began to stroke her stomach, she shut her eyes, trying to control her trembling, which came from anger, but also from excitement. His fingers moved into her vagina. "Yes, my little Lu, your name is too German. We need something softer, as soft as you are right here . . ."

Her breathing quickened. She began to stir and sigh as he worked his way inside her. An orgasm was approaching. She began to move her body when he abruptly withdrew. "Leave the table. Go inside and get ready for me," he ordered. "I want a new woman in bed tonight. Her name is Louise Towers."

*   *   *

In two months the shop, formerly a gourmet bakery, one block away from Alexandra's store, Petals, on East Sixty-second Street, was ready, transformed into the Louise Towers Skincare Institute, one of the first intimate salons in New York to specialize in the treatment of skin.

The decor was unusual, too. Unlike the frills and furbelows of the vast, multistoried marble mansions of the beauty queens Arden and Rubinstein, dispensing services and pampering from top to toe, the Louise Towers Institute was clinically white, cool and linear, from the immaculate reception area to the analyzing consultation room to the extra-large treatment rooms at the back.

Each of the four staff members—two aestheticians (as Louise insisted they be called), both with Eastern European backgrounds, an assistant for odd jobs, and the receptionist—had been hired because of the excellence of their skins. A condition of their employment made it clear they were never to be touched, let alone covered by, makeup.

Ludmilla, at Benedict's firm suggestion, officially changed her name to Louise, although, as she told Alexandra without a trace of a smile, her closest friends were allowed to call her "Lu" or "Lou"—"provided it sounds the same"—as her husband continued to do.

Also at Benedict's direction, Louise Towers had applied for a patent for the Sukova family's ancient botanical anti-wrinkle cream, though he well knew the formula was a concoction derived from something Louise remembered her mother making from buttermilk and herbs and some basic raw materials, augmented by cerersine wax and mineral and sesame oils, as suggested by one of the younger Towers Pharmaceuticals' chemists, David Reemer, who had been told to make himself available to Mrs. Towers until the new venture got off the ground.

"The patent will probably not be granted," Benedict told Louise cheerfully, "but to tell the press your special potion has a patent pending adds cachet, and by the time you hear from the patent office, the Institute will be off and running."

He didn't really believe it, but it was a joy for him to return to the Park Avenue apartment every evening and see how happy and unusually vivacious his young wife had become.

The opening party was planned for the end of September, but a week beforehand, the most influential members of the press were invited for a private preview. They all accepted—Antoinette Donnelly of the *Daily News*, the paper with the greatest circulation in the country; the brilliant, widely read and copied Eugenia Sheppard of the *Herald Tribune*; Virginia Pope of *The New York Times*; Ann Yates of the *World Tele-*

gram; Pat Lewis of the *Journal American*; and the editors-in-chief and beauty editors of *Vogue* and *Harper's Bazaar*. If they wished, they were offered a free consultation and treatment, too.

Only two of the newspaperwomen said they had time for the two-hour treatment, which immediately alerted Louise to the fact that perhaps two hours was too long, although most of the Rubinstein treatments in London had taken at least that amount of time. Perhaps New York women were busier than their languid London counterparts. She added the thought to the notebook she now carried with her everywhere.

The idea of the private visits for the top journalists also came from Benedict, who explained, "during the dry run, when your aestheticians or beauticians or whatever you call 'em are getting used to the products and the work, it's helpful to have some press. When you're launching anything, large or small, early publicity—but not too early, or people forget—whets the public's appetite, which is further stimulated by the second wave of press coverage, which comes with the official party."

On the day of the opening, Eugenia Sheppard devoted her whole column to a glowing write-up of the Institute and its unique owner, who preferred to work instead of living the life of absolute luxury and leisure she could have, being married to one of the country's richest men. Sheppard suggested cheekily that Towers Pharmaceuticals could be about to have an even bigger future in the cosmetics business than in the drug business, running a close-up photograph of Mrs. Benedict Towers with the caption, THE OWNER OF THE MOST BEAUTIFUL SKIN IN THE WORLD SHARES HER SECRETS.

That same morning the PR agency reported that both *Vogue* and *Harper's Bazaar* wanted to send photographers and models for upcoming stories, and *Life* magazine had expressed interest, too.

"I'm so nervous," Louise told Benedict as the car approached the Institute just after five. On both sides of a wide red carpet stretching to the curb, photographers were already waiting. "Oh, Benedict, do you think anyone will come? I mean, the list is full of the most important names, all because of you . . . but will they really turn up just to see a new shop, my shop?"

Benedict laughed, but still corrected her. "Never say 'shop.' It sounds cheap. Don't say 'salon,' either. You have an institute, the Louise Towers Institute. Now don't slump. Sit upright, and look as you usually do in public—as if you have something slightly contemptible under your nose. As for the guests, of course they'll come. They may be powerful, but they're freeloaders, like most of the people in this city. With the kind of champagne we're serving tonight, we'll have a job getting rid of them." He paused frowning. "If anything, I must make sure security has sent along enough people to check names. We haven't the space for gate-crashers, but with Miss Sheppard's rave review today, I think we have to expect them."

"Gate-crashers?" Louise had never heard the expression, but before she could ask what it meant, the flashes of the cameras as she stepped out of the car startled her so much she jumped. Benedict whisked her inside, where her four employees were waiting with pale, strained expressions in immaculate white starched uniforms.

In minutes, pouring them glasses of champagne and toasting their success, Benedict had relaxed them all. Even though the official start of the party was still forty-five minutes away, Louise felt faint as she went through the rooms, inspecting every detail, running her finger along the ledges for even a speck of dust.

Perhaps it was the scent from the bowers of white roses everywhere, even tied in small bunches on the white hangers in the cloakroom. She pressed her head against the large picture window at the back of the Institute.

Benedict came up behind her. "I'm very proud of you, Lu," he said softly. "Give me your wrist."

He was opening a dark blue velvet box. Inside was a gleaming gold bracelet, engraved on one side with the name Louise. "Oh, darling, it's so beautiful."

"Look inside." Engraved there was the name Ludmilla. "I really like both your names, little Lu," he said, looking into her eyes.

How young and vulnerable she looked. He felt a surge of love. God, he hoped the day wouldn't come when she thought he was too old for her.

There was a familiar voice behind them. It was Alexandra Sanford. "Bravo, Benedict! Congratulations, Louise!" she purred. "It's like being in Switzerland, it's so white, so pristine, so perfect."

By six-thirty the shop was filled with people, overflowing out onto the pavement, with cars drawing up, disgorging women whose names were constantly in the gossip columns (like the three Gabor sisters and Tallulah Bankhead) as well as those who rarely were, the rarefied ladies who were known to lead society, many of them the wives and relations of Benedict's friends and business associates.

As *The New York Times* reported, the guests varied in age from girls in their early teens (Alexandra's fourteen-year-old twin daughters) to grand matriachs of over seventy, including the sister of Benedict's father, the formidable Ursula, who traveled from Maine to see what her favorite nephew had become involved with now. They quoted from the press release, too, commenting on its originality. "Only neglect is aging. Good skin care should be a daily habit, as familiar and easy as brushing one's teeth." There was a lot more, which would be picked up in magazines in the months ahead: "It is not the chronological passing of time that ages the skin; it is bad habits and poor care. The skin is the largest organ of the body and deserves the proper respect and attention." Louise had found the last piece of information in one of the anatomical tomes she constantly studied, and with Benedict's encouragement she had added it to the release when it came over for her approval.

For the next few months Benedict allowed Louise to spend most of her days at the Institute, which had clients storming the doors from the first day. After the first month she cut the treatments down to ninety minutes long and added five dollars to the charge. Still the waiting list grew. It was phenomenal, and even some of the women who had shown her the most disdain following her marriage were now calling for appointments.

Benedict thought she would be upset when one piece in the *Mirror* quoted an indignant Madame Rubinstein, who for once remembered names very clearly. "Ludmilla Sukova learned everything from me," she was quoted in a long article by the women's editor, Alma Archer. "She was a junior executive in my London salon, but of course she never gives me credit, no credit whatever, and yet she has taken many of my ideas, but of course she has none of my formulas. This anti-wrinkle serum of hers, why, it is nothing but scented Vaseline. Now, my Wake Up Cream, that is something to get excited about!"

Lying in bed, Benedict watched Louise as she unplaited the braid she now often wore on top of her head to keep her long hair in place, and brushed it out to flow down the back of her virginal white nightdress. "But Alma Archer followed that up with a glowing account of her visit to the Institute, pointing out—which, of course, Madame didn't do—that the Ludmilla she kept referring to was me, Louise Towers. That's surely good for business, isn't it?" She jumped into bed to curl up beside him.

"Business, that's all you think about now," he said, absentmindedly stroking her hair. "I think it's time I took you away somewhere. I hear Winny Aldrich, our new ambassador in London, is giving a ball for the Queen of England. How would you like to go?"

She was hardly listening. She was thinking about adding something else to sell at the Institute, another product or service that could be written about in the papers, something else to make the old empress sit up and take notice. Benedict pinched her.

"Oh!"

"Pay attention!"

"Oh, darling, I'm sorry. Where is the ball?"

"London, of course. The only problem is it's in January. Such a godawful month over there, with all the pipes outside the houses, freezing, bursting, the weather stripping away your flesh ..." As he spoke, he started to growl and strip away the straps of her nightgown. "Can your magical cream cure man-bites?" He growled and started to make little bite marks on her skin. She shifted restlessly, wanting to move away, but not daring to.

She could smell a faint trace of the brandy he liked to drink after dinner on his breath. She didn't want to make love; she wanted to think about the next business step she should take, but she quickly stifled a sigh and turned toward her husband. She had to do her duty, but now every time she prayed she wouldn't get pregnant. Not now, not yet ... she had too much to do, and at twenty-eight she still had plenty of time left for motherhood.

Jan Feiner's all-efficient secretary, Marge, who seemed to read every newspaper and magazine she could get her hands on, always clipped pieces for him about Helena Rubinstein. If it hadn't been for her, it was doubtful that he would have learned so quickly about Ludmilla Sukova's transformation into Louise Towers and her proprietorship of a skin-care institute apparently so successful it had goaded the old beauty empress into print.

Jan took the *Mirror* article home when he reluctantly left the laboratory at around nine-thirty that night, back to the old house high above the Palisades, with its spectacular view of Manhattan across the Hudson.

He'd often thought of Ludmilla living somewhere over there in luxury, because of course he knew she had married Benedict Towers. Victor had made sure, informing him with venomous satisfaction, that he also knew that Ludmilla had once worked for the Towers family as a maid. The news had disturbed him for months.

So the Cinderella he had realized he loved too late had been found again by her prince of industry and turned into a princess. Where was the crime in that? Yes, he had been bitterly hurt that Ludmilla hadn't had the courage or ability to meet him as she'd promised that weekend to tell him face to face about this astonishing change in her life, but then she had always been a woman of mystery. He had never once complained to Victor how hurt he had been; there was no point in adding fuel to Victor's inexplicable burning dislike of her.

Looking back, Jan realized he'd known practically nothing about her and had never asked any questions. Perhaps that was why Ludmilla

had trusted him. Victor had been pleased to point out that he'd thought
from their first lunch together that there was something sinister about
her. He'd even found out somewhere that Benedict Towers's wife had
been killed only one year before Benedict came to London to claim
Ludmilla as his bride.

Tonight Jan wasn't hungry, although his housekeeper had left him
some excellent consommé. Instead of heating it up, he took out the
vials he'd brought home in his briefcase. For the last few days he'd
hardly had them out of his sight—or should he say *smell*?

He showered, washing his face thoroughly, scrubbing his hands as
meticulously as if he were scrubbing up before an operation. Only
then did he put on a freshly washed cotton kimono to sit in the room
he kept bereft of draperies and furniture, except for the one wooden
chair he'd had specially designed with exceptionally wide arms, drilled
with holes into which the vials fitted perfectly.

He placed the vials in the slots; on the other chair arm was his pad
and pencil. For the next hour, Jan continued what he had been doing
all day and for several days now, sniffing, inhaling, analyzing the contents of each vial, adding new observations to those he'd already made.

By now he was recognized as a "nose" in the fragrance and—much
bigger—flavors industries, a "natural" perfumer who knew instinctively
when a mélange of essences belonged together or did not. He had
never smoked, which he now knew was lucky because smoking could
disastrously affect the olfactory cells in the nose. Since his arrival in
the States to work for the still small American subsidiary of the Dutch
Vreinsdrof flavors and fragrances company, he'd sent his nose into
"training," eating only bland food, avoiding anything spicy or even
tasty because he'd soon realized any piquant or special taste could
interfere with his work. Taste and smell were so intimately linked that
he had learned never to order chili or his favorite curry or even much
fish. He had become autocratic about what his few meal companions
ordered, too, except for Victor, but then Victor never needed to be
told anything.

He was on to something. He was sure of it now, although he'd told
no one, not even Victor, who nevertheless sensed that his little brother
was about to "deliver," as he put it.

He'd left these particular vials alone for several months, much as
they'd originally excited him, learning on the job that it was impossible
to keep sniffing the same thing day after day, hoping to reach perfection. Instead, you reached nose fatigue.

He'd learned he had to work on several jobs at once in order to get
fresh perspectives. Now he was almost there. The night before, he'd

thought he'd reached it. Now he would wait one more day, but following the subtle change he'd made today, he was certain vial number five contained an exceptional, revolutionary scent, every bit as creative as the most famous No. 5 in the world from Mademoiselle Chanel.

Number four, in a different strength, was evocative too, but with the most minuscule yet important change he'd made today in the middle note, he was sure number five was the one. Soon he would be ready to make his peace with the great Madame Rubinstein, who was still a remarkable "nose" herself, despite her great age. Yes, she would open her arms to greet him when he told her he had created a scent that would add to her reputation as it added millions to her coffers—as well as to his own!

Jan felt excitement building, but forced himself to go to bed. He knew better than to tell a soul, not until he had Madame Rubinstein's name on a contract. Before he turned out the light, he thought again of Ludmilla and the Louise Towers Institute.

After his meeting with the great Helena, if all went as he hoped and expected, he would drop by Sixty-second Street, he told himself. If, as the article suggested, Ludmilla was often there herself, to set eyes on her again would be a wonderful way to celebrate. Perhaps she would allow him to take her out for coffee. Perhaps they could even do some business together. Perhaps he would return to New Jersey with two new clients instead of one—one huge, one fledgling. The idea kept him awake for hours.

Three weeks later, as the hour of his appointment for 10:00 A.M. chimed from the belfry of St. Patrick's Cathedral, Jan arrived at the majestic eight-story building on the corner of Fifth Avenue and Fifty-second Street that was Helena Rubinstein's worldwide headquarters and flagship salon.

Although it was a chilly day, he was dripping with perspiration. The wind had already sent the black derby hat he wore to business meetings flying out over the Hudson as he'd left home that morning.

It had taken ten days for his two telephone calls to be returned by a frosty secretary, who nevertheless had been told to grant an appointment if one was asked for. Jan was as amused as he was nervous. He was sure Madame Rubinstein was expecting him to come with cap in hand, asking for his job back. Well, she was in for quite a surprise.

He had been told to come to the business entrance on Fifty-second Street, where he gave his name to the receptionist, who was dressed in lavender to match the walls. She led him down a long corridor to a suite of offices where several secretaries were drinking coffee out of cerise-colored mugs that matched their typewriters.

It was unusually silent, and Jan was surprised the secretaries were not working busily, as he was so used to seeing in the London office whenever Madame was in residence. He soon knew why.

He was asked to sit on a tufted sofa that, he reflected, would have looked more at home in a boudoir than in an office. Before him was a copy of the latest *Vogue*, in which he saw the usual gold paper clips placed in the front section to indicate Rubinstein advertisements, and two silver paper clips indicating Rubinstein editorials. Madame had instituted a similar practice in the London and Paris offices.

No sooner had he turned to read the first editorial than a brisk young woman came out of an adjoining office and said, without a trace of apology, "I'm Madame Rubinstein's secretary, Ruth Hopkins. She has had an emergency. She had to go to her factory in Long Island City. She told me to take you along to our personnel director, who . . ."

Jan jumped to his feet. He had never been so angry. He didn't know what he was saying. "I didn't come here to see a personnel director. As usual, Madame Rubinstein is displaying her bad manners and ignorance of human nature. How dare she!" The young woman didn't seem at all dismayed by his reaction, although the other secretaries openly stared at him.

"Well, I'm sorry," she said, not sounding it. "Is there somebody else? A marketing person? Advertising? Are you interested in becoming a supplier of some kind?"

Jan snorted. At that moment he realized the futility of his dream. If he sold his unique perfume to Madame Rubinstein, that was how she would regard him, as a supplier, and he'd heard enough of her opinion of suppliers, whom she regarded as cheats and conniving idiots, to last him a lifetime. No matter that his fragrance could earn both his company and hers hundreds of thousands of dollars over the years if the fragrance was a success, not to mention his own personal royalties. In Madame Rubinstein's eyes he would be a supplier, not an artist; he might as well be selling bottle tops or powder puffs.

Victor was right. Rubinstein hadn't the ability to treat people who dealt with her in business as equals. He would be putting his head right back into the noose from which Victor had rescued him.

Although Ruth Hopkins followed him down the corridor, sensing somehow that her boss was not going to be happy that she had allowed him to escape, Jan was so furious he didn't even answer her until he reached the elevator. Then, as the doors opened, he said, "You can tell Madame Rubinstein her rudeness gave me a sudden revelation. She has missed the opportunity of a lifetime. Good-bye."

Across the street was a coffee shop. Still seething, Jan drank two cups of coffee in quick succession, something he would normally never have done. Now depression overcame him. There were many houses he could go to. Elizabeth Arden was the most obvious choice, but he felt instinctively that it was too different a scent for her.

He had planned to visit the Louise Towers Institute around the lunch hour, expecting his interview with Rubinstein to last at least two hours. Now it wasn't even ten-fifteen. Well, he wasn't in the city that much. He might as well go take a look, even if he didn't venture inside.

In a funny way, because he'd already expended so much emotion, Jan didn't feel as nervous as he'd expected, arriving at the small store-front ten blocks north. In fact, his anger, still deep inside, steeled him. He'd been fooling himself; he should have known he'd go in once he saw the place.

He gingerly opened the door, releasing a gentle chime of bells. How refreshing and how different it was from the florid pink establishment he had just left. A girl with a sweet smile and delectable-looking skin asked him softly, "May I help you, sir?"

He didn't know what to say. The word "supplier" still stung his brain. He stuttered, "Is Lud—Mrs. Towers here today?"

"Yes, but I am afraid she is busy, sir. You would like to make an appointment for somebody? A skin consultation, perhaps?"

He shook his head and fumbled inside his pocket for a business card. He was about to give it to the girl when the woman of his dreams opened a door and came into the reception area. If he'd thought she was beautiful before, now there was a radiance about her, an aura of majesty. He wanted to run away. Instead he stood tongue-tied, knowing he looked as he felt, totally overwhelmed.

There was a split-second hesitation, then she ran up to him. "Jan, Jan Feiner, what an absolutely wonderful surprise! I can't believe my eyes. What are you doing here?"

"I read . . . read about your Institute. I . . . congratulations. It's . . . impressive."

Ludmilla clapped her hands happily. Jan knew she had never been like this in London, never so happy, so sure of herself, above all so beautiful. "Do you really like it?" She looked at her watch. Jan noticed it had diamonds around it.

"We are so busy! We're booked from dawn to dusk. I'd love to show you the rest, but of course we have appointments all the time, and the rooms are occupied. But what are you doing? No, wait, don't tell me. Martine, let me see the book."

She was wearing a simple white wool suit, perfectly cut to show off her wonderful body. Jan had never seen her wear white, had never seen her wear anything so stylish, obviously made by a leading fashion designer, but then, of course, she could afford anything and everything now.

He could feel the pain building. What a terrible day it had turned out to be. He felt a total failure, although he knew he was not. Thank goodness he was wearing one of his two expensive suits.

"Ludmilla, I have to go. It was wonderful seeing . . ."

She turned, smiling the smile that turned his stomach over as it always had. "You mustn't call me that anymore, Jan. I'm Louise now, privately and professionally. There are lots of reasons, but let's go and have some coffee." Without waiting for an answer, she said, "Martine, this is a dear friend. I am going out now, but I'll be back in an hour. If my husband calls, say I had to run an errand and I'll call him before lunch."

They walked toward the East River, where Louise, as Jan practiced thinking of her in his mind, said she knew a restaurant in a small hotel where they could talk privately.

Had she always been able to make him tell her everything? Jan didn't remember, but as the hour stretched to an hour and a half, as usual he was telling her far more than she was telling him. Not that she had to tell him anything. Success was written all over her, the subtle kind of success that carries with it the intoxicating, undeniable smell of big money and power.

He tried to describe his 10:00 A.M. appointment in the lighthearted, amusing manner in which he'd often recounted Madame Rubinstein stories, but it didn't come off.

At first, Ludmilla-turned-Louise didn't speak. Then she touched his hand lightly as he finished the story of his humiliation. "May I smell the perfume?" she asked, her dark eyes never leaving his.

She mesmerized him. It was something he had never dreamed he would do, but he passed her the secret vial. This time he didn't speak either as she first inhaled it in the vial, then, to his surprise, applied the scent the way professionals applied it, to the pulse point just below the heel of the hand, waiting a few minutes before she brought her nose down to inhale again. At least three or four minutes passed. Then she spoke quickly. "Jan, as I've told you, and from what you have read yourself, you know I am married to a very powerful man. What started as a business to amuse me has already had a success my husband can hardly comprehend."

She didn't see him wince as she used the word "husband," and perhaps it didn't show. The intense note in her voice was reflected in the look of concentration on her face. "You told me once that you believed one day American perfume could rival French perfume, that American women would begin to buy it for themselves, not just receive it as birthday and Christmas gifts. I think you were right. I'm beginning to learn a lot about women, American women, who are years away from understanding what European women know about beauty. They don't even understand how much better their makeup would look if they took better care of their skin. They only understand that makeup can cover many sins. Makeup, that's all they really know about, but things are changing. I'm changing things in my small way, and I'm going to get much bigger, much!"

Her cheeks were flushed; a tendril of silky black hair had escaped to brush her cheek. Jan felt more depressed than ever, realizing how far out of his reach she was now. But, oh, she was magnificent.

Louise knew he wasn't listening to her as she needed him to listen. She clutched his arm. "Jan, I want to buy the rights to your perfume. It's irresistible, and you've already named it for me and the women of America . . ."

"Named it?" He was stunned by what she was saying. She had no idea that this was a perfume that was going to revolutionize perfumes, that it had to be sold to the highest bidder.

"Yes, remember you just said you'd had a revelation. Revelation—it's the perfect name. It's exquisite. I will wear it from now on. I will get every society woman in America to wear it. It will cause a sensation, and I will sell it from my Institute and all the Institutes I intend to open across the country."

"Across the country?" he echoed, dumbfounded.

"Yes," Louise, who from now on would never be Ludmilla to him again, spoke as if everything were already decided. "Benedict took me with him last week to see Northland. Do you know what that is?" Her eyes, her teeth, her skin were gleaming. She was like a creature from another planet.

Jan shook his head dolefully.

"It opened last March. It's the world's largest shopping center, with already one hundred stores, designed by a genius called Victor Gruen, whom Benedict knows well. It's all undercover. You walk and shop until your feet fall off. Benedict says it's going to revolutionize shopping in America and throughout the world. He's already investing in areas where other Northlands will be built, and in every shopping center will be a Louise Towers Institute."

She was unstoppable. She went on and on about the future of her company.

"And this is what Benedict . . . your husband . . . really wants?"

Jan asked, as he wondered how any man in his senses could want such a beautiful wife to devote herself to anything other than their marriage.

"Oh, yes," Louise lied. "He is as dedicated to building my business as I am. We are partners," she added proudly.

One month later, after Elizabeth Arden and Coty had turned the fragrance down, Jan received a firm proposal from Leonard Towers, the bachelor brother whom Benedict had assigned to investigate sundry business matters relating to the Institute, from the hiring of staff to insurance to investment of profits from what was proving to be a little gold mine.

Louise had hardly been off the phone, asking Jan about Revelation every day, but she didn't think it was wise at this juncture to explain to Benedict that the next step in her business, the introduction of a small, exclusive Louise Towers perfume, had anything to do with the Jan Feiner who had been such a good friend in London. She didn't think it would ever be necessary. She would make sure their social paths never crossed, and Benedict was far too tied up in major pharmaceutical affairs to pay much attention to her minuscule expansion plans.

Jan, on the other hand, was finally persuaded to give Revelation's American rights to Louise Towers, not only because it was, as Louise had stated, a company that was growing incredibly fast, and not only because Leonard Towers offered superbly advantageous royalties. If the perfume was the success Jan expected it to be, his royalties would grow much more rapidly according to sales than most agreements between essential-oil houses and cosmetic manufacturers provided for.

No, the way Jan sold the idea to himself was that in forging a business arrangement with Louise Towers, Inc., so early in its life, he could look forward to a long and satisfying relationship with both the company and its founder. He accepted that Ludmilla was never meant to be his partner in marriage, so he would settle for the next best thing: Louise would be his partner in business, and certainly always a close and beloved friend in whom he could confide when necessary.

Louise overlooked one thing. Leonard, often Benedict's whipping boy, now that Charles was safely out of sight and earshot overseas in London, was always trying to win approval. He did this by preparing long and laborious reports on companies he was dealing with on behalf of his brother or, in this case, his brother's exotic, strange young wife.

In studying Vreinsdrof, Leonard discovered to his excitement that it was a sturdy company with excellent real estate in Holland and Germany that appeared to be seriously undervalued. He tried for weeks to get Benedict's attention, but he was flying to London to show off his wife at a ball for the Queen of England, so he had to make do with Norris, who also had other things on his mind, like alimony payments and kiss-and-make-up time with his children.

As it was, months passed before Benedict learned that the mind—or the nose—behind Louise's new toy, the Revelation perfume, was none other than the "dear friend who means absolutely nothing to me," Jan Feiner, the Rubinstein chemist in London. It had nothing to do with Leonard's attempt to gain a moment in the sun with his information and suggestion that Vreinsdrof would make a good acquisition for Towers. It had everything to do with the success of Revelation itself, which, after a shaky start as a perfume, began to take off when Louise decided to market it as the first body skin treatment, selling it in bath oil and lotion form, advertising it as a miracle treatment in three-inch boxed ads in the newspapers.

They were both in Europe when frantic calls started coming in, first from Martine and then from David Reemer, saying there was an avalanche of orders, with major stores calling up to see if Louise Towers would be interested in selling the Revelation bath oil to them on an exclusive basis.

"Even Neiman-Marcus is interested." Louise exulted, pirouetting around the room in the nude. They would be late for a dinner at the Elysée Palais, but Benedict didn't stop her. He was so proud, he thought he would burst.

The next day, while Louise was shopping, Norris called to answer some questions about an indigestion pill Benedict wanted to introduce in Scandinavia.

"Perhaps you should take a look at Holland, too," Norris said, after they'd been talking for about twenty minutes.

"Holland. Now that's an interesting idea, but why did you think of that?"

"Well, your brilliant other half is causing a sensation here with her Revelation. Leonard has been pestering me for months, but before I put on sackcloth and ashes, I gather he's apparently been pestering you, too, to study the facts and figures behind the Vreinsdrof company in Holland, whose American subsidiary supplies the Institute with the juice."

"So? What do we want with an essence house?"

"We have orders for nearly two hundred thousand dollars' worth of the stuff, and more are coming in every day. It's emergency time here, but Jan Feiner is doing a great job. He . . ."

"Feiner? Jan Feiner, did you say?"

"Yep! He's the nose, the perfumer who made the scent and formulated the bath-oil and lotion versions. Well, he's more than that. Together with a financial head put in by Vreinsdrof, Feiner more or less makes the big decisions as far as the U.S. market goes."

"What else do you know about him?" Benedict's voice shook Norris. He recognized that tone; it spelled trouble.

"Not much. I only know he has a big reputation in the smell area. I'm not a hundred percent sure, but I believe his brother is Victor Feiner, the guy we've been hearing so much about at K. Avery, but again, I'm not sure. Why? Something wrong?"

"No, nothing."

When Louise came in, Benedict told her sorrowfully that he had to make a quick twenty-four-hour trip to Scandinavia. He didn't think it would be worth her going with him for so short a time.

"Would you like to go back to London, and I'll join you there for a few days with Charles?"

There was something strange about him, something Louise couldn't pin down, but she didn't comment on it. "No, darling," she said. "I've found the most wonderful facialist on the Faubourg. I want to spend more time with her. I've booked all her appointments tomorrow." She laughed mischievously. "I've paid her double to cancel the ones she had. My, but the French are avaricious. I'd kill my girls if they ever did that."

Benedict never mentioned his conversation with Norris, and by the time they'd returned to New York, Towers Pharmaceuticals had a controlling interest in Vreinsdrof. He didn't tell Louise that, either. It was Jan, who still had to be invited to meet Benedict, who told her over the telephone, although he'd asked her to meet him for lunch.

"Alas, Jan, dear, I can't have lunch for weeks. I'm having to pay for my playtime away in Europe. As you know only too well, we're flooded with orders. I'm meeting with Saks and Lord & Taylor and Neiman-Marcus. I can't believe it. Already we're taking the floor upstairs, and next week I'm looking at space in Washington because Benedict says the First Lady wants a Louise Towers Institute near at hand." She paused, then added in a little-girl voice, "I told you, Jan, I'm really changing things. Aren't you thrilled with Revelation's success—mine and yours?"

Jan spoke quietly. "You own your supplier now, Louise, but of course you know that."

There was silence, then she said, "I don't understand. Own my supplier? Who? What do you mean?"

"Vreinsdrof. Towers Pharmaceuticals now owns a controlling interest in the company, with an option to take it over completely. I am being transferred to the head office."

Louise grew cold. "Why?" she asked tremulously.

"Why don't you ask your husband?" Jan answered bitterly. "It's called a promotion, but whatever it is, I am contractually obliged to agree to the move."

"Where is the head office? The Hague? Amsterdam?"

"What interest can it possibly have for you? Good-bye, Mrs. Towers." There was a click, and the line went dead.

"You imbecile! I asked you months ago, what on earth possessed you to do it? I told you it would end in disaster." Victor paced up and down Jan's large living room, packed with boxes and files.

Jan sat with his head in his hands. "I don't know. Well, I do know. I was living in a fool's paradise. It was a good deal for the company." Seeing the expression on Victor's face, he didn't pursue that direction. "Perhaps I could have made a better one, I don't know, but I can't lie to you. She mesmerized me. I felt ..." He actually felt like crying, but he would never let Victor know that. "I felt that perhaps we could develop a partnership, a friendship and a business partnership." He got up and punched his hands together. "I believed her when she said it was possible, but of course now I realize how insane I was."

Victor saw his anguish. He put his arms around him. "Look at it positively, Jan. It is a promotion. You'll be supervising all the lab operations ..."

As he hesitated, Jan burst out, "But I know Towers is responsible for my being sent back. For some reason, Benedict Towers doesn't think I've done a good enough job here."

"It can't be that. I'm certain of it. I'm going to get to the bottom of why you're being transferred, if it's the last thing I do," Victor said grimly. "How much longer is your contract?"

"Two years . . . two and a half."

"They'll have to pay you a lot of money to get rid of you, but that's hardly likely."

"It's a dead end. How can I think creatively in Holland?"

Again Victor embraced him. "You're a genius, my dear brother. You'll think creatively wherever you are. But . . ." again he paused, a ferocious look on his face. "Don't give your best ideas to Vreinsdrof—or should I now say Towers? How I loathe the name." Victor spat on the carpet. "That's what I think about Towers now. In three years' time, if something hasn't happened long before that, I'll make sure you come back here in a bigger and better job."

There were tears in both brothers' eyes, but they were for very different reasons. Despite everything I'll always love her Jan thought.

I'll never forgive her for hurting my brother, thought Victor. Never. Never. One day I will get my revenge.

Prague, 1958

LYING ON HER wooden bed, its headboard delicately stenciled with ballerinas, Natasha contrived with a loop of string to construct a cat's cradle of amazing complexity. With her legs in the air, she transferred the string from hands to feet and back again. She concentrated on trying to tie knots with her toes as she had read the Maestro Houdini had been able to do. It passed the time.

Waiting. This was an intolerable waiting, worse than anything she'd dreamed a human being could experience. Worse than waiting, at eleven years old, to learn whether she'd been chosen to play Clara in *The Nutcracker*. Worse than sitting by the telephone in the post office, waiting for her sister's telephone calls from America or Europe or wherever she happened to be in the world, calls that sometimes didn't come for days, if at all; worse than the endless waiting for her breast exercises to produce noticeable results.

Pieter! Natasha tried to twist the string into the letter *P*, and the cat's cradle disintegrated.

"Na-tash-aaa . . ." Why did her mother have to call out her name as if she were at the other end of the Charles bridge? "Na-tash-aaa . . ."

"Coming . . . I'm coming, Mama." Natasha looked at the white china clock on the mantelpiece, crowded with her collection of ballerina dolls, sent from the States, that had arrived via the American legation in the last few years.

Five minutes past six. Another seventeen hours and fifty-five minutes before she would see Pieter again. It was so strange. Two months ago, before she knew him, after hours of barre exercises, ronds de jambes sauté, and turnouts, she had been too exhausted to eat even a piece of buttermilk bread or drink a cup of coffee with the other students in Madame Brouetsky's ballet class, let alone . . . Natasha shut her eyes, determined to spend another few minutes dreaming of what "let alone" had begun to mean.

How endlessly fascinated Pieter was by her body, as proud as she had been herself that her "turnouts" were so perfect. He had knelt before her recently in his own home while his mother was out, begging to fasten her toe shoes, stroking the tapered toe, seeming to understand, as if he himself were a dancer, how the shoe was designed to complete the line that ran along the top of the instep, to cross the ankle up to the knee and hip. She had gone up on pointe for him and then, dizzy with his admiration, had demonstrated one of the most important fundamentals of ballet, placing her heels together with the feet splayed out at an angle approaching 180 degrees, rotating her thighs so as to effect the necessary pose.

Thighs.

Natasha shivered at the delicious thought of Pieter's hand on her bare thigh. She had permitted it and she was not ashamed, although it had been he who had moved away. She hadn't wanted him to stop whatever he had been about to do.

As the familiar smell of her beloved father's favorite meal, *zverina*, venison roasted gypsy-style on the kitchen spit, drifted up the staircase, Natasha reluctantly got up from the bed. It was time she helped her mother play hostess, but she was already bored at the thought of the evening ahead with their shrill neighbors, her mother's brother, Uncle Ivo and his busybody wife, Kamilla, endlessly curious, endlessly jealous of all the good things Ludmilla managed now to provide. Aunt Kamilla made her uneasy. Sometimes she felt she should warn her mother not to tell her anything. Aunt Kamilla was just the kind of person to report their food parcels to the authorities. These days nobody, not even a relation, could be trusted.

Natasha began to open her door, then closed it again. Once, when the ballet had been all she ever thought about, the smell of the venison on the spit would have revolted her, and her mother would have spent the evening, she knew, sighing despairingly as she pushed the hard-to-get food around her plate. But she had no need to starve herself any longer. Two days ago, although her mother didn't yet know it, Madame Brouetsky had broken the news that because she'd grown another inch over the summer, it was unlikely she would ever become a ballerina, even in the back row of the corps de ballet.

If it hadn't been for Pieter, she would have jumped into the river, sure that only a future as a beautician forever tied to the Sukova Beauty Salon loomed before her, but Pieter had helped her look at things differently.

It was Pieter who'd reminded her that she was different from most seventeen year olds in Prague, that because she had an enormously successful sister, Ludmilla, now called Louise, married to the richest man in the world, one day she might be able to escape. He'd pointed out lovingly that just as her sister had now somehow miraculously arranged for them to receive food parcels every few months from the U.S. Army base at Grafenwöhr, parcels full of cheese and fruit and butter and meat, including the venison her mother was cooking tonight, so one day she might be able to arrange an exit visa.

Of course, they still had to wait on line for hours to get other basic necessities, but these unexpected luxuries had brought a smile to her mother's face that she hadn't seen there since her father died, but an exit visa—that was another thing entirely.

"Perhaps one day your sister Ludmilla can help you escape to America where, because you're so beautiful, you can become a film star in Hollywood," Pieter had said without the trace of a smile on his face or a sarcastic note in his voice.

Film star? Beautiful? Hollywood? Was she really beautiful? She'd never been told so before; she had grown up accepting that the beautiful one in the family was Ludmilla, who'd flown away on a magic carpet and had all her dreams come true. She pretended to everyone she remembered exactly what her big sister looked like, but of course she didn't. How could she, after so many years?

Before going downstairs, Natasha looked at herself in the huge cheval glass that had once been in her parents' room, but had been moved to hers when her father died. Madame B. had insisted she resist the habit of the mirror, to learn to dance without the constant comforting partnership of her reflection. Now she could look in the mirror without guilt; now she was consumed with her reflection, desperate that her appearance would always meet with Pieter's approval.

She lifted her arms high in front of the mirror. The Magyar sleeves of the dark blue dress her mother had just finished sewing fell back around her shoulders, and if she turned slightly she could see, through the deep arm hole, the soft, small curve of her breast. Soon she would wear the dress for Pieter. She would show him this position from *Giselle*, by far her favorite ballet, and without saying a word, she would command his hand to touch the pale white flesh where her breasts were at last beginning to swell.

On the wall of the bedroom, a poster of the American film star James Dean looked down on her. She curtsied low to the floor. "I'm going to be a film star. I'm going to go to Hollywood and make rock-and-roll films with the King of Rock, Elvis Presley," she sang softly to James Dean as, down below, the doorbell rang.

The smell of soft coal, which permeated Prague's city air as cooler weather arrived with fall, came through the door with the visitor. Natasha ran to peek over the banister. She was relieved to see the rosy bald head of Father Kusy. It meant the evening ahead wouldn't just be one of the neighbors' and her mother's lamentations about the past and Aunt Kamilla's inquisition. There would at least be music, because Father Kusy loved to play her father's violin, and after a few glasses of beer, perhaps there would also be some gossip about the indiscretions of Party members.

"Well, well, well, so here is my favorite ballerina, Slecna Natasha. And when am I going to see you at the Prague Opera House? I don't want to have to stand in line in the cold Wenceslas wind. As the oldest family friend I can expect better, *ze jo?*" Father Kusy laughed heartily as Natasha played her part in a pantomime that had been repeated many times, assuring him that he would receive the first engraved invitation to her first opening night. When her aunt and uncle arrived a few minutes later, she excused herself and went into the kitchen to help her mother.

As she added garlic to a bowl of grated potatoes ready to be made into pancakes, she said, "Mama, do you think one day I'll be able to join Ludmilla, to escape to the free world? Do you think there's even the slightest chance that Ludmilla could arrange that miracle?" She hadn't meant to say it. The words had tumbled out without her thinking. Natasha was horrified to see her mother's face grow pale and look even more drawn than usual.

She quickly went to her, ashamed. "Mama, forget what I just said. I'd never leave you behind. But ... I don't know ... I was daydreaming, silly daydreams about a lot of things, if and if and if ..."

She saw tears on her mother's cheeks. "Oh, Mama, I'm so sorry to upset you. Forget every word I said. I didn't mean anything."

"No, Natasha. You're the one who's right. When we listen together to the Voice of America, when I hear what other children have ... you child ..." her mother's voice broke.

"I'm not a child, Mama. I'm nearly eighteen. You've given me everything a child could wish for, and I've grown up, well, happy because of you."

There was the sweet sound of a violin. Father Kusy had begun to play. Natasha hugged her mother, angry with herself for putting a blight on the evening she knew her mother had looked forward to since the venison arrived. What could she say to make everything all right again?

Again the words tumbled out. "Look, Mama, at how happy I look, and yet I had bad news this week."

Setting the table, Blanka Sukova pushed her hair, badly in need of new color, out of her eyes. "Bad news?"

Natasha gave a wide, impish grin to make sure her mother knew she was fine. "Yes, Madame Brouetsky told me I'm now too tall to be a ballerina, so I suppose I was born to be a beautician after all."

Her mother gave a wry smile, then turned abruptly as the venison started to sputter on the spit over the blazing kitchen fire. "We'll see, we'll see . . . if we have any customers left. We're out of peroxide, out of perm solution, I don't know." She sighed deeply, the sigh Natasha lived with every day. "Oh, well, tell everyone to come in. Supper will be ready by the time Father Kusy has said grace."

The venison was delicious, and Natasha found herself hungrily eating every scrap from her plate. It could be a long time before they had anything like it again.

As more beer was poured, Father Kusy leaned back contentedly and lit a cigarette, watching the smoke curl up to the old wooden chandelier. "I hear Hungary's ex-premier Nagy is the latest one to be executed."

"Everything comes to him who waits," Uncle Ivo mumbled.

"Well, I'm prepared to wait if I can be sure Novotny will get his one day," the next-door neighbor moaned.

"Sssh . . ." Aunt Kamilla warned, glancing around nervously. "You never know who might be . . ."

"Listening?" Blanka snorted. "You think we're bugged in here, my dear sister-in-law? Please! If we can't speak in our own homes . . ."

"Kamilla is right," Ivo retorted. "Why, just the other day Merivalo was arrested after a dinner in his home. They say he was talking against the Party and they found a dozen eggs in his larder."

Natasha tried to block out their voices, to relive moment by moment her meeting with Pieter that afternoon, but it was impossible. The old grandfather clock just outside the front parlor, which was also the beauty salon, was erratic. Sometimes it chimed the hour; sometimes it didn't. Tonight Natasha jumped when the chimes rang through the house. Nine chimes . . . Now only fifteen hours separated her from her date with Pieter at noon the next day.

Tonight she would sleep with Pieter's handkerchief on her pillow, with the strong *P* embroidered by his sister next to her face. She would sleep and she would dream of escaping to America, where, with the help of her brilliant, powerful sister, she would become a film star in rock-and-roll films with Elvis Presley.

*   *   *

Less than a thousand miles away, Natasha's brilliant and powerful sister, Louise Towers, looked bored. After six years of near asphyxiation from boredom, living with Mr. Alex Fiestler in Geneva, Switzerland, no one knew the signs better than Suzanne.

If those subtle signs had been accompanied by the reddened eyes and careless appearance that she had regularly exhibited in her last year of marriage, nothing would have made Suzanne happier. But her father's wife didn't look unhappy, because obviously there was no reason on earth why she should. Her idiot father still acted as if she were a national treasure that he had created and was lucky enough to possess totally.

No, Louise wasn't sighing or drumming her fingers or even fidgeting with the huge diamond that now decorated the ring finger of her left hand. It was the faraway look in her eyes that Suzanne had noticed before, a look that to her said, "My thoughts are far more entertaining than any conversation I might have here." It was an I-want-to-be-alone look.

On the way to the table, Suzanne had been impressed to see the woman who'd made "I want to be alone" part of her persona, Greta Garbo, dining in a small group that included Maria Callas and the Greek who had one of the most magnificent yachts in Monte Carlo Harbor, Aristotle Onassis. She had been impressed, but when she'd pointed them out to Louise, she'd shown complete indifference. How dare she be so superior!

Suzanne's anger grew as she stared across the table at Louise, apparently completely at ease in one of the most sophisticated restaurants in the world, the Chateau Madrid, built on a rocky plateau hundreds of feet above the Mediterranean. It would be almost impossible for anyone to believe this vision had been a housemaid ten or eleven years ago—*their* housemaid! To her chagrin, Suzanne had to accept that the slut had learned fast how to conduct herself in the upper echelons of society. Although the first course of the sumptuous birthday feast was only just being served, Suzanne realized she'd lost her appetite.

There were thirty people around the table on the fabled terrace, the best table, oval-shaped at her father's request, so that as many people as possible could talk to each other. Her father sat in the middle, facing the Mediterranean, with Princess Grace of Monaco on his right, looking more like an out-of-reach film star than ever in a silver evening dress that sparkled each time she moved her slender body.

On her father's left—a distinct breach of etiquette, as Suzanne had felt she had to point out to him—was his wife, Louise, her breasts only just covered by an intricate swath of pale primrose, white, and gold chiffon in a spectacular dress Givenchy had designed especially for her to wear this evening. And what breasts they were, so white, so perfectly shaped. No wonder that at the small cocktail party before the dinner, every man in the room could hardly keep his eyes away. It didn't seem to bother her father. On the contrary, he seemed to revel in the fact that they could look but never come near, let alone touch.

"It's my birthday, my pet," he'd said when she'd finished remonstrating with him about the seating plan. He'd looked so boyish and fit it was incredible to think he was fifty. "It was my idea to celebrate it here, and I'm doing the seating. I want the three most beautiful women on the Riviera all within reach."

Suzanne knew he was including her in the three, and she was certainly seated within reach, almost opposite him, to the left of Prince Rainier, who had so far been singularly unimpressed with her beauty, having only grunted in her direction, twice, before turning to talk animatedly with the lady on his right, the wife of their new ambassador to France, Amory Houghton.

Her father blew her a kiss and she blew one back as her favorite champagne, Cristal's rose, was poured. That would help save the evening—and so would David Reemer who, thank God, when the ambassador had to cancel, had been invited at the last minute because he was so important to the brilliant and beautiful Louise. They were going together to Grasse later in the week, where Louise would soak her nose in some apparently extraordinary new smell. It was a pity they hadn't seated David next to her, or at least across the table, because she knew she might not be beautiful, but she looked pretty good tonight—even without the help of Ludmilla, a.k.a. Louise, to do her hair.

Charles had almost had a heart attack when she'd whispered that in his ear after receiving his usual darling compliments. "Now, Suzanne," her adorable brother had said, wagging his finger at her, "you've been behaving like an angel. Surely you're not going to spoil things for yourself—and for Dad—on his big night, are you?"

She had no intention of doing so. Since her divorce and return to New York, she had been proud of her performance as the prodigal daughter returning in sackcloth and ashes. Louise probably knew she still hated her guts and always would, but she couldn't prove it because her manners had been so impeccable that Dad had even started throwing out hints that she might like to work in what he now called "the Louise Towers division of the business."

Fat chance! If her brother, Charles, was prepared to kowtow to Madame Louise and put on a show as if he actually enjoyed the cosmetics business, she certainly wasn't about to join him. Dad had given her three months to settle back in New York. After this special birthday sojourn in the South of France, she had an appointment to meet him in the office after Labor Day and give him the good news that she was ready to start her orientation period at Towers Pharmaceuticals, perhaps in advertising or marketing or new drug development.

Dad had already told her it took from five to ten years to market a new drug, and that out of several thousand compounds tested, on average only three new products were realized. By the time a new drug came into being, she hoped there would be a new man in her life and she could gracefully "retire" from active duty, having earned her rightful place on the board as a diligent, informed member of the family.

As giant shrimp grilled with coriander, cumin, and fennel arrived, Suzanne caught David Reemer looking at her from the end of the table. He winked. Things were looking up. Perhaps they could go dancing after dinner. If he didn't suggest it, she would. He could hardly say no to the daughter of the boss.

Benedict woke with a rare hangover the next morning. Perhaps it had something to do with being fifty. With his eyes still closed, he reached over for Louise, but she wasn't there. He eased himself up gingerly to sit on the edge of the bed and called out, "Lu, Lu, come here. I need you."

Through half-closed eyes he was surprised to see that when Louise came out of the bathroom she was already dressed. "What time is it?"

"Nine-fifteen, nine-twenty."

"Where the hell are you going so early?"

"I told you last night." She used the tone of voice he particularly loathed, as if she were talking to a spoiled child. "David Reemer told me he'd heard—"

"Heard what? Like hell you told me. Do you think I'm losing my memory? Come back to bed. Now! This instant." He groaned. "Oh, I feel like shit."

She began to massage his neck and shoulders. Her hands were as they always were, cool, strong, taking away some, but not much, of the hangover pain in his temples.

After a few minutes she took her hands away. He saw she was looking at her watch. He scowled. "Louise, whatever you told me or didn't tell me last night is unimportant. You are not going anywhere now. Come back to bed and massage my back. I'll expect to find you there when I return."

He padded wearily into the bathroom. Louise must have opened the heavy shutters, because brilliant Mediterranean sunshine sent a stab of new pain through his head. He slammed the shutters shut, brushed his teeth, and splashed cold water and Guerlain's Imperiale cologne over his face and neck. That would have to do for now. He was suddenly, urgently in need of her. In the past few weeks they'd hardly made love; he'd meant to the night before, but he must have fallen asleep. He yawned. He could hardly remember getting back at all. The restaurant had lived up to its reputation, but it had taken much too long to get there. God knows what time they'd returned to the hotel.

He leaned against the marble sink. The problem was they were both too busy. He had always been busy, but now she was more preoccupied than he. No wonder she didn't get pregnant. She continually told him she wanted a child; she'd had everything checked out and there seemed to be no reason she didn't conceive, except her increasing work load. It was ridiculous. The powder-and-paint business had become for him a cause for both pride in her accomplishments and intense irritation. Sometimes he felt like getting out of the whole thing, although its growth continued to be phenomenal.

From one tiny acorn of a shop on Sixty-second Street, a whole tree had taken root. He was the one who, out of self-interest, had begun to curtail distribution and put an embargo on any more Louise Towers Institutes for the time being. With four established in the East and the Southeast, and franchises in Neiman-Marcus and Saks Fifth Avenue, Louise was already far too involved. Thank God, he'd had the idea of bringing Charles back to help out when they'd begun to have cash-flow problems because Louise was in over her head. And thank God, too, that Charles had taken to the business as if he were Charles of the Ritz, looking after the books as well as doing the foot-slogging and on-the-spot checking that this crazy cosmetics business seemed to need.

Benedict inspected himself in the mirror. A few gray hairs, but a slight tan gained fast in the last forty-eight hours made him look better than he felt. Lack of virility wasn't his problem . . . Still, Louise seemed to be drifting away, or was he imagining it because he himself got so caught up?

He drank down an Alka-Seltzer, although he hated using the competition's antacid. Why couldn't they come up with something to match Miles Labs' tablet? His thoughts drifted back to Louise and the huge amount of time she was now devoting to Louise Towers, Incorporated. She didn't know, of course, but he had asked Norris before he left to investigate quietly the possibility of a buyer for the cosmetics company. If the right group could be found, and they offered a good price, he would discuss it with her, but the decision to sell, he would make perfectly clear, was his and his alone. It all depended on her behavior in the weeks and months ahead.

Benedict's mood darkened when he returned to the bedroom to find Louise still dressed in what he now recognized as the pale gray and white linen suit she'd occasionally worn this summer to business meetings in New York. The way she held her head, not so much defiant as haughty, maddened him further, but he said calmly, "Well, why aren't you in bed?"

"Benedict, I told you about this last night before the party and you didn't seem to mind at all. David Reemer's learned that a French group is outbidding us on the new fragrance in Grasse. He asked my permission to move our Friday appointment to today if possible, because the essential-oil house isn't taking us seriously. I told him to go ahead, and he did. It will take at least two hours to get there. I really must leave now, then I'll be back in good time for dinner." There was no suggestion of asking his permission. A wave of nausea passed over him. He wasn't used to being crossed, and certainly not by a woman, let alone his wife. Obviously her success had gone to her head. She was changing. She would have to be taught who was in charge.

"No," Benedict said softly, though he felt like shouting out the word. "No, my dear Lu. Let Reemer go there alone; that's what he's paid for, to evaluate and negotiate on your behalf. This is our vacation, short as it is. I will allow you to go to Grasse on Friday when I leave for Zurich. I can assure you the fragrance will still be there. But in any case, that isn't the issue. I want you now. Grasse and its stinking fragrance can go to hell, for all I care."

Her obvious reluctance stimulated his desire, even as it angered him. This wasn't the first time her business had interfered with his plans. He'd thought it was the pressure of New York. Now thousands of miles away, on the Riviera, he knew it wouldn't matter where they were.

She stared at him with those impenetrable dark eyes of hers, then said, as he'd known she eventually would, "Very well."

If she hadn't acquiesced? Well, he would deal with that problem if and when it happened.

He put his hand heavily over hers as he went to pick up the phone. "I'll deal with Reemer."

He watched her unswervingly as she unzipped the tailored skirt and unbuttoned the sleeveless jacket. His eyes never left her body as Reemer came on the line. "Mrs. Towers cannot come with you to Grasse this morning," he said sharply. "I have work for her here for me."

His pleasure grew as he saw Louise flush slightly at his words. She stepped out of her stiletto-heeled red sandals as Reemer answered, and then unfastened her lace garter belt and peeled off gossamer-thin stockings as pale as her skin.

"You can surely handle it, Reemer," Benedict added. "Keep everything on hold. Don't make any commitments." As Louise unfastened her bra and stepped out of her silk briefs, Benedict beckoned her to come over to him. Her nipples were erect. She was biting her lip.

"If they're playing a little game, we can play it too." As he spoke, he casually caressed her buttocks, without looking at her, running his finger inside the crease. She was stiff, resistant, but he would soon change that. "Yes, Mrs. Towers will, I am sure, keep her appointment on Friday, as originally arranged. You can report to us—to me— tomorrow. Come to the suite about noon."

He put the phone down and, without speaking, continued to fondle her behind. She had begun to tremble, probably with rage. Good, good. He didn't want continual conflict, and he was going to make sure it didn't happen, but on occasions, like today, it could make for better sex. He was big and getting bigger. He pulled her roughly down to the bed and penetrated her at once.

Since the Tuesday display of attempted independence, Louise had been much more like the Ludmilla he'd fallen in love with and trained to become the perfect wife. They'd made love at least twice a day, and she hadn't mentioned the cosmetics business once.

As he tied his tie on Friday morning, Benedict felt refreshed and sexually satisfied, knowing that when they met again in Paris on Sunday evening, he would want her as much as ever, and she would be pliant and ready for him. Perhaps he'd even take her to a club he hadn't been to in years, one he'd been introduced to by a particularly creative French *poule de luxe*. His penis stirred as he thought of another beautiful woman touching his wife. They'd been married for over six years. He didn't have a seven-year-itch or anything like it, but every marriage needed new stimulus at times. Well, he'd think about it.

"I hate leaving you, darling," he said over his shoulder. "But I think for once it will be worth it. This Swiss guy has never wasted my time yet. The land he wants me to buy is on the main line linking Zurich with the south—with France and Italy. A major road borders the property, and there's plenty of good water. More important, the government has lowered taxes in the area because they want to develop it commercially." In the mirror he could see Louise listening attentively. She was wearing the gray and white suit again, ready for her business meeting in Grasse.

"What will you use it for? You already have such a beautiful plant in Switzerland."

"It's an investment. Right now there's nothing there but cows and grass. Ruetger thinks even a new town could be developed." He turned to face her, laughing. "You need lots of good water to formulate cosmetics. Perhaps it will become the site for the first Louise Towers plant overseas."

He thought she would laugh too, but she didn't. "Why not? We could easily be ready in three to five years." Her voice was serious.

He was going to tell her he was only joking when the phone rang. She was leaving before him. He had another hour before he had to leave for Nice airport.

"It's Charles," she said, smiling. "He's waiting for me in the lobby with Reemer." She paused, then added casually, "Suzanne asked if she could come too. I didn't see any reason to say no. She wants to see the famous town of perfume, she told me, so she will sightsee while we deal."

Benedict was delighted. "I'm happier than you'll ever know to hear that. It seems that at last Suzanne is beginning to respect you as she should." Louise nodded, still smiling, knowing nothing could be further from the truth. Reemer was the big attraction, but Benedict didn't need to know that.

"Really, Lu, the best news I can get is to hear that the kids are happy and settling down. I can't get over how quickly Charles has adapted to the cosmetics business, obviously with your help. He really seems to have matured. Now if only we could find him a wife . . ." Benedict kissed the back of her neck. "Poor fella, he doesn't know what he's missing."

He pulled her to him to kiss her again before she left. "What's the name of the place again, where you're all staying tonight? Or is the Rolls bringing you back here? You could easily sleep in the car on the way."

"Remember I told you, Charles knows this wonderful artists' inn in a little village called St.-Paul-de-Vence? We have reservations there, but we'll decide after the meeting whether we return here or not." She indicated a small overnight case by the door. "I'm taking this, but if I'm not too tired the driver will bring us back. Wish me luck. There's a lot of competition out there."

The large suite seemed empty and silent after Louise left. Her wardrobe door was slightly open. Benedict opened it wider, visualizing Louise in the beautiful dresses hanging there, seeing the row of handmade shoes she now had, the matching handbags in soft chamois cases, thinking back to the days of Ludmilla with the single yellow silk dress.

The large crocodile handbag that she usually carried on transatlantic crossings was half out of its protective case. He bent down to push it back inside. There was a stiff envelope preventing it. As he pulled it out, intending to leave it on her bedside table, something dropped out. It was something he'd never seen before, although he'd heard enough about the unusual packaging to recognize it. In a slim white container, no bigger than a comb case, was a blister pack of tiny white pills, numbered from one to twenty-one.

He sat down heavily in an armchair, all the energy drained out of him. The envelope, addressed to Mrs. Mellon Sanford III, was crossed through and the words "Dexter, deliver to Mrs. Towers at the salon as usual," had been added in big letters. Dexter was the Sanfords' chauffeur.

There was a brief note inside, scribbled on a page from a prescription pad. He couldn't decipher all the words, but two sprang out to burn his mind: "Regular supply." The doctor's name at the top of the slip of paper was John Rock, a Boston gynecologist who, as Benedict knew well, had been conducting tests with a new birth-control pill for a competing pharmaceutical company. The tests had been so successful, it was expected the government would shortly allow the pill to be available on prescription to everyone.

"Oh, Lu." He said her name aloud in pain. She'd been lying to him. Not only didn't she want to have his baby, but with the help of his oldest friend's wife she'd been secretly obtaining the medication to ensure it never happened.

The road to Grasse was terrible, full of hairpin bends and dangerous corners, winding round and round and up and up a mountainside. "They should have warned us," Charles said as the large Rolls slowed almost to walking speed. "Are you feeling all right?" he asked solicitously.

Louise smiled reassuringly at him. "Yes, yes, the bumps don't bother me. It's like getting a massage." If only he knew. She wasn't only "all right," she was ecstatic to be free for the next few days, looking forward to the business meeting ahead just as most women, she supposed, looked forward to yet another cocktail party or shopping expedition. Only the presence of Suzanne put a damper on the day, but Suzanne for the moment was engrossed in fascinating David Reemer, who looked as if he might be carsick any minute.

A soft laugh escaped her.

Charles looked at her with real affection. "What on earth can you find to laugh about on this nightmare journey? You are such a good sport," he added admiringly as the car lurched over a pile of stones, stopped, and then started its uphill climb again.

"You'll never know."

As he turned to look out the window at the spectacular view unfolding below, Louise saw in his profile the young Benedict. Had Benedict ever been as gentle, as compassionate, as patient as she'd now discovered his son to be? She doubted it.

There was an omnipresence about Benedict that she doubted anyone else in the world possessed. It frightened her even as it dazzled and impressed her. However much she learned, Benedict made her realize in seconds, it was nothing. At the same time, when she least expected it, he could make her feel like a star. She was a possession he continually liked to re-create. He could be cruel in his words, his actions, his lovemaking; he could also be the most caring of men—when it suited him. She still never knew what to expect, but she knew she had to obey him and it was beginning to wear her down.

Why was she thinking this way? Benedict had made her what she was. Why did she now have to remind herself of that so often?

David Reemer was white-faced. "Do you mind if we stop the car? I'm afraid I'm going to be ill."

Louise was glad to get out too. The mountain air was scented with lilies of the valley. She could hear rushing water. A soft breeze tousled her hair, tendrils falling onto her face. She longed to unwind it, to let it fly behind her as it had in the carefree days of her childhood, riding ponies in Bohemia.

Charles said, "You're enjoying this, aren't you, Lu? You're really wonderful. You look like a schoolgirl playing hooky."

Charles was taller than his father, she hadn't realized how much before. They stood together at the edge of the road, looking down into a darkly wooded ravine, watching a waterfall skip down a cliff to a silver stream, threading its way through dark green trees like a snake.

The wind was stronger now, whipping her hairpins out. She quickly put her hands up to stop her chignon from falling down, and Charles scooped it up at the back, laughing, pushing the pins back in. "Mustn't let you lose your executive image." He was like a gentle giant, smiling down at her with warm brown eyes. For one strange moment, Louise felt like putting her head on his shoulder. He was such a peaceful person, happy-go-lucky, always anxious to put people at ease, so different from his demanding father.

A sharp gust of wind made her sway. Charles quickly put his arm around her to steady her, pulling her back toward him. "Whoa, there, we're too near the edge."

His touch was like an electric shock on her skin. Had he felt it? Young Charles, her stepson? Was she crazy? Still with his arm casually around her shoulder, Charles was looking away to where David Reemer was sitting on a rock, less ashen-faced now. Staring at both of them was Reemer's would-be nurse, Suzanne. Louise could feel the blood coursing into her face, but when Charles turned back, he looked no different from before, smiling the same cheery, giving smile, no indication on his face that he had felt what, for an insane moment, she had felt.

She walked over to David Reemer. "Do you think you can make it?"

Suzanne scowled. "I certainly think it's time you attended to your business."

Louise ignored the barbed remark, but she could feel her heart beating faster. Had she shown to her enemy so clearly what she'd felt? She couldn't have; she didn't know what it meant herself. She was drained, that was it, exhausted after the last few days of striving to prove to Benedict that he came first, before everything and everyone else in her life.

As the Rolls approached Grasse, they passed field after field of flowers—roses, violets, jasmine, jonquils, mimosas, acacias—all growing in orderly profusion. "It's paradise," Louise murmured.

The eighteenth-century town itself, with its picturesque squares, cobblestone streets, and plants and flowers everywhere, tumbling over walls, climbing staircases, made her feel like a new person. Charles seemed equally enchanted, excitedly pointing out a statue decorated with a crown of orange blossoms, a street cart vivid with roses.

They were nearly forty minutes late for their appointment, but Henri Petissier, head of the old, established essential-oil house, did not keep them waiting long in the lofty reception room, where a floor-to-ceiling bottle-filled showcase portrayed the liquid history of the company, dating back to 1830. There were Baccarat crystal flacons and embossed decanters of colognes and infusions created for the court of Napoleon III, along with modern, streamlined bottles with names Louise immediately recognized. She was awed, as tongue-tied as she had been at the first black-tie dinner party she'd attended as Benedict's wife. All the straightforward business proposals she planned to bring forward if she liked what she smelled seemed inadequate in this house of history.

An English-speaking secretary came in after a few minutes. "Madame Towers?"

"Yes."

"I have a mes-sage for you." She pronounced the last syllable of "message" like "sarge"; it sounded charming. She handed Louise a slip of paper. "Please call your husband in Zurich this evening after 9:00 P.M."

The iron grip of tension was back, but only momentarily, as the secretary then asked them to follow her to Petissier's office. Tall—as tall as Charles—and totally bald, Henri Petissier greeted them in a long white laboratory coat and an equally long white linen apron. "*Bonjour, bonjour . . .*"

Coffee appeared, served in fragile porcelain cups. On an enormous oak desk was a strange object that looked like a wheel with long spokes of blotting paper jutting from it. Petissier saw her studying it.

"Yes, yes, there are different strengths of Amore on those pieces of paper." His voice was languid, yet musical. "Amore is, as I believe you already learned in the United States, our code name for this exquisite work. When it works here . . . and sometimes it takes two thousand tests . . ." His eyes twinkled. "It works."

Reemer started to talk about the success of Louise Towers and their Revelation bath oil in the States. She wanted to stop him, although it had been their plan. Perhaps in another life she had been a perfumer, she felt completely happy in this environment. Only Benedict's message in her suit pocket disturbed her serenity.

"Perhaps you would like to see our establishment before we approach Amore?" As he led the way, through an immaculate laboratory that adjoined his office, then along a wide, sunny corridor to the factory, Petissier explained some of the mystery behind the creation of a great perfume. "First, of course, will be the selection of raw materials, then their preparation, soaked in alcohol for six months before being filtered, cooled, and stored. And, of course, we are not speaking only of flowers here, but of other essential natural ingredients"—he spoke as quickly as he walked—"from the civet cat of Ethiopia, the musk deer of Tibet, ambergris, which is an essential fixative part of perfume, from the sperm whale . . ." They passed huge vats where millions of rose petals were being prepared. "Two hundred million are needed to distill only one kilo of the essential oil of Bulgarian rose." Petissier tossed facts at them, adding with a twisted smile, "Perhaps this will explain to you why great perfume formulas cost so much."

The tour took almost an hour, but far from being tired, Louise was elated, asking permission to note down some of Petissier's lyrical explanations. They would be invaluable in press releases later. "A perfume is like a portrait, and a portrait is not a photograph. Both are interpretations of a person, something that instantly brings character, personality to mind. But nothing stimulates the memory more than perfume!"

Louise was keenly aware of Charles's presence, behind her, in front of her, often beside her, listening as eagerly as she to everything the perfumer had to say, asking as many questions as she, and often the most pertinent questions. She couldn't understand how, to her, he had suddenly become a different person. Was it because everywhere they went, irresistible fragrances surrounded them? She told herself yes, that was the reason; it was an exotic, erotic dangerous bower of nature, relaxing the senses, penetrating the civilized frontiers of behavior.

Back in the office, Petissier went to a safe and took out five or six small vials. "Each of us is divinely different, with different odor receptors, different skin and bodily functions, which is why we all see and smell and perceive the world in different ways. This knowledge is the basis for understanding that every fragrance will smell differently to different people."

Ceremoniously, Petissier dipped one of the blotters into the first vial and gave it to Louise, her eyes bright and curious like a child. "Amore," he said with a funny little half-bow.

Louise smelled a strange, disturbing note, sexual, arousing, followed by a keen, sharp sweetness. It had not been named Amore for nothing. Vials number two through four had too much impact, five not enough, but six . . . "Oh, yes, yes . . ." she breathed, inhaling again.

"Now on your skin, Madame Towers."

"What is that strange note?"

"Perhaps it is vanilla, the first known aphrodisiac, touched with orange blossom and a special synthetic compound as close to lilac as we have so far been able to get." Petissier looked at David Reemer as if he would understand his frustration. "The smell of lilac has been broken down into two hundred different ingredients and still defies analysis." He looked again at Louise. "But I think what we have achieved here, we like this better. *Oui?*"

"*Oui*, yes, we do, I do." This was it, she thought excitedly. Now she knew why it had been so important to come. Louise Towers would market this unusual, evasive, disturbing perfume as a true love potion. Why not? Fragrances had been used to seduce and attract since ancient times. This formula would be the twentieth-century equivalent of what Cleopatra had used to lure Antony into her arms. She could already see the display, the promotional copy, the press attention.

"Then we must discuss our terms. Now you will understand why the rare fragrance Amore is so expensive. Now you have seen for yourself, Madame Towers, what enormous quantities of raw materials—and in this case, rare raw materials—are needed to produce only a fraction of concentrated oils."

*   *   *

In the old inn in St-Paul-de-Vence later that night, David Reemer had no qualms about telling Suzanne how much money he'd saved her father, after Suzanne had spent an hour telling him the incredible story of Louise's background. At last he understood why, from the beginning of Louise Towers, Incorporated, Benedict Towers had repeatedly told him never to agree to anything his wife wanted until the head office looked it over.

"This bald-headed frog could have sold Mrs. Towers lavender water for a million dollars," Reemer told Suzanne over a late-night drink. "He had her totally in a spell; I've never seen anything like it. I thought we'd never get out of there. Talk, talk, talk, and then, when she smelled the stuff, she almost swooned. I tell you, when she gave me the go-ahead to accept any terms Petissier wanted, I nearly threw up. It was the most flagrant bullshitting job of salesmanship I've ever seen."

"Doesn't she ever deal with the financial side of the Louise Towers business?" Suzanne asked.

"Only the small, day-to-day stuff in the salon. No big deals. She knows that's not her métier. That's why your father brought your brother Charles in, and why I've spent so much time with her."

"What happens when you or Dad—I mean the head office—doesn't go along with something she wants? A new location or something big like that."

"There's usually a convincing reason. Your father, however, doesn't seem overeager to expand at the rate we could easily afford now. I know she's been disappointed in a few situations where he's said no when perhaps he should have said yes during the past couple of years, but she's too smart herself to question his decisions."

Suzanne glared at him. "Smart? I've got another word for it. Does she know that neither you nor Charles signed the Amore contract? I thought over dinner she seemed sure you had. She certainly wouldn't have been in such a good mood if she'd known she hasn't yet got the rights to the formula."

"And may never have," Reemer replied, putting his hand confidently on Suzanne's knee. "Petissier was trying to pull a fast one. He knows an American sucker when he sees one. His problem was that because neither Charles nor I could get a word in, he thought we were of no account. Did he have a surprise!" Reemer appeared to be absent-minded as he began to stroke her skin, continuing, "No, Mrs. Towers doesn't know. She thinks we're home and dry with Amore, but your father apparently warned Charles last night not to finalize any agreement before discussing it with him. If the price isn't right—and believe me, it is far from right—Charles was told to procrastinate."

"Wasn't she there all the time? I mean, how is it she doesn't know what finally happened?"

"Charles and I had it worked out. He said it was time to pick you up, as it was getting so late, that I could take care of everything, and of course that's what she was expecting to happen. She's used to the men in the company finalizing the major decisions."

Suzanne looked lost in thought for a minute or two. "I wish my brother Charles weren't involved with her business. You never know what to expect from her," she added fiercely.

"You don't like her, do you?"

"Like her! I detest her!"

Reemer moved his hand an inch higher. "Do you like *me*?"

"I could . . ."

Fifteen minutes later he was in her bed, making sure of it.

In the bar of the hotel, overlooking Lake Zurich, Benedict was allowing himself to become pleasantly intoxicated. He'd run into Audrey Walson, an exotic-looking young lobbyist he'd met a few times in Washington over the years and who, he had learned, had just joined the Food and Drug Administration.

He'd invited her to join him for a quick drink, anything to take his mind off Louise's betrayal, and what the hell, she could also turn out to be a good contact.

After thirty minutes he was wondering why he'd never realized how attractive she was, a bit on the skinny side for him, but probably enjoyably athletic in bed. He ordered two more cognacs.

"So, Audrey, what's with this new amendment to the Food, Drug and Cosmetic Act of 1938?"

"The Food Additives Amendment?"

"Can't think of any others. No food additives to be permitted other than those used widely for years and 'generally recognized as safe,' unless the FDA agrees after a thorough review of test data that the new additive is safe at the intended level of use. Isn't that how the gobbledygook you folks use goes? Have I got it right?" He looked at her intently, knowing what an effect he was having, pleased that his tan was emphasized by the crisp whiteness of his shirt.

Despite her sleek, sophisticated looks, Audrey was unused to sophisticated men. She laughed nervously. "I can't tell you anything more than that."

"Well, now, I bet those breakfast-food boys are giving you a hard time. You ever had a bath in a tub full of cornflakes? It's a really crunchy experience."

Over the bar he could see the time. It was nearing eleven o'clock. He expected, when he went to get his key, to find a message from Louise, if not two. He'd called the Grasse plant impulsively, leaving her a message to call him. Now he wished he hadn't. He didn't intend to speak to her again until Paris. Come to think of it, he might skip Paris and let Louise Towers of Louise Towers, Inc., cool her heels there for a while, wondering what the hell was going on. He needed time to think, perhaps a lot of time. Perhaps he'd take Audrey for a little trip somewhere, a drive into the Albis, where the Alps began their magnificent climb, or a visit to the Towers Pharmaceuticals' plant outside Geneva, ending up in Prangins for some extracurricular activity.

Audrey had dark red hair, the kind that blazed under lamplight. He idly wondered what color her pubic hair was, and what she tasted like. He hadn't thought about any woman this way since he'd fallen in love with Louise, although he knew, except for her new job with the part of government that influenced his business the most, Audrey would keep his interest for about five minutes.

"What do you hear about the new birth-control pill?" he asked.

Stupid young woman. She was blushing. Did she really think he was asking the question out of a personal interest in fucking her?

"That's not . . . not my area. I'm compliance in food," she stuttered. "You probably know more than I do. The Puerto Rico tests last year were successful. I believe . . . no, I'm not sure . . . Searle has a program planned for England, I think . . ."

He was no longer listening. Pain had slowly changed during the day into deep-rooted anger—and fear, as he began to accept that he himself was responsible for obliterating the Ludmilla who'd once said and then proved over and over again that she was willing to give herself to him, body, mind, and soul. As thoroughly as he'd done away with the name Ludmilla, he'd also, without realizing it until now, thrown away the girl the name had stood for, the selfless, innocent, uneducated girl he'd trained to become Louise.

This was where the fear came in, for who was this Louise? He no longer felt that he knew. On the surface she was a sophisticated, incredibly beautiful enchantress who, he'd been proud to see, had learned under his direction how to use the mystery and melancholy of her Eastern European past in business. At the same time she'd developed the necessary New York toughness and tenacity to make the business grow. Now he had to face the fact that she had also developed New York guile and deceit.

Miss Compliance Officer was babbling on, flattering him in the same breath on the success of the Louise Towers Institutes as well as Pavadrin, their latest answer to headaches.

"The first causes headaches; the other takes them away." He wasn't making any sense, but he didn't care. He beckoned the barman to refill their glasses. Should he take Miss Compliance Officer to bed? Her breasts were too small, but her tight behind, as flat as a boy's, suggested an interesting place to try a forced entry.

Audrey Walson was, he noted smugly, trying without success to regain her composure, returning his suggestive glances with dark, smoky eyes.

A shadow hovered over him. It was a page boy.

"Yes?" He continued to stare insolently at Audrey's body, smiling the thin-lipped smile the girls had always fallen for in the good old days, before he'd lost his mind.

"Sir, there is a telephone call for you, sir, from Madame Towers in the South of France." Above the bar, the clock showed 11:40. Was this the first time she'd called? It couldn't be.

He didn't take his eyes away from Audrey, still smiling the same smile. "Tell Mrs. Towers I can't be disturbed. I am going to be tied up for a very long time." He knew he slurred the words, but their choice was deliberate. The page hovered uncertainly, then went away.

He clinked his brandy glass against Audrey's. "Would you like to be tied up for a very long time?"

She squirmed on her nonexistent rump as if a bee were stinging her there. "Literally?" She tried to laugh lightheartedly, but there was a nervous undertone.

"Literally," he said coolly.

To his surprise, she stood up. "I don't think so." Again, there was the nervous laugh. "Not with a married man, anyway."

If he'd wanted to, he could have persuaded her. She stood over him, rocking on high heels, still not sure whether he meant what she thought he meant, not sure whether she was walking away from the opportunity of a lifetime. He saw a ring of perspiration under her arm, darkening the cheap silk of her blouse. It sickened him. All women sickened him.

He slumped back in the deep chair and waved good-bye. "Sweet dreams, Audrey. I'll look you up sometime at the FDA." He watched her tight little behind as she walked disconsolately out of the bar.

There were plenty more where that came from, but first he had to decide what he was going to do—with Louise Towers and with his wife. They were no longer the same person.

Zurich, 1961

"THE AMERICAN FOOD and Drug Administration has a law that says drugs are different from cosmetics. There are legal definitions here—and the American Congress passed the laws in 1938. Until they are changed, the FDA has to enforce the act. The type of testing required to support cosmetics claims, you must realize, is drastically different from that needed to persuade the FDA to approve a new drug." Jan Feiner, senior vice-president of research and development for K. Averbach, paused, wondering if anything he was saying was sinking in.

The journalist, who looked as if he needed a shave, glanced at his notes. "You mean the kind of product a Louise Towers might describe as an overnight sensation will actually have been years in the making?"

"No, no, no."

Thank God, Victor wasn't here to hear him making such a mess of things. He tried to think of a simple way to get across what, above all, he knew Victor wanted him to get across, namely a contemptuous dismissal of Louise Towers's nonsensical claim for their latest skin product.

Jan tried another tack. "We are one of the world's leading pharmaceutical companies, above all concerned with drugs for health care, sold in every country of the world. However, no matter where else they are sold, in order for our drugs to be sold in the United States, all drug test results must be submitted to the FDA." Jan thought of a perfect example. "Last year an FDA researcher refused to allow a tranquilizer called Thalidomide, made by one of our competitors, a German company, to be sold in the United States, wanting further proof of its safety, although it was and still is on sale in Europe. Now, in fact, the German Ministry of Health has just issued a warning to physicians that it may cause birth defects. I doubt very much it will ever be allowed in the United States."

The journalist fidgeted and used his pen to scratch his forehead. Was he straying too far off the subject? Wearily, Jan went on. "What I'm trying to point out is that there are *never* any overnight sensations as far as drugs are concerned; it is a long and laborious route, whereas cosmetics don't need FDA approval. They . . ."

The hirsute reporter interrupted, "So, when a company with Towers's reputation brings out a product and calls it a revolutionary skin discovery, it could be suggested they are trying to avoid the lengthy drug-application procedure by passing it off as a cosmetic?"

How he longed to be back in his lab. "Or it could mean it's not revolutionary at all. That it's just a pleasant variant on the cosmetics out there already." His thoughts went to Helena Rubinstein. Louise was certainly following closely in her footsteps. "Calling it revolutionary isn't that unusual. As I recall, it's a word that has been around in cosmetics parlance for quite some time."

As the journalist probed and persisted in making him say the same thing in a dozen different ways, and then tried to imply that he already knew Victor and Jan were working for Averbach on both sides of the Atlantic on an "overnight skin sensation" themselves, Jan became more and more distant. How he loathed and detested interviews. He'd only given in to this request because Victor had been so insistent. He knew why.

Time magazine was working on a cover story about youth creams in general and Louise Towers's new "revolutionary discovery" in particular. They were doing a thorough job, asking their correspondents worldwide to report on anything that seemed significant in the cosmetics area. Somehow they'd found out that K. Averbach, the Swiss pharmaceutical giant, was working on something, and they'd tried to find out what it was, first from Victor, who was now head of research in the United States division, known as K. Avery. Victor had played dumb until he'd learned they were planning to put Louise on the cover. Then he allowed himself to be "persuaded" to give them the name of the researcher in Zurich, also working on the "secret project" code-named AC3, the researcher who just happened to be his own brother.

Once again Victor had rescued him, selling his talents to K. Averbach, where he himself had been steadily moving up the ladder, though Jan often warned him about too much self-promotion. Two years ago Jan had moved from the Dutch purgatory of Vreinsdrof's HQ, where Benedict Towers had had him "relocated," to Averbach's Zurich HQ. Now he headed their new cosmetics and toiletries division and even had a few press clippings of his own.

Paulina Sygorski, the buxom, Polish-born girl he'd been sleeping with on and off during the past year, and his right hand in the lab, had pasted them carefully in a book. "One day for your brother to see."

He didn't care about Victor seeing them. Victor knew how good he was, and how AC3, the project he was working on with vitamin-A derivatives, was moving along at an extremely hopeful pace. Work on this vitamin of such benefit to the skin had been going on since the forties, but only recently, through his contributions, had there appeared to be a light at the end of the tunnel. It was his secret prayer that one day Louise would learn that the man who was carrying out the most promising skin-care research in the world was the man she'd allowed her monster of a husband to ditch.

Louise was not the Ludmilla he burned for in the middle of the night, but he burned with hatred, not love. At least that's what he told himself—and told Victor, mostly to shut him up when he got on his favorite subject. "Why don't you settle down, Jan? Get married. Have someone to come home to, to look after you, the way Elise looks after me. I think you could do better than Paulina, but she's not bad. You could do worse. At least she's a good cook."

He wasn't interested. He was happy that his brother seemed content with a marriage that would have bored him into an early old age. Victor had told him he wanted a wife who could cook and sew and had "no grand ideas," and Elise fitted the job description perfectly. That wasn't for him, and neither was Paulina, although her hints about a more permanent relationship were becoming too obvious to ignore. The problem was, after the initial few months of intense sexual excitement, he couldn't stop himself from losing interest. Paulina was just another substitute for Ludmilla, as Katherine and Ivy had been before her. Would he have tired of Ludmilla if she'd come home with him that day? Would he suddenly have lost interest in her body, once she'd allowed him to explore it? No, he knew he never would have. She was his first and last true love.

As Jan returned to the lab, he was already trying to think of an excuse not to go up to Engelberg for the weekend to ski. Paulina was always nagging him about not getting enough fresh air, but it was just an excuse to get him to herself, away from the test tubes, away from what consumed him, the vitamin-A derivatives, the retinoids, the most exciting group of compounds to come to dermatology in a hundred years.

Who knew where his research was going to lead? What if he was the one to lead the way to a cure for aging skin? If he developed the first real youth cream? What would Louise have to say then?

*   *   *

Even though Suzanne was three months pregnant, she insisted on dancing the twist at the reception Benedict and Louise threw at New York's latest fancy restaurant, the Four Seasons, following the wedding of Benedict's longtime bachelor brother.

Benedict was relieved to see that Suzanne didn't look pregnant yet, though it wouldn't be long before people began counting. It was no use signaling to his impossible, wayward daughter to stop jiggling around the dance floor. Nor was it any use signaling to her asinine new husband, Reemer, to make her sit down. As Benedict had seen and heard too many times during the rollercoaster, on-again, off-again courtship, Suzanne ruled the roost totally in their household.

When she'd told them over dinner that she'd finally decided to make it legal, and he'd been fool enough to ask her why, she'd had the perfect answer, smiting Louise, knowing in her uncanny Towers way that he wouldn't be sorry or angry. Hell, no. Suzanne had been perfectly right to answer as she had.

"I'm pregnant, and since it doesn't look as if you're going to have any other heirs, Daddy, I think I'd better go through with it and have a legitimate baby before I run out of time. With any luck, it will be your first grandson."

Benedict frowned as, across the room, he saw Louise join everyone dancing the new dance craze, whirling round like some teenager, her Oleg Cassini tiered skirt billowing out to show her incredibly long stems. Charles was twisting along beside her, with another gorgeous piece of work, one of the Sanford twins. As Benedict watched, he saw Louise twist around until she was dancing with Charles and her partner was with the Sanford girl. It was a pleasure to watch them, but enough was enough. He walked through the twirling couples and said to his son, "Excuse me, Charles."

Instead of attempting the twist, he took Louise into his arms, keeping time to the music, dancing a fast quick-step. Smiling broadly for everyone to see, he whispered, "You're making a fool of yourself. Every time you twist around, you show your ass, so cool it."

She tried to move out of his arms, to go back to their table, but he hissed, "Keep dancing, but this time act your age. Leave the twist to those young enough to enjoy it."

So that was how her husband was going to behave today. Louise never knew anymore, but the pain his perfect verbal darts caused never lessened.

When they returned to their table, Marlene, Leonard's bride, was sitting there alone, her shoulders rounded, looking as if she wished she could hide somewhere. Louise felt sorry for her. No one knew better than she what it was like to become a member of the high and mighty Towers clan. Leonard, the one family member whom nobody paid much attention to, always overshadowed by Benedict, had surprised everyone by marrying for the first time at forty-five, not someone from the social register, but an unsophisticated "hick from Tennessee," as Suzanne described her, a twenty-eight-year-old nurse who'd looked after him when he'd broken his leg while skiing in Colorado.

"Let's have lunch when you get back from your honeymoon," Louise said impulsively.

Marlene blushed. "Ooh, I'd love that." She spoke with a soft drawl, which fascinated Louise, who still spent time practicing her English accent. She was glad to see that as she looked at her, Marlene straightened up. Perhaps she would learn quickly how to "fit in." She would help her as much as she could.

A beaming Leonard came over with a heavyset, swarthy man whom Louise recognized as Emilio Vicani, the head of Towers Pharmaceuticals in Italy. She saw Benedict's face brighten. Vicani was for the moment a favored employee, who had more than doubled profits in his area during the past year.

"Here is my little bride, Marly," Leonard said excitedly. "Marly, meet Signor Vicani, the brilliant Emilio. He's the one I told you about in the hospital, who always makes me laugh. He should have been a comedian, eh, Emilio?"

"Sit down, sit down." Benedict beckoned the Italian to sit beside Louise. "Glad you could come over for the festivities." Louise forced back a smile. As if he could have refused. It had been a royal command, a Towers reward for services rendered. Benedict went on jovially, "Bet you were surprised to hear there was at last a saintly girl out there who'd put up with my brother." He threw an arm around his brother's shoulder. "Well, Len, you sure proved one should never give up hope. Life begins at forty-five, eh?"

"*Gallina vecchia fa buon brodo,*" the Italian said silkily.

Both brothers said together, "What does that mean?"

With a decorous little bow, Emilio answered, "Old chicken soup makes better broth. It is an Italian saying." He hesitated, then added, "Usually made about ladies of a certain age." All three men roared with laughter.

Benedict winked. "I can vouch for that." He turned to indicate Louise with a wave of his hand. "Not exactly old, not exactly young, now that's the kind of broth every man would go to the well for."

Louise felt her body go cold. She could see that Marlene was embarrassed, not sure whether to join in the male laughter, not sure how to react or what to think. Louise wanted to get up, to go the ladies' room, and stay there until she was sure she could smile without sobbing, but she did nothing.

Charles was twisting away in front of their table now, spinning the Sanford girl around, laughing gaily, looking like a movie star. Swiftly, out of nowhere, came a stab of jealousy to make her pain worse. How she longed to be dancing, twisting, twirling with him, laughing freely, with no pretense, no hidden agendas or meanings, feeling the support of his presence as she often did during the working day.

Louise clenched her hands together beneath the tablecloth as she heard the Italian say, "Your son is so handsome, such a great asset to the company. He is not yet married, no?"

Benedict shook his head ruefully. "No, I'm afraid not, my friend. It seems the Towers men are often late starters."

"May I ask how old he is now? He looks so young."

"He is young." She hadn't meant to say it. Benedict shot her a quizzical glance.

"My wife is getting sensitive over our jokes, but she's right. Charles is young, and so is my beautiful wife. What's the difference between your ages? Five years, six?"

Leonard, in his usual ponderous manner, said, "Charlie was born in 1930 . . . so he's about to be thirty-one. And Louise? I don't know the year you were born, my dear." He tried a clumsy compliment. "I'd say you're ageless."

Benedict was tired of the conversation. He cut in with a note of finality, "No beautiful woman talks about her age. It's unimportant except when a man is looking for a wife because he wants an heir." He swiveled around and yelled, "Waiter, waiter, we need more champagne over here."

Of course, they'd had it out. Why didn't she want his child? Why had she deceived him? Things between them had never been the same since Benedict found the birth-control pills she'd so carelessly left in the hotel room in the South of France. Benedict hadn't contacted her for almost a week. She'd been frantic, because first Charles and then Suzanne and David Reemer had been called away on some company business never fully explained, and she'd been left alone, trying to reach Benedict for over twenty-four hours. When she'd arrived at their rendezvous in Paris on Sunday to find that Benedict wasn't there, she'd been convinced he was dead.

It had been the worst day of her life. Guilt had swamped her, remembering the strange, inexplicable attraction she'd felt for Charles on their trip to Grasse, feelings she'd stifled, feelings she'd never understood. The evasive answers from the Towers French office when she'd tried to discover Benedict's whereabouts, the embarrassed attempts to convince her he was perfectly all right, had made her realize his absence was deliberate, that she was being taught a lesson, that something had happened to put their marriage in jeopardy.

She'd stayed in Paris, not venturing out of the hotel suite, sick and afraid. A courier had brought her an airline ticket to New York with a terse note from Benedict telling her he would meet her at the New York apartment on her return. He never told her where he'd been; she never asked. He had been cold, aloof, unmoved by her total capitulation, begging for his forgiveness, attempting to explain the necessity to give herself a little more time, a few more weeks, a few more months to get the business going before trying to get pregnant.

Although Benedict had to know that Alexandra Sanford was involved—he'd told her he didn't want her to see so much of the woman she felt was her only real friend—didn't blame Alexandra for introducing her to the pills, for suggesting she take every protection she could, so she could become the star she was destined to be, and not be saddled with children and houses and housekeeping as Honey had been.

No, it wasn't Alexandra's fault. It had been her decision. Nothing Alexandra could have said would have persuaded her to take the pills if, from the day the Louise Towers Institute opened, she hadn't decided she wanted no interruptions, no pregnancies, no children—at that time—to hinder her on the way to building her own beauty empire.

Louise had tried to equate it with fate. She'd told herself that God must have wanted her not to have a child because, despite the amount of lovemaking they'd made day in, night out, before the magic pill became available, somehow she had never conceived.

The terrible confrontation had happened that September. Benedict hadn't touched her then or for some time afterwards, often not coming home, never telling her where he was going or where he'd been. She had cut down enormously on going to the Institutes, leaving much too much to David Reemer. She had waited submissively at home, studying as she'd studied in the past, but this time not subjects dictated by Benedict to make sure she could make good conversation at dinner parties. Oh, no, she didn't study foreign affairs, French plays, or English literature, but chemical manuals, old-fashioned treatises about the skin and the body, the skin, and the brain, learning everything she could about the skin, as she patiently waited for Benedict to change, to forgive her—and one night the old Benedict had come home.

At least she'd thought so at first. It was a couple of days before

Thanksgiving, and she'd been sitting in the library, feeling as solitary and lost as she'd felt in the early days in Palm Beach with Milos. She'd worn a new yellow cashmere dress, a straight sheath with pearl buttons on the high collar. It had reminded her of the yellow cardigan she'd worn the day Benedict came to the apartment in London, but when she thought of Benedict making love to her, it was Charles's face in her mind, supplanting the stern, reproachful Benedict she was now living with.

That night, when he'd seen her sitting by the library fire, eyes closed, lost in memories, he'd carried her upstairs and gently unbuttoned the high collar, lifting the soft wool over her head.

She'd been ecstatic, sure all was going to be well again, but when she was naked, he'd lain on the bed and pushed her head down, directing her mouth to bring him to orgasm, leaving her wanting, frustrated, explaining carefully that from now on, that was the way it was going to be.

The edict hadn't lasted, but even wrapped in Benedict's arms with his penis deep in her, Louise no longer felt the security of his love. As his moods swung from one end of the barometer to the other, neither was she sure anymore how she felt about him. She had fallen into a behavior pattern, hypersensitive about displeasing him, carefully following his instructions at home and at work, as everyone around him did. At the same time she grew in need of solace, of a confidant or at least a trusted companion, but there was no one to trust—except Charles.

For the past year, since it had become obvious that Suzanne's affair with David Reemer was serious, she'd often felt that Charles was the only person working for Louise Towers she could really rely on to tell her the truth about corporate decisions, about long-term plans. Because she had hurt Benedict so deeply, he retaliated by refusing to discuss what was going to happen to the company, now frequently referred to in the press as "the extremely profitable cosmetic division of Towers Pharmaceuticals."

"We're running one of the biggest drugstores in the world, Lu," Charles told her over lunch a couple of months after Leonard and Marlene's wedding. They had traveled to Washington, D.C., together that morning to look at a larger location for what the family called "the White House Louise Towers Institute."

Since the Kennedys had moved in, the town seemed full of vibrant, attractive young men and women, and the original Louise Towers salon was now woefully inadequate to cope with all the increased business that an early visit from Jacqueline Kennedy had guaranteed.

They were lunching at the exclusive F Street Club, where Charles had just become a member and where Benedict had been a member since the Truman days. "Whoever sits in Dad's chair has to make all the final decisions. It's such an awesome responsibility, I still wonder how Dad can sleep at night," Charles said. "I sometimes can't sleep, just thinking about what he has to do. I can't imagine I could ever do it. I mean, look at us now. Can you imagine Dad taking time out to celebrate the kind of insignificant real-estate deal we just pulled off?" Charles looked at Louise sheepishly. "Frankly, I didn't expect you to agree to my suggestion that we take advantage of my new status as an F Street Club member and treat ourselves to a leisurely lunch."

"We deserve it, Charlie. We never have lunch together. Today is a treat." As Louise looked at him across the perfectly starched, snowy white cloth, she wondered if he was aware of her as a woman at all. Did he think of her only as his father's wife, or as the creator of Louise Towers? How did he think of her, if at all? Did he realize the difference between their ages was only three years, seven months, and nine days? Something she was ashamed she'd taken the trouble to work out one day. Could he see how happy she was, just sitting alone with him, eating fairly indifferent lamb chops? Could he see the difference between the tense Louise in New York and the relaxed Louise off duty here?

She sighed inwardly. Probably not, thank God.

Benedict was arriving late that afternoon because they were attending a dinner at the White House in honor of the President of France. Their presence would be noted in all the society columns. "The supremely successful (or soignée or sophisticated) Mr. and Mrs. Benedict Towers," it would say, or something similiar. Whatever adjectives were used, they would certainly be laudatory because Mr. and Mrs. Benedict Towers had become one of the most admired, talked about, and envied couples in America, part of the Camelot court around the Kennedys, but Louise hadn't given much thought to what she would wear at 7:00 P.M. when she had to be on parade. She had cared how she would look now, her hair painstakingly coiled into a braided topknot, tied with a jaunty emerald green bow that exactly matched the collar and cuffs of a pristine white linen suit.

She tried to concentrate on what Charles was saying.

"Do you feel overburdened sometimes, Charlie? Is that what you're trying to tell me? Do you feel too much is expected of you as the son and heir?"

He gave a wry little smile. "You know, it's funny, Louise, but I've just realized I've begun to talk to you the way I only used to talk to Suzanne." He hesitated, then added quickly, "I'm not complaining or anything. Suzie's too preoccupied with all her mother-to-be stuff, her natural childbirth classes and all that jazz." For a moment Charles looked at Louise so intently she became nervous and at the same time excited that the look meant something, something special between them, but no, the look meant nothing, as it certainly had to mean nothing, nothing at all.

"It didn't take me long to understand why Dad wanted you with him . . . why he married you. You're probably the reason he can do all he does." He laughed sunnily, once again, without a care in the world. "You've kept him young."

How she would have treasured those words once. Now, knowing how adrift her marriage was, she felt an impostor, a sick-in-the-head impostor, seeking something that was unattainable, a younger, kinder, above all gentler Benedict, the kind of man he could have been and perhaps long ago was, the kind of man his son, Charles, who bore him such a strong physical resemblance, had turned out to be.

Louise sat with what she hoped was an understanding smile on her face as Charles poured out his aspirations, his dreams. "I really enjoy working with you, Louise. I love the way your mind works. I know you love the cosmetics part of the business, and so do I. As I've told you before, it's the only part of Towers I feel thoroughly comfortable with. I do believe I understand something about women and their lack of confidence about their looks. You've taught me that. I enjoy the product planning, the consumer reaction reports, the focus groups. I don't think Dad would understand how much I enjoy it; that's why I don't tell him. I don't want him to transfer me into another division. You're the one who's shown me where I should concentrate my energies."

Louise felt she was blushing with pleasure. "I'm so happy to hear that, Charlie. It's like . . . like getting a present, a bonus."

"A bonus?" He looked at her searchingly again. "You must get bonuses all the time for what you've done and are doing with the beauty products." He moved awkwardly on the chair. "I hope you don't feel badly about not being on the main board." He hesitated, then said quickly, "Of course, my mother never was, but then she took no part in the business. Perhaps you don't know, but neither was my grandmother. Dad's told me many times how many ideas she contributed to the company, when Granddad really started building Towers into something sizable—although, of course, not in the incredible way Dad has done. As I grew up, I often thought it must have riled Grandma plenty, seeing the husbands of Granddad's five sisters being invited onto the board just because they married the right women. It's lucky he didn't have any brothers!"

A tottering old waiter, who looked more like a family retainer in an English country home, came to ask them solemnly whether they would like a savory, a dessert, some splendid Stilton, or, he added with a toothy smile, "A little of each, sir? Mr. Towers, Mrs. Towers?"

Louise knew she was blushing now. Mr. and Mrs. Towers. She shook her head quickly. "Just coffee, please."

Charles ordered the savory, mushrooms on toast, to be followed by a piece of Stilton. "May I suggest a fine old port, Mr. Towers?"

"You certainly may." When the waiter went out with their orders, Charles and Louise laughed together like conspirators. "A fine old port at lunch? I think I'm going to enjoy being a member here," said Charles. "It's like being back in London. What were we talking about? Oh yes, the board. You probably know that Dad has always had problems with Norris over that. My grandfather set Towers up as a family business to keep outsiders out, but he couldn't have dreamed how huge the company was going to become." Charles leaned back in his chair and checked off on his fingers, as if to remind himself. "Let's see, there are at least fifty factories around the world, ten research centers, a network of thousands of salesmen and detail people—you know, those who call on doctors and hospitals to sell them drugs."

Louise nodded. Of course she knew everything he was telling her, but she didn't stop him, waiting for him to get to the point. She had already guessed what it was.

"Frankly, I feel that Dad should consider allowing someone as exceptional as Norris on the board. When I joined last year, I even mentioned it, but got my head bitten off, so it probably won't happen, at least not . . ." Charles didn't finish the sentence. There was an embarrassed silence, then he said, "But you are the perfect exception; perhaps one day the rules will be changed for you—as the most valuable member of the family."

Louise could see he was beginning to look uncomfortable, probably wishing he hadn't brought the subject up. Was he testing her? Would he report her reaction back to his father? "I mean, you're never going to rock the boat by wanting to sell any stock," Charles continued earnestly. "As you know, it can't be sold—it's a closely held corporation. Only if all the board members agree could that happen. And Dad would never agree."

It was time to stop him. "I've never expected to be on the board, Charlie, dear." She meant it. It had never occurred to her. All she hoped was that Benedict hadn't changed the original arrangement they'd made when the first Louise Towers Institute opened on East Sixty-second Street. "We're partners, fifty-fifty," he'd said. "Your talent, darling, my money." She hadn't thought where the money was coming from then—from Benedict's own money or Towers Pharmaceuticals; to her it had been one and the same. She hadn't thought about a lot of things because she'd been so green, so naive.

Although the last person she was going to tell was Charles, more and more she lay awake in the middle of the night herself, wondering what the financial situation really was as far as Louise Towers was concerned, now that in its own way it had grown as phenomenally as the original Towers Pharmaceuticals company had grown following Benedict's return from the war.

Outside the family, Louise knew, all their friends and acquaintances assumed the beauty business was as much hers as Benedict's, but she had no control over the financial running of the company and didn't even know how it was set up. Was it still a separate company?

In the beginning, she knew, Benedict had viewed the Louise Towers Institute as her plaything, an attitude she hadn't wanted to contradict. She blamed herself bitterly for the amount of time it had taken her to realize that once the sales of Revelation went through the roof and first David Reemer and then Charles came to work full-time for Louise Towers, perhaps the company would be swallowed up by its mighty parent. She still didn't know, but one day, not too far off, she was determined to find out exactly where she stood.

She was ashamed, as she knew she should be, to admit to anyone that she received no actual salary, but only a limitless expense account, and what until recently she had considered a huge bonus on her birthday and at Christmas. It was ironic how thrilled she had been even to have her own bank account, with the statements sent to Benedict's office so that she never needed to balance her account. When it was below five thousand dollars, Benedict simply called to tell her he was "topping it up." No independence for her in that situation, but it had taken her all this time to know it.

"Well, I'm glad about that." Louise jumped as Charles spoke in a hearty sort of way. Glad? About what? Oh yes, her answer to his question about the board. She couldn't help being amused. However she felt about him, attracted to him or not, at that second she was keenly aware of how much of a Towers Charles really was. *Well, I'm glad about that.* Louise could hear Benedict's end-of-discussion note of finality in Charles's voice. It signaled the end of his worrying about her feelings as far as board membership was concerned. She was not a born Towers, not a male relative by marriage, so he accepted immediately that she had never expected to be considered.

"What I'm getting at is, I can't see how I could ever take over from

Dad and run the whole shebang," Charles went on, between bites of his Stilton. "It just isn't in me to control an empire, and that's what Towers Pharmaceuticals is, a bloody empire, with many regions run by able presidents, in many cases far more able than I, all looking to that certain chair in New York City for the final word."

When Louise said nothing, he leaned back, scrunched up his eyes, and smiled. "Let's hope and pray Suzanne gets what she wants most in the world, a son. She's sure it's going to be, because the bulge is hanging low and the baby never stops kicking, or something weird to that effect."

Louise smiled back. "You mean because a grandson could be groomed from birth to sit in your father's chair in New York one day?"

"You've got it. Don't think for a second that my beloved sister doesn't have that in mind." Charles put a commiserating hand lightly on Louise's arm. "I'm not going to talk about the board again, but I have to tell you that probably one of these days, as Suzanne's husband, David Reemer will be invited on, but don't let that trouble you. Reemer will be more concerned with the earnest, serious side of the Towers business, with drugs, animal nitrates and adhesives, pesticides and . . ."

Flushed from the port, Charles tried to think of another product made by Towers, beginning with *p*. With a flourish of his arm, he found it. "Pesticides and plastic explosives. But you and I can have a very good time running the profit-making Louise Towers cosmetics company together. I'd be very content with that, wouldn't you?"

Christopher David Towers Reemer, weighing in at a hefty ten pounds, was born two weeks before Arabian Nights, the first Louise Towers perfume to be heavily advertised, was launched.

At the elaborate christening party held a month later, Eugenia Sheppard was given an "exclusive" from Towers Pharmaceuticals's public-relations department and so, without being invited to attend, was able to divulge in her much-read column that "bottles of Louise Towers's new elixir, specially packaged in gold filigree with the christening date engraved on the bottom, were presented to every one of the female guests along with the christening cake."

What she wasn't able to divulge—because nobody, including the main participants, knew it at the time—was that the date of the christening party was destined to be remembered for another reason.

Suzanne, still plump from overeating during the pregnancy, was nevertheless glowing with pride in her son, with exquisite new pearls from her father around her neck, and the knowledge that she had scored a notable victory over Louise. She held court, receiving scores of friends, relations, and business associates in the drawing room of the Park Avenue apartment where she had grown up.

"He's di-vine . . . oooh, baby, baby, boo-ti-ful baby . . ."

"Can I hold him, Suzanne?"

"I wouldn't if I were you. He's still a kicker and a wetter." Screeches, squeals, gales of laughter, and baby talk filled the air as champagne glasses were refilled over and over again by the dutiful Thorpe and his core of well-trained waiters. When Master Reemer added howls of protest to the cacophany, a crisp Norland nurse, hired from England before the birth, scooped him up from Suzanne's lap and looked around the magnificent room for an escape route.

"Where can nanny change the child?" David Reemer asked Louise coolly. She wanted to slap his thin, arrogant face. Instead she ignored him and beckoned to Thorpe. "Please show the nurse the way to the primrose guest room. I believe she will find everything she requires in there."

Louise's head was aching violently, as much from the effort of smiling her good-hostess smile as from two interviews Benedict had insisted she agree to do earlier that day with members of the powerful British press, one with the U.S. correspondent of London's *Daily Telegraph*, followed an hour later by one with the women's editor of *The London Sunday Times*.

There was to be the first Louise Towers Institute in a store, not just any store, but the most famous store in the world, Harrods of London. Louise had had to learn it from David Reemer, who, she discovered, Benedict had sent to London to negotiate the deal.

It hadn't been difficult to appear before the journalists as Benedict directed. "Be cool, mysterious, full of secrets that only you know to help a woman's skin and appearance." It would have been impossible for her to show any excitement or enthusiasm for a project she knew so little about. Things couldn't go on like this for much longer.

Louise looked around the room for Charles. He had been in the Midwest when she received the Harrods news, but surely he must have been aware of the purpose of Reemer's trip. Why hadn't he told her? The only explanation was that his father had told him not to. She had to find out for herself, but he'd only returned the day before for the christening, where he'd been obviously proud to be one of Christopher's godfathers.

Louise couldn't see him in the crush. Then she heard his voice behind her. He had his back to her. She couldn't see his face as Suzanne was saying, "But I can't believe you've never met Blythe. She's

Maisie's famous little sister. Well, not so little. I had no idea all those overhead serves could make one shoot up as tall as a beanstalk . . ."

A slender, ash-blond girl was smiling good-naturedly at Suzanne as she prattled on. Charles interrupted reprovingly as Louise joined them. "Beanstalk! Watch your language, sis. I think we can come up with a more appropriate description than that. Of course, I've heard all about you, Blythe, but somehow I don't think we've actually ever met."

Louise put a light touch on his arm. He wheeled around, his face lighting up. "Oh, now here is the famous one in our family, Louise, my father's wife, Louise Towers herself. Louise, meet the next American Wimbledon champion, Miss Blythe Robertson."

Again Louise dutifully smiled her good-hostess smile, wondering how she could get Charles to herself for a few minutes to discuss Harrods. She barely observed the girl being introduced. To her she was just another all-American girl. The drawing room seemed full of them, all taller than average, lightly tanned, with perfectly shaped haircuts and nails and whiter-than-white teeth, exuding breeding, a life of privilege, lived in the freshest of air, the most comfortable of backgrounds. It made Louise sick to see their easy complacency with everything they had, comparing it to her sister Natasha's heartrending letters of appreciation for the little she was able to send her.

"Are you still training at Teach Tennant's tennis clinic in La Jolla, Blythe?" asked another blonde in the circle around Suzanne.

"Oh yes, you never stop training."

"I read somewhere that Teach is pretty demanding. Don't you have curfews or something like that? And horrible diets with no ice cream or martinis allowed?"

Still good-naturedly, Blythe responded, "Something like that, but it's not so bad."

"You two should get to know each other," Suzanne cut in, looking at Charles in an exaggeratedly pointed way.

Blythe laughed carelessly, about to turn away, when to Louise's surprise Charles said quickly, "I'd like that. How long will you be in New York, Blythe?"

"Maybe longer than I want to be." Louise hated the cool, disinterested note in the girl's voice. "I've sprained a tendon, so I'm under doctor's orders for the moment. I have to check in again in a few days."

Louise wanted to shout, *No, stop, no!* as Charles laughed and went on, "Maybe that's my good luck. Are you free for a tendon-resting dinner tonight? I hear the new French place, La Grenouille, is pretty good despite its froggy name."

Suzanne cackled. "Blythe, you'd better say yes before my brother changes his mind. He doesn't give out those invitations so lightly since he started working for his slave-driving stepmama here." There was no missing the malice in Suzanne's voice as she nodded at Louise.

Charles said airily, "Don't believe a word of it, but perhaps we do have a product for your tendon, Miss Robertson. After all, Elizabeth Arden created her Eight-Hour Cream for her fillies' tendons. We can do better than that. Louise Towers concentrates on people, not horses, right, ma'am?"

As he winked at Louise, everybody laughed. To her horror, Charles slipped his arm through Blythe's and very obviously started to move her out of the circle around Suzanne. Over his shoulder he winked at Louise again, oblivious of her strained expression as he said loudly, "Let's go somewhere quiet, Blythe, so that Dr. Towers from the Louise Towers Institute can prescribe the best miraculous lotion and potion for your condition."

How she got through the rest of the afternoon, Louise didn't know. She ached inside and out as she saw Charles and Blythe first sit together on a window seat in the library, chatting away animatedly, and then, soon afterwards, slip out of the apartment. It's nothing, it means nothing, she told herself. And then, This is healthy. He has been working too hard. Thank God, this girl is a replica of hundreds he must have gone out with, friends and college roommates of Suzanne, duplicates of Suzanne he must have been dating for years, probably even slept with. They're all the same; this one is no different . . .

What business was it of hers anyway? Why did it hurt so much to see Charles enjoying the company of a girl at least ten years younger than she? Was it because Benedict made a point of telling her she was no longer so young? Alexandra had once told her that was because Benedict himself was afraid she would grow more and more aware of the age difference between them. Was she jealous because she'd never had a happy-go-lucky youth, because she wanted to go dancing, dining, dating? Or was she jealous for a sicker, more serious reason? She didn't know.

Two weeks before the gala Harrods opening of the Louise Towers Institute in London, Benedict flew down to Washington with Charles on the company's new Gulf Stream aircraft to attend a ceremony at the White House. President Kennedy had invited them to a reception for Frances Kelsey, a researcher with the Food and Drug Administration who was to receive a medal of honor for what the *Washington Post* described as "her courage and devotion to the public interest, in preventing thalidomide-produced birth defects in thousands upon thousands of U.S. infants through her actions in denying approval for the infamous drug to be sold in this country."

"We're the only outsiders here, Dad," Charles whispered nervously as they waited for the President to arrive. "I can't see anyone from the competition, nobody from Eli Lilly or Pfizer or Squibb, and frankly I'm not surprised. In fact, I'm amazed anyone from the drug industry was invited, despite our snow-white reputation."

"That's right, Charlie, we're here because we're friends of the family, but that doesn't mean our industry isn't going to be damnably affected by this thalidomide disaster."

In the audience was Audrey Walson, who Benedict knew would not attempt to acknowledge him. She was looking particularly chic in a beautifully cut navy suit that emphasized the flatness of the rump he now knew so well. He presumed the last check he'd given her had paid for the suit. It was the only way she could look halfway decent on the ridiculous salary she received from the FDA. On the lapel was the small diamond owl he'd given her the year before as a tribute to the long, drawn-out sounds she made when she came. "Like some fucking owl," he'd told her the first time. "What's with you with all that whoo-whooing?" She couldn't help it, she'd told him. "I held my breath because it hurt so much at first, then when I began . . . began to come, well, I guess my breath came out like that." It amused him, and her tight behind still excited him because he rarely had time to spend there.

He waited for the surreptitious look that he knew would not be long in coming, and casually, without smiling, appraised her from across the room. He knew she was hopeful he would see her sometime today. He knew her pants would be moistening. She would be trying to control the quickening of her breath. She ran her tongue over her lips and slowly moved her hand to touch the brooch. It was a clear message, but he hadn't made up his mind. He looked away. He would not look at her again. He knew she would be waiting for him in her apartment if he felt like sex later on.

The ceremony was brief but beautifully handled by the handsome President, who, to Benedict's eyes, looked younger and more relaxed than ever, despite what had to be the huge weight on his shoulders with the increasing menace of the Russian presence in Cuba.

"We're going to have to put some extra police on you guys," the President said to Benedict affectionately as he mingled with the guests. "God gave us Frances Kelsey to look over this country, but we've got to introduce some kind of consumer protection to ensure that we don't have to rely on the brilliance of one person anymore. It's ludicrous. We've got to pass a consumers' bill of rights to prevent you guys from confusing buyers of prescription drugs, to introduce the whole truth and nothing but the truth in packaging. Don't you agree, young Charles?"

As Charles began to mumble in embarrassment, Benedict answered for him. "Mr. President, sir, I agree the consumer needs every bit of protection he can get, but I'd love it if you would allow me to explain to you sometime, sir, exactly the testing procedures we go through before we even begin to submit our new-drug application to the FDA . . ." But the President's attention was already being directed elsewhere.

Later, as they left the White House, Benedict spotted Senator Kefauver, who had been at the ceremony, getting into his car. "There's the stone in our shoe, son. After this sorry state of affairs, with what thalidomide has done to our industry's image, Kefauver's going to be able to push through legislation regulating the introduction of new drugs as easily as a knife sliding through butter. And that's just the beginning. God knows what else he's going to dream up to harass us, and Congress will go along with everything the man says."

Benedict looked at his watch. It was too early for dinner. Should he pay the tight little owl a visit? Although the President's tone had been bantering and light, he felt anxious and tense, which could mean he might not even be able to get an erection. Only Louise . . . He stopped that train of thought as long ago he'd schooled himself to do. "What are your plans, Charlie? I have a couple of appointments here in Washington, but we could meet for a quick dinner at the F Street Club before flying back to New York. There's the Harrods opening to discuss, and the Arabian Nights' sales figures, among other things."

As they waited for their car, he saw Charles's hangdog look. It was an expression he hadn't seen on his face for quite some time—in fact, not since he'd joined the Louise Towers division. In the old days, just after Honey's death, when Charles had first come back to New York to struggle along in the main drug division, he'd seen that expression on his son's face every day. "What's up, Charlie?" His voice was sharp. He couldn't help it. He always sounded sharp when he was anxious about his children, as he was now.

Their car was three away in the line up to the portico. "Nothing, Dad. Well, yes, there is something I'd like to talk to you about. The problem is, I can't have dinner tonight."

"You've got a date in New York?"

"Yes, sir."

"Well, don't look so miserable about it. That's good news. What else is on your mind?" They climbed into the car. "Where do you want to go? I imagine National Airport? You have a reservation?"

"Yes, Dad, but I've got lots of time yet. What time's your next appointment?"

To hell with it. Benedict dismissed all thoughts of seeing Audrey. Some other time. Without explaining his change of plans to Charles about staying in Washington, Benedict said to his driver, "Call Wes, tell him we'd like to take off in an hour." He turned to Charles. "We'll go back together on the Gulf Stream, and you can tell me what's bothering you."

His eyes misted over unexpectedly as Charles tried to get out what Benedict had already guessed. They were well up over the capital, and his son was telling him the oldest story in the world, a love story. "I know it sounds crazy, Dad, but I can only say it was love at first sight. We met at the christening four months ago and we had dinner that night and I knew right away this was it. So did she. She's Maisie Robertson's sister, Blythe. Maisie was Suzanne's roommate in . . ."

"I know, I know. Suzanne told me you'd met your match at last."

"She did?"

She hadn't, but Suzanne had mentioned to him how thankful she was that Charlie was seeing one of their own sort. He knew it was a crack, even if Suzanne hadn't been aware of it herself. Perhaps not. She'd been making cracks for so many years about Louise, she probably didn't even know when she was doing it now. Well, so was he thankful. Blythe Robertson was an outstandingly suitable candidate as a wife for his son and heir.

"You want to marry her?"

"Yes, Dad."

"Well, what's wrong with that? I think it's an eminently sensible idea."

"Our schedules."

Benedict frowned. "What do you mean?"

"I don't want to go to London for the Harrods opening because Blythe is playing in the U.S. Open, and it's the biggest match of her life. Then, if she wins, there'll be other tournaments that don't work with my commitments and we have to find a date that works with both our schedules. She lives for tennis." Charles paused and then said hesitantly, "Blythe isn't like other girls. She doesn't want a fancy wedding. She just wants to get married quietly so it doesn't interfere with her training."

"You mean you've already proposed and she's accepted?"

"Oh yes, that's not the problem." Benedict started to laugh at Charles's matter-of-fact voice.

Charles looked puzzled. "What's so funny?"

"You wouldn't understand." Benedict buzzed for the steward. "Open a bottle of Krug."

He leaned forward earnestly. "Forget about Louise Towers and Harrods, son. Why don't you elope?"

Charles began to feel elated. Here was the father he'd gone to London with so long ago, the father who'd confided in him about Ludmilla. God, he hadn't thought of Louise as Ludmilla for ages. This was the father who was his pal, his partner, who'd once treated him as a conspirator, the father he often forgot had to be there underneath the tense, fast-acting, brilliant tycoon businessman who was also his boss.

"No, we don't have to elope—I don't think Blythe would like that. She's ... well, she's quite old-fashioned in many ways, but I know she'd like to do it with a minimum of fuss, particularly since her dad died last year."

"Do you have a plan?"

"Yes, well, Maisie's apartment sometime before Thanksgiving ... Maisie's married quite well, to the middle son of the Parr Dobson banking family. They have a swell apartment on Sutton Place. Then we'd go down to the Parr Dobsons' house in Hobe Sound for our honeymoon before Blythe has to start on the '63 circuit. It means I couldn't attend the California cosmetics and drugs convention you asked me to attend, and since I already said I really want to be at the U.S. Open to give Blythe support, that means Harrods is out, if you really don't mind."

Benedict let Charles talk on, spilling out dates that would have to be overturned and Blythe's tennis tournament schedules. By the time they'd finished the bottle of Krug and the seat-belt sign was flashing, he'd given Charles his blessing and, looking at his own calendar, they worked out a November wedding date between them.

Louise was curled up on the sofa in the library when Benedict walked in. His heart jumped. She looked so lovely, vulnerable, and, yes, it struck him forcibly, lonely. There was so much distance between them. It was her fault for deceiving him; it was his fault for punishing her for so long. Talking to Charlie about being in love had made him remorseful, remembering his overwhelming passion for the innocent Ludmilla.

He never wasted time. It wasn't his style. He went and knelt beside her. She looked startled—no, afraid. He wasn't surprised. He knew how he dominated her life, and that was the way he knew it had to be for him, but he wanted her love too, not forced as if a pistol were at her head, but the total, selfless love she'd shown in the beginning.

"What is it? I didn't think you were returning tonight. Is something wrong?"

The words chilled him. Honey had used those words, and rightly so. Now there was no other love in his life. He'd used Audrey Walson to release his misery—and also to gain a close contact at the FDA, the most important agency in the world as far as his business was concerned—but she meant nothing. It was Louise who meant everything to him.

Now that his son was in love and preparing to share his life with a woman, Benedict realized the depth of his anguish, of his feelings for Louise. He wanted to share his life fully with his wife again. He'd spent four years punishing her, and the end result was that he'd punished himself just as much. It was ironic to think his own son had opened his eyes to that.

"No, nothing's wrong, my darling. In fact, everything is suddenly all right again. My son has just taught me a lesson. Can you imagine that, Charlie teaching me something?"

She looked at him guardedly, her dark eyes showing him she still expected the worst, poor girl.

"I've been too hard on you. That's going to change."

There were tears glistening in those dark eyes now, but she said nothing, did nothing.

He put his head on her lap, suddenly tired. "Charlie's in love," he said softly. "He made me realize how much I am still in love with you, although I've been trying for the past few years not to be . . . since you let me down so badly. Well, enough of that." He couldn't see her expression as he went on. "Yes, my son's in love at last, with the most perfect girl for him—just as you're the perfect girl for me."

He could feel Louise's body tense, and smiled, thinking her reaction was because at last he'd lowered his defenses and told her the truth about his love for her. "It's Blythe Robertson, a young tennis hopeful. Suzanne's friend Maisie's younger sister. They're going to get married in November in Maisie's apartment. He was worried, poor boy, because he thought I'd be mad that he does't want to go to London for the Harrods opening. He wants to stay in New York to support Blythe in her first important tennis match at the U.S. Open . . ."

Benedict went on talking dreamily about his conversation with Charles on the plane. He kept his head on her lap. He didn't see Louise's face. It was just as well.

Natasha

Prague, 1965

"DEAREST LUDMILLA, I have wonderful news . . ." Natasha threw down the pen in exasperation as the ink grew fainter and fainter. She tried to lick some life into it with her tongue, but it was dead, and Pieter had warned her he probably wouldn't be able to filch another one from City Hall soon, because they'd begun to count the stationery supplies again.

The expiration of the pen dispirited her. She lit a forbidden cigarette and went out onto the tiny roof garden, where a solitary flowering apple tree scattered its blossoms over the oxblood-red roof tiles below. She was three months pregnant, but looked more like six, because she'd developed such a passion for rolled waffles filled with whipped cream, a Prague speciality that, for some reason, were still easily available.

Soon Pieter, her loving husband, would be home from his deadly dull job, climbing the stairs to the two-room top-floor flat they'd been so incredibly lucky to be offered the year after their wedding. Pieter agreed with Natasha that somehow Ludmilla must have arranged it with undercover money slipped to an easily corrupted member of the housing bureau, because even in Czechoslovakia, Ludmilla, under her new name, had become a subject of national pride.

The flat was in Mala Strana, the street right under Hradcany Castle, the seat of the wretched Czech government. How Natasha wished she could put a bomb under the castle and see it and the Czech Communist party, a mere front for the real rulers in Moscow, go up in a glorious cloud of smoke.

They—she always thought of the government as "they"—were responsible for Pieter's lack of advancement, first depriving him of a university education and keeping him stuck in a dead-end job, where he was little more than a sticker-on of stamps. It was all because his father had spoken out once or twice and had spent time in prison for reading the totally forbidden Kafka. Well, at least Pieter hadn't been ordered to become a window cleaner like his cousin, who spoke six languages and had a degree in foreign studies.

Natasha took a few satisfying puffs of the cigarette Pieter had asked her not to smoke because of the baby, and went inside to find a pencil to continue her letter to her famous sister.

From Ludmilla's careful answer to the news of her marriage to Pieter, Natasha had sensed she wasn't as overjoyed as she'd hoped she would be to know they had at last been able to save up enough to get married. She suspected it was because her mother hadn't been overjoyed either and, although she denied it, had probably written to Ludmilla herself to say she thought Natasha could have done better.

As she wobbled out to sit beneath the apple tree to resume her letter, Natasha tried to imagine Ludmilla's face as she read she was going to be an aunt. The letters often took a long time to get to America. She hoped this one would reach her sister quickly, so that she could hear from her before the baby was born. She wanted reassurance that Ludmilla was happy to receive her mementous news. She wanted somehow to convey to her that she wasn't to worry, that she had done the right thing in marrying Pieter.

Natasha sucked the end of the pencil, thinking of how to write down in words the feeling of joy that was in her, joy to be carrying Pieter's baby, joy to be living away from the beauty salon with her own husband in a sweet if shabby little home with its own tiny garden, where apple blossoms fell like wedding confetti.

At half past five, Pieter came home. His supper was ready under the apple tree, set out on a clean, darned cloth on the rusty garden table. Natasha had prepared his favorite meal, two pieces of cheese and pickles and two pieces of salami, pale with fat. Not that she had much chance to vary it. Except for the rare parcels from Ludmilla, most food was getting increasingly hard to get. Also on the table was the letter to Ludmilla, sealed and stamped, ready for its journey across the seas to the land of the free.

"Did you tell your sister how happy you are, pusskin?" Pieter asked, ruffling her hair as she sat on his lap after he'd eaten.

"No, I told her you beat me and kept me locked up in a cupboard," she teased.

Pieter frowned. "I hope not."

Natasha laughed sunnily. Poor Pieter, he always took her so seriously, no wonder she liked to tease him. Her mother thought his lack of humor about their relationship showed a basic lack of intelligence, but Natasha knew better. It was because her Pieter loved her so much, he couldn't see or hear straight when she talked about their marriage.

"Don't be silly, of course I didn't. I told her you treat me like a princess, sit me on a silk cushion, and feed me too many waffles."

Pieter didn't respond. Then, "Petr Chramostova has been disgraced," he said in a tired voice, shifting Natasha's weight from one knee to the other.

Her eyes grew wide. Petr was one of her husband's immediate bosses, an attractive, flirtatious man who'd obviously admired her, one of the few party members she really liked. He had even come to supper one evening and asked her with obvious admiration about her sister's huge success in the United States.

"Why? What happened?"

"He was transferred last week, although I didn't know it. Something about a pamphlet he was distributing. Today I heard he had been sent to the coal mines in Bratislava, to become a stoker."

Pieter sighed heavily. Stoking was a regular punishment meted out to outspoken professors and impertinent intellectuals in Czechoslovakia. Through the underground, the word was out that it wasn't quite as bad as it seemed, except for living in permanent pollution, because with little coal to stoke and few supervisors around, there was often free time in which to write and think and exchange ideas with other opponents of the government.

Natasha threw her arms around Pieter's neck. "Oh, I don't like it, Pieter. It frightens me. Nothing ever stays the same. If anything ever happened to you I'd die." The young man cradled his wife like a baby.

"Nothing's going to happen to me. I'm too unimportant. I stay very, very quiet, don't you worry." He stared over her head as night began to fall and lights began to sparkle on the domes and steeples below them. "It's so beautiful . . . so beautiful . . ." he murmured.

Natasha stared out across the river, where blue electrical sparks off the tram wires looked like fireflies dancing in the dark. "And so ugly, too. Will we ever be free?" It was a familiar rhetorical question no one ever expected to be answered.

Pieter sighed again. "There is some sign. There are some people in the Politburo who I sometimes think could help bring about change . . ."

"But look what happened in Hungary when Nagy tried to bring in reform. We've only just begun to understand that was the reason he was executed, and now they say conditions in Budapest and everywhere are worse."

"No worse than here." Pieter kissed his wife's cheek. "Your face is cold. Let's go in." With his arm around her waist, they went into their little living room, where Pieter brought Natasha her calcium pill, put her feet up on a footstool, and switched on the radio to listen to Smetana. The radio, once his parents', had been their wedding present to them. As they listened to the music, Pieter began to unwind Natasha's braids, stroking her reddish-brown hair as she rested her head on his shoulder.

At half past eight, as he did every night, Pieter washed the dishes and prepared the pot for the coffee he would bring to Natasha in bed in the morning before he left for work. Then he went into the bedroom to switch on the lamp and turn down the heavy coverlet. "It's time for bed, my beauty," he called out as he did every night.

Natasha, who had recently found herself dozing more and more, struggled to her feet and, yawning, started to undress. There was only one big cupboard in the apartment, just by the front door, so that was where she kept her clothes. Pieter's hung from an old-fashioned hatrack in the corner of the bedroom.

She sighed with relief as she unfastened her tight skirt and climbed out of her voluminous cotton knickers. In the long mirror she'd brought with her from home, she saw the reflection of her burgeoning white belly. "Oh, I'm getting enormous," she moaned. "I don't know how you can still look at me, let alone love me. I won't be able to see my toes soon." She moaned self-pityingly. "And to think I once dreamed of being a prima ballerina."

She crossed her arms coquettishly over her stomach, as Pieter looked at her. She smiled as he came over, as she knew he would. He went down on his knees and began to smother her belly with wet, noisy kisses.

"There can never be too much of you for me." He buried his face in her pubic hair, first his nose burrowing down into her, then his mouth.

"Oh no, no, Pieter," she laughed, but she didn't mean it. As he began to suck her, her excitement mounted and she leaned back against the wall, grabbing his hair for support. She cried out with ecstasy as his hands reached up to clutch and squeeze her full breasts and his tongue went on probing her into a long, sweet orgasm.

Just before the board meeting, Benedict broke the news to Suzanne that he would be announcing the successful results of a feasibility study he'd commissioned to turn their family estate in Palm Beach into Louise Towers's first spa.

Suzanne was only half listening. She was annoyed with her children's nanny that day, and even at the board meeting she had had trouble concentrating on Towers business, particularly when her father asked his brother, Leonard, to give them the good news about Towers's new appetite suppressant, Temperate.

Leonard had such a lackluster way of speaking that as his voice droned on about the pill exceeding its projected first three months' sales, Suzanne's thoughts were miles away.

The meeting only came to life for her when her husband, newly elected to the board, was asked to position Temperate against all the other drugs available to help Americans lose weight. "I have just received these figures. Sixty million dollars is spent annually in the United States today on weight-loss-related drugs, exactly double what was spent five years ago. Americans' new preoccupation with keeping in better shape is also reflected in the phenomenal success of a Queens housewife, Jean Neditch, who founded the Weight Watchers organization over two years ago. This is a small operation we might consider acquiring, but first we have to address how our Louise Towers division can best take advantage of this new American pursuit of happiness. It appears to me . . ."

Suzanne was so proud of David's maiden speech as a board member that she didn't realize until her father began to speak that Temperate's wild success was one of the reasons for the Palm Beach feasibility study.

As Benedict analyzed the enormous public-relations value—though it was a small financial addition to the balance sheet—of Elizabeth Arden's Maine Chance Spas, open in Maine in the summer and Phoenix in the winter, the horror of what was going to happen descended like a black cloud.

"Next year you won't recognize my beloved winter home for all these years," she sobbed to Maisie over lunch. "During the summer it's being totally gutted, expanded, and turned into one of those pampering palaces for the overweight nouveau riche. Oh, Maisie, it means my children will never, never know the carefree winter vacations in the sun that Charlie and I enjoyed."

Maisie tried to calm her down. "Darling, you must admit none of the family have spent much time in Palm Beach since . . . since your darling mother's accident." Maisie cooed on. "If you really love it so much, why don't you buy a place down there for yourself?"

Suzanne shuddered dramatically. "Impossible! The Towers name will stand for commerce in Palm Beach from next year on." More angry tears came to her eyes as she spat out, "I can't bear to think of it! Imagine all those fat, over-jeweled, blue-haired matrons being massaged on our patio, exercising in our pool, sleeping in our bedrooms! I just can't bear it. My darling mother must be turning over in her grave!"

To placate his daughter, Benedict ordered David to take Suzanne on a short vacation, "away-from-it-all" in Lyford Cay, a private enclave on the island of Nassau in the Bahamas, where a well-manned entrance gate kept out anyone who was not at least a millionaire. "It will do you good to have a rest," Benedict said guiltily.

Was Suzanne happy to be away from her fifteen-room Fifth Avenue apartment? Away from supervising her staff of five, which included not only the Norland-trained nanny, but also nanny's Puerto Rican assistant, now that baby Fiona, born scarcely a year after brother Christopher, was also in the nursery?

"No," said David Reemer, scarlet with the sun, and irritible after an unsatisfactory day on the immaculate Lyford Cay golf course. "You're never happy, never satisfied, for longer than it takes me to turn around, are you Suzanne? What's eating you up today?"

"Oh, nothing, nothing. You'll never understand my feelings about Palm Beach. It's just as much your fault as Louise's for turning my home into a spa."

When David ignored her, she knew how to make him pay attention. "Since we're here, I'm going to talk to Harold Christy about that island he's got for sale, Moat Cay, it sounds too good to be true."

David Reemer threw his hands into the air in despair. "You'd be bored out of your mind after twenty-four hours living there. The idea makes me want to throw up."

"I talked to Maisie about it today," Suzanne said, cutting across him as if he weren't speaking. "She'd like to come in on the deal if I like it. I tried to reach Blythe, but as usual there was no one home and no one who spoke any known language to take a message. Charlie is in Paris again. I wonder when those two ever see each other. No wonder there's no sign of Blythe getting pregnant. They can only fuck once a month, if that."

"Oh, be quiet! You're beginning to bore me with that long-playing record. Can't we have a conversation without your using that word? It's . . ."

Again Suzanne plowed on. "Be quiet yourself. Let's see, I made a list somewhere. I thought if we got the right group together we could build a compound and all the children could grow up with the right people, the right friends, at least on vacation."

By the time the vacation was over, Moat Cay was Suzanne's, despite

David's repeated warning that it was in reality Remote Cay. The first thing she did on her arrival back in New York was to ask her father if he'd like to build a "cottage" in the Towers-Reemer compound.

In death she seemed to have shrunk even smaller than her diminutive four feet ten inches. She looked like a small, exquisite doll dressed in an ornately beaded tunic, which newspapers later recorded had been designed by Yves Saint Laurent, her fingers wearing the ruby and emerald rings Louise remembered so well.

As Louise paused beside Helena Rubinstein's casket, tears choked her throat and filled her eyes, hidden by dark glasses. Madame's features in death were so noble and strong, while her skin, astonishingly unlined, shone translucently, veiled in a delicate violet powder.

Louise blinked back the tears. She could hear that rasping voice, which could also be so cajoling. "I svear, if I live to be a hundred, there is no better cream in the world than my vake-up cream! Here, feel it on your skin. Is it not the cream of angels!" Well, Madame Rubinstein had almost made it to one hundred years, and her skin was indeed the skin of an angel.

Thousands of people had come to Campbell's Funeral Home in New York, where the beauty empress had lain in state for the past two days. Though she'd had to return earlier than planned from a California business trip, something had driven Louise to come. Until this moment she hadn't known why.

The old witch had been criticizing her publicly since she'd opened the first Louise Towers salon, almost eleven years before. She'd accused her of everything from stealing formulas and staff (only the latter was true) to "slavishly modeling herself on me in thought, vord, and deed." She'd refused every invitation Benedict and she had ever proffered; she'd shown her anger and enmity right up to her last gasp, but Louise now realized she would never have forgiven herself if she hadn't come to say her own private thank-you and farewell to the woman who had shown her a way to find her own identity.

But for Helena Rubinstein, Louise told herself, she would have been swept up by Benedict's ardor and become his mistress—and how that would have ended, she dreaded to think. Without the spur of a career in cosmetics with Rubinstein she would never have been able to resist Benedict's first proposal that day in London. Instead, she had become not only Benedict's wife, but now, after a stormy beginning, his trusted partner in a business that showed every sign of one day becoming as important and influential around the world as Rubinstein's own.

Among the sea of faces in the chapel, Louise thought she saw someone familiar, someone she had often wished she could see again, to make peace with him, even though she knew it would be impossible to resume their friendship. Could it be Jan?

Her heart beat faster as she tried to get through the crowd to where she thought she had seen Jan Feiner. Strangers, acquaintances, and business associates kept stopping her, trying to engage her in useless pleasantries, trying to find out how she felt, why she was here. The man she thought was Jan was now at the end of the room. "Jan, is it you? Jan . . . Jan . . ." Her voice was lost in the hubbub. He turned to speak to someone. It *was* Jan. She impulsively waved her hand, trying to attract his attention, but it was no use. He obviously couldn't see her. He was leaving.

She'd read somewhere only recently that Jan Feiner was now in the running for the top job with K. Avery. In the last few years at the parent company's head office in Zurich, Jan had apparently been building an enormous reputation for his work on skin care.

She hadn't mentioned it to Benedict because for all she knew he still harbored the strange jealousy against Jan that had led to his transfer to Holland years before. Well, there was nothing Benedict could do to him now, but there was no chance of any renewed ongoing friendship, even if the two companies weren't in competition. Jan's brother, Victor, also a K. Avery executive, had never ceased taking every opportunity to denigrate Louise Towers in print and in public. From the beginning, she knew, Victor had never liked her as a person and loathed the company Benedict had allowed her to build under her own name.

Louise decided she would call Jan at K. Avery—if not today, sometime during the week. She would call to wish him luck and congratulate him on all he had achieved. She hoped they could have a civilized, pleasant conversation. Perhaps she might even risk seeing him, if only for a few minutes, to tell him how happy she was about his incredible success. She had vowed never to keep anything from Benedict again, but this was different. She owed it to Jan to explain how she would always be grateful to him, not only because Revelation's success had proved to be the foundation stone on which the whole company had been built, but for giving her hope and courage during her dark days in London.

It was Benedict who had phoned her in California to tell her Madame Rubinstein had died. But, as he'd made clear in his inimitable way, Madame's death was only part of the reason for his call. "The Rubinstein business grosses nearly a hundred million throughout the world, but it's taken seven decades to get there. We're already well on the way, baby, and we're only in our second decade," he'd told her happily. "As you know, I thought seriously of buying Rubinstein once, but now I've got my own home-grown star. Now what do you think about that movie star's ranch property? It's buggy, but the guy who Suzanne and David told me drained the swamps successfully around Nassau for Lyford Cay could probably do the same for us. I like the idea of Louise Towers spas on both coasts, one for winter, one for summer."

"I think it's too hemmed in by the hills. It's still spring, but there's not much air," Louise had told him. "In summer it could become stifling. I think perhaps we should think of a cooler climate as a contrast to Florida. I'd say Maine, except that Elizabeth Arden is already there. Perhaps Colorado or Vermont or somewhere near to New York—in Connecticut. If it was Colorado, we could open year-round and in winter offer skiing as part of the spa program for those who prefer the snow to the sun."

He paid attention to her now in a way he never had in the past. And she, well, she made sure that Benedict never had reason to doubt that her every thought, awake and asleep, was for him and about him.

It was, she told herself, the reason she had suggested, and Benedict had concurred, that Charles should run the international division of Louise Towers, in order to spare her the constant traveling that the job demanded. There was no way Benedict could be without her for such a considerable amount of time. Charles was doing a wonderful job for the company, though the traveling had unfortunately not helped his marriage.

"There's trouble in paradise," Benedict had warned her at Easter, when Blythe hadn't turned up for the traditional Towers Pharmaceuticals Easter lunch. Held at company headquarters, it was an annual event at which Benedict, at his most expansive, announced a huge financial gift to the city's hospitals and kicked off an Easter egg hunt in Central Park. It was a command performance for the family, attended by Suzanne and David and their two babies, Christopher—now always called Kick—and Fiona; Leonard and Marlene and their chubby toddler, Zoe; as well as assorted cousins, nannies, servants—and Charles.

He had been closeted with his father for an hour after everyone, in various degrees of intoxication or exhaustion, left at about four, and hadn't needed to be persuaded to come back to the Park Avenue apartment for a glass or two of special brandy from Benedict's private reserve. Louise had known better than to mention Blythe's name. Benedict had even complimented her on her ability to cheer Charles up and take his mind off his marital worries after he'd finally staggered into the Towers limousine to be driven home at around seven-thirty.

She was still taking his mind off unhappy things. She'd asked him to accompany her today on her sad mission, and he was waiting for her in Campbell's main lobby as she emerged from the elevator, pale, beautiful, downcast.

"I didn't realize how much she meant to you," Charles said softly as, in the car, she took off her glasses and he saw what few people in the world ever saw, tears glistening in Louise Towers's eyes.

Charles looked miserable too. He'd lost weight, but he was better looking than ever, more and more a softer, sweeter, younger version of his father. He looked at her tenderly, compassionately, thinking, she knew, that her rare tears were for the old warhorse in the coffin she'd just left. They were, but they were also for herself. It was still the same. Whenever she saw Charles alone, which she didn't allow herself to do much anymore, she had the same insane sensation. She wanted to put her head on his shoulder and forget the world. She wanted his young, strong arm to crush her to him. She wanted . . . she didn't allow herself to think of what she wanted.

Louise put her suede-gloved hand in his and said, "I didn't realize how much she meant to me, either. I feel very, very sad that she never allowed me to thank her."

She was startled when Charles laughed, just as she was often startled when Benedict laughed for no reason she could understand.

"I'm sorry, Louise, I couldn't help it, but I mean how could you expect Madame Rubinstein willingly to receive your thanks for stealing away so many of her customers? She had nothing to thank you for, and she certainly didn't want to be thanked *by* you, either." Charles shook his head in wonderment. "That's what makes you so special. You really don't think the way most people do. I don't think you even realize how important you've become to women. Helena Rubinstein died knowing that Louise Towers had become a major threat to her business. I bet she thought about you every day."

"Do *you* think about me?"

How had the words escaped? It was because she was so vulnerable today, too much in touch with the painful past.

Charles was saying nothing she wanted to hear. "Do I? You must be joking. I work like a lunatic for Louise Towers, the company and the person." He squeezed her hand. "You mean the world to me. I told Dad"—he gulped like a child—"I told him only at Easter how much I'd hoped to have a marriage like yours and his, how much of a failure I feel." He looked at Louise hopelessly. "I'm sure Suzanne has told you if Dad hasn't. Blythe wants a divorce."

He let go of Louise's hand and stared straight ahead, his mouth fixed, bitter. "She blames Louise Towers, says no marriage could survive a travel schedule like mine, but that's not it. She's met someone else, another tennis player, a stud, a jerk . . ."

The words would come back to haunt her in the following months, but now Louise said, "What are you going to do?"

"I don't know. Dad says I shouldn't give up if I still love her. That I should take her away somewhere for a month or two, if I want it to work."

"Do you?"

"That's the trouble. I don't know. When we're apart I miss her—terribly. I want her—terribly."

Louise wanted to shut out his voice. She couldn't bear to hear him say any of this, but she sat upright, poker-straight, hoping he'd see she didn't want him to go on, but he didn't notice.

"Then when we meet it's so tense, so full of tension—hate, I suppose—I just want to cut loose." He put his head in his hands, his voice tearful, muffled. "I don't want to lose her, but I don't think we can live together anymore."

"Why don't you go away by yourself for a few days? Forget about business, go somewhere to think things out by yourself." As she spoke, Louise was telling herself, he doesn't really love her—it's his pride. They were never suited; she has no sensitivity; she was always only interested in the Towers name. She was never a real wife to him, always away on some tennis circuit, although she's never come near succeeding there, either.

"No, I've tried going off on my own. I even . . ." Charles leaned back against the seat with his eyes shut. "I shouldn't be telling you this, but I even slept with someone I met when I went skiing in February after closing the research agreement in Geneva. It was one of the few times Blythe came with me on a business trip. That's when I found out about the tennis player. I was so crazy, so out of my skull, I wanted to shoot him or someone. I left Blythe at the hotel and went to this little village up in the Alps and just . . . just slept with the first pretty girl I could find."

Crazy? She was going crazy too, just listening to him. He'd slept with someone . . . just like that . . . the first pretty girl. The car was pulling up to the main Towers building. She'd forgotten there was a research-and-development meeting she'd said she would attend, since she was back in New York. She was drained, sick, never more aware of the total difference in their perceptions of each other.

As if he wanted to instill it in her still further, Charles, grinning ruefully, said, "Sorry, Mother! I'm sure I've shocked you, but, you know something, you've made me feel better just talking about it." They began to walk into the building, when Charles stopped, looked at his watch, and said, "I'm going to take Dad at his word. I know exactly where Blythe is, for a change. I'm going to see her now and find out once and for all if we still have a chance together."

"But, Charles . . ." He wasn't listening. He turned and ran toward Park Avenue.

Louise went to the Louise Towers executive offices in a trance. "I don't want to be disturbed," she told her secretary, even as the girl was saying, "Mr. Reemer has arrived and would like to begin the meeting."

She closed the door and leaned against it, trying not to cry. What was wrong with her? She had everything in the world. Benedict seemed to trust and love her again. She was proud of that love, proud to be his wife, and determined to do everything to become Madame Rubinstein's successor as the leading beauty authority in the world. And yet she had to accept that she hungered for something that was and always would be—had to be—unattainable. Her stepson.

Was she fated for self-destruction? Was there a psychiatrist in New York she could trust to find out what was going on in her head? Was she in love with a younger version of Benedict? Or was she like every other woman in the world, in search of something to perpetuate her own youth, or what was left of it? Was it a younger Benedict she really desired? If so, why? Her husband was still virile, and just as demanding and commanding as ever.

Louise stumbled over to her desk. It was a beautiful desk, cut from one piece of amber-colored Carrara marble. Benedict insisted it should be kept uncluttered, free of mail and papers, as his desk always was. It was a sign of being in command, he had told her. Papers were brought to the boss by underlings when the boss wanted to see them, and not before. Clutter on a desk led to a distracted mind, a loss of focus on the major planning that had to occupy the brain of the commander in chief for the time when he was alone. He had told her more than once that on his rare visits to her office he wanted to see only the handsome ornaments he had specially commissioned for her out of tortoiseshell, pieces of a desk set resting on top like sculptures.

One piece was in the shape of a woman's torso. There was an unopened letter resting between the shapely breasts, a letter her secretary knew she would want to be there, no matter what Benedict said. It was a letter from Prague, a letter from Natasha.

Five floors above, in Towers Pharmaceuticals' executive suite, Norris had just given the chairman a disturbing progress report on K.

Averbach's AC3 project. "Seems our nemesis, Feiner, or perhaps I should use the plural, *nemeses*, the Feiner brothers, one here, the other in Zurich, have been carrying out clinical trials on the use of AC3 for psoriasis at twelve medical centers around the world and they're now confident that tretinoin, one of the most active derivatives of vitamin A, prevents skin cells from clustering in pores, thus leading the way to an acne cure. There is, shall we say, controlled excitement among the big boys in the Alps, all of whom are well aware of what is going on with retinoic acid research here in Pennsylvania."

When Norris left the report from one of the company's top private investigators on his desk, Benedict read only the first two pages before he dialed out on his private line. He leaned back in his chair, looking forward to the appointment he was about to instigate in much the same way he looked forward to a fine meal at Lutèce or a good, strong Havana cigar.

"Audrey, you little vixen, why have you been hiding from me?" His voice was light, humorous. He knew Audrey would be grateful to him for the opportunity to go along with what was a flagrant lie. He hadn't been in touch with her for weeks, hadn't seen her in more than five months, and, although she didn't know it, he hardly thought of her at all, except when he needed some inside information on the FDA, as he did now.

Audrey jumped at the chance to appear to be the hunted as opposed to the huntress. "It's good to hear your voice, Ben." She knew he hated the diminutive of his name, but she thought it emphasized her indifference, her independence.

He decided to do away with the banter. For what he wanted to know, he would have to see her. "I have to come to Washington on Thursday. If I send the champagne, will you supply the foie gras?"

There was silence at the other end, but it didn't bother him. Unless she had an FDA meeting, he knew she'd break anything to have a tête-à-tête with him. "Well?" His tone was deliberately curt.

"Friday would be better."

"If Friday still follows Thursday, you can have me on Friday, too. Shall we say around nine-thirty."

She never quite got him the first time. "A.M.?" She laughed uneasily.

"No, Audrey. Nine-thirty P.M., Thursday evening."

"I'll chill the champagne, sir," she said in a low, shaky voice.

"Don't chill anything else."

Of course, Jan had seen Louise. He'd half hoped, half dreaded that she might be at Campbell's Funeral Home. When he'd seen her raise her arm, trying to attract his attention, he'd reacted involuntarily, the way chemicals react in a test tube. He'd found his body turning away in flight, his skin growing damp as if with terror. It was only when he was walking fast down Madison Avenue, not watching the lights, getting yelled at, that he fully realized what he'd done.

He'd been given the perfect opportunity. An accidental meeting with his enemy on the most important day in his entire career. It would shortly be announced in the newspapers, but he would have been able to tell Louise face to face that he was being brought back to the United States in the new year to head up the fast-growing U.S. division of K. Averbach. Fourteen years after Louise and Benedict Towers had shown what they thought of him, forcing him out of the mainstream, exiling him to a job with no future in a backwater in Holland, he was not only returning to New York as president of an important company, he was returning with a major mandate.

It wouldn't be announced, of course, but he had been given the go-ahead either to acquire or create a cosmetics company, one that as far as he was concerned he would spend his life building to outsell, out-smart, and outstrip Louise Towers, Inc.

Well, he'd blown the chance, but, he told himself over a strong espresso, it was just as well. Louise, witch that she undoubtedly still was—and from across the room, just as beautiful—would probably have had him telling her far more than was prudent. Their paths would cross more than once in the world in which he would shortly be a major player. He could hardly wait for the warfare to begin.

Benedict was late getting to Audrey's apartment, much later than he'd intended, but he'd run into a couple of senators he liked at the F Street Club and had tried to get a clear picture of what the situation really was in Vietnam. Audrey was smoldering, which didn't bother him at all. He would soon take care of that. It was all part of the game, not real life. Real life was Louise, and he never intended to forget it again.

"It's nearly ten-thirty."

"I'm sorry, ma'am. Affairs of state." She was wearing diaphanous pajamas, a pale pink skin color that, when she stood directly in front of the lamp, made her look as if she was naked underneath. Perhaps she was. If so, she'd made a mistake. He'd told her from the beginning that mystery was what aroused him.

She bent down to pour the champagne—he'd sent a case of Dom Perignon over earlier that day—and he saw the pajamas caught in the crease of her tight little behind. He decided to dispense with foreplay and to hell with mystery. The sooner he got the first part of the evening over, the sooner he would learn what he'd come to find out.

"Come here, you little vixen."

She turned a sulky, angry face to him and saw that he was dangling a necklace in his hands; it looked like a gold necklace. It was a gold necklace. "Oh, Ben-e-dict . . ."

"It's your birthday next month, isn't it? Are you going to be a good girl and stop giving me a hard time?"

He could see the indecision in Audrey's face. Should she move toward him or make him wait the requisite time that single women in her age group felt had to pass before taking the irrevocable step? She wanted him, all right. She was hungry for it, but—Benedict sighed inwardly— he was already bored with the scene that had to be played out to ensure that she didn't think she was "being taken for granted."

She was a fool, he decided, a fool who, for all her backbreaking days of tedious work for the agency, would never move up the ladder. She lacked the necessary spark, the imagination, and, yes, the courage that everyone had to have in the business jungle to go forward. She was the kind of employee he despised, full of potential, quick and intelligent, but too willing to toe the line, unable to go the extra mile for progress. For all that, despite the fact that he knew what she was going to say and do before she said or did it, he would put up with her because she was the only source he could entirely rely on at the FDA, which made her a very useful fool indeed.

She slowly brought the glasses of champagne over to the low settee. They clinked glasses, and Benedict never took his eyes away from her, willing her to drink. "Bend your neck down." He fastened the necklace. "Now look at yourself and bring the bottle of champers over here." In thirty minutes Audrey had drunk half a bottle of the Dom Perignon, while Benedict had taken only a few sips.

He loosened his tie, put his feet up on the coffee table, and slipped a casual arm around her thin shoulders, appearing to unburden himself of the problems and grinding toil of his overpacked agenda. He effort- lessly drew a picture of the life he knew she hoped he led, a life that also explained, without his putting it into exact words, why he saw her so seldom: overworked, overtraveled, with no relaxed home life, living with Louise Towers, a woman who was as ambitious as any man, if not more so.

When the clock chimed midnight, the second bottle was half empty and Benedict's handsome head was on Audrey's lap. She felt a sense of pride that she had been able to make the great Benedict Towers relax sufficiently to confide in her some of his problems. How amazed her bosses would be to know she had this power over one of the most important industrialists in the country. She was longing for him to take her to bed—it had been so long, she'd begun to think it would never happen again—but much as she desired him, she was euphoric to sit just like this. They were like a happily married couple, she told herself, as he told her ruefully—even boyishly, she thought—how aggravated he'd been to learn recently that Jan Feiner, the man he suspected had once been his wife's lover in London, had emerged from oblivion to be credited as the mastermind behind an important new Swiss skin-saving drug, code-named AC3.

As he spoke, Benedict reached up to play with the necklace. He could feel her body respond, but he didn't move his hands—it was not time yet. He continued to talk on drowsily about their own research, starting and stopping as Audrey opened her foolish mouth to tell him what he wanted to know. "Yes, Averbach's clinical trials are causing a stir in Europe, but Kligman's on to something here, too, at Penn. Aren't you funding some of his research? Oh, that feels lovely . . ." Audrey squirmed as Benedict's finger traced a path from her chin down to the necklace and back again.

"What do you hear?" he asked lazily, dropping his hand to rest on her thigh.

"We've heard Averbach is about to make an announcement for a European launch . . . but they're not ready for us yet, and Kligman may beat them to it here. No, of course it isn't you funding his research. It's Johnson and Johnson's Ortho, isn't it? All the same . . ."

"Is it Feiner?" He began to stroke her thigh.

"Yes, that's the name I hear all the time. Jan or John Feiner, who I hear has beaten his brother Victor out of the top job over here, to run Avery. His brother's brilliant but too pushy, too fond of self-promotion. Oh, don't stop. Averbach is definitely going to expand its U.S. subsidiary; if AC3 is what everyone says it is, we'll certainly be hearing from them, but you don't have to worry, oh, don't stop . . ." Audrey moaned.

Benedict sat up abruptly. He hadn't expected to hear that about Feiner, though it made perfect sense. Did Louise know? The jealousy he hadn't thought about in years surfaced. Did Louise know her puny chemist beau was coming back to expand the U.S. operation of Towers's major competitor in Europe? He felt physically sick at the thought.

As Audrey tried to put his hand back on her thigh, he knew he had to get out of the apartment. He'd learned enough. He didn't—couldn't—play the game he knew like the back of his hand for one moment longer. So he'd leave the woman frustrated and furious. It wouldn't be the first or the last time he'd treated a woman that way. He'd just have to work harder the next time around, if, God forbid, there had to be a next time. All the same, he still knew how to leave without a scene. He didn't want to go back with any telltale scratches.

He picked Audrey up, feeling her bare flesh through the flimsy pajamas. She heaved and sighed all the way to the bedroom, where he laid her down gently on the bed she'd christened an "occasional two" size—bigger than a single, but not quite a double bed—which was all the room could contain. Audrey slithered out of her pajamas and turned obediently onto her stomach, but even that didn't arouse him.

He had to find out if Louise knew about Feiner's return to the States as a formidable competitor. He bent down and kissed the tight little behind, but even as Audrey began to yelp with pleasure, he started to back out, saying, "Darling, I've got to go ... got to fly back to New York for an early meeting ... I'm sorry, but I'll be back ..."

Her yelps turned into a wail, and she cried, "Over my dead body! Over my dead body."

He could hear her crying and cursing as he waited for the elevator. As he stepped inside, she flung open the front door and hurled the necklace at him. As the doors closed, it bounced back into the hall.

Benedict felt he was gasping for fresh air as he left the apartment building. He inhaled deeply for a second before heading toward his car. As he did so, he heard a window go up, followed by a clang. It was the necklace hitting the pavement in front of him. Audrey didn't call out, and he didn't expect her to. The guiding force in Audrey's life, he knew, was what people might think.

He bent down to retrieve the necklace, now broken in two. He would get it repaired and return it to her with a matching bracelet and the kind of note that would allow her to keep her image of herself as a femme fatale. He had to. He knew he'd need the useful fool again one day. As he drove toward the airport, where his plane was standing by, he mentally made a note to check Averbach's trading price. From what Audrey had told him, it was obvious it was going to jump. He loathed the reason for the jump, but at least he'd make some money on it.

Prague, 1968

WHEN PROFESSOR JUTA asked to see her before she left for the day, Natasha immediately thought he was going to tell her that Pieter had been pardoned, that he was coming home to Prague and life, which had been in limbo for fifteen months, two weeks and one and a half days, could start again.

As she ran up two flights to the professor's austere office in the stark white dermatological clinic where she was completing a course in skin and scalp care, she sang under her breath, "Pieter's coming home; Kristina's daddy's coming home, Pieter's coming home . . ."

There was no one in the secretary's office. Natasha was too excited to sit down. On the table was the daily paper with more news of what the amazing Alexander Dubcek was accomplishing. Neither her mother nor she could really believe what they were reading, with censorship abolished.

Now, in their own papers, they could read what papers overseas were saying about them. They were calling it "the Prague Spring of Marxism with a human face," but now it was the beginning of June, summer! Since Dubcek's surprising appointment in January as First Secretary, his new programs were still, to everyone's bewildered joy, gathering strength, with political prisoners being released and fresh milk in the stores last week.

Pieter hadn't returned home from work one terrible, bitterly cold March night the year before. At eleven o'clock she'd been told he'd been relocated to Chomutov, one of Czechoslovakia's most polluted industrial towns. Since then she'd spent every penny they'd saved, and every moment she could, trying to find out how Pieter had transgressed and how to obtain his release. All to no avail.

Pieter's co-workers had been too scared to talk, and all she'd learned was that he had in some way collaborated in the distribution of "subversive documents against the party." She knew it wasn't true, but a week later she'd been given two hours to leave their beloved rooftop apartment, told that she and Pieter had lived there illegally, and that she was lucky not to be under arrest herself.

With baby Kristina she'd moved back to her mother's house, and the beauty salon. There, last summer, out of the blue, she'd received an invitation—an order was more like it—to take an advanced skin and hair-care course at the prestigious Prague Clinic, three days a week. She'd been sure Ludmilla had somehow arranged it, though her name had never been mentioned, and on the rare occasions when she'd been able to get through on the telephone, Natasha had totally forgotten to bring the subject up.

There was no doubt that studying at the clinic had helped ease the pain of separation from Pieter, and had lessened the tedium of looking after her mother's increasingly old and garrulous customers. Because Professor Juta was so brilliant and he had managed to assemble some talented teachers around him, for the first time Natasha found she loved skin care and hair care. Last year the classes had often run out of supplies to practice with, but even that had been a challenge; Juta and the small staff had shown the students how to use botanicals and sour milk and fruit to create emulsions, potions, and lotions. One of the most amazing of these had been a bandage of cobwebs used to cover a scratch on a student's arm. How awed they'd all been to monitor the healing process and discover that the cobwebs actually seemed to promote healing.

Natasha jumped as Professor Juta put a friendly hand on her shoulder. He smiled at her dancing eyes, her dimpled smile. What a lovely, wholesome, unspoiled girl she was. "I have some interesting news for you, my dear," he began.

"Yes, yes. Is it . . . it must be . . . Pieter . . ."

Juta frowned, then quickly smiled again. "Not yet, not yet, but yes, I am sure we can expect news of your husband's return soon, very soon. For the moment, I have an opportunity for you that I can safely say is unique."

Natasha's expression had exchanged immediately. What could the professor possibly tell her that was interesting, if it wasn't news of Pieter's return. She had only received half a dozen letters from him since his banishment, admittedly two in the last month, but even those read as if someone were dictating their contents.

"You have a very famous sister, a great credit to our country." The professor had a sonorous voice that made Natasha think of church, where she hadn't been in years. Perhaps she should go again, to pray for Pieter's return. Yes, she would go this Sunday.

She was hardly listening to Juta. Everyone knew she had a famous sister. So what? Ludmilla hadn't been able to save her husband from the horror of living in Chomutov. She hadn't been able to save their apartment, either. Too many miles separated them.

"It appears that our Dermatological Clinic is held in great esteem in the United States. It has been proposed by their government that we exchange ideas, that a group should come from America to study what we are doing, and a small group, headed by myself, should take a mission to the United States, to New York, to discuss mutual interests and goals. It has been suggested that you should be part of that mission."

Natasha looked at Juta in disbelief. A mission to New York? To see her sister? Tears were running down her face. Not knowing what to say, one word was choked out. "When?"

"Well, of course, this will take a long time to prepare. I have written this draft proposal. It has to be approved. Later this year, perhaps, but to be ready at a moment's notice it has been suggested you apply for a passport now. Here is the application form. Please return it to me with six photographs of yourself. Go to this address tomorrow morning, where the photographer will be waiting."

Natasha went home in a daze. She hardly knew how to tell her mother that she had been selected to go on a special mission to America because her sister was the famous Louise Towers, born Ludmilla Sukova, from Prague. If it hadn't counted before, now with Dubcek, it counted for everything.

As if her day had not already been splendid enough, her two-year-old daughter, Kristina, greeted Natasha at the door with another letter from Pieter. Usually she would have scooped the child up and rushed upstairs to the bedroom she'd grown up in to read every word out loud, hoping in some way that the cherub-faced Kristina would remember her father more, but today the arrival of the letter was eclipsed by Professor Juta's news.

"Mama, Mama, where are you, Mama?"

Blanka Sukova was where she always was at around five-thirty in the afternoon, in the front-parlor beauty salon, rolling sparse hair high up onto perm rods attached to an archaic perm machine, washing heads in one of the two cracked basins that had leaked for as long as Natasha could remember.

She didn't look up as Natasha stood in the doorway with Kristina in her arms. When Natasha saw that one of the three clients was Aunt

Kamilla, she waved her hand in greeting and retreated. If she even hinted at the news in front of her aunt, it would be all over town in hours.

The first few paragraphs of her husband's letter held little that he hadn't written before. "The weather is bad. Every breath tastes rancid. The toxic wastes gather in clouds above the rooftops, and then the rain brings them down on our skin. I have been moved to the steel plant." The last paragraph, however, made her hug Kristina to her and cover her face in kisses until the child howled in protest.

"The best news is that I asked if and when we could be reunited with our loved ones, and I was told everyone's case is under review and certainly we should be home before the end of the year. "I love you and our beautiful daughter more every day."

Would Pieter be home before she left with the mission? Would he be upset that she was going so far away? No, of course not. He always wanted the best for her. She would write to tell him the incredible news tonight, after Kristina was in bed, and write to Ludmilla too, although Professor Juta had intimated that her sister probably knew all about it.

Natasha found it difficult to sleep that night after she'd written the letters. Now that the shock was wearing off, she found she was afraid, but she didn't know of what. The unknown, she supposed, the meeting with the sister she had idolized for so long. What if her sister didn't like her? Since Pieter's expulsion to Chomutov, she had lost most of the enormous weight she'd put on during her pregnancy, but she was probably much rounder than Ludmilla would like. She vowed she would go on a diet the next day.

It was easy to do. The tension of waiting for Professor Juta to tell her what was happening as the days went by diminished her appetite until she could hardly take a bite. Her mother didn't help. Natasha could hardly put a foot in the door without her mother appearing, her face gray and strained, asking, "Have you heard anything? Do you have a date for the mission's departure yet?"

It wasn't until the third week of July that Professor Juta called her to his office once more. This time Natasha didn't race up the stairs. Since Monday there had been an ominous feeling in the air, as rumors had surfaced of Moscow's annoyance over Dubcek's liberalizing process going too fast, getting out of hand.

Uncle Ivo, who, Natasha privately believed, delighted in passing on bad news, had come by to say he'd heard from business associates that Soviet troops had been seen on the Czech borders carrying out maneuvers. "I don't like it," he moaned. "If Dubcek throwing us the occasional bone means we've got to live with Russian troops on our land,

I'd sooner live with an empty cupboard. We've never had 'em. It can only lead to worse times, not better."

Juta's face didn't allay her sense of pessimism, though his words, spoken in the same sonorous tones, should have. "I have some good news, my dear. I have been asked to attend a conference to be held in Slovakia early next month, at Comenius University in Bratislava. It is essentially to discuss the effects of living in industrial zones on the body, the skin, and aging. Representatives will be there from the Ana Aslan Geriatric Institute in Bucharest—I believe they have interesting developments to report—and a team from Hungary." He broke off, staring at her in a way that made Natasha feel uncomfortable. "I was supposed to take Swavzek, but her father is in the hospital. I want you to accompany me as my assistant. It will give us an opportunity to discuss an agenda for our mission to the United States."

"Do I have to go?" Natasha knew she shouldn't say it, but she felt uneasy. Every time the doorbell rang at home, she expected to find Pieter standing there. It was all right to be in the United States when he returned to Prague, but Bratislava? He would surely find that strange. There were other staff members. Why wasn't Professor Juta taking one of them?

"I can't make you, but it would . . ." He hesitated, then went on, "It would be helpful to me, to our country. Your sister is famous throughout Eastern Europe. Perhaps you don't realize the extent of this."

She didn't, but at this moment she didn't care. Juta's face was reddening. She accepted without further questioning that Juta was under some kind of duress to get her to accompany him. In any case, she had no option. He wasn't only her professor; in a sense, he was her boss. She had grown up knowing that not following orders could lead to disgrace, if not death. She had grown up knowing that it was not only useless to ask questions, to try to find out what was behind certain words and actions; it was also dangerous.

"How long is the conference?"

"Three days."

"When do we leave?"

"The first week of August."

When she told her mother, and Blanka reacted with obvious joy and pride, Natasha tried to put out of her mind any uneasiness.

A week before her departure, while she was helping her mother in the salon, the long-awaited call came through from Ludmilla. As usual, Ludmilla, never knowing when they might be cut off, spoke very fast, urgently, not about the wonderful news in Natasha's letter, the proposed mission to the United States, but, to Natasha's amazement, about the Bratislava conference. How on earth did Ludmilla already know about that?

"It is very important that you attend, little sister." To Natasha's ears, Ludmilla sounded slightly nervous. "Do exactly what the professor tells you. He is a very important influence on your future." She then asked to speak to her mother, as she always did. They were lucky; they did not get cut off, though the line kept fading. She then asked to speak to Natasha again before hanging up.

"Even if you don't understand everything, promise that you'll trust me, Natasha. Everything is going according to plan, and that includes Mama, Pieter, and of course Kristina, too. Follow instructions and trust me."

Trust her famous sister? Of course she trusted her. What on earth did she mean? Afterwards, Ludmilla's words kept coming back, troubling her. When she asked her mother about it, Blanka was unusually evasive.

The next weekend her mother had a small dinner for her, inviting a couple of school friends and their husbands, as well as Aunt Kamilla, and Uncle Ivo. If only Pieter were home . . . Natasha tried to relish the *svickova*, beef braised in the oven with spices and served with a rich cream sauce, cooked to perfection by her mother, who knew it was her favorite dish.

When everyone had gone home and they were washing the dishes, Blanka suddenly burst into tears. "My God, Mama, what is it?" Natasha asked.

Her mother shook her head furiously and rubbed her eyes with the damp dish towel. "I'm sorry, I'm sorry . . . they're tears of . . . of joy. Everything's going to be so good for you . . ."

Natasha forced her mother to look at her. "Is there something I don't know? Did Ludmilla tell you something? I don't like this. It worries me. Perhaps I shouldn't go to Bratislava."

The sudden fierce expression on her mother's face frightened her. "You *must* go. For all our sakes. In case things change here . . . You're our only hope."

"What do you mean?" Now Natasha was really frightened. "I'm only going for three days . . . aren't I?"

Her mother, still rubbing her eyes with the dish towel, spoke in whispers. "I was going to explain everything tomorrow, but I can't wait. Let's talk now." Like a sleepwalker, Natasha followed her mother to the old sofa where, over the years, so many mother-and-daughter conversations had taken place. All the long-familiar things—the grandfather clock, her father's wooden rocking chair, the old-fashioned photographs of aunts and uncles, grandfathers and grandmothers long gone—were suddenly unbearably important, beloved. She felt a sense of foreboding as her mother began to speak.

"I had a visitor. I was going to tell you tomorrow, before you left on Tuesday. I didn't want to give you too much time to think, to worry, to fret. It was a visitor from the American Embassy." Her mother stopped talking, seeing the anguished expression on Natasha's face.

"What, Mama? What did he say? Oh, Mama, please, please tell me . . . or I won't go . . . I won't go."

"It's all a plan. First you, then Kristina and me, then Pieter . . ." Natasha could see her mother's hands shaking. She covered them with hers.

"A plan?"

"Bratislava is only some thirty miles from Vienna." Her mother spoke in whispers. "Vienna and freedom. Professor Juta is your pass to freedom. When you're in Bratislava, I am told you will receive your passport stamped with an exit visa to attend another meeting in Vienna." Her mother's voice broke, but through her tears she croaked, "A meeting with your sister to discuss the mission to the United States. By the end of the year"—her mother tried to sniff away her tears—"we'll all be together, free, free, out safe and sound, thanks to what Dubcek is achieving and your sister's husband's money and influence."

Now Natasha was sobbing. "I won't go. I won't go and leave Kristina behind . . . if what you're saying . . ." Her mother held her arm again, so tightly it hurt.

"See here, girl, this isn't just for you. It's for the whole family. If you went with Kristina now, there are jealous people opposed to everything Dubcek is doing. They would be suspicious. It has to be slow, careful, cautious, but as your sister told you, trust her. It has all been arranged. Kristina and I have our papers ready to submit." Her mother got up abruptly and went to the coal cellar, where Natasha knew that beneath the coal was a loose board under which her parents had been hiding money and papers for as long as she could remember.

Blanka returned to hand Natasha a large manila envelope. Inside were a bunch of documents, passport applications, neatly filled out in her mother's handwriting, with the correct-size photographs of herself and Kristina.

"Where is Pieter's?" Natasha cried bleakly.

"He has been sent the application paper. He is getting his photographs. The man from the American Embassy, a Mr. Fle . . . Fletch"— her mother had difficulty pronouncing the name—"Fletcher told me not to be worried, that it was probable Pieter would not return to Prague, but would be allowed to leave from . . ."

Natasha interrupted her, crying, "How can we be sure? How can I do this? How can I? Oh, Mama, I can't leave Kristina behind . . . I can't . . . I can't . . ."

Her mother rocked her in her arms, the passport papers falling to the floor. "It won't be long. Flet . . . Fletcher said that before autumn Kristina and I will receive our passports and exit visas, then Pieter. By Christmas we will all be together somewhere in the free world, wherever Ludmilla wants us to be. And then, if everything works out here as Dubcek says it will, we will be able to return to Czechoslovakia, to come and go as I'm told people in the free world are able to do."

Louise had just been elected to the International Best Dressed Hall of Fame. It wasn't surprising, according to a left-wing French newspaper, which, along with satirizing Americans' insatiable need to categorize people, inaccurately printed how much Madame Towers had spent on clothes during the past year. In fact, she'd spent more. And here she was, at the couture collections in Paris, where, because of the intolerable French attitude toward air conditioning (deploring it) and hair under women's arms (applauding it) she felt nearly asphyxiated by the heat and the odor of perspiration mixed with expensive perfume, emanating from the women surrounding her. Some of them, also on the best-dressed list, were wearing the hit dress of the season, wraparound, made of silk, and sleeveless!

As the bride appeared on the Pierre Cardin runway, Louise let out a small but still audible sigh of relief. She couldn't wait to get back to the Ritz for a cool shower and an iced tea. Then she would try again to get through to Prague, to make sure Natasha had not backed out of going to Bratislava with Juta. After Benedict's hard work on her family's behalf, Louise had longed to scold Natasha for her lack of enthusiasm on the phone the week before, but of course she couldn't because Natasha didn't understand what was going on.

From what Benedict had told her, time was of the essence. Dubcek's days were numbered, and nobody knew who or what was going to come after him. It was vital to act as if Marxism with a human face were still being tolerated by the Russians, to act as if an exchange of dermatological information between their two countries—and perhaps even the United States and the Eastern European bloc—could become a reality in terms of what the Russians wanted most, hard currency.

As Louise stepped out of the Rolls at the Ritz, she heard someone call her name. She turned and her heart leapt. It was Jan Feiner, a grinning, self-assured-looking Jan Feiner, despite his crumpled light denim suit and askew tie, which made him look more like the research scientist he was at heart than the big-time executive he had become. He was not only president and chief executive officer of K. Avery, but, as the press had recently reported, still only approaching forty years old this year, he had received equity worth hundreds of thousands of dollars in K. Averbach, the giant parent of K. Avery, for his part in producing the remarkable acne-fighting drug AC3, which after years of clinical trials, had just received the blessing of the Food and Drug Administration.

"Jan Feiner! What are you doing here?"

The last time Louise had seen Jan was a few months back at an industry dinner honoring Benedict at the Waldorf-Astoria in New York. Benedict hadn't been at all happy to discover Jan on the dais, even though he was only one among twenty men in the pharmaceutical industry considered sufficiently distinguished to salute him.

Louise would always remember the evening because, at the small VIP reception before the dinner, the ice had been broken between Jan and herself. In fact, there hadn't been any ice. Although, as she'd predicted when Jan returned to New York to take up his K. Avery, post, it was inevitable that they should run into each other, this was the first time Jan had been relaxed enough to treat her as an old friend and colleague instead of as an enemy. Perhaps it was because Jan had been with a gorgeous-looking, voluptuous model. Even so, she'd been pleased that after a few minutes of small talk, he'd ignored the beauty and hung on her words just like the old days—until Benedict had come over to say it was time to make their grand entry into the ballroom.

"What luck! I'm here for just twenty-four hours from Zurich," Jan said happily. He had a slight tan. It suited him. "I was going to call you on my return to New York this week. I have something I want to discuss with you."

Louise smiled. "Lucky for me, too." She turned to the chauffeur. "I won't be needing you tonight, Terence. Please call me in the morning, at about eight."

Jan took her arm. "What about having dinner with me tonight? I'm leaving for the States in the morning. Can you and Benedict join me?"

Louise shook her head. "Benedict's not here. He's in New York, concluding a deal. I'm meeting him in Vienna this weekend."

Jan's expression was wry, impish. "Well, then, just the two of us. I promise not to talk about the past. It's the future I have on my mind."

Louise realized Terence was still standing behind her. "Terence, you can go. I won't need you tonight." She turned to Jan with a bemused expression. "Well, why not? If you're leaving for the States, an early dinner would suit me, too. I am in Europe on a special mission, one that you will understand very well."

They arranged to meet in the Vendôme Bar at six-thirty. Louise showered, washed, and dried her new wash-and-wear Vidal Sassoon haircut, longer in the front than in the back—prominently displayed in spectacular pictures of her by Richard Avedon in the current issue of American *Vogue*. She realized she was sorry, but also intrigued, that there seemed to be no trace left of the shy, besotted Jan of the past. Had she lost her power to attract men? Had her successful attempt to bury what the psychiatrist had called "her sexual infatuation" for Charles stunted or shriveled something in her?

Charles and Blythe had divorced. Blythe had petitioned on grounds of cruelty: "He was away more than he was at home; he was more in love with Louise Towers, Incorporated, than with me." How ironic that had been for Louise to learn. Benedict had insisted they all spend much more time together "to help Charlie get over it." It had been torture for her to see how wounded Charles was, and how helpless she was to help him recover.

She'd gone to see a pyschiatrist secretly. It had helped. He'd made her realize that much of her desire was, as she'd suspected, related to a lost youth, that for everything she'd gained in life, she'd had to pay a price. Above all, apart from being married to a much older man, she was also married to an extremely dominating one. Because she was a dominating woman herself, who also wanted her own way, this had caused her inner conflicts.

The psychiatrist had helped her lose what she'd come to recognize as a dangerous self-pity, showing itself in sexual fantasies involving her stepson. She was all over that. She had learned to stand up for the important things in her relationship with Benedict and obey him totally in all the unimportant minutiae of life, and their marriage was all the happier for it. So she was happy now, wasn't she? As the psychiatrist had also taught her to do, when she asked herself that question she deliberately turned her thoughts to something else, to something worthwhile.

As Louise put through a call to her mother's house in Prague, Terence the chauffeur was reporting by phone to Monsieur Prelintoin, head of security for Towers Pharmaceuticals in Paris, what time he had picked Madame Towers up, where she had been, whom she had met or visited, and what instructions she had given him for the evening and the following day.

This was something he was used to doing every time Madame Towers came to France. At annual get-togethers for Towers's European employees, he had learned this function was also performed by his counterparts in other countries. He supposed it was in case of kidnapping or, as the chauffeurs joked among themselves, because Madame Towers was such a luscious honeypot, despite her often icy demeanor, and so much younger than her husband, old man Towers, that he wanted to be sure there were no outside bees buzzing around.

Because he prided himself on never missing a thing, Terence repeated what he had heard almost perfectly, making only the natural mistake of pronouncing "Jan" as "Jean."

Monsieur Prelintoin knew how to carry out orders, too. He dispatched a security motorcyclist to the Ritz to keep tabs on Madame Towers that night, and filed his usual report to the New York head office.

It was unlike her, but Louise put on another dress before deciding to go back to her first choice for her dinner date with her long-lost friend. She was aware that it was an act of defiance. The dress she returned to was one she knew Benedict disliked—not because it wasn't pretty, but more likely because it was exceptionally so, with its bell-shaped skirt and bodice of ice-peach faille, and shoelace tulle shoulder straps with matching tulle bolero. Courreges, who had designed the dress, hadn't liked making the hemline an inch longer, but Benedict had given her an ultimatum about skirt lengths he would tolerate, and she knew better than to ignore him.

Even though the length was correct, just touching her knee, never above it, the bell of the skirt billowed out as she moved, revealing her long, slender legs, which, in the new kind of pantyhose, requiring no girdle, no garters, and ice-peach to match the dress, looked as if they went right up to her armpits.

At 6:20, as she was powdering her pale shoulders with a new version of a luminous powder from the lab, the phone rang. Her mother's voice was so clear she might have been in the same room. Before Blanka told her what she was longing to know, Louise could hear tears in her voice, and already the ache of being separated from her only other child. "Yes, Natasha has gone to Bratislava. It was difficult, I tell you, Ludmilla. The questions! So many questions. But of course I couldn't blame her. It was difficult for me, very difficult to convince her we had to believe in all you have said, in all you are trying to do, very difficult for me, Ludmilla."

Hearing her mother call her by her old name always unnerved Louise, surrounding her with ghosts she hated to remember. As much as she longed for her phone calls to Prague to go through, it was always the same. No sooner did she hear those familiar family voices than Louise longed for the conversation to be over, to be restored to her existing safe and secure world.

"I suppose it's because I feel guilty," she told Jan, explaining why she was arriving in the bar nearly forty minutes late. "I want to hang up almost as soon as I hear my mother start to speak. I suppose it's because the sound of gratitude in her voice for the little I'm able to do tears me apart . . . because I'm so aware of what I escaped from, what I have and what they have, Dubcek or no Dubcek."

Five minute before, Jan had been about to leave, no longer certain that Louise Towers had lost the power to awe him, no longer proud that on seeing her he had felt so much in control that he had been able to act naturally, asking her to dinner as if all he'd ever felt for her had been camaraderie and friendship. He'd started to hate her all over again, but then without seeing her arrive, he'd known she'd come into the bar.

He'd seen others turn and whisper, seen men at the bar look approvingly as she passed, and then she'd been standing before him, the ice maiden in ice-peach, her ivory shoulders and the deep cleavage of her breasts showing through the silly tulle wisp of a jacket.

There were tears in her eyes as she apologized profusely for her lateness, telling him her deepest feelings, the emotional upheaval of talking to her mother in Prague about her little sister, Natasha, starting out on the most momentous journey of her life, a journey west into her arms, into a life of freedom.

Had she changed that much? Could this possibly be the same Louise Towers he'd tried to hate for so many years, the out-of-reach, superior Louise Towers with whom he'd vowed to get even, who'd scorned and spurned him? Or was it that just as she was the only woman in the world who could immediately seduce him and make him forget all the terrible things she'd done, perhaps he was the one man she could relax with, let her hair down with, confide in?

"I've booked a table at Taillevent," he said after he'd ordered another martini for himself, a Perrier for her.

"Oh." There was disappointment in her voice.

"You would prefer somewhere else?"

"Well, yes, if you don't mind. Of course, it's one of the greatest restaurants in the world, but . . . well . . ." She didn't finish the sentence. She didn't need to. It was probably Benedict Towers's regular hangout, Jan told himself. It wasn't that she didn't want to be seen with him; she just didn't want to create an unnecessary problem for herself. In a way he didn't blame Benedict Towers. Strangely enough, it was Paulina Sygorski, the Polish girl Victor had nearly talked him into marrying, who'd once suggested that Benedict Towers had exiled him because he was jealous of his relationship with his wife, not because he thought he was untalented or inferior.

Now when he looked at Louise, who if possible was even more attractive than when he'd seen her last, he couldn't blame any man for being jealous. If she were his . . .

Her dark eyes were watching him. "We can dine quietly here."

"No," he said firmly, determined to take charge, to be the man with her that he was now, effortlessly, with other women. "We'll behave like good old-fashioned boulevardiers. We'll stroll around the Place Vendôme and window-shop at Cassegrain for stationery, at Selleries de France in case you'd like another ostrich handbag, Madame. We'll study some of the finest fragrances in the world in Guerlain's window, and inhale the charcuterie at Gargantua around the corner on the rue St.-Honoré. Then . . ." Jan wrinkled his brow. "I've got it. We'll dine on St.-Honoré at number twenty-four, L'Absinthe, Belle Époque decor, the chic-est, prettiest people in Paris, and delicious duck. What do you say?"

She'd caught a glimpse of the old bewitched Jan, but it had fast disappeared, supplanted by this funny, fast-talking, quick-witted charmer who had somehow managed to marry his Old World Polish manners with New World American action. She liked him all the more for it. "It sounds wonderful."

Jan summoned a waiter, wrote a note to Claude, the celebrated bartender in charge of the Vendôme bar, and in fifteen minutes received word that L'Absinthe awaited their arrival.

It wasn't until Louise had finished telling Jan about Natasha's marriage and the birth of Kristina and all that Benedict was now predicting about Czechoslovakia, that he teasingly told her she'd forgotten how to hold her tongue. "Once I could never get a word out of you about your family, your life. Are you telling me all this because you're frightened I'm going to ask you about your R.O.I.?"

"R.O.I.?" Louise looked startled.

"You can't fool me, Louise. You know all about R.O.G. return on investment, but in fact that is what I want to talk to you about. I thank you, dear lady, for all the nice compliments you've been giving me this evening about acne research and Averbach's clinical excellence. Now it's my turn. I've been watching Louise Towers, Incorporated, very carefully for some time now. It's my opinion that despite your brilliant ideas, your obvious appeal to the public—particularly whenever you yourself make a public appearance—if I haven't been there, believe me, I have had every one of them documented and reported to me, along with the resultant sales—I believe you are at a standstill. Louise Towers doesn't seem to be moving."

As Louise started to protest, Jan wagged a finger at her. "I'm not insulting you. I just think Towers Pharmaceuticals doesn't have Louise Towers high on its priority list. You aren't expanding because either your parent company doesn't want LTI to expand, or it's too busy with its multiple other businesses to give your company the attention and financial support it deserves and now desperately needs.

"When Pfizer bought Coty a couple of years ago, I thought we'd see some action from Towers, but no, we haven't seen any changes at all. I know Squibb and Lilly are making shopping lists of cosmetics companies they want to acquire. They may not know how to run them, we don't know yet, but it's just too tempting. Wall Street keeps saying it, and many are listening out there. 'The cosmetics industry is inflation-proof and recession-resilient.' What a beautiful combo, and what could be a more natural partnership than one between a modern pharmaceutical company, with its in-depth research facilities, and a cosmetics company?

"Up to now it's been little more than a cottage industry dominated by two old ladies, Arden and Rubinstein, who held their autocratic fingers out the window and said 'Think pink,' and the world of women blindly followed. Whether our pharmaceutical competitors come in and join the party or not—and I'm sure they're going to—there's already serious competition for Louise Towers from this lively newcomer, Estée Lauder."

Louise, who had been sitting still, moved her body as if she wanted to leave but Jan took no notice.

"I'm sure you've seen what Lauder's doing with her new Clinique company—fragrance-free, allergy-proof, all products vetted by this tony New York dermatologist Orentreich, all copy written by that brilliant ex-beauty editor from *Vogue*. It's clever, very clever, tapping into women's nameless fears about their skin. And the packaging's brilliant too, streamlined, with almost a medical connotation, and this weird but wonderful slide-rule contraption at the counter to answer consumers' questions in the most basic, oversimplified way. It's perception that counts. If women believe in the thing, they'll start buying because of it. Lauder will lose money at first, but you'll see Clinique grow into a monster, and there will be many copycats from other companies, Revlon for sure, all of which will nibble away at Louise Towers's reputation as the numero-uno skin maven. Now, I have a proposal that may come as a surprise to you, but I don't want you to say anything until I've finished."

Jan beckoned to the sommelier, who came over to refill their glasses. He leaned back against the deep-cushioned chair and saw that Louise was upset. Exactly why he wasn't certain, but he thought he knew. Without intending to, he had touched a nerve. It scarcely seemed possible, yet it explained a lot of things that had mystified him about the Louise Towers company. Benedict Towers didn't want his own wife's company to be too successful. If Towers had been jealous of him, then so lacking in confidence, puny, poor, and totally insignificant in Louise's life, could it be that Towers was also jealous of his own wife?

Jan drained all the feeling from his voice, to be as businesslike as he could be with this woman, who would never know how he really felt about her. "As you probably know, Averbach is now determined to acquire a cosmetics business either in Europe or the United States. From our studies it is eminently clear that this is the industry with the greatest potential. It is in its infancy. We are committed to investing heavily in its growth. I have proposed, and it has been agreed to by my bosses in Zurich, that we purchase Louise Towers. As part of the purchase price, we want to offer you ten-percent equity, a five-year renewable contract at a beginning salary of three hundred thousand dollars a year, with a guaranteed annual increase of not less than ten percent, a sizable expense account, and a nondiscriminatory pension for life."

It was a remarkable compensation package. They both knew it, but Jan's admiration for Louise grew as she gave no indication of being either impressed or unimpressed. How lucky Benedict Towers was, he thought again. Not because his wife was so exquisite, but because she naturally possessed one of the most important assets for a beauty empress—mystery. Despite an ungainly, squat figure, Madame Rubinstein had learned to acquire that sense of mystery—until she opened her mouth. Jan knew, as few people did, that Louise had always possessed it and that in her years with Benedict Towers she had honed it to perfection. In one way she was like a great movie star, up on a pedestal for all the world to worship and admire, but she had far more power. One gracious, helpful word from her, and the public opened their pocketbooks and bought and bought whatever magical potions she recommended.

Jan congratulated himself that he had been right to push for such an extraordinary deal for Louise. He had examined his conscience for an ulterior motive and had found none. Louise Towers was a bankable asset, a perfect fit with Averbach. If Towers Pharmaceuticals wasn't that interested in the cosmetics industry, it should fall over itself to accept the price Averbach was willing to pay for Louise Towers.

As Jan and Louise strolled back to the Ritz, neither was aware of the motorcyclist following them at a discreet distance. When Jan accompanied Louise inside, the security guard waited outside, having been told that Monsieur Feiner was not staying at the Ritz but at the Crillon, and that he should report on how much time elapsed between their arrival at the Ritz and Feiner's return to his hotel.

"Not even fifteen minutes," he was able to write in his log. "Monsieur Feiner arrived with Madame Towers at the Ritz Hotel at 2120 hours and left the Ritz Hotel at 2132."

Only twelve minutes, but long enough for Jan to forget his business-like manner, to hold Louise's tulle-covered shoulders and look longingly at her as he said, "We've both come a long way from Revelation. Now I hope we will go still further together. I want to make you the number-one name in the world of beauty, just as you are the most beautiful woman in the world." He tried to sound carefree, laughing, but it didn't come out that way. "I want to, I can, and I will if you support everything I've said tonight."

Her eyes were shining. She looked exhilarated. "Thank you, Jan, dear. I have never been more flattered. Let me talk to Benedict about it."

"As soon as you say the word, my financial people will contact yours." Jan kissed her quickly on the lips, then turned and walked stiffly out into the Place Vendôme, where the motorcyclist followed him as he walked aimlessly around Paris for over an hour before returning to the Crillon.

Louise was waiting for Benedict when he arrived at Wien Schwechat Airport. She had told him she would be there because she missed him so much and Benedict waited during the drive to the Imperial Hotel for his wife to mention her dinner with Jan Feiner.

He had been waiting for her to mention it on the telephone since he'd read about it in the security report five days before. Of course he told himself her mind was focused on Natasha's arrival. Of course that was uppermost in her mind. Nevertheless, she knew how he felt about Feiner. When was she going to tell him why she'd had dinner with the president of a competing company, a man who had meant something to her in the past, a man she knew he loathed? And what had they talked about during their tête-à-tête?

She looked strained, anxious for news of Natasha, who was still in Bratislava, delayed, as far as he had been able to find out, by some stupid bureaucrat who was not happy with Juta's papers and who was not prepared to let Natasha travel out of the country for a meeting with her famous sister without him.

Benedict wasn't going to add to Louise's fears, but although at first it had appeared as if Dubcek had won a reprieve for his liberalism, now the Russians were berating the Czech leader again for "betraying international socialism" and other garbage put forth as serving the "imperialist cause."

Benedict gave Louise the only good news he had, hoping to unlock her mind and thus her mouth, to talk about something other than the escape mission he'd worked on with the American Embassy in Prague since early spring. "The first thing you can tell your little sister is that her husband is back in Prague with her mother and the baby."

"Oh, how wonderful." Louise looked at him the way he wanted her always to look at him, like a savior, a god, a man to whom she would always be indebted. She tucked her arm through his and rested her head on his shoulder. He was glad that he'd allowed her to cut her hair, though it had been a sacrifice not to have her heavy tresses to play with. Because the haircut followed the perfect symmetry of her head, it had aroused him sexually from the first moment he'd seen her new look. It returned the vulnerability and innocence of the Ludmilla he'd fallen so crazily in love with.

They made love as soon as they arrived in the lofty Imperial Hotel suite. Because of his jealousy and suspicion, Benedict found himself more aroused by Louise than ever. She was unlike any other woman he had known, in that he rarely felt he totally possessed her, even when he heard her crying out in her own ecstasy or when he cruelly withdrew as she approached her climax, only to take her again when she least expected it, sometimes hours later when she was dressed to go out, when he knew that beneath her fancy clothes she would still be throbbing, wanting. Nothing excited him more than the knowledge that beneath his wife's cool, often cold exterior was a heat, a greedy fire, more passionate than any he'd ever experienced.

Freshly bathed and dressed, they ordered dinner in their suite. He ate silently, not answering her when she spoke, willing her by his withdrawal to tell him about the Feiner dinner. She would know what he was waiting for, and she didn't disappoint him, though he distrusted the offhand, casual way she began to refer to their meeting.

"Did I tell you I ran into Feiner in Paris?" He remained silent, toying with his fork, his eyes not leaving her face, watching for some telltale sign of unease. There was none.

"He said he wanted to talk business, something that would interest us. He invited us to dinner and then, of course, because you weren't there, I decided to see what he had to say, knowing how important Averbach is to us in Europe."

When she hesitated, Benedict nearly gave himself away. "Why didn't you . . ." He was about to say ". . . eat at the hotel." He couldn't believe his stupidity. He changed the question ". . . call me about it before you agreed to meet him?"

"Frankly, my mind was—is—so full of Natasha, I didn't think. I should have called you, but, well, I don't think this is the time to go into every detail of what he said, but in short, he had been to Zurich to discuss Averbach's acquisition interests. They are—he is—very high on the cosmetics business."

Louise gave Benedict a quick précis of what Jan had said to her, omitting the fact that he felt Towers was not giving enough attention or financial support to its own Louise Towers division.

"Averbach is interested in acquiring Louise Towers," she finally said with an almost helpless wave of her hand. "Jan"—she corrected herself—"Feiner mentioned an extraordinary salary for me." She looked at Benedict shyly. "Three hundred thousand, with a guaranted ten percent increase each year for five years. I could hardly believe my ears. It leads me to believe Averbach is prepared to pay a great deal for the company. I haven't given it much thought because, of course, who knows what would actually happen if the financial teams were to meet, but only one thing came to my mind. If you're not interested in selling, they are certainly going to buy something and put a lot of money behind it. It would create fierce competition and . . ."

"Do you want Feiner for a boss?" Benedict couldn't hide his hostility, his growing anger, as he interrupted her.

"Of course not. I didn't even think of that. If it—" The phone rang. Since Benedict had given orders not to be disturbed unless it was an urgent call, he picked it up and listened with a grim, set expression. Louise began to feel sick.

"Yes, yes, we'll be there." When Benedict put the phone down, he was smiling again. "We can expect Natasha in two days. Her exit visa has been stamped for the eighth. We are told to be at the border at Osterre by eighteen hundred hours."

Tears streamed down Louise's face as she ran to embrace him. He cupped her face in his hands. "I'm not going to let you be crushed, destroyed by that Swiss money machine. We'll talk about this later. I want to hear every detail, but you're not for sale, my darling. Never, never, never, over my dead body."

Louise hardly heard what he was saying. Every nerve in her body was tingling. All she could think about was Natasha and the eighth of

August. "Did . . . did you hear anything else? How will she arrive? With Juta, of course, but how? By car, of course, yes?" Strangely, for the first time in years, Benedict heard a foreign accent in his wife's voice.

He put his arms around her protectively. "Juta and she will be in a pea-green Tatra driven by a commie from Bratislava University—"

"A Tatra!" Louise looked alarmed.

"So? What's wrong with that?"

She spoke slowly, as if the words were accompanied by pictures in her mind. "I can remember my father warning us about Tatras. 'Where there's a Tatra,' he would say, 'there's the secret police.' They all drove them. It was a sign of influence, of power." She shivered.

"Well, now it's a sign of freedom. You wouldn't know this, you're too young . . ." For once there was no trace of sarcasm in Benedict's voice when he mentioned their age difference. "The Czechs used to be known for their car manufacture. They were the envy of Europe. In fact, I vaguely remember hearing that Hitler's car for the people, the VW, was modeled on the Tatra. Yes, I'm sure I'm right."

Again Louise wasn't listening. Another momentous change was about to happen in her life, something she had been awaiting for twenty years. How she was going to get through the next two days she didn't know.

Although Benedict didn't mention Jan Feiner's offer to her again, he didn't waste time acting on it. The next day he rang the man he still trusted more than any other in the company, the faithful Norris. He briefly recounted what Louise had told him. "I want a stern official warning sent to this fucking upstart by our lawyers. It should say un-equivocally that Louise Towers is not for sale now, nor will it ever be. It should also say that I will take it as a personal insult should I hear that any approach or proposal is ever made again to my wife, or for that matter, to any Towers employee. Make it clear in the strongest possible way that the subject is closed forever."

Norris hadn't heard the old man so angry in years, but he didn't need an explanation. He knew how galling it was for Benedict to see how far the chemist who'd created Revelation, Louise's Towers's first triumph, had come. Physically, Feiner had always looked like a pip-squeak to him, but who knew if at one time in her life Louise Towers hadn't found him attractive? Not in comparison to Benedict, of course, but he understood the old man's ire, all right. Since his own remar-riage, Norris understood what it was like to be jealous.

Benedict hadn't finished. "When I get back from this nightmare, Norris, I want to sit down with Phillips as soon as possible. I want to make sure that whatever happens to me, there is no way that slimy bastard Feiner can ever get his hands on Louise Towers. I want to rethink the way the cosmetics division is set up. To protect Louise, of course, but also to make sure she has no chance of doing anything foolish, should I not be around to guide her. I want to go over everything, my will, everything."

It was raining heavily when they reached the Austrian border at 6:00 P.M. on the eighth. It was impossible to see across the no-man's-land that was the bridge across the Morava River, a tributary of the Danube, to the heavily guarded Czech sentry gate.

Louise couldn't sit in the car. The chauffeur unfurled an enormous umbrella, and Benedict and she stood close together beneath it, looking into the distance. Thirty minutes, then forty minutes passed, but Louise was not aware of time. The rain made her think of what was supposed to happen when you were drowning—that your life passed before your eyes. She tried to think of what her father looked like, her mother, even Milos, the man she had treated so abominably, like a stepping-stone, an inanimate foothold to take her to another place, another life. When she thought of Natasha, it was as the solemn little girl of seven or eight that she'd last seen, a cherub with red-gold pigtails and a wide vivid smile, pirouetting by the fire in the kitchen, wearing the tutu her mother had made for her.

It had been impossible for Louise to connect the slim girl in the wedding picture with that little girl, just as it had been impossible to see any trace of the eight-year-old Natasha she remembered in last year's formal picture of Natasha as a mother, much chubbier, with a baby in her arms, her husband standing behind her.

Benedict was speaking, stroking back a piece of her damp hair from her forehead. "I can hear a car."

Louise looked at her watch. Diamonds and gold, from the great Swiss watchmaker Türler of Zurich. It would be the first thing she gave to her sister as she stepped onto free soil. Ten minutes to seven. Slowly, like a photograph appearing in a darkroom, a car came into view. Louise gulped down tears. It wasn't a Tatra, all fins and looming rear-engine bulk. It was the pathetic, often-laughed-at Czech Skoda, which, even translated into English, meant "pity" or "shame." Who was daring to take the place of her beloved sister in this forlorn apology for a car?

Louise turned away, painful tears coursing down her face. When she looked back, the car was still beside the Austrian guard box. After ten minutes it inched ahead. The door flew open. A tall, ungainly man in a suit that was too big for him was helping someone out. A tall, slender woman in an old-fashioned, garish mauve raincoat. The woman looked around nervously, toward Benedict and Louise standing under the umbrella. She took an uncertain step toward them. It was then that Louise noticed the Skoda was pea-green. "Natasha . . ." Her voice was a whisper. "Natasha!" Now it was a scream. The two women ran toward each other.

"Ludmilla, is it really you?"

"Yes, little sister. It is really me."

Las Vegas, 1970

"CHEER UP, Natasha."

Charles was used to her silence, which she'd told him was more because of her lack of English vocabulary than from not having anything to say. She hadn't needed to tell him. He already knew, as did some others in the company, that Natasha was opinionated.

In her own way she'd made clear, lack of the correct English words or not, that she considered the training of skin-care personnel in the United States to be inferior to the training even now being taught at the impoverished Prague Dermatological Clinic, that in Czechoslovakia the profession of aesthetician was aspired to, took years to achieve, and therefore was treated with much more respect than it appeared to be in America. From Louise, Charles had learned that that included Louise Towers's personnel, although she had been tactful enough not to say so publicly.

"Sorry, Charlie."

He liked the way Natasha said his name. Louise had pronounced it "Sharlie" once, but years with a voice teacher had changed all that. Natasha still had a long way to go, and he, for one, hoped she would retain something of a foreign accent. It was good for business. Customers seemed to know, or at least believe, that most Eastern European facialists who managed to get to the United States were well trained, and Natasha was no exception.

In fact, she was exceptional. His brother-in-law David had told him that even the blasé girls on the executive floor clamored for a facial from Natasha, so perhaps she was right about their training programs. He wasn't going to get into it.

They'd been on the road for over an hour, driving from Los Angeles to Las Vegas, where the largest ophthalmic convention ever to be held was about to take place. There, at the Las Vegas Hilton, Louise Towers was going to put on three spectacular beauty shows to announce the wonderful marriage between Opteck, the world leader in the optical field, and Louise Towers, to solve forever the eye makeup problems of girls who wear glasses. Using an innovative demonstration, a new line of Louise Towers shadows, liners, and mascaras was going to be introduced, along with a matching or coordinating new line of eyeglass frames in various designs, for different-shaped faces. From next month on, for the first time, eye cosmetics would be on sale at Opteck vision centers in selected markets—but, of course, only Louise Towers eye cosmetics.

It was just one promotion among many that the marketing division was going to roll out in the coming months, a result of the increased competition that had led to the Towers board's decision to invest more heavily in the beauty division. Charles had never been busier, and he had so much business on his mind, it was only in the last few minutes he'd noticed not only how silent but how downcast the little Czech looked.

"Why the long face today? This is supposed to be a treat, a break." Charles laughed, though he didn't feel like laughing. It was a downer he didn't need, being with someone who was invariably depressed. "Why, Natasha, don't you know that women would pay a fortune to be sitting here with me at the wheel of this demon of the road? Don't you know that *Esquire* just announced I am one of the ten most eligible bachelors in America?"

"S. Quayer?"

Charles sighed. He wished he hadn't mentioned it. "It's a magazine. Forget it. It's a joke. But I still want to know why you look more miserable than ever, when you've told me I'm one of the few members of the family you can talk to."

As Charles accelerated past ninety miles an hour, Natasha fell against the door of the Porsche and gripped the dashboard. "It's the music. It hurts me too much," she said in a low voice.

Charles immediately felt ashamed. He switched off his favorite station, which was playing Simon and Garfunkel's big hit "Bridge Over Troubled Waters." No one could understand more than he how Natasha felt. He hadn't been able to stand any love songs after his breakup with Blythe. It had taken a couple of years before he'd been able to listen without wanting to bawl like a kid . . . and Natasha had much more to cry about than he'd had. If he'd lost a child as well as a spouse, he couldn't imagine ever recovering.

In the last couple of months he'd been spending much more time in the States helping to build the domestic business. Louise had encouraged him to take her little sister on field trips, to show her something of America. "Charlie, I'd be grateful for anything you can suggest to take that agonized look off her face," she'd said, with something of an agonized look herself.

Did Louise feel guilty? Dad had told him Louise had felt guilty about his marriage breaking up, wondering if his long absences abroad, building up Louise Towers internationally, had caused it, but he didn't blame her one bit. Blythe could have accompanied him if she hadn't been so fixated on becoming a tennis star—in fact, if she hadn't been so fixated on a male tennis star.

His father had worked him like a slave driver. "To help you get over the mess, son," he'd said. He'd been resentful, but work had helped, and Charles knew, without Benedict saying "Work her ass off, Charlie," that his father considered hard work the answer to Natasha's understandable grief.

Well, no one had to order Natasha to work. She worked like a maniac, delivering the best facials in the shortest time at the Institutes, receiving the most compliments at the Palm Beach Spa, the biggest tips, the most demands for new appointments. Research and development had told him recently she was an idea girl, too. At the right moment he intended to talk to her about that, but he had to be careful. He wasn't sure yet what long-term role in the company Louise had in mind for her sister. He didn't want to step on any toes.

Charles slowed down as he saw a sign ahead. "Not too long now, Nat." He pressed her hand briefly. It was ice cold. He turned the air conditioning down. "Do you want to talk?"

She shook her head and stared out the window.

She'd started to open up a little bit on their second field trip together to Atlanta, where they were launching their new Big Glow Foundation at Rich's. Natasha had been billed for the first time as "a leading makeup artist from Europe," and he'd been impressed with her makeovers at the counter. The line had grown so long that Rich's had asked whether, if they ran an ad in the *Atlanta Constitution*, she could stay another couple of days, and Louise had said yes, and it was the first time Charles had seen Natasha smile.

She had a beautiful smile. It was the only time you could see a resemblance to her superstar sister, mainly because Natasha had such different coloring, much warmer, more golden, with all that wonderful red-gold hair and soft freckles over her nose. Although around the office they still referred to her as "Louise's little sister," she was almost as tall as Louise, but rounder. Reemer, showing off his new interest in art, had for once used the right analogy, describing her as "a Reubens as opposed to Louise's Renoir."

Before they'd flown back to New York, Charles had taken Natasha out to lunch, determined somehow to console her with the truth: that there was no one in the whole of the United States who could do more for her family than his father, except the President himself, with whom his father was on very good terms, just as he'd made it his business to be on good terms with every President since Truman.

The problem, as he'd quickly realized during that lunch, was that Natasha was frightened of the Towers family in general and his father in particular. He couldn't blame her. The transition from her life in Prague to her life as a member of the Towers entourage had to be traumatic, even if it wasn't overshadowed by so much tragedy.

From the terrible days of waiting in Vienna for the rest of her family to join her, Charles understood only too well how Natasha must have learned to fear his father. He sympathized with him, too, having to stay day after day in a hotel suite with two desperate women, both clinging to every false promise that Natasha's husband, baby, and mother would soon be there, when instead things were getting worse, culminating in Russia's invasion of Czechoslovakia with thousands of troops at the end of August.

His father wasn't used to roadblocks, blind alleys, expending massive effort to no avail. He wasn't used to placating people when things went wrong, either, not even his wife, as she watched her sister collapse with nervous tension, guilt, and anxiety when the world's press reported that Dubcek and his liberal Communist colleagues had been flown in manacles to Moscow, that the Prague spring was over, and that over half a million Soviet troops would occupy her country.

Pieter, Natasha's husband, had not been seen since he'd attempted to flee with the baby. Charles could well imagine how short his father's temper must have become in that nightmare atmosphere, particularly the day Natasha had tried to bolt back across the border to Czechoslovakia, when they'd had to sedate her and put her under a doctor's care in a Vienna hospital until she came to her senses. No wonder Natasha was wary of what Charles knew many of the employees called his father's famous "Towers temper twitch."

Apparently Blanka Sukova, Louise and Natasha's mother, hadn't helped. It was practically impossible to get through to her on the phone now, but his father had told him that in a letter received late the year before, Blanka had written that her brother, Ivo, had been told that

Natasha's husband and baby had been caught in an exchange of gun-fire in a place called Brno, on the way to the border. The mother had written bleakly that it would be better if Natasha considered them dead, which in many ways she wished she were herself!

They were approaching the famous Las Vegas Strip. Charles began to tell Natasha about the city in the desert, about the round-the-clock gambling, about the "one-armed bandits" positioned by the checkout counters of supermarkets, so that few shoppers ever returned home from grocery shopping with any change. He told her, as they approached the Hilton, how Nevada differed a hundred and eighty degrees from Utah, the state next door.

"In some little border towns, like Wendover, half in one state, half in the other, at one end of the main street guys are gambling their paychecks away, and girls are dancing topless in bars that never close, while at the other end—in Utah—even coffee is considered a dangerous stimulant and people say grace before eating a hot dog. This is America."

He found it a strain, trying to fill the silence with conversation, but his reward, as they drew up at the hotel, was one of Natasha's beautiful smiles.

She was a genuinely sweet person, Charles decided. Only time would help her mend, time or the wonderful news that somehow her uncle was wrong, that her loved ones were still alive somewhere in Czechoslovakia.

During the convention, more than three thousand women came to the Las Vegas Dinner Theater to hear about the Louise Towers/Opteck "marriage" and see for themselves, on a huge television screen, dramatic before-and-after transformations being carried out on stage by Natasha and a team of Louise Towers makeup artists and Opteck technicians. It was the first time they'd used this new, expensive Project-TV technology in before-and-afters.

As the last show ended to thunderous applause, Charles rushed to the phone to call New York. He'd been worried because he'd recommended they spend the extra money on Project-TV, and now it had succeeded beyond his wildest dreams.

"Orders for the new eye line are, if you'll excuse the expression, out of sight, Dave," he told David Reemer excitedly. "We've got to move to get an exclusive on Project-TV for cosmetic use as soon as possible. Nothing can sell makeup better than this. Every move, every stroke made on stage was simultaneously projected to movie-size proportions on the screen. It was just incredible. When they split the screen to show the final before-and-after effect, the audience went wild, and today, like every other day, we've had to bring in extra help to cope with taking orders at the booths."

"I know Madame Louise will want to know how Little Sister performed. Was she okay?" Charles was used to the laconic, supercilious note in his brother-in-law's voice. Charles shook his head in distaste as he answered him. Couldn't Reemer understand that Natasha wasn't going to fail? That whatever Suzanne said or predicted, if not as talented as her sister, Natasha was definitely an asset to Towers. In fact, Charles had been stunned upon seeing Natasha on the big screen. Made up by a professional Hollywood makeup artist for the occasion, she'd looked like a movie star herself.

He told Reemer so, adding, "Frankly, I was more than pleasantly surprised. There may be a way we can utilize her in special Project-TV promotions. I think we should have a meeting to find out if Louise has any objections to using Natasha for this kind of public appearance. If not, someone has to advise her how to dress, how to move, but I tell you, Dave, she's got it. She's a natural. The women loved her, foreign accent and all."

When he put the phone down, Charles was sorry that he'd even mentioned to his brother-in-law the need for Natasha to learn how to dress. Of course he would immediately repeat it to Suzanne. Well, it couldn't be helped, and in a way he was surprised that Louise hadn't already done something about Natasha's dreary-looking black and gray color schemes and strange accessory combinations. Perhaps she felt it was insensitive and frivolous to talk to her sister about clothes when she was still suffering so much. On the other hand, perhaps it was exactly what Natasha needed to begin to live again. She was too young to give up on life.

Back in New York, Project-TV provided Charles with a print of the Las Vegas show for Louise, Benedict, Reemer, and a group from marketing, so they could see for themselves what a success it was. "I like the makeup team in white doctors' coats," said Benedict, smiling. "A neat touch."

"Yes, we thought they gave the girls more clinical authority than the usual Louise Towers uniforms," Louise explained earnestly. "The white coats underline the link between beauty and medicine, between advising the consumer on which eyeglass frames to choose for their face shape and which eye makeup to glamorize their eyes behind the prescription lenses, which, of course, tend to magnify every wrinkle, every defect."

Benedict smiled. "Men never make passes at girls who wear glasses—"

"Unless they're also wearing Louise Towers eye makeup." David Reemer interjected smarmily.

Benedict ignored him. "I must say Natasha looks incredible. For the first time I don't feel so sorry for her, having you as a sister. Competition, my dear . . ."

Charles smiled, watching Reemer watch Louise, hoping for some sign of jealousy. There was none. On the contrary, Louise shone with pride. "She certainly does. It just shows you the magic of a professional makeup. She even looks a little happy." She turned to Benedict anxiously. "Charles tells me she's doing very well, especially when dealing directly with the consumer. Perhaps we should work out a special promotion program around her, using Project-TV."

"Let's work up some numbers," Benedict said. "Let me see a P-and-L on the Las Vegas promotion."

"We're working on the figures now," said Reemer. "Charles suggested Natasha might need some grooming if we're going to feature her in any prominent way, and Project-TV is nothing if not prominent. She's bound to get publicity, which means she needs a suitable wardrobe."

Charles saw Louise looking at him thoughtfully. He couldn't fathom what she was thinking, but then that was nothing unusual. He hoped she didn't think he'd been criticizing her sister behind her back to Reemer or Suzanne.

"I've tried to get her interested in her appearance, but except for doing the very minimum for store presentations, she's resisted." Louise looked troubled. "Except for the Louise Towers uniform and now the doctor's coat, as I don't need to tell you, she's refused to wear anything except black or gray. She told me last month she wants to remain in mourning until she finds out"—Louise gulped as if she were going to cry—"what's happened to her husband and . . . and . . . her little daughter, Kristina."

One of the marketing product managers, Dee Possant, said hesitantly, "She seems to work very well with Charles. I know she values his opinion. Perhaps if he talks to her it may seem more impersonal. If she knows she's going to have a larger role for the good of the company, perhaps he could persuade her to see Edie, the personal shopper we use at Saks to get clothes for our photo shoots."

"That's a good idea," said Reemer.

"Let's look at the cost involved with Project-TV first," said Benedict.

That night, as Benedict and Louise were getting ready to go to the theater, he asked her a question he'd been thinking of asking her for some time. "Do you ever regret not selling out to Averbach?"

Louise gave a short laugh. "Do I? Did I have any say in it? It was entirely your decision, wasn't it?" Before he could reply, she went on quickly, "No, Benedict, of course not. I always believed you when you said Feiner would destroy the heart and soul of the company. I've never liked the Swiss anyway."

What about the Poles? he thought. How much does she like the Poles?

As she sat at the dressing-table mirror, he pushed down her camisole top to cup her breasts and fondle her nipples, enjoying the reflection. "How did you feel when you saw your young sister looking like a femme fatale on the screen? I wasn't even aware she had breasts until I saw her in that Las Vegas film."

"If I believe that, I will believe anything."

"Are you jealous?"

"Of what?"

"Oh, I don't know. Her youth, her future, certainly not her beauty. You are a thousand times more beautiful."

"Her future?" Louise tried to move out of his grip, without success. "I only pray she thinks she has one. In the first few months, when we were so close, she confided in me and cried with me, day after day, night after night. Now she seems distant. Perhaps I'm imagining it, because I'm so worried about her. I still can't believe Pieter and Kristina are dead, but I don't want to hold out any hope. Frankly, I don't know what to do, and you tell me the situation in Czechoslovakia is even worse, if that's possible."

Benedict bent to kiss the nape of her neck. "I'd love to leave a mark there. Remember?"

"Of course I remember, but there's not much hair to cover it." She laughed again. "Perhaps it would give us a chance to test the new concealer?"

Benedict wasn't laughing. He continued to stroke her breasts, then said, "Sometimes I look at Charles and feel so old. You still look so young, more beautiful if possible, and there's Natasha, another version of a younger you, reminding me of the past. The years are going by so quickly, I don't know . . ." Benedict sounded unlike himself; Louise was startled.

She tried to get up to look at him, but his hands kept her down. "Do you think of me as old?"

"Of course not. I've never thought, never think of age when I think of you. You'll always be the most exciting man on earth for me."

If only he could believe she meant it. "You never wish I was younger? When you look at Charlie, for instance? Don't you ever wish

I was nearer his age, which is nearer your age, or that you were ten years younger? Like Natasha?"

Louise felt cold inside, but she shook her head as she watched her husband's hands still covering her breasts. There were now veins clearly visible on his hands, yes, old hands, but still as powerful as they had always been . . . as Charles's strong tanned hands were. A sound escaped her. Benedict misunderstood what it meant. It pleased him. "I'll always be able to arouse you, won't I, my pet? Shall we stay home?"

"But what about the Rockefellers? I thought we were meeting them?"

"Damn, of course we are. You make me forget everything." Benedict looked at his watch. "A pleasure deferred, my love." As he tied his tie, he seemed to be thinking aloud, but Louise wasn't sure. "I wonder what kind of love life Charlie has. It's time he found himself a new woman, don't you think? Well, first he'll do his duty and look after getting Natasha groomed and ready for stardom, then we'll give him some time off to look around and see what talent's available. Maybe I'll give Suzie a call and see if she has any candidates. It's time she came to her brother's rescue."

"That's a great idea," she said. She was proud of herself. It sounded as if she meant it. Perhaps she did.

It seemed to Natasha that she now spent most of her time traveling, by car, by train, by plane, crisscrossing the gigantic United States, making "personal appearances for Louise Towers," building the company's reputation as the number-one skin-care company with demonstrations using the amazing Project-TV. Without realizing it, she was building her own reputation too, albeit as "Louise Towers's sister with the magical touch."

She got used to keeping an overnight bag packed. With the help of Edie, the Saks personal shopper, she now had a small wardrobe in subdued but not, thank God, said Louise, funereal colors. Edie described them in language Natasha barely understood: "Perfect for taking you anywhere, anytime, from work to play, from dawn to dusk." But she didn't "play." Nor did she want to "play."

From breakfast time to bedtime, work was what she did and what she wanted to do. It was only in the last six months, since her success in Las Vegas and Louise's decision to use her on the road with the Project-TV promotion, that she'd started to come alive. In order to get through the hours and days and weeks before, ever since her arrival in America, she'd had to pretend to herself that she didn't really live there; that she was on an extended visit to her famous sister; that she would wake up one day and find it was time to go home to Pieter's outstretched arms.

But one morning she'd woken up—she couldn't remember where it had been, one of the "small towns" on her itinerary, so grossly misnamed by the promotions department, and she'd simply forgotten to "pretend" and play a role that day. She'd overslept for the first time since her arrival. More accurately, she'd been able to sleep all through the night instead of tossing and turning most of it away. Instead of 4:00 or 5:00 A.M., it had miraculously been 8:15 A.M. and she was being picked up at eight-forty-five to appear at a downtown hotel. It was funny how all American towns, big and small, had "downtowns" where apparently the "business" was. In her rush to be on time and to do her homework about the store and the products the sales department particularly wanted pushed that day, for the first time Natasha hadn't thought about whether there would be any news from Prague. She'd lived that day like every other Louise Towers employee, living and working in America.

Of course, not every day had been like that, but there were more "real" days now, fewer "pretend" days. She still had sleepless nights, many of them, but she could sometimes even take out the memory of Kristina without falling apart. She still had hope, but now her hope was tied up with making it in America, not as a star like her sister, but making it the way most Americans she worked with wanted to make it, with money, enough money to conduct her own search for her loved ones.

Because of her relationship with the Towers family, it had been decided that instead of reporting to a vice president of marketing, as most promotional sales employees did, Natasha should report directly to top Towers management, to Charles. She was relieved they hadn't chosen Suzanne Towers's husband, David Reemer. Suzanne, she felt, eyed her with suspicion, whereas she believed that Charles really cared about her welfare.

From time to time, when it was an important "door"—cosmetics companies called the stores they supplied "doors," she had learned—Charles accompanied her, amused and charmed by her reactions to the "small towns" she was told to appear in. "They're not small at all," she told him with a mixture of awe and annoyance. "Here in middle of nowhere is another city, full of skyscrapers, department stores, fancy hotels and, yes, lots of customers, asking same questions all the time."

"It doesn't seem to matter whether rich or poor," she related wide-eyed after record-breaking sales followed her demonstration in Dayton, Ohio. "During our tat-a-tat at counter after appearance and demonstration, however pleased with selves or good dressed they look, they all want to know how to look young or how to take away the wrinkles."

"Tête-à-tête," Charles corrected her automatically, not aware that he was doing it. "And *well* dressed, not *good* dressed." He had flown in especially because Natasha was making her first television appearance on a talk show the next day, and during the week it had been reported that she was terrified.

Now she looked at him beseechingly. "Do I have to do this silly thing? I can't. My English ... my mistakes ..."

"Your English is just fine. The more mistakes you make, the prettier it sounds. You just have to do in the television studio what you've been doing for the last few months in stores and hotels around the country. For most people, appearing on stage, as you've been doing, would be much more frightening." He was walking her back to her hotel room. When they reached her door, he chucked her under the chin. "It will all be over in a minute, you'll see. You'll wonder why you made such a fuss."

"You sound like my mother when she took me to dentist as little girl. 'It won't hurt. It will all be over in minute.' That's what this television is like ... like going to dentist."

It was the first time she had mentioned her mother or anything to do with her past life when she hadn't looked desolate. Did she realize that? A warm feeling came over him as he looked at Natasha's upturned face. She was a brave girl. She was smiling. There were no tears in her eyes. She was getting better. Her wounds were beginning to heal. It made him feel like a giant, like a bloody great giant, that he had been the motivating force behind this course of action, which was turning out so well for the company, but, much more important, was helping Natasha get back on her feet.

Impulsively, Charles bent down and kissed her cheek. "If you're a good girl and don't cry, I'll buy you a present after the show."

He saw she was blushing. It made her look even prettier. "Oh no, you don't have to do that, Charlie ..."

He repeated "Sharlie" to himself as he strolled back to his room, the warm feeling still there, wondering what on earth he could find the girl that she might like.

Natasha didn't do so well on the local noontime talk show. She was so nervous she dropped the new nourisher on the floor and spent too long trying to mop it up, despite the attempts of the show's hostess to dissuade her. Charles didn't attempt to pretend she'd handled it well. She was far too smart to accept any hogwash, but to his delight he found it didn't take her long to see the funny side of it.

"That studio floor never looked so good," he said, as he drove her to the department store where she was going to appear that afternoon. "Towers has a floor-wax business too, you know. Perhaps we should add a little L.T. Nourisher to the formula—floor rejuvenator, something like that." He wasn't at his funniest, but perhaps out of relief that it was over, Natasha laughed at everything he said.

When he drew up at the store's staff entrance, he took a small box out of his pocket. "I promised if you didn't cry, I'd give you a present, so here it is."

"Oh, Charlie, no!"

"Oh, Sharlie, yes, yes . . ."

He watched her as, with obvious excitement, she unwrapped the paper. "It's nothing much." Suddenly he wished it were something more than the gold key ring in the shape of the letter N that he'd bought that morning. At the time it had seemed appropriate, suitable; now he was embarrassed by her little-girl glee, opening the box.

He needn't have been. Natasha was obviously thrilled, though he couldn't think why, but at least it was gold, and of course she was thoroughly unspoiled, so unlike most of the predatory women he took out.

Charles had a satisfactory meeting with the store president that afternoon, when an agreement was reached not only to move the Louise Towers counter to a more advantageous position in the cosmetics department, but also to double its size. They strolled through the aisles together later, hoping to catch the end of Natasha's special demonstration in the store's large promotion arena. They were too late. The store's obviously elated promotion director said that Natasha had, like a Pied Piper, already led the audience to the Louise Towers counter, where the beauty consultants were being run off their feet selling whatever Natasha decreed.

From the back of the crowd around the counter, Charles could see Natasha, flushed, excited, in her element, her English getting more broken by the minute, as women, their voices rising to be heard, asked for her personal recommendations. There was no one like her. He corrected himself. He had seen only one other person have such an effect on women, on consumers, and that, of course, was Louise, who conducted herself so differently, but who also knew how to make sales soar through the roof. Towers Pharmaceuticals had really lucked out, with two such priceless assets.

He called his office and found that a budget meeting with his father had been postponed to the following week. He moved a few other appointments around, deciding he wouldn't return to New York that night. He'd take Natasha out to dinner to celebrate her success with Hudson's before she moved on to do her thing at her next stop, Marshall Field's in Chicago.

But they didn't go to dinner. On the way back to the hotel, they passed a billboard advertising *Love Story* at the Northway Drive-in. "What's a love story at a drive-in?" she asked innocently.

"Would you like to see?"

"Oh yes!" There was still something of the small child about her. She was on a high from her success with the customers. Either she'd forgotten about the TV debacle, or he'd convinced her it didn't matter. Her hair, so carefully coiffed for the TV appearance, the Project-TV demo, and the in-store public appearance, was now unraveling in red-gold fronds over her forehead, and freckles were showing through on her nose, which was shiny.

"You look about twelve," he said.

"Oh, I must look a muss!" Muss! Charles laughed, watching as she hunted through her bag for her compact, an antique one with small diamond chips he remembered she'd received from Leonard and Marlene at the usual Towers gathering around the Christmas tree. How much more assured she was now, how delightfully feminine and kittenish. The more she smiled, the more he wanted to make her smile.

It happened at the drive-in. He didn't know how; he would never know how. Perhaps it was because he soon realized it was totally the wrong kind of picture for her to see. How could he have known? He never read reviews, he wasn't much of a moviegoer, but *Love Story* was a thousand times worse for the heartstrings than listening to "Bridge Over Troubled Waters."

He looked at Natasha's profile, her serious, intense eyes fixed on the screen, and was about to whisper that he was sorry, they didn't need to sit any longer watching such sentimental, mawkish junk, when she turned to him with a funny little crooked grin. Suddenly she was in his arms, and his mouth was on her mouth, and she was kissing him as much as he was kissing her, and he was dizzy with the smell of her sweet sweat and the softness of her body and he knew the only thing he wanted to do was protect her from all the pain and misery in the world and take away forever the guilt and pain from her eyes.

They didn't see any more of the movie. Perhaps it was true—he'd often read it—that drive-ins were for lovers who had nowhere else to go. They kissed for so long, he could see the skin around her mouth was red, sore. They hardly spoke, except to murmur each other's names. They held on to each other as if they'd just been rescued from disaster. Only when the huge spotlights around the movie parking lot went on did they come back to earth. She stared ahead, biting her lip as he slowly drove back to the hotel.

He didn't know what to say. He didn't know exactly how he felt—a little ashamed, but not too much, strangely nervous, or perhaps awkward was a better word.

As he parked the car, Natasha said in a shaky voice, "I . . . I don't know, I'm sorry, Charles."

Instead of calling him Charlie or "Sharlie," as she usually did when they were on the road working together, the use of the more formal "Charles" was her way of showing him she knew he was, of course, her boss. It touched him, but saddened him too. He was the one who should apologize.

"Don't be sorry, Natasha. I don't know what came over me, but . . . well, you know we're two wounded birds. I thought all my misery was behind me, but perhaps that stupid movie got to me. I turned to comfort you, and I guess . . . I guess I must have wanted some comforting myself."

Her face was pale, tense with shadows under her eyes emphasized by the harsh parking-lot lights. "Forgive me, Nat," he heard himself saying, although that wasn't what he wanted to say.

She didn't answer. They walked stiffly back to the hotel and shook hands like strangers in the lobby. Neither of them slept well that night. Charles gave up the attempt at about three o'clock and tried to bury himself in paperwork, but again and again he remembered the softness of Natasha, the sweetness of her mouth, and the feeling came back that he wanted to protect and guard her against any further unhappiness.

Natasha lay awake staring at the ceiling, wondering how and why she had allowed Charles to kiss her, to hold her, not just once but for hours, had not only "allowed" him, but had responded so fully, so completely. She had needed him, but was it the need for any warmhearted, sympathetic male? Was it because the ache for Pieter's arms had grown so great she would have fallen into anyone's arms, watching the two American movie stars make such tender love up on the screen? No, that wasn't true. It was because Charles was always so sweet and thoughtful to her. He had explained it perfectly. She wasn't the only one in the world who had suffered. His wife had left him for another man. It had taken him years to get over it, and every so often he hurt just as she hurt.

In the morning there was a note waiting for her. "I don't regret last night, and neither should you. I'll see you back in New York next week. Love, Charles." She reread the note several times on the way to

Chicago. She didn't realize it, but every time she read it she was smiling.

Although Suzanne still felt exactly the same about Louise, it didn't stop her from pestering Benedict and everyone in the family to come to Moat Cay for Thanksgiving, instead of the usual gathering in the Park Avenue apartment.

Louise absolutely didn't want to go. She hated Suzanne for being in control of her life as much as she knew Suzanne reveled in it, but finally, when she heard to her surprise that Charles wanted to go, once he knew for certain that Blythe would not be on the island with her sister Maisie, and then Natasha told her she would love a few days of sunshine, she relented.

Louise was worried about Natasha, who she knew had been working herself to exhaustion. She hadn't seen her sister in weeks, as Natasha traveled from one end of America to the other. When Louise finally put her foot down and demanded that somebody else take Natasha's place in the Project-TV program, she was shocked to see how thin and drawn she looked.

"Do you realize this is the first time we've been alone together in months?" Louise chided her sister gently over lunch at La Grenouille. "I am very cross with Charles for working you so hard."

"It isn't Charlie's fault," Natasha replied quickly. "I asked to be kept busy. Charlie . . ." She corrected herself, not knowing that a soft pink had come to her cheeks. "Charles would like me to do less, too, but he knows it helps." Natasha was trying to summon up her courage to ask Louise about Blythe, but she didn't know how to do it. Charles had told her a lot now, but she wanted her sister's view of why the marriage had failed.

How could anyone leave a man like Charles, she continually asked herself. He was so gentle, so thoughtful, as well as being the most sophisticated man she'd ever known. Every instinct told her to trust him. They hadn't kissed again, or at least not as they'd kissed at the drive-in. He had kissed her good night on the mouth four times since, and each time he had been the one to move away. He was right, of course, but she knew that he knew the more they were together, the stronger their friendship grew. When he didn't visit her on the road, she missed him—a lot. He told her he missed her, too.

It was the reason he'd told her to tell Louise she'd like to go to the Bahamas, since Suzanne had invited the whole family and he had decided to accept, though Suzanne had told him her best friend, Maisie Parr Dobson, would also be in residence. Maisie was Blythe's sister, but Charles had explained that he'd remained on good terms with Maisie and her husband, whereas apparently after the divorce Blythe had not.

Louise saw her sister blush. It puzzled her, but she squeezed Natasha's hand as she said what she thought Natasha wanted most to hear. "Benedict is still working with the State Department to try to get some information, but there is so much confusion in Prague, and the new, severe censorship laws aren't helping. It appears there were no actual eyewitnesses to what Uncle Ivo told Mama. It was established that Pieter was trying to get out with Kristina and was definitely in an area where the Russian tanks were firing, but so far no one is talking. There's a definite underground in Prague now, and that's where the State Department is concentrating its efforts, but I don't need to tell you how frightened people are to speak." When Natasha didn't answer, Louise went on, "If work helps, you know we want whatever you want. Helena Rubinstein used to say, 'Work is the only excitement which lasts.' I used to think, 'Poor woman, she doesn't know any better,' but I think if the word is excitement, she was probably right. I've always found work a great panacea."

Natasha looked uncomfortable. "I don't know." She stared at her plate, where a delectable salad of tiny shrimp and artichoke hearts awaited her attention. "There are ... other excitements," she finally added slowly.

What was going on in Natasha's head? Louise knew that everyone in the company thought they were so different, she the inscrutable, mysterious one, Natasha much more open and easy to read, but she could tell them Natasha could act like a closed-up clam, too.

Louise decided to change the subject. She started to talk about the business, about customers' comments, about increasing competition from Estée Lauder and the specter of K. Avery, who, Louise told her uncomprehending sister, along with two other big American drug companies, was now interested in buying Elizabeth Arden, after having once expressed interest in Louise Towers. Mostly, Louise talked and Natasha seemed to listen.

It was only when Louise mentioned the upcoming Thanksgiving visit to Moat Cay that Natasha brightened up, especially when she learned that Leonard, Marlene, and their daughter, Zoe, were Suzanne's latest recruits. "I like Marlene. She is very kind," Natasha said.

"Yes, she is. It hasn't been easy for her, fitting into the Tower clan."

"Was it easy for you?"

Had Natasha ever asked her such a direct question before? Louise didn't think so. They had never talked about Louise's arrival in

America. By now Louise was sure Natasha knew more than she'd ever written home to Prague about her divorce from Milos, her move to work in London, and then her move back to America and her marriage to the mighty Benedict Towers. With so much on Natasha's mind and too many years between their ages, there had never been any need, Louise had decided, to tell her baby sister many details about her own agonizing past. Now was certainly not the time.

A silence fell, one Louise didn't like. It wasn't the kind of silence that family members could live and relax with. Something was wrong, something new.

"Nothing is ever easy when you move to another country."

Another pause. Should she ask Louise now about Blythe? Something told Natasha that Louise wasn't the one to ask. Perhaps Marlene could tell her something when they were all in Moat Cay together. Perhaps she'd learn something just by studying Maisie, Blythe's sister.

David Reemer had won a concession from Suzanne when at last, after nearly four years of delays and breakdowns in communication, two houses, each with three guest cottages, had finally been completed in the Moat Cay compound, one for Maisie and her brood, and one for the Reemers, while a third stood half-finished, for her father and Louise to occupy one day.

"We have to get our own plane. We can't be dependent on the air taxis down here," David had said to his wife from the beginning. "The pilots may be okay, but I don't trust the mechanics, and, knowing you, you won't want to be dependent on any blacks, either." The year before, Suzanne, who always said she hated small planes, had agreed, and they'd bought a 1968 Cessna in mint condition for twelve thousand dollars.

David had immediately enrolled in flying school and now had his pilot's license, something Suzanne moaned about when he spent "too much time playing with his new airplane toy," or trumpeted about when they island-hopped together or, as now, when David taxied in on the rough Moat Cay airstrip, bringing over from Nassau some extra pairs of hands to look after the swelling number of Thanksgiving guests.

After a lunch of barbecued fish and tropical salad, Suzanne led the way to a large, shady veranda overlooking the sea. "Iced coffee and a snooze for the grownups, yes? Who wants coffee, iced or otherwise? Hands up." She counted languidly as Benedict, Leonard, and her husband raised their hands. "Four for coffee, then." Her eyes flickered maliciously toward Louise, who sat cool and composed in a cream cotton dress on a chaise longue. "This is perfect for the grownups in the afternoon. It gets all the breeze, and we can see what the youngsters are up to, who today seem to include my brother and your sister, Louise," she said through tight lips.

While around them Suzanne's children, Kick and Fiona, played a noisy, quarrelsome game with little Zoe Towers and three of Maisie's children, Natasha and Charles stood looking out to sea, seemingly oblivious of everyone else.

As Louise watched them and Suzanne watched her, they turned and waved to the group on the veranda. Charles came nearer to shout, "We're going shelling. I told Natasha about the trophies I found for your shell cabinet last time I was here, Suze."

To everyone's surprise, including her own, Louise stood up, calling out, "Wait for me. I'd like to stretch my legs after that lunch." She turned to Benedict. "Darling, would you like to ... " She stopped. Benedict was already dozing, his head fallen onto his chest.

That night the entire Towers group went over to Maisie's for dinner, walking along the path that bordered the perfect white sand beach. Natasha was happy to walk with Marlene, who, often the last to arrive, never knowing what to wear, was at the tail end. Hesitantly, Natasha asked, "Did ... did you ever meet Blythe, Charles's wife—ex-wife—Maisie's sister?"

"Of course I did. Lots of times ... well, on family occasions. I can't say I ever really knew her. Too Wasp, too sporty for me." Marlene spoke casually, more at ease with Natasha than with anyone else in the family, but nevertheless looking anxiously ahead, walking faster to catch up with Leonard, who was already approaching the wide white stone steps to the Parr Dobsons' beachfront patio.

Suzanne, holding on to David's arm, was taking a pebble out of her sandal as they arrived at the steps. To Natasha's embarrassment, Marlene said, "Natasha was asking me about Blythe. She's not going to be here, is she? I mean, that would be dreadful!"

Suzanne looked at Natasha in much the same way that Louise had looked at her yesterday when they'd gone shelling. Not idly curious, but speculative. Natasha felt guilty because she'd been disappointed when Louise had joined them, though Charles had obviously been delighted. She hadn't enjoyed the expedition as she knew she would have if Charles and she had been able to go alone.

"Of course Blythe isn't here," Suzanne said sharply. "Do you think I'd be such a fool as to ask the family down if she were! Maisie would never ask her. Anyway, she's very pissed off with her. Now she's off

somewhere with an Argentinian polo player or hockey player or someone equally suspect."

Again Suzanne looked at Natasha, before they climbed the steps.
"Charlie took the breakup very hard, but he's over it now. He's having
a ball with lots of beautiful young wanna-be's." Natasha didn't know
what she meant, but she wasn't going to ask. When the moment was
right she would ask Charlie what a "wanna-be" was.

It was a trying evening for her. After dinner they played charades,
"for the children's sake," but it seemed to Natasha that the adults
enjoyed it more, even Charles, who rolled on the floor to enact something she finally understood to be a play called *Death of a Salesman*.
Luckily, after proving her English wasn't up to it, Natasha was excused
from joining a team and went out on the patio for some fresh air.

The patio ran along the bedroom wing of the low-lying house, and
all the louvered doors were open, revealing bedrooms and anterooms
with streamlined white wicker furniture, colorful, chintz-covered cushions and covers, and softly lighted primitive paintings. She wandered
into a bedroom, looking for a bathroom. There were dozens of photographs on a side table, photographs of the family, of good-looking,
confident people having a wonderful time, laughing into the camera,
some of whom Natasha thought looked familiar; they were famous
faces, but she couldn't put a name to any of them. Which one, if any,
was Blythe?

The door opened behind her, and Fiona, Suzanne and David's nine-
year-old, came in, also looking for the bathroom. Natasha smiled at
the solemn-looking child. "Aren't these pretty pictures?"

Fiona didn't answer, but just stared at her. Then she said, "Are you
really Loulou's little sister? You don't look like Loulou."

"No, I know I look different," Natasha said gently. "But yes . . ."
She laughed, liking the name Suzanne's children had somehow grown
used to calling Louise. "Yes, I really am Loulou's little sister."

"Can you imagine, Natasha then asked the child if Blythe was in
any of the photos!" Suzanne exclaimed to her husband the next day,
as she emerged from the shower to dress for their Thanksgiving dinner.
"Of course, Fiona could hardly remember—why should she?—she was
only about four or five when they broke up, and Charlie and Blythe
were hardly together for more than a week at a time. But why this
sudden interest on Natasha's part? You don't think there's going to be
another Czech invasion of the Towers family, do you?"

"God, no!" David exclaimed. "Why on earth would you think that?

She's pretty, but very much an also-ran, next to her sister, although I know you hate me to say it. She's Miss Beauty Consultant 1970. Surely you don't think your brother would be interested in that."

"My father was," Suzanne snapped. "How many times do I have to tell you Louise was Ludmilla the upstairs maid—or was it downstairs?"

"And how many times do I have to remind you that Ludmilla was and still is a knockout! As trained by your father, Louise is certainly as beautiful as any movie star—and that's very good for business, our bottom line, your inheritance, m'dear." When Suzanne glared at him, he shook his head as if she were an idiot. "If I've told you once, I've told you a thousand times, accept your stepmama for what she is, and you'll save yourself a lot of grief."

In the largest guest cottage, as Benedict and Louise dressed for dinner, they chatted about Natasha, too. "Your little sister is coming out of her shell at last," Benedict said as he buttoned up a white piqué shirt. "I thought it would never happen, but I've actually seen her laughing on this trip."

When Louise didn't answer, he said, "Hey, did you hear me?"

"Sorry, darling. Yes, of course, you're right. Well, it's time. You've done so much for her." There was a hard note in Louise's voice that took Benedict by surprise.

"What's up? You hardly sound ecstatic. Surely you don't expect her to wear sackcloth and ashes forever, do you? I'll never understand women. Now you sound as if you don't want her to be happy. I can tell you it's embarrassing for me to owe so many favors at State. I'd love to stop putting the pressure on and forget all about your Czech connection. What's wrong? Is she stealing too much of your thunder out on the road? Sales have been phenomenal!"

"Oh, really! Of course not. How could you think like that?" Her voice was much sharper than she'd meant it to be. Quickly she went over to him and put her arms around his neck. "Sometimes I just don't think Natasha's as appreciative as she should be for all you've done and are doing for her—buying her the apartment, bringing her here on the private plane to stay on a private island, buying her new clothes when she wants them. I worry that she takes all this incredible luxury for granted. Being a member of this family is so special, I just want her to show that she's aware of how lucky she is, despite all the horror she's endured."

"It's another generation, my dear. Well, okay, not really, but she so often looks like a teenager, I forget Natasha's real age. All the same, she didn't have any time to grow into life with the Towers family as you did." Benedict began to laugh at the cross look on Louise's face. "You did have to earn your way in, no? Whereas Natasha arrived as a full-fledged member. But let's face it, she's certainly earning her way, working as she does for the company. Charles is thrilled with her performance."

What kind of performance? No sooner had the thought crossed her mind than she threw it out. If she was beginning to suspect her own sister, she was obviously in need of a refresher from the psychiatrist!

"I saw them holding hands."

"That's not all he's been holding, from what I've been told."

"Well, what else do you expect? They've been thrown together so much. They're always out of town, on the road. He's been supervising her for months."

"They call it something else where I come from."

"What else is new? It's natural. Like father, like son. Bringing in fresh peasant blood, that's the way these dynasties go. Don't think Madame Louise didn't have that in mind for her little sister from the first."

"Some people get all the luck. She arrives as a washed-out refugee and ends up with the boss's son. He's a dish, apart from having all that dough."

"I'm not so sure she'll end up with him. He could just be having a fling."

"Not if Madame Louise has anything to do with it."

"Well, Madame Suzanne won't be too happy. Haven't you heard her go on about the Czech invasion?"

Hardly daring to breathe, still in her pale turquoise Louise Towers robe with matching paper slippers, Marlene sat motionless in the back cubicle until she heard the two chattering employees leave the spa's changing room. It wasn't the first time she'd heard innuendos about Charles and Natasha. She had become friendly with one or two people in marketing who'd made the odd wisecrack, but she'd never taken anything seriously, knowing how people in New York loved to gossip.

Recently, though, she'd heard some stories, and now, trying to get in shape at the Palm Beach spa after the Christmas holidays, here she was, over a thousand miles away from the head office, and the employees were gossiping about the same thing.

Something had to be done. Whether there was any truth in what she'd just heard, Marlene didn't know or care, but the family name was at stake, a name she, as a small-town girl from Tennessee, was fiercely proud to call her own.

Marlene made a decision. It was no use telling Leonard. He would immediately tell Benedict, who was always too hard on Charles anyway, and God knew what he might do. She had no influence on Natasha, and in any case it would be embarrassing if there was really nothing to the talk. Charles was an exceptionally thoughtful, kind young man. Perhaps Natasha misinterpreted that kindness for something else. On the other hand, Marlene reflected, as she knew only too well, coming as she did from a town of gossips, there was usually no smoke without fire. The only one who could put an end to whatever was going on was Louise, who could talk to both Natasha and Charles and tell them their behavior was causing talk.

Her sister-in-law unnerved her with her ability to stay silent for so long during a conversation, to make her feel as if her shoulder strap was showing or her lipstick was smudged when she looked at her with her dark, soulful eyes, but Marlene told herself she had to summon up courage for the sake of the family.

Under Leonard's orders, she had asked Louise to lunch a few times over the past few years. "Duty" lunches that somehow she'd endured without making a complete fool of herself. Now she would ask her to lunch for the good of the Louise Towers company; at least this was something Louise would be able to thank her for.

Marlene chose the Colony Club because, as she told herself, the dining room was so discreet, so quiet. In fact, she was immensely proud of her membership, which had taken quite a while to arrange, and felt it added to her stature to arrive there with someone as celebrated as Louise. After a while, though, she wished she hadn't chosen the Colony. In a trashy novel she'd read the phrase "the silence was deafening." It was only after sitting through three courses with Louise in the still atmosphere of the second-floor dining room that she realized the sentence did, in fact, make sense.

They'd discussed Zoe and her reading problems, Leonard's occasional painful bouts of gout, whether Louise thought the house on Moat Cay would ever be ready for them, the new Louise Towers perfume, Veil of Night, which Marlene was proud to be wearing before it went on sale, and now, with coffee, she knew the time had come to discuss what had been on her mind all through the consommé, sole meuniere, and fruit compote.

"I was just at the Palm Beach spa, as you know," she began. Instead of telling Louise about what had prompted the invitation to lunch, she found herself praising the facials, the massages, the sumptuous rooms.

It wasn't until they were walking down the staircase to the cloakroom that Marlene blurted out, "Louise, I haven't known how to say this, but you have to talk to Natasha and Charles."

Her sister-in-law stopped in mid-step, an alarmed look on her usually phlegmatic face. "About what?" she asked coldly.

"I think they're having an affair, but whether they are or not, people think they are. There's a lot of unfortunate gossip in New York, and unfortunately in Palm Beach, too."

Marlene was talking to Louise's back. She was continuing to walk down the stairs. When they reached the bottom, Marlene saw that Louise looked as if she were going to faint, her normal paleness changed to an abnormal pallor. "Oh my dear, oh Louise, I didn't mean to upset you. I'm sure Natasha would never do anything to disgrace you, us . . ." Marlene fluttered her hands around, aghast at Louise's reaction.

She followed her into the cloakroom, where Louise sat down carefully on the sofa, as if in pain. She closed her eyes, took a deep breath, then seemed to regain her composure. "Tell me what you've heard, Marly."

Marlene recounted most of what she'd heard sitting in the cubicle, along with various comments heard over the past few months in New York.

"I wish you'd told me this before." Louise's voice was even lower than usual, but now she didn't look as if she were going to faint.

"Are you going to tell Benedict?" Marlene asked fearfully. "If you do, please don't involve me."

"Don't worry, Marly. I'll handle this myself."

Natasha and Charles . . . Natasha and Charles . . . How she had stopped herself from being sick, she didn't know. By the time Louise arrived in her office, she thought she was in control. "Bring me the Project-TV calendar," she ordered.

Yes, she was right. Natasha was going to be in the New York and Connecticut area for the next week, before going down to work at the Palm Beach spa for a month. She buzzed for another file and frowned when she found what she was looking for. Charles would be attending the National Association of Drugstores' three-day convention in Boca Raton, just down the road from Palm Beach, the week Natasha arrived at the spa. She pushed the file away, feeling sick again. He was then intending to spend a couple of days in Palm Beach, working with the architects on a proposed extension, and all through the month his appointments were in comfortable proximity to Florida. Natasha and Charles . . . She was screaming inside.

Where was Benedict? Her mind was blank, then she remembered he was in Washington at an economic advisory meeting with the President. "Don't wait up for me," he'd said.

"Please ask my sister to come to the apartment when she finishes work. I have something urgent to discuss with her."

She could no longer concentrate on work herself. Even the thought of a facial at the Sixty-second Street Institute, often a fast way to relaxation, was out. Although it was raining and chilly, she left the office without summoning the car, wanting to feel the sting of rain on her face, cold air on her legs. Nothing seemed real. She walked as fast as she could, punishing her body, her mind a nightmare of all the pain she'd lived through, all the dreams of rescuing Natasha and her husband and baby and, one day, her mother too, meaningless. Instead of love, she hated Natasha—and Charles—but most of all she hated herself.

"I don't know what you mean." Natasha was pale, defiant, angry. "Who's been talking? Gossiping?"

Louise tried to remain calm, to act like the wiser older sister who had called the meeting to guide an errant, unworldly girl away from danger, but she knew she was failing. Her voice shook as she asked, "Natasha, are you having an affair with Charles?"

"No, no, no! How dare people say so? Charles is . . . always is . . . my friend, a wonderful friend . . ." angry tears streamed down her face.

Louise couldn't stop. "Have you made love? Been seen together? I'm trying to help you. I'll fire anybody who dares to talk about you, but I must know the truth."

Natasha put her head in her hands and now burst into noisy tears. "No, no, not love, not like . . . like . . . not exactly . . ."

Louise bit her lip. "Has Charles taken advantage of you?"

Natasha lifted her tear-stained face. "Never! Never! We're like . . . how did he say . . . two wounded birds . . . we comfort each other. We are very close." She looked at Louise with a strange, cautious expression, as if not sure whether to trust her or not. "I love him like a friend. I need him. He needs me. That is all, until I know what the future holds."

"What do you mean by that?" Louise knew she was shouting, but she didn't care.

Natasha was shaken, but she returned Louise's angry shout with one of her own. "Until I know about my Pieter . . . what happened to my Pieter and my baby. Charles is my protector . . . he has told me so . . . he wants to help me until I find out the truth."

As Louise glared at her, Natasha wiped her eyes and then said coldly, "I thought you would be pleased to know that. You've always said you wanted me to make new friends, to build a new life in America, to stop always thinking about past. Charles is helping me do all those things. Why should you want to stop it? Are you jealous I like Charles so much? I don't understand."

Louise fought to regain control, but she couldn't make her tone warmer. "For the good of the company, it would be best if you didn't see so much of each other. I'm going to change your schedule tomorrow. You probably didn't even realize it, but while you were going to be at the Palm Beach spa, Charles was planning to spend some time in Florida. It's that kind of thing that feeds rumor and gossip." She prayed as she spoke that perhaps it was all a terrible mistake, one of those coincidences in life that bring nothing but trouble, but Natasha's behavior immediately made her lose hope.

"How can you! We . . . we . . . Charles planned his calendar around my stay in spa. You can't do this to me. You can't, you can't. You pull strings like I am doll. Take me away from home, husband, baby, then when I have friend, take me away from friend. What do you want from me?" She was screaming, throwing her arms up in the air. Louise had never seen her like this, had never witnessed anything like it from anyone. As Natasha grew louder and angrier, Louise grew quieter and colder. So this was the gratitude she received for rescuing her sister from repression and poverty. "Control yourself." Now her voice was like ice. "You're behaving like an imbecile." Like a tramp, a slut, she wanted to cry, but now all she wanted was to be left alone, to think through what this short confrontation with Natasha meant, in all its implications.

"I won't let you order me about anymore!" Her sister was still screaming. "I'll ask Charlie to talk to father. He's real boss, not you." As quickly as she had turned into a fireball, Natasha crumpled and collapsed on the sofa, her shoulders shaking, talking to herself in Czech. Louise could only hear a few words, interspered with *Pieter, Kristina, Mama.* She wanted to feel the familiar sense of guilt and pity rising in her, to go over to her sister and rock her out of her grief as she had done in the first few months of her arrival, but she couldn't. She sat like stone, waiting for Natasha to recover her composure, waiting for her to leave so that she could give in to her own sense of loss.

New York, 1972

LAST YEAR HAD been the worst Benedict could remember for business. Not a day had seemed to go by without a new problem, a new lawsuit, another nosy parker from one government subcommittee or another, poking their usually uninformed noses into Towers's affairs, and, last but far from least, unusual pressure from the banks to reduce their spending.

A BITTER PROFIT PILL FOR BIG DRUG MAKER, the *Wall Street Journal* headline had screamed at the end of the year, topping an article that had listed Towers's woes in an altogether too accurate way.

Two of his biggest pharmaceutical competitors had finally muscled their way into the cosmetics business, but it wasn't even Lilly's successful purchase of Elizabeth Arden, after a battle with Cyanamid, or Squibb's acquisition of Charles of the Ritz that troubled him. Sure, he didn't like it. It meant the struggle was intensified to keep or find the few really talented people in the crazy cosmetics business and step up the industrial espionage to find out what, if anything, was going on in their labs that Louise Towers wasn't already working on. There was no Ponce de León or fountain of youth around—yet.

What made Benedict most bilious was the ongoing, extraordinary success of K. Avery's acne-fighting drug, AC3, now available by prescription, and sending Avery's stock sky-high. The fact that he'd invested in it himself after his evening meeting with Audrey Walson, long before the FDA approved Avery's clinical trials, didn't sweeten his temper. He'd made a few hundred thousand dollars already on his investment, but it meant nothing.

There were two people on whom he would like to put out contracts he thought grimly as, back from a brief New Year's holiday in Moat Cay, he arrived at his office for his first day's work in 1972. One of them was the so-called consumer activist Ralph Nader, who, he knew, many of his contemporaries running other different businesses would also cheerfully eliminate. The other was Jan Feiner.

According to Audrey, Feiner was now the FDA's blue-eyed boy who could do no wrong. He received endless kudos in the business and pharmaceutical press, often for things he had nothing whatever to do with, and was treated like a celebrity on the society pages, as was any girl he ever took out more than once.

Was Feiner still in touch with Louise? Benedict hadn't been able to establish that he was, but sometimes, despite having the best investigators in the world at his disposal, he woke up in the middle of the night wet with perspiration, believing that somehow, something was still going on.

Benedict groaned when he looked at the first report in the file on his desk marked PRIORITY/URGENT, sent to him by the company's lawyers. A subcommittee of the House Small Business Committee was recommending a more rigorous review and monitoring system for over-the-counter drugs, now that consumers were increasingly turning to self-medication to reduce health-care costs.

In the same "urgent" file was a note to call Stephenson, now on the Czech desk at State. Benedict sighed. Whatever the news, he didn't want to hear it, didn't want to have to think about what both he and Louise had begun to call "the Czech problem."

He cursed the day he'd ever been persuaded to undertake the hazardous task of getting Natasha out from behind the Iron Curtain. It hadn't brought Louise any happiness. Since he'd learned the year before that Charles had taken his job of helping Natasha over her misery a shade too conscientiously, there had been nothing but rows.

Not between Charles and himself. As far as he was concerned, provided Charles wasn't serious and acted discreetly, if he wanted to take the full-blooded, full-bodied young Czech to bed, it was fine with him. After all, she sprang from the same genes as Louise, so that didn't surprise him. Of course, it was time Charles found himself the right partner in life, but while a man was looking, he had to relieve himself somehow.

It was the dissension in the company he didn't like. From what Suzanne had told him only a few days ago in Moat Cay, there were now two camps in the Louise Towers cosmetics company, Natasha's and Louise's. He'd talked to Louise about it. She'd appeared to be shocked, had said she didn't think it was true, but had told him she'd look into it as soon as she got back to work.

Suzanne had also told him that Louise had made it her business to keep Charles and Natasha apart professionally, but as he'd explained to Louise on the island, what they did privately she couldn't really do anything about.

On the spur of the moment, though he'd kept the day clear to catch up, Benedict asked his secretary to see if Charles was in town, and if so, to tell his son to join him for lunch.

Although he had flown in that morning from an overnight business trip to Chicago, Charles was only ten minutes late arriving at the executive dining room. Benedict felt proud as his son approached him. Charles had gone skiing over the holidays, and as he strode toward the table, tanned, flashing his warm, wide grin, Benedict was reminded of himself at Charles's age. Yes, people were right when they said Charles resembled him. He was glad about that. Suzanne's son, Kick, looked all too much like his father, David Reemer. If Charles had a son, Benedict hoped he, too, would resemble the Towers side of the family.

After Benedict had moaned on for a while about the economy, he brought the conversation onto a more personal level. "Suzanne tells me Natasha's brought the Cold War with her from Prague. There's a cold war going on between her and Louise, and it's getting worse. Is it really true? I know there's an embargo on you two working together. I kept right out of that decision, but what's up, what's behind it all?"

Charles looked embarrassed, a slow red blush creeping up his neck from his white collar. "Dad, I think Suzanne's probably right. I thought when Natasha was sent to work on the college campus skin-care program she did a wonderful job. It doesn't matter what age the customer is, this kid . . ."

"Kid!" his father interjected humorously.

"Okay, okay, I can't helping thinking of her that way. She's so unsophisticated for her age. Perhaps it is her innocence that attracts people, but because she is so much older than she looks, and therefore knows so much, it's an incredible combination, and . . ."

"I didn't bring the subject up for a salary review, son," Benedict said sarcastically. "What I want to know is whether we can afford to have Natasha working for Louise Towers if the minions know there's so much bad blood between the sisters. It beats me why there is. Do you know? It all started last winter, when your extracurricular activities together came to light."

Charles's mouth tightened. "That's so goddamned unfair. Yes, sure, as I told you at the time, I do like the girl—in fact, I'm very, very fond of her, but who wouldn't be? I admire her bravery, after all she's been through. She puts in more hours without complaint than anyone I know—except perhaps Lousie herself. She doesn't ask for anything, yet she's lost all those closest to her. I've tried to discuss it with Louise, but I get nowhere. Frankly, at first I thought it was Suzanne's mischief-making. I don't need to tell you how she still feels about the 'Czech invasion,' but no, I don't think any blame can be attached to Suzanne here."

"Could it be a case of plain, old-fashioned green-eyed monster?"

Charles looked startled. "Of what? Louise is the star; Natasha is . . ." He hesitated.

"Just another employee," his father said firmly. "Well, something's got to change. Suzanne says there are now two camps—Natasha supporters and Louise supporters. At a time like this, when Lilly and Squibb are sending their scouts out looking for talent, we can't afford any dissension. Are you still seeing Natasha?"

The question took Charles by surprise. "Yes—well, no, not that often, but from time to time, yes. Why shouldn't I? She needs someone to look out for her. What would have happened to her over Christmas if I hadn't asked if she could go to Uncle Leonard's? She may have been welcome in one of the 'camps,' as you put it, but that would hardly have calmed gossip down, and she obviously didn't feel she was welcome in her own sister's home."

Benedict said sharply, "That's bullshit. If that's the story Natasha puts out, no wonder things go from bad to worse. Whatever happens privately between Louise and Natasha, she is still a welcome guest in our home, even if it's a question of putting on a happy face for the sake of propriety."

When Benedict returned to his office, Stephenson had called again. Wearily he asked his secretary to get him on the line. As always, there was a note of embarrassment in Stephenson's voice. As he relayed the information, it was clear it was something he felt his office should not have to deal with; at the same time it was also clear that he realized he was relaying it to one of America's leaders of industry, and this was the reason his desk was involved in the first place. Also as always, the exchange between them was brief and to the point.

"Our years of payola are at last paying off," Stephenson said dryly. "We have reason to believe that Kristina Mahler is alive. Her grandmother, Blanka Sukova, contacted our source over the Christmas holidays. We had been concentrating our efforts around Brno again. Sukova reported she received a greeting card that implied the child was well and being cared for by nuns in a convent near Brno. We have just received word that appears to confirm that the child is the daughter of Natasha and Pieter Mahler. At this point there seems to be no opposition to returning the child to her grandmother."

"Any news of the father, Pieter Mahler?"

"No."

"I appreciate this. Please keep me informed when you hear the child has been returned to Prague."

"Of course." To Benedict's irritation, he heard the receiver being replaced before he could hang up himself. Well, at least perhaps this was news that could solve everything. Blood is thicker than professional jealousy, he told himself as he dialed Louise on the private house phone that connected only their two offices. "Can you come up, darling?"

His request was a formality. He knew that she knew on the rare occasions when he asked to see her personally, nothing and no one could be allowed to stand in the way.

As they had left the apartment together that morning, Louise had been wearing yellow, his favorite color, "a touch of sunshine," he'd told her, perfect for such a wintry Monday morning. Her hair, a little longer than the original Sassoon bob, was a simple, silky, jet frame around her beautiful face. She looked apprehensive. He was looking forward to telling her the news.

"I've just received the most wonderful New Year's present for you . . ."

She sat facing him across his giant desk, more like a hopeful applicant, he reflected, than his cherished wife. It was, of course, the reason he did cherish her. After the shock of her first—and, he prayed, her only—deception, Louise had been a perfect wife, rarely disappointing him.

He had resigned himself to the fact she had not given him a child. He knew only too well how much he hated it when she was not giving him her full attention. If they had had a child, children, she would have had less time for him, so perhaps it was all for the best.

She was silent. He enjoyed it. It proved she had learned well what he had taught her—that her silence could be as eloquent as words, and was often more so when she was not sure what she was going to hear or what was going to happen in a business transaction.

"Stephenson has been trying to get me. The State Department believes the baby, Natasha's child, Kristina, is safe. It appears she's been in a convent near Brno, where heavy fighting took place in '68, and where Natasha's husband and the child were last seen."

Louise put her hands to her face. "Ahh!" It was a guttural sound, as if dragged out of the depths of her. She said it again, "Ahh!"

Benedict came over to put his arms around her heaving shoulders. Gently for him, he said, "Isn't this the perfect olive branch? Isn't this the perfect news to give to Natasha, to achieve peace between you two?"

She didn't seem to hear him. "And her husband, Pieter? Any word of him?" There was an agonized appeal in her voice that he didn't really understand, but then, would he ever understand his wife?

Still gently, he said, "No, I'm afraid not, no. No news of the father of the child, but I think the fact that it appears the child is alive is hopeful. Someone had to place her in safekeeping at the worst moment of the Russian invasion, someone who thought first of her in the middle of a battle. That person would be her father, but we mustn't say that to Natasha. We mustn't offer her that hope. For the moment, let's stay with this wonderful news." Benedict told Louise that Stephenson would keep in close contact with what happened in the next few weeks, during which time he'd been told, Kristina would be returned to Prague, to her grandmother's care. "I thought you would want to tell Natasha yourself." He kissed his wife's forehead. It was ice cold. "Whatever has been wrong between you, surely it will be forgiven and forgotten with this news."

"Natasha's in Palm Beach, training some new spa personnel. She'll be back at the end of the week."

"I'll leave it to you," Benedict said. He gave her a playful tap on the behind. "Now, back to work with a smile."

That afternoon, Louise began a short letter in Czech to Kristina. "I am your loving aunt, who has worked with your loving Uncle Benedict to return you to your beloved granny . . ." She stared out of her corner office windows at the spectacular New York view. Kristina was approaching six. Louise knew her mother would read every word to the child several times over—if the letter ever reached Prague. Was she wasting her time, beginning a correspondence with a niece she might never see? Something told her to persevere. From now on she would write to Kristina every few months.

The lawyers suggested that Benedict meet with the head of the Small Business Subcommittee, and later that week he flew to Washington, expecting to be away overnight. As it was, the meeting was so frustrating he brought it to an abrupt end and was back in the Park Avenue apartment by early evening on Friday.

As Thorpe took his coat and umbrella, he heard raised voices, which seemed to be coming from the first-floor landing. He looked questioningly at Thorpe.

"Madame is meeting with her sister, Mr. Towers. She arrived about a half hour ago. Madame asked me to show her up to her private sitting room."

The last thing he felt like doing was sitting in on that emotional exchange. He wasn't in the mood for any tearful expressions of gratitude; he certainly didn't want to referee what he supposed Louise was also going to tackle—the "two camps" issue. Benedict sighed heavily. He would change his clothes and pour himself a stiff drink before deciding whether to make his presence known.

Because his dressing-room door wasn't quite closed, as he slipped into casual slacks and a sweater, Benedict heard Natasha follow Louise into their bedroom next door. He was shocked to hear the tone of Natasha's voice. It was cold, bitter. He stood stiffly, forgetting he had been about to pick up the whiskey decanter. "And what about Pieter? Where is Pieter?"

To Benedict's amazement, he heard Louise say, just as coldly, "Pieter is alive. They don't know where, but he is alive." He was about to join them, hoping in some way to add a note of caution and doubt to what Louise was saying, obviously to console Natasha as much as possible, when Natasha's response stunned him into immobility.

"How happy that must make you, Louise, to know my long-lost husband is alive, that I am not free to belong to anybody else . . ."

Benedict heard glass smash, as if something had been thrown. When Louise answered, it was in a voice he hardly recognized. "What are you trying to say, you ungrateful little peasant? What are you trying to imply?"

"You know as well as I do, Louise." Now Natasha's voice was choked. "You are happy Pieter is alive because I am not free for Charles. You try to stop our love because you love Charles yourself. Long-time girls tell me in office you want both Charles and his father. You don't want Charles happy with other woman . . . you want him for yourself . . . you made sure his marriage fail, sending him away all the time . . ."

Benedict had heard enough. He threw open the bedroom door. "Get out, you little slut!" he boomed. "Get out, and never dare to speak to your sister again until you can . . . you can . . . prove you've washed the sickness out of you. You fool, you little fool!" His voice shook as he went toward her. Louise rushed to restrain him. He wanted to strangle the girl. There was evil in her soul; the commies had poisoned her; Louise and he hadn't realized it, but Natasha wasn't fit to live among civilized people.

Natasha backed to the door. She was white, trembling, but defiantly she said, "You're fool, Benedict. Can't you see with your own eyes how your wife looks at your son?" She fled from the room.

Roaring with rage, Benedict was about to go after her, but Louise put herself against the door, imploring him, "Let her go, let her go. It's better for all of us."

He couldn't think straight. On the floor was a broken perfume bottle, the contents seeping into the Aubusson carpet. Without realizing what he was doing, slowly and carefully he picked up the shards of glass and then the remains of the bottle. He slowly looked up at Louise as he saw the name on the bottle. It was Revelation.

Four weeks later there was an early evening family party at "21" for the eleventh birthday of Christopher David Towers Reemer, now known as Kick to everyone, even to Benedict, who had reluctantly been forced to accept that his grandson preferred his nickname to his given names. Kick had chosen "21" for his grown-up party, just as he had asked for and received as one of his presents the new Polaroid SX-70, capable of producing instant color prints that developed outside the camera.

The following day, at Suzanne's request, Benedict was again at "21," this time lunching alone with his daughter. As she opened her purse to reapply her lipstick after the first course, one of the Polaroid photos taken at the dinner fell out.

Benedict picked it up. "Why did you keep this one?" he asked idly. Fiona, Kick's ten-year-old sister, was scowling, sitting between her Uncle Charles and Louise, neither of whom looked very happy.

"Oh, give that to me." Suzanne tried to tear it up, but unlike regular photographs, the Polaroid paper was too tough. "I kept it to show Fiona how ugly she looks when she shows what she's thinking. She didn't want to sit next to LouLou."

Benedict didn't pursue the subject, though he knew Suzanne probably wanted him to. He also knew only too well that Suzanne hardly encouraged her children to like or even respect Louise. He had protested when they'd begun to call Louise "LouLou," but when she'd told him she really didn't mind, that in fact she quite liked it—"much preferable to 'Grandma'!"—he'd decided to hide his irritation. It was too bad, but he had too much on his mind to worry about that. When they grew up, they would learn for themselves what a jewel Louise really was—or at least he hoped so.

"So what's worrying you, Suze?" His daughter was already looking older than her age. The tan that had looked so golden on the Moat Cay beach in January, a tan she had tried to keep with the use of a tanning lamp in her apartment, now in April looked yellowish, leathery. He wondered whether he should try one more time to persuade her to stop baking her skin in the hot Bahamian sun and to throw away her sunlamp. If Louise's smooth, flawless white skin—never exposed to the sun—hadn't served as an example to stop her sunbathing, he supposed nothing would do it.

To his surprise, Suzanne put her hand over his. She wasn't very demonstrative, not like Charles, who always liked to hug him. "So?" he repeated, puzzled.

She was hesitating. Also unusual. Suzanne usually wanted to bite her tongue after she'd spoken. He'd never seen her try to do it before she opened her mouth. "Dad . . ."

Here it came.

"Dad, you know we talked at New Year's about the Natasha problem, the camps, then you told me she'd been unacceptably rude to Louise without ever explaining exactly what it was she'd said that forced you to . . . to . . . release her from the company?"

"Yes." He was curt. It was the last thing he wanted to discuss, yet he'd had an uneasy suspicion Suzanne was going to bring it up. " 'Release' was a safer word to use than 'fire.' As a condition of her release and the annual allowance that goes with it, the lawyers had her sign a confidentiality letter saying she would not discuss the situation or the company. Why?"

Suzanne sighed. "Dad, you know I've never been able to . . . to be as fond of Louise as I know you want me to be. Because you're such a wonderful father, you've always understood that it was because of Mom . . . and everything . . ."

Benedict began to feel ill. Suzanne's eyes were glistening. Even after all these years, she still couldn't mention her mother without goddamn tears. He didn't know what to do. He hadn't wanted to drink because he had a heavy afternoon ahead. Now he had to have one. "Get out what you want to say, Suzanne. You know I dislike this kind of conversation intensely. I don't know where it's leading, but I should warn you I'm not in the mood for more rumors, more calumny." As he spoke, he was remembering the look on Louise's face when he'd picked up the bottle of Revelation. There was hardly a day that went by when he didn't remember.

"Dad, this isn't rumor. Natasha told Charles what happened that night, and Charles told me. Do you know what I said?"

She didn't wait for him to answer. She gripped his hand as she said, "I'm not surprised. That's what I had to say. I'm not surprised because, as I told Charlie, since that trip to Grasse back in the fifties, I've always suspected Louise liked him more than she should, and . . ."

Even though David Mahoney of Norton Simon was looking at them from his usual table, Benedict pulled his hand violently away. "You make me sick." He pushed the table away and went to the men's room, but he couldn't throw up. He splashed cold water on his face. He wanted to leave. If it had been anyone but Suzanne, even Louise, he would have left, but he couldn't leave his daughter sitting there with tears in her eyes, starting a story that would find its way into the columns that there had been another falling-out in the Towers family.

His appetite had gone, but on his return he managed to pick at the sole when it arrived. "Suzanne," he began, his voice low and controlled, "your enmity toward Louise has been a constant source of pain to me. You have influenced your children against her; you have tried in every way you know to turn me against her; but there is a big difference. I live with Louise. I know her."

Did he believe what he was saying? Of course he'd been tormented by the horrifying accusation Natasha had hurled, and Louise had been as shocked as he, agreeing that Natasha must have lost her mind with grief and could obviously no longer remain with the company. Once that decision had been made, neither of them had mentioned her name again. Out of sight, out of mind? Not out of his mind, and certainly not out of Louise's, either.

If he hadn't heard Louise lie about knowing that Pieter was still alive, it might have been possible to block out the memory of the ugly scene. Instead, he'd begun to look back and realize that Louise had never shown any of her usual tenacity in urging him to find out whether Pieter Mahler could be declared legally dead. Why was that? Was it because she preferred to think he was legally alive, an impediment, as Natasha had said, to her being free for anyone else?

Even the night before, at his grandson's party, he'd had to force himself not to watch Charles and Louise for any surreptitious glances passing between them, now sharply aware that they looked more or less the same age—because they were!

Suzanne was looking at him intently. "Dad, Charlie was horrified when Natasha told him what she'd said to Louise. He thought she'd gone crazy. We had quite a row when I finally got it out of him and told him I agreed with Natasha. Now he thinks I'm crazy, too." Again she gripped his hand. "He wants to leave Louise Towers. He thinks we're all mad. He's fed up, he says, he wants out. He was going to tell you this week, but I begged him to think it over and in any case not to spoil Kick's party." Her grip tightened. "He's been offered something on Wall Street. He'll hate it. He knows he'll hate it, yet he thinks it's the only answer to the mess. He says he wants his independence— to see if he can make something of himself away from the company, even if after a few years he comes back. You've got to talk him out of it, Dad."

"Why?"

Suzanne's eyes widened. "Why! Because he's a Towers, that's why. He's your only son. He loves you. You can't blame him. I could tell when I opened my big mouth that whatever Louise may feel for him, he has never, never, never reciprocated or . . ."

"Shut up." His voice was hoarse with emotion, with pain, with shame and anger. He'd never spoken to her that way before, yet he repeated, "Shut up, damn you, shut up."

They sat in silence while Benedict signed the bill. Only when they stood outside in the cool late-spring sunshine, waiting for their respective cars to pull up at the curb, did Benedict trust himself to speak. "I don't want this to happen, but if you ever mention this again, despite what it will do to me, I will no longer be able to recognize you as my daughter."

"But . . . but . . . what about Charlie?"

"There are no buts. I mean what I say. If your brother wants out, as you say, good luck to him. He's welcome to go."

"You can't mean that." Suzanne's voice broke. "If he left, could he ever come back?"

As his chauffeur held the door open, Benedict looked down into his daughter's face. He felt sick again. She looked terrified, but she also looked so much like Honey.

"I repeat, I mean every word I've said."

She may have looked terrified, but Suzanne was not her father's daughter for nothing. "If he tries Wall Street and it's the big mistake I know it will be, can he come back?" she persisted.

"It depends," he said.

"On what?"

He climbed in the car and closed the door. He couldn't answer because he didn't know.

It was still light outside, which was the reason Charles had lost track of time as he tried to tie up as many loose ends as possible before he left the company. It was the third night he'd worked late. Tonight he'd promised Natasha to call her by eight if there was a chance they could meet.

Through his window high in the Towers Building, he saw the time flash on the Newsweek Building, 7:42 P.M., followed by the temperature, seventy-four degrees. No wonder he felt so hot. His shirt was sticking to his body. His secretary, who had long since gone home, was right to call it the silly season, the period just a few days short of the official date for switching off the central heating and switching on the central air conditioning in the massive skyscraper. In common with hundreds of other Towers employees, she never realized how much the utilities cost the company, how much they added . . . God, what was wrong with him, wasting time thinking about it? He didn't have to worry about Louise Towers's profit-and-loss picture anymore.

Charles leaned back in his chair, yawning. How quiet the office was. The silence added to the depression he hadn't been able to shake off in weeks. He sighed and tried to absorb the figures in front of him.

He jumped in fear as someone tapped on the door.

"Come in."

He took a deep breath as Louise walked in, not the Louise Towers he was so used to, compelling in her beauty and self-assurance. For the first time in years he was reminded of the girlish Louise he'd first met in London years before, the Louise who had been Ludmilla. To-night her dark hair was tied back carelessly; she was wearing slacks and a simple white shirt; a white sweater was slung around her shoulders, emphasizing the whiteness of her face, which, without lipstick, looked as young and as vulnerable as . . . Charles revised his thought . . . no, not Natasha, but someone very like her.

Even the hesitant, shy way Louise approached his desk was different. It made him more nervous, not less so.

He could hear his voice shaking as he said, "Louise, what on earth is it? What's wrong?"

"What's wrong! What's right anymore?" Tears began to stream down her face.

Charles looked behind her to the door she'd left open. Was his father about to march in? He went quickly to shut the door, and she read his mind. "I'm alone. Your father's in Washington. I had to come . . . Charles . . ." As he came toward her, she held out her arms beseech-ingly. "Charlie," she repeated. He could swear it came out "Sharlie," just as it had in the days long gone. "Please don't leave . . ." There was a long pause. "Don't leave me . . ."

He couldn't move. His mind was so agitated, he felt he might be sick. He couldn't recognize the mighty Louise Towers in the entreating woman before him. There was something in the sadness of her eyes that filled him with guilt. "Louise . . ." He stepped nearer, near enough to smell the delicate scent of lilacs.

He put his hands on her shoulders, then her arms, gently lowering them. "What is all this about?" he whispered, longing for an answer that would make the world sane again. "You know I only wanted to help, to do what I could, as you asked me to, to make Natasha feel at home here. Why has it all gone so wrong? What did she do to make you turn against her? What did I do?"

"Oh, Charlie, nothing, nothing . . ." The lilac scent was enveloping him; he could smell it on her hair, on her skin. He looked into Louise's

tearful eyes. With a trembling finger he touched her lashes. She turned
her face upward, the lovely face he knew so well, but that now showed
suffering, with dark shadows beneath her eyes. Suddenly she threw her
arms around his neck; he felt the swell of her breasts against his damp
shirt, the soft wool of her sweater brushed his skin. His penis hardened.
Her mouth was half open, like a bird's, hungry, in need.

He couldn't help himself. He kissed her fiercely, wanting to bruise
the mouth that was tempting him to ruin. His tongue probed open
her lips. She responded so passionately, he almost lost his balance. She
was like a starving child, cramming his kisses into her mouth, but the
more she threw away her restraint, the more his desire became a mixture of lust and anger. He wanted her, yet he wanted to punish her
for the longing every movement of her body conveyed.

As she covered his face with kisses, all guilt left him. She was everything Suzanne had always said she was, nothing more than a whore,
a witch, an evil temptress who had lured his father into her clutches
as easily as she was now trying to capture him. They were both betraying his father, but as her hand began to open his trousers, to caress
his bulging penis, he couldn't stop. She was a woman in heat, a pliant
piece of flesh in his hands, a servant, a slave.

He tore open her shirt; she wasn't wearing a bra. *Help yourself*—the
phrase ran through his head as he bent his head to suck and bite the
erect nipples, dark red against impossibly white-as-milk breasts. His
passion grew as he molded them, his fingers like pincers, knowing he
was marking the white skin, hurting her. He wanted to show his contempt through inflicting pain, but her cry was the cry of a woman
needing more, and she drew him to the sofa, panting, urgent, crying
out to give herself to him in whatever way he wanted her.

The phone rang, once, twice, shrilling through the darkened office
like an alarm bell. The room swung around as he jumped to his feet,
filled with self-loathing and fear. Natasha! He knew it had to be
Natasha calling him, miserable bastard that he was. What in God's
name had possessed him! What in God's name had he allowed to take
place in the space of a few minutes? If Louise was a witch, he had
turned into the devil. He wanted to weep. Even as Louise tried to grab
his leg, he rushed over to his desk, but he didn't, couldn't, pick up
the receiver. It rang six, perhaps seven more times. Louise sat silently,
looking at him, not attempting to hide her exposed breasts, luminous
like moons in the fading light, her jet hair around her face. Now she
looks like the witch she is, he thought, a bewitching, wicked witch.

He was breathing heavily, as if he'd been in a race, but when he
spoke he sounded composed. "I didn't believe Natasha, I didn't believe

Suzanne, but now I have to believe." He leaned on the desk like an old man. Still Louise said nothing, her face impassive, as quietly and firmly he went on, "For everyone's sake, I implore you to understand that whatever sickness is in you, I'm not the cure. Whatever you think you feel . . ."

Louise stood up to move toward him, tears running down her cheeks. Charles put up a forbidding hand. "Keep away from me, Louise. Don't you think you've caused enough pain, enough trouble? This can only lead to something tragic and . . ." The phone began to ring again.

Charles picked it up. He turned his back. "Natasha, yes, darling. I'm sorry . . . Yes, I was probably in the men's room. Yes, I'm going to quit now. I should be with you in another half hour . . . I can't wait either. Be ready for me, as you always are. Yes, I need you badly, too. You don't know how much I miss your lovely face. Yes, I do, too . . ."

When he turned around, the office was empty.

David Reemer remembered being told during his first flying lessons that you can tell an eastern pilot from a western one because the eastern pilot flies looking straight down at the instrument panel, while the western pilot tends to focus on the distant horizon. Well, he was certainly acting like an easterner today.

Having Suzanne along as the sole passenger wasn't helping things. Perhaps because after an early start she'd slept most of the way to their first refueling stop in Jacksonville, she now hadn't drawn breath since takeoff. In one way he was glad she seemed oblivious of the haze surrounding them, as she delivered a monologue about Charles's unhappiness on Wall Street, her father's apparent disinterest, Louise retreating more and more into a shell, and a few tasty morsels about Natasha and Charlie becoming more of an item rather than less of one.

Although he could hear her voice, David was no longer listening. At 7,500 feet he'd been about a thousand feet above the inversion, where cold air capped the haze and all the miscellaneous crud rising from the ground, but now the haze was beginning to mount an assault, growing denser below and around him, until imperceptibly, as had happened to him once before, the beige plain of the inversion had become his horizon, with the earth's horizon lost in a dim glow.

He adored flying, which was the reason he'd been so enthusiastic when, on the most perfect fall day the week before, Suzanne, in one of her now infrequent sentimental moods, suggested they fly down to the Cay, just the two of them, to celebrate their anniversary. They'd taken off on an almost perfect day in New York, too. As far as he was concerned, everything had been perfect until now.

"Miami Radio two-four-eight-seven, do you have the Nassau weather?"

"Five-zero-five-P stand by."

"Five-zero-five-P."

"Two-four-eight-seven. Nassau weather is three hundred broken, fifteen hundred overcast, visibility one-half mile in rain, altimeter two-nine-point-nine-six, thunderstorms are reported northeast of the field. Are you instrument-rated and instrument-equipped, sir?"

"This is five-zero-five-P, roger the weather and roger the instruments."

The gray beyond the windshield darkened as the controller informed him that he was predicting some "moderate to heavy precipitation along the route for the next twenty minutes."

"Goddamn," David muttered under his breath. "Is your seat belt fastened, Suzanne?" he asked curtly.

"No, oh, yes, loosely. Why?" She suddenly became aware of the lack of visibility outside. She had grown used to flying with David. Except in turbulence, he had to admit, she was usually a good passenger. As rain began to pelt against the windshield, she said, "Is everything okay? God, I hope it's not raining on the Cay." Fractiously, she said, "Hobart told me yesterday it was a blissful day. I'll give him hell if it's raining." She peered out the window. "Hell, I can't see anything."

Although the plane was behaving and it took little effort to keep all of the instruments precisely where they belonged, David still felt tense. Should he request a change of route? The storm struck, and suddenly it sounded as if a million steel balls were pelting a metal drum just outside the cockpit, determined to get inside. The airspeed shot up into the yellow arc. David saw the altimeter wind up at a rate that was startling. As he reached forward to reduce power, the engine quit momentarily and the Cessna was subjected to several quick, violent jolts. Suzanne started to scream.

As David struggled to control the aircraft's altitude, abruptly there was a feeling of weightlessness. The airspeed lazily drifted back to 100 mph. As he sighed with relief, there came another series of rapid, violent jolts that blurred his vision, making it all but impossible to read the instruments. He tried to hold on to the seat with one hand, but the quickly alternating G forces acting against the weight of his arm caused unwanted constraints on the controls.

With both of his hands on the control yoke, the altimeter indicated he was now below his assigned altitude. He wasn't about to do anything about it. His entire world was centered on the altitude indicator, even as Suzanne began to sob and scream, "Where are we? Can't we land?

Can't you call SOS or Mayday or whatever you have to call? Do something!"

The turn coordinator was wallowing from side to side, giving absolutely no useful information. In the midst of the maelstrom, David boiled over with anger and frustration. There was the controller down on the ground safe and secure, talking about "moderate to heavy precipitation," and here they were, being tossed about by what felt like a goddamned tornado. He vowed to invest in the new, extremely costly airborne radar as soon as he got back to New York.

"Miami two-four-eight-seven, this is five-zero-five-P. Do you hear me?"

There was silence. He'd lost radio contact. He knew he had to be approaching the coast. The combination of dense haze ashore and the blending of gray sky with gray water had now effectively destroyed his entire horizon. He had run out of all visual references. He'd have to rely on instruments until he could pick up the radio again.

God almighty! He stifled a scream. The altimeter was falling rapidly. He struggled to keep the plane upright and level. He overreacted, increasing speed too fast as a flash of lightning hit the aircraft and the small plane went out of control, diving down, down, down.

Search parties found 505P late the next afternoon. Investigation of the wreckage revealed that 505P had crashed in a clump of trees at the northeast corner of the Florida Everglades. The wreckage was less than two and a half miles from a wide-shouldered highway. The engine had stopped prior to impact, and the fuel tanks were empty. In the official report, the cause of the crash was given as "pilot error." The plane had been fighting heavy headwinds, and the pilot not taking this into account, may well not have realized he didn't have enough gas to reach Nassau. Somewhere between Jacksonville and the end of its flight, 505P had eliminated its alternatives, passing up another en route fuel stop, and passing over an excellent two-lane road on which to attempt an emergency landing.

It was a tragedy that would be referred to for many years by people who had known neither of the Reemers. It was used as a warning to point out that no parents of young children should ever fly together in a small private aircraft, especially if it was piloted by one of the parents. It was used by flying instructors and aviation journalists to point out David Reemer's fatal piloting errors in dealing with what all too often became major hazards—increasing haze and embedded thunderstorms.

As for the family and everyone close to Suzanne and David, it was like the day JFK was assassinated; they would remember for the rest of their lives where they were and what they were doing when they first heard the terrible news.

Because thunderstorms around Moat Cay temporarily put their telephone lines out of order, and there was some confusion in the Nassau control room about who owned and who was actually piloting 505P, there was a good fifteen-hour delay before anyone in New York was alerted that the Reemers' Cessna had not arrived and was missing.

A night watchman at Towers Pharmaceuticals was the first person to be called. Because the airport police mentioned only David Reemer's name, he gave them the home number of Reemer's secretary, Colleen. She was not unduly alarmed. Although she had made most of the calls regarding the anniversary trip, all too often the Reemers changed their plans at the last minute, without telling her. Invariably the plans were changed by Mrs. Reemer, but Colleen had grown used to planes not caught, hotel reservations not honored, and even occasional disappearances by one or the other Reemer, disappearances that were never explained to her by either party.

Because of all this, before passing on the disturbing information, Colleen, who prided herself on her initiative and on keeping cool in all eventualities, first telephoned the Reemer residence to confirm that the Reemers had indeed left the day before, Sunday, for Moat Cay. She then telephoned Teterboro Airport, the New Jersey home base of 505P, and established that David Reemer had taken off at 8:45 A.M. the morning before, with his wife as the only passenger.

Now pale and nervous, twenty minutes after receiving the news, hardly believing what she was about to say, Colleen set about passing it on.

It wasn't easy. During the next thirty minutes she learned that Louise Towers had flown to London the day before to join her husband on a ten-day European business trip.

Colleen didn't have the courage to call Claridge's, where the Towers were in their usual suite. How could she break the news to the big boss that his daughter was missing somewhere in the Bahamas in a plane piloted by his son-in-law? There was no way. Instead, she called the man she knew Mr. Benedict relied on the most, Mr. Norris, but he was en route to Chicago.

Her nervousness was turning into terror. Charles. It would have to be Charles who made the call. She knew he was not on good terms with his father since his move out of Louise Towers cosmetics into Wall Street finance, but there was nothing else she could do.

Charles was in the shower when he heard the phone ringing. Because he thought it might be Natasha, whom he had only kissed good night eight hours before, he jumped out and, dripping wet, rushed to his bedroom to pick it up. The television was still on. Forever he would remember that "The Today Show" was on, and that as he said "Hello," half his mind was on the screen where Bob Woodward and Carl Bernstein were being interviewed about their Watergate story in the *Washington Post*.

For a confused moment, Charles didn't know who was on the other end and what on earth the nervous-sounding woman was talking about. As the horror of what she was telling him sank in, he held on to the bed. The room was swaying. He made her repeat it. He made her repeat the telephone numbers he would have to call next. All the time "The Today Show" was going on, while the room was swaying so that he couldn't see straight.

With trembling fingers, the first person he called was Natasha. Now for the first time he understood the hell of not knowing whether someone you loved was alive or dead. "Shall I come over?"

"No, I don't know what's going to happen. I'll . . . I'll try to keep in touch." As much as he realized he wanted Natasha there, not speaking, just sitting somewhere in the apartment, he also knew how much she would be in the way of all he had to do.

He was on the phone for over an hour, to both the Bahamian and the Miami airport authorities; to his secretary, to make arrangements to fly down to Miami; to the Reemers' nanny and butler; to the headmaster of the school where Kick and Fiona were already in class; to his Uncle Leonard, who was at home with the flu; to Marlene, to ask for her assistance with the children; to the head of Towers's public-relations department, to stall off all press inquiries; and, after a second's hesitation, to Maisie, also to ask for her help with the children.

Finally he could put off no longer the most important call of all, the one he dreaded to make, to his father in London. He waited for the call, sitting on sheets now soaked through from his still-wet body.

It was a replay in reverse of the day when he'd been in Europe and his father had telephoned from New York with the news of his mother's death in the Philadelphia train disaster. Now his father was in Europe and he was calling from New York with . . . He began to sob. They were cursed. The Towers family was cursed. He could see Suzanne's angry face, eyes blazing, spitting out her suspicions and accusations about Ludmilla, suspicions that had all turned out to be true.

He could hear Suzanne's voice earlier this year, two decades on, biting, cold, with new, incredible, insane accusations: she, his own sister, agreed with Natasha that his father's wife, Louise, who had been Ludmilla, was half in love with Charles herself. It had led to the first serious row between them, a row that had never been patched up, because it had been impossible for him to risk trusting Suzanne with what had happened that night during his last week at Louise Towers.

The phone rang.

"This is White Plains. Your person-to-person call is going through now, sir." A rush of air, a sound of the ocean, a gabble of unintelligible voices emphasized the distance. His father was not yet on the line, but Charles was crying like a child over the wire, lonely and afraid.

He had no memory of what he actually said, how he explained the terrible facts. All he would ever remember was that he heard his father crying for the first time, crying and shouting over and over again, "Oh my God, oh my God, no, no, no, don't let it be true, no!"

The funerals were private, but even so, some enterprising paparazzi must have used cameras with telephoto lenses to obtain fuzzy pictures of the family and close friends grieving at the graveside, where Suzanne was buried beside her mother. The pictures ran in many major newspapers around the world, tugging at heartstrings, showing young Kick standing like a little soldier, holding the hand of his ten-year-old sister, Fiona, while one of the most important industrialists in the world, Benedict Towers, behind dark glasses, stood stooped like an old man, with a hand on each child's shoulder. Some papers even commented on the enduring beauty of Benedict Towers's wife, Louise, in her own right one of the most famous women in America as founder and guiding force of the beauty company bearing her name.

It was reported that she was wearing Balenciaga as a tribute to the great couturier who himself had just died, but the reports were wrong. Her black suit and cloche hat were designed by an up and coming American designer named Bill Blass.

One of the most revealing facts was entirely missed by the press, because it was a closely guarded secret known only to Benedict, Louise, the president of the funeral home, and Benedict's most trusted employee, Norris. Although the family naturally believed the double casket being lowered into the grave contained the bodies of both Suzanne and her husband, they were wrong. Suzanne alone was buried in the Towers family plot. David Reemer was cremated at Benedict's direction; it was the way he chose to extinguish the memory of the man who he believed had killed his beloved only daughter.

Benedict had told Louise, on the agonizing trip back from Florida to New York, that they would, of course, adopt Kick and Fiona. It didn't cross his mind to discuss it with her. He hadn't been able to speak for hours after Charles's phone call. It was Louise who had called the head office to make all the arrangements to fly from London to Miami, to cancel ten days of their engagements on the packed European itinerary, and to bring a secretarial staff to Claridge's to deal with the calls that started flooding in that same day. It was Louise who agreed to the corporate affairs office's suggestion that once the inescapable facts were confirmed, a day of mourning should be ordered in Towers offices around the world.

Adoption! Benedict seemed obsessed with the idea almost from the moment he had to accept the fact that the broken bodies in the Florida swamp belonged to his daughter and her husband. It was the only thought, Louise believed, that kept him sane in the days that followed. It was the only subject he wished to discuss when he emerged from one alcoholic binge after another.

"At least Kick and Fiona will be brought up as Towers and not as Reemers." If he said it once, he said it a hundred times. It was a tragic, agonizing accident to everyone except to Benedict, who, for weeks and even months after, she would hear shouting in the early morning and late at night, "Murderer . . . murderer . . ."

It was the same at the office. He never wanted to hear the name Reemer again. Those people known to have been especially close to Reemer in the organization shivered with anxiety, sure they were in danger of losing their jobs unless they could prove that they, too, believed Reemer had murdered the boss's only daughter.

It was Norris who had to put up with the most. "I gave him my greatest treasure and he abused it, Norris. He didn't take care of my daughter, Norris. We've got to be sure her children are brought up to recognize this, to recognize the honor of bearing the Towers name. Norris, you've got to help me in this. I can't do it alone."

Six weeks after the tragedy, they were in Benedict's office at the end of the day, Norris nursing the same glass of brandy Benedict had poured over forty minutes ago, while he was already nearing the end of his second glass.

"What about Charlie? Will you let him come back to Louise Towers or one of the divisions now if he wants to?"

"How can I rely on him?" Benedict snarled. "He wouldn't listen to his sister. She begged him not to leave the company. Suzanne . . ." He choked up. "Suzanne . . . she knew that when the going gets tough, the tough get going . . . she would never have deserted the ship. But what does my son and heir do as soon as we learn we've taken a snake into our family? He wants out. He wants to keep the same cunning cunt on tap for whenever he wants a fuck." Benedict ground his heel into the floor to emphasize his disgust. "But he doesn't want to put up with any unpleasantness, any signals from us that we think he shouldn't join the excrement in the gutter. He'd rather be 'independent.' Even he knows Wall Street's not for him, but he'd rather be 'independent.' "

The sardonic tone Benedict used when he said "independent" made Norris wince. He was fond of Charles. In fact, he thought Charles was a remarkably unspoiled, hardworking young man, considering who his father was. As he had never been told what had been said to cause the estrangement between the sisters, followed by Charles's exodus from Louise Towers, Norris now didn't know what to say. He didn't want to know. In dealing with Benedict Towers for over thirty years, ignorance, he knew, was sometimes literally bliss.

"The fact is, Norris, old friend . . ." To Norris's dismay, he saw Benedict pouring himself another generous glass of brandy. ". . . the fact is I despise my son and heir. It was Suzanne who should have been born with balls—she was the one who always showed courage. I hope to God Kick has his mother's temperament. If he doesn't now, I'm going to make it my business to see he grows up like a Towers. I didn't pay enough attention to Charlie's upbringing. With the war and everything, I left too much in Honey's hands; that's why he's such a wimp. I've learned my lesson. Kick is going to get my full attention, do you hear me?"

There was another major change about to be made. Over breakfast one morning, Benedict told Louise he could no longer tolerate living in the Park Avenue apartment.

"There are too many memories here now of loved ones lost before their time in hideous, unthinkable accidents. As much as I loved this apartment once, I'm beginning to hate the sight of it now."

He stared at Louise without really seeing her, without saying what else was in his mind, that it hadn't been difficult to wipe out Honey's memory because of the sexual excitement of living there with Louise in the early years, years when he'd hardly been able to come near her without wanting to possess her. She could still excite him, but, of course, it was different now. No woman, not even someone like Louise, who never seemed to tire of creating new ways to arouse him, could obliterate the pain he felt now every day in the home where Suzanne had grown up. There wasn't an inch of the place that hadn't once contained her. Everywhere he looked, there was a memory of Suzanne.

"Spend what you like," he told Louise. "Call the best realtors in town. Check with Abbotson at the office for the names of the best residential realtors. Look at town houses, triplexes. When you've found something you like, take the kids along to be sure they like it, too."

When Benedict left for the office, Louise walked slowly around the enormous apartment where she had once lived and worked as a servant. Those memories had been stored away for so long that they had no more power to affect her. Instead, burning into her brain, as if it had only just taken place, was the memory of her humiliation in Charles's office, a memory she was sure she would live with forever. Even the shock of the Reemers' death and all the changes that had followed hadn't lessened the pain. If no one else had noticed, Louise was certain Benedict had seen how Charles barely acknowledged her at the funeral.

In the coral and white guest room that was now Fiona's bedroom, Louise's pent-up anger and anguish escaped. "Take the kids along to be sure they like it." Benedict's order rang in her head as she saw Fiona's tiny printed mules on the floor. She violently kicked them halfway across the room. When she turned to leave, she saw the British nanny, Miss Hobson, looking at her sternly from the adjoining small study that Fiona now shared with her brother.

"Can I help you with anything, Mrs. Towers?" The voice was unfriendly, even condescending, a voice that reminded Louise that this was a woman who'd spent years hearing unflattering stories about her from Suzanne. Louise left the room without answering.

It was bad enough that the children were so sullen and unfriendly. Even the way they pronounced "LouLou" sounded deprecating, careless, as if she really didn't count. Years ago, Jan had called her Lulu, short for Ludmilla. It wasn't the same.

Louise kept telling herself, give the children time; be patient; they've lost their parents; it will take a long, long time to win their trust, let alone their friendship. But did she have to put up with an insolent servant, someone who could influence her own household? No, she didn't. When she found their new home, she told herself, no matter what the children said, she would be adamant that the nanny, "Hobby," as the children called her, would not be moving with them.

There was silence in the boardroom as Benedict pored over the papers in front of him. Norris, in his usual seat by the oak double doors, could see that many of the people around the boardroom table looked unusually tense. Charles, whom he hadn't seen in months, but whose presence had been demanded, no longer resembled the laughing-faced young man he often thought of. He looked white, ill.

In a cool, steady voice, Benedict began to go over the problems the board had been listening to for the past two to three years, the lawsuits, the constant government interference and investigation, the heavy expansion in the good years that had led to a number of large short-term loans.

"Following the tragic events last year . . ." For a moment Benedict's voice wavered, and Norris saw Charles grip the arms of his chair. "The tragic events," Benedict repeated, looking slowly around the table at every board member, all of whom were related to him in some way or another, "have led me to think of my own mortality. I have come to the reluctant conclusion that I have no crystal ball, I can no longer feel confident that our company's problems will go away with more hard work, more relentless moves against our competitors."

He stopped and held up a bound sheaf of papers. "We must reorganize our company by selling Towers stock to the public while they still believe in us."

Everyone started talking at once. For a few moments Benedict allowed it, then he gave a sharp rap on the table. "For many reasons, but mainly because I have decided for once to listen to my financial and legal advisers, the Louise Towers cosmetics division will not be included in the stock offering. Those assets are currently being evaluated and separated out in order for me to purchase them privately and then incorporate Louise Towers as a separate private company."

It wasn't true. No one had advised Benedict to do this, and it was news to Norris. He was stunned, and so, he could see, was Charles. But not the rest of the board, apparently. There were no questions; they all knew where the cosmetics division had come from, and in the past Norris had heard many of them grumbling about its extravagances. How shortsighted most of the Towers board members were.

For the next couple of hours the board divided into three groups to study and discuss the complicated statements prepared by the company's financial advisers. The names of the brokerage firms and the right share price to aim for were gone over again and again. It was understood that it would take several weeks to finalize the offering.

As they began to break up, it was obvious to Norris that Charles wanted to stay behind and talk, but that Benedict just as obviously did not. "I'll call you in a day or so," he told his son offhandedly as he left the boardroom to walk into his office. The next day Norris understood why he hadn't wanted to prolong any conversation with Charles, least of all about Louise Towers, Incorporated.

Benedict summoned him to his office at about two o'clock, where Greg Phillips, the lawyer in charge of his personal affairs and one of the officers of the Benedict Towers Foundation, was sitting patiently in the large club chair by the window. Benedict waved Norris toward the other chair beside Phillips, and continued to read the document on his desk.

Finally, after about fifteen minutes, he lifted his head to look at Phillips and then steadily at Norris. "With Louise Towers restructured as a separately incorporated company, it is my understanding from this document that Charles Towers is eliminated from the picture entirely, that on my death the controlling Louise Towers shares will be held in trust for Christopher Towers, known as Kick, to receive on his thirtieth birthday, provided the Louise Towers board attests that he has been a conscientious employee, working in every area of the company, for a minimum of the five preceding years." He paused and then added with a wry smile, "It is also my understanding that, should I die before Kick reaches the age of twenty-five, he will not be told of his eventual ownership of the company until a time decided upon by Louise, should she survive me, and by you, Phillips, as the legal officer."

"That is correct," Phillips said.

"This clause . . ." Benedict moved the document over to Phillips. "Are you sure this prevents in every way the sale of Louise Towers after my death? That Louise Towers will continue to be a close-held corporation, held by the Towers family issue, and that none of its stock can be sold without . . ."

"The only way it can be sold—and then not to a competitor—is with Kick's approval on attaining the controlling interest, together with the full consent of the board."

"And the board will hopefully then include Fiona Towers, on her twenty-eighth birthday, provided she meets the same employee requirements? And Zoe Towers, my niece, too? And the husbands of both, provided the entire board approves of them, whoever they may be?"

"Yes." There was no sign of irritation or weariness in Phillips's voice, though he had already been over these points more than once.

Benedict smiled thinly. "Well, Norris, I'm glad you've already reached the age of wisdom. We do not need to wait for you to reach any age. I want you to know now that in your case, as the family's oldest friend, I intend to ask you to join the new Louise Towers board as soon as the intricacies of setting up the company as a separate entity have been accomplished. Nothing has given me more pleasure than making this decision. I intend to remain as chairman, and Louise will be named officially president of the new company. To really run the show, today I am asking you to become Louise Towers's chief executive officer."

Norris hoped he didn't look as shocked as he felt. "Does Louise know . . . wish this?"

To his relief, Benedict smiled broadly, then laughed as if he'd made a good joke. "Of course she does, my dear fellow. Of course she does. She is delighted, and both of us have no doubt that we will beat out the competition and reach the number one spot in this decade."

Norris gave Benedict a similar smile in return. It was a major step for Benedict Towers to decide to appoint him to the board of anything bearing the Towers name. If he succeeded in filling both Charlie's and Reemer's shoes—and he didn't doubt that he could—he would become even richer than he already was, and in a few years he would retire to sail around the world with the wife he still called his bride.

"Charles received a sizable piece of money from his mother, you know . . ."

Norris was surprised to hear Benedict bring up Charles's name again—probably, he thought, to justify what he had just done, cutting his son out entirely from the cosmetics end of the business, the one Norris knew Charlie loved the most. God knew what else he was cut out from, as far as Benedict's personal will was concerned.

When neither of them spoke, Benedict went on, "If he doesn't lose his shirt on Wall Street, he can take it easy whenever he wants to. I just want to make sure I don't make it easy for him now to subsidize my wife's enemy. When I see that that dangerous attachment is over, I will start considering him as my son and heir again. If it's ever over . . ." He sighed heavily. Again, no one spoke.

"Well, Norris, I think that's all. This stuff"—he indicated another thick document on his desk—"this is my personal will. There are a few points I have to go over with Phillips here."

As Norris left, he heard Benedict say, with more enthusiasm than he'd heard in a long time, "This won't take long, will it, Phillips? I'm picking the kids up myself to take them to the new Louise Towers manufacturing plant in New Jersey this afternoon. Can't start them off too early, you know."

It took Charles less than a year to accept that his instincts had been right from the beginning: his future didn't lie on Wall Street. He missed the cosmetics business; it was a natural métier for him, and now that Louise Towers was newly incorporated as a separate company with Norris running the show, he wondered if perhaps he could take on the international side of the company again, provided he didn't have to run into Louise too often. And there too, he consoled himself, perhaps after all that had happened, she'd come to her senses. Perhaps the embarrassing encounter in his office had had something to do with menopause or some weird thing that happened to women of her age.

He took Norris to lunch to ask his advice, and at the coffee stage Norris told him without preamble that if he wanted to return to Louise Towers, he was sure there would be a condition.

"You know your father. He feels very strongly about certain things, certain people. He doesn't change, once he's made up his mind, and he's made up his mind Natasha is trouble, the cause of your leaving the company, the cause of a lot of things. I don't want to go into it all; frankly, I don't know what's at the bottom of the rupture and I don't want to know, but I'm certain Natasha couldn't still be part of your life if you came back to the company."

Charles erupted. "The days when my father dictates what I do with my private life are over, and perhaps what I do with my professional life, too." He got up, shook Norris's hand stiffly, and stalked out. Norris didn't blame him, but he knew he'd been right to mention Natasha.

In the fall of 1973, after a lunch with too many brandies, Benedict told Charles some of his plans for the future of the Louise Towers company after his death.

"You left too soon, Charlie boy," Benedict said, relaxed, leaning back as if he hadn't a care in the world. "I told Norris I couldn't rely on you to grab hold of the reins and keep Louise Towers going full steam ahead once Louise and I are gone. I had to secure the company for the next generation." He looked broodingly at his son. "It's all going to go to Kick eventually, you know. If you'd hung in there, it could have been yours, but all your values are cockeyed; you're too mixed up with that woman . . ."

It was too much. Charles jumped up, red-faced, angry. "I *did* 'hang in there,' as you put it. I worked my guts out for the company, and you didn't lift a finger to stop the idle, stupid gossip; neither you nor Louise did one positive thing about the venal—"

"Oh, go to hell." His father spilled some brandy on the desk. "Go to hell with your Czech slut." He shut his eyes; he didn't seem to comprehend what he was saying. "Suze was right . . . the 'Czech invasion' . . ." But Charles wasn't prepared to listen to any more.

That evening for the first time, Charles didn't shut his ears to Natasha's plans for a future she often talked about, one they might share professionally if not personally. He had money from his mother's estate. Even if he never received another penny from his father or Towers Pharmaceuticals, he was in a position to move on his own.

"Just small skin-care business with good, clean, honest manufacturing arrangement," Natasha said dreamily, as she'd said before. "Let's start to look around. American woman, she needs so much help; not all can pay fancy department store, institute la-de-da prices. We can find something small, something already selling in drugstores—how do you say, mass marketplace—like Formula 405. One special skin product . . . something we can build on slowly. We can do it."

Charles was listening through a haze of pain, but something about Natasha's enthusiasm and conviction was getting through. He had to accept that following Suzanne's death, instead of drawing closer, his father and he were practically estranged. As for Louise, once bitten, twice shy, he could never trust her to help him—or certainly Natasha—in any shape or form. He had never told Natasha about the scene in the office with Louise, and he never would. One thing it had proved: Natasha was obviously never going to be accepted into the Towers family. Louise would see to that. Once again he remembered his father's words after lunch. They burned into his mind. It was as if his father hated him.

He tried to concentrate on what Natasha was saying. She was making sense. He could obviously never enter into competition with his own family's beauty company, but in the mass market, where Louise Towers had never been, and never would be, why shouldn't he be a player there? He knew he thoroughly enjoyed the beauty business. If he succeeded on his own, perhaps his father would recognize that he had something in him after all. Perhaps one day it could provide a bridge to reunite them.

He cupped Natasha's earnest face in his hands. Her skin was like velvet, like a velvet peach. He ran his tongue down it, loving the way she squirmed with delight, the way she would soon squirm deeper into his arms. He had never made any promises, and she hadn't asked for any. He comforted her when she cried over Kristina, growing up without her in the Communist hell of Prague; she comforted him when he cried over the loss of his family.

"Tomorrow," he said with a confidence he didn't feel. "Tomorrow we'll begin shopping for a small skin-care company." As her face lit up, he parroted her: "A small skin-care company for mass marketplace."

Tokyo, 1976

FROM A HIGH-BACKED chair provided by a grinning yet also unmistakably deferential store employee, the honorable young gentleman, who was somehow both the adopted son and the step-grandson of the most important guest of honor, Madame Louise Towers, gave little sign of approval or disapproval of the opening ceremonies. This was as it should be, as far as the Japanese dignitaries were concerned.

Equally impassive, the owners of the huge Takashimaya department store, with their wives in elaborate kimonos standing one step behind them, applauded softly as Louise cut the white silk ribbon garlanding the first Louise Towers Beauty Institute and counter in Japan.

Even as he acknowledged how glamorous LouLou looked, in a pale silk turquoise suit with matching shoes and minute veiled hat, Kick was writhing inside with the hypocrisy of it all. As part of the itinerary his grandfather had personally drawn up for him, "to continue your Louise Towers education," he'd had to get up at the crack of dawn to meet with Dougy Faseff, head of creative design for Louise Towers International, to see something of what went into such an occasion to make it perfect.

Now he knew, as if he cared, why LouLou's skin had an almost eerie, pale moon glow as she turned to face the audience, the kind of flawless paleness Dougy had told him Jap females craved and would give plenty of yen for. He also knew why not one crease appeared in the turquoise suit, though LouLou had been wearing it for well over an hour. It was the lighting from two tungsten spotlights that had taken an age to position, starting at around eight o'clock that morning. Now, shining through a backdrop of perfectly white seamless paper, they cast exactly the right shadows of drama on two pillars erected just for the opening ceremony to hold the white silk rope outside the Institute.

And, as Dougy had explained, the spotlights defined "in a ravishing way Madame Towers's cheekbones." *Ravishing* was one of Dougy's favorite words.

Kick tried to look at his watch without anyone noticing. He put his left hand on his knee. Drat it. His sleeve covered the watch. If he'd only looked when he'd stood to join in the applause, but he hadn't, and his grandfather's lecture on using the right body language and maintaining the correct eye contact in Japan had been drummed into him too much for him to throw caution away now.

As he often did to pass the time during interminable official Towers events, Kick began an imaginary conversation in his head with the Takashimaya executive now making yet another fulsome welcoming speech, translated agonizingly slowly into halting English.

You silly, yellow-faced little drone, Kick said to himself, *don't you realize where the rejuvenating cream you'll be selling really comes from? Made especially for you from water lilies grown for Louise Towers by nuns in a nonspeaking order in France? What a joke! It really comes from a Towers Pharmaceuticals factory in Elizabeth, New Jersey!*

Although he remained totally still, Kick's dark blue eyes flickered around to the long, docile line of female customers encircling the new Louise Towers Institute. They seemed to be absorbing every word as they waited to make their first purchases. *And as for you, my slit-eyed friends, don't you know that rich emollient lipstick you can't wait to pay five dollars for—or whatever five dollars is in your filthy currency—only costs ten cents to make?*

LouLou knew what he was going through. She was smiling at him. He wasn't going to give her the satisfaction of smiling back, though he knew it wasn't her fault he was there, at an important Louise Towers opening in a sweltering Tokyo department store, when he could have been sailing on the Sound or fishing in Maine with one or another of his best friends from Dalton. It wasn't her fault that Granddad had had to fly home because Uncle Leonard had taken a turn for the worse.

All the same, he blamed Louise in the same way he knew his mother would have blamed her. Because she existed. Because she had brought Louise Towers into being. Because, as he'd been told over and over again by so many members of the family, now that Uncle Charlie had severed his connections with the company and—worse—set out on his own, all of his grandfather's dreams for the future were centered on him and, to a lesser extent, on his sister, Fiona. It was so unfair.

Kick surreptitiously moved in the chair as now, again through an interpreter, Louise began what he knew was the last speech of the day.

"I am privileged to be able to reveal to you that this week Her Royal Highness, the Princess Chichibu, sister-in-law of your great Emperor Hirohito, will honor Louise Towers by making a royal visit to our first Japanese Louise Towers manufacturing facility, in Gotemba. To celebrate this glorious occasion, the city of Gotemba has created a reconditioned road to connect our facility with the main highway . . ."

More hypocrisy! Kick knew, because he'd overheard more than one conversation on the subject, that his all-powerful grandfather had bribed the Gotemba authorities to put in the small stretch of road. Oh well, what did it mean to him? Nothing.

Oh no, what was LouLou saying now? She was saying what he'd pleaded with her never to say. Worse, she was stretching out her arm in a prima-donnaish way, making it impossible for him to ignore the command to join him in the tungsten spotlight. "I would like to introduce you all to the next generation of Towers men, my son, Christopher Towers."

How dare she call him her son! Nevertheless, he bowed as his grandfather had taught him to do. "Just one obvious, courteous bow of respect. All over Japan you'll see both sexes make goddamned fools of themselves trying to out-bow each other, but never forget, son, that's for the Japanese. Just one bow for Americans."

Kick was deliberately cool to Louise for the rest of the Tokyo trip. It didn't matter that she apologized and said his grandfather had insisted he be acknowledged. It was probably true, but as he said during his daily call to his sister staying with the Parr Dobsons in Nantucket, "Mom was right. You can't ever trust LouLou. Just when you think she's okay, boom, she breaks her promise and the ground opens right under your feet."

Benedict knew his sister-in-law, Marlene, would never have called him in Tokyo if things weren't really serious. Leonard's cancer had been diagnosed the year before, and at first, after the operation, everyone thought he was going to be okay.

"He's got ten more years of youth than I have to fight the damn thing," Benedict had said to Marlene more than once during the ups and downs in her husband's progress report.

He doesn't realize that even when he talks about my Leonard, he always refers to himself, Marlene sighed. What was to become of her? She'd seen for herself how implacable Benedict Towers could be to those he was supposed to love the most, like Charles, his own son. If Leonard was no longer there to provide the link, would Benedict still treat her as a member of the family?

Sure, she knew Leonard had provided for Zoe and herself. She'd never have to worry about money, but the yawning loneliness of life without her husband made her realize more every day that she had no identity except as Mrs. Leonard Towers.

As it was, Louise and Kick had long returned from Japan and Kick was halfway through the next term, when, with Marlene sitting on one side of the bed and Benedict and Louise on the other, Leonard died.

She was as shocked as if he'd never been ill. She didn't cry. She just refused to leave the room, clinging to his poor cold white hand, until Louise and Benedict somehow managed to walk her out. "What's to become of me? I've got no reason to live. I want to die." She said it over and over, all the way back to the enormous brownstone mansion on East Seventy-third Street where Louise and Benedict now lived.

"Zoe . . . there's Zoe. You've got to be strong for little Zoe," Benedict said with a terrible look of grief.

Even in the midst of her own agony, and not for the first time, Marlene thought Benedict was a changed man since Suzanne's death. "Where is little Zoe?" he asked in a broken voice.

"She's . . . I let her stay with her best friend, Ginny Somner, out on the island. I don't know how to tell her," Marlene said woodenly. "I don't know anything anymore."

"You've got to be strong for the company, Marly. For Louise Towers."

"Louise Towers . . ." she answered haltingly. Marlene didn't know who looked more shocked, Benedict or herself. What had got into Louise? Was she mad? How could she be so unfeeling as to mention her wretched company at a time like this?

Louise put her arm around her. It was the first time Marlene could ever remember her doing it. "We won't talk about it now, but one day, when the timing's right, I know you could be a great asset to the company. Leonard and I have talked about it during the last year."

It was then the tears came, from all of them, but most of all from Benedict. After all he'd been through, it wasn't surprising.

They tried to persuade her to stay overnight. "Benedict and I will drive out and bring Zoe back to you," Louise volunteered.

"No, no, it will frighten her. I'll have to go . . . I want to go."

"I'll call the Somners, then, and if you're sure you really want to go yourself, one of the drivers . . ."

"No." Marlene was surprised that she was interrupting Benedict, surprised by the firmness in her own voice. "Our driver, Tate, will take me. I like Tate. Zoe likes Tate."

Something of the old Benedict came back. He looked at his watch, then said in a tone she knew she couldn't argue with, "It's much too late for you to go anywhere tonight. You will stay here, Marly. I will call the Somners and get Tate here first thing in the morning. Louise will go with you, and I will make all the arrangements that have to be made."

When Louise was sure the sleeping pill she insisted Marlene take was working, she found Benedict in his study, his head down on the desk. "Darling . . ."

He raised a haggard face. "It's too much, Lou, too much for me to bear . . ." It was a cry she had become used to hearing.

As she had done so many times, she began to massage his neck, whispering to him as if he were a child, "Close your eyes, don't fight, rest against me."

As her cool fingers worked on his neck muscles, he began to feel better. "What did you mean about Marlene and Louise Towers? Were you serious?"

"I was serious. She gets on well with the staff. She's one of those dedicated creatures who'd give her all to . . . to . . ."

"To what?"

"I'm not sure, perhaps training programs. She's always been like a mother hen, a nanny, a tireless sort of busybody who remembers birthdays and anniversaries of maids and beauty consultants." Louise paused. "She's so proud of being a Towers, did you know that? Leonard tried to explain it to me when I visited him in the hospital a few months ago. I think he was trying to ask me to make sure we never left her out if anything happened to him."

Benedict stood up abruptly. "Pride in the Towers name isn't in too much supply. I guess that's enough of a reason to give her a big job!" He picked up a clipping and asked grimly, "Did you read this?"

Louise saw the headline: WHY BUY A CORPORATE LOSER? She hadn't read it, but she could guess what it was about. She shook her head.

"I learn more every day about that serpent's-tooth son of mine. Read it. It will make you want to throw up, but it's an education."

He walked slowly out of the room, saying over his shoulder, "Better work out a deal with Marlene before Charles gets to her. He and she have always been pretty close, I believe. Nothing would surprise me anymore."

Her hand was shaking, the outward sign of the deep reservoir of bitterness and pain inside, caused by Charles and . . . she wouldn't even think of her sister by name. After skimming over the first few paragraphs of the article, which came from *Fortune* magazine, Louise read:

Why would anyone want companies that were such intractable losers? They were certainly cheap; some corporate dogs went for less than their presumed liquidation value.

For instance, take the now promising future of the two-year-old Aesthetique company, purchased by Charles Towers, son of Benedict Towers, the all-powerful chairman of the Towers Pharmaceutical giant. Young Towers worked out a lucrative deal, agreeing to pay $8 million with a down payment of $1 million, the rest payable over ten years. As Towers explained in this, his first interview since his surprising purchase, "My father helped me develop an eye for value at an early age. From my training at Towers Pharmaceuticals, I learned it was a lot easier for an individual entrepreneur to make quick decisions and respond to changing market pressures, to fire unnecessary staff and ignore Wall Street's need for ever-increasing quarterly profits. All this can help turn a laggard into a champ."

In Aesthetique's case, Towers's partner, Natasha Mahler, spotted the potential in one product, Smooth-Soap, which accounted for 38 percent of total sales. Shortly, Towers tells us, there will be a line extension for SmoothSoap—no longer hyphenated and already in new and impressive glossy white packaging—based on Natasha Mahler's unique knowledge of skin care. It is not generally known that Miss Mahler is the sister of . . .

Louise tore the paper into several pieces. There had to be retribution. But when? How long did she have to wait before this hell came to an end?

It was well after midnight. Before reading the article she'd felt drained, longing for bed. Now she knew any chance of sleep was gone. She took a piece of cream-colored writing paper from the antique stationery stand, and began to write:

Dear Mama,   Your letter, which took three weeks to arrive, broke my heart. As I have written to you so many times and told you on the rare occasions we have been able to speak on the telephone, I feel so responsible for Natasha abandoning you, leaving you with the burden of bringing up her child when you are sick, old, and tired.

I still cannot comprehend how Natasha could change from the little angel she was into the devil she is today, concerned only with money and her own self-aggrandizement. I must take all the blame, but as you know, I suppose to bury her guilt, she has repaid the endless kindness of my husband with terrible accusations against me, even to the extent of opening her own cosmetics business (which is, between us, a bit of a joke), enticing my husband's son away from his proper place as heir apparent in the Towers company, to join her and back her foolish enterprise. Her ambition seems to have no bounds. While you slave away, I weep over all that has happened. But as you know from the facts, not from the fantasies you hear from Natasha, we are still tirelessly working for your freedom and Kristina's. Please don't let Kristina stop her English practice with Father Kusy's friend. One day I swear she will be able to use it . . .

When the letter to her mother was finished, Louise found a postcard in the stand showing a picture of the imposing Towers Building. *"Kristina, it is very late and silent here in New York City, but I am thinking of you as always,"* she wrote across the back in clear, small letters. *"I am proud to learn from Grandmama that you are behaving so well. One day, you can be sure, your loving aunt and uncle will find a way to bring Grandmama and you here to live with us happily ever after. Although your mama left you, we never will."*

She had been writing similar notes since Kristina had been found in Brno and returned to Prague. As communications from her mother had grown more bitter, so Louise's responses had slowly indicated her own disapproval of Natasha. Her mother had all too eagerly accepted that she had been abandoned, promising to read to Kristina every word Louise wrote.

Louise shut her eyes and leaned back in Benedict's chair. Although he complained, she knew that Benedict was still, for her sake, trying to find a way to get her mother and Kristina out, but the Iron Curtain was clamped down even more firmly than it had been in the years before the '68 rebellion. She herself sometimes called a contact on the Czech desk at State, Brian Lasker, whom she'd met at a State Department reception and who had been flattered by her attention. She had told him not to bother her husband, but to call her directly if he could ever find out what had happened to her sister's husband, Pieter.

She dreaded to hear that Natasha was taking steps to have Pieter declared legally dead. It was eight years since Natasha's escape—an escape that had been greeted with so much joy, but had ended in so much misery for her.

Louise reread her letter to her mother before putting it with the card into an airmail envelope. *Which is, between us, a bit of a joke.* But Natasha Aesthetique had never been a joke to her. Until it failed dismally in the most public way, the knowledge of its existence was a constant thorn in her side. Most of all, she longed for Benedict to open his arms and welcome Charles back into the Towers fold, but it could never happen until Natasha was out of the way.

*   *   *

Although it was early spring, it was warm enough for Jan Feiner to have breakfast on the wide terrace of his suite overlooking Lake Zurich. It was his usual suite, the best one in the best wing of his favorite hotel in Switzerland, the Dolder Grand. On his last visit he had been with his wife. Now they were divorced and, as he inhaled the fresh mountain air, he realized, not for the first time, how relieved he was to be single again.

If he hadn't been living in America, he knew he would never have gone through with the marriage. Americans were insanely suspicious about men in their late forties who'd never married. Although the tabloids had made sure everyone knew who his current girlfriend was, there was a suggestion that there was something not quite normal about him. It was preposterous, but his brother Victor had warned him there were even rumors that he was homosexual.

If he'd continued to live in Europe, his bachelor status would never have been questioned. He'd allowed Victor to push him into marriage at the height of his sexual infatuation with a young Hungarian model who, in the beginning, had reminded him of Louise. Not for long enough. Well, he'd done it; it had been an eighteen-month disaster, and Victor now knew he never dared interfere in his personal life again.

On the contrary. Now the tables were turned. Victor was brilliant but erratic, too anxious for praise, too loose-tongued with the press. Jan had saved his job once before. Now one of his tasks, meeting with the chairman of Averbach this morning, would be to reassure him that Victor's ill-advised attack on Louise Towers's latest coup, printed in the much-read trade paper *Women's Wear Daily*, wouldn't in any way affect the interesting conversation he had just begun with Charles Towers and Natasha Aesthetique.

Jan didn't begin to understand the relationships between the Towers father and son and the two sisters. There had been halfhearted attempts to paint "family divided" stories in the press, especially when, in a surprise maneuver, it had been announced that Towers Pharmaceuticals was going public, with the exception of the Louise Towers cosmetics division, the assets of which had been evaluated at $130 million, and purchased by Benedict Towers himself.

Jan remembered every minute of the evening he'd spent in Paris with Louise. He remembered her agonizing over Natasha's imminent arrival at the Austrian border, something she had been longing for and planning for so long. He had been very touched by her obvious love for her little sister. What had happened to change that love? If everything proceeded as he wished with the Aesthetique company, perhaps one day he would find out.

As the Averbach chauffeur drove him swiftly to the head office in downtown Zurich, Jan glanced at the papers waiting for him on the backseat: the *International Herald Tribune*, the *Financial Times*, and the Swiss papers. The *Tribune* had picked up a straightforward article from *The New York Times* on what Louise Towers was calling "the first anti-aging cosmetic," Wrinkle Fighter, which, in its first week at Louise Towers counters, had made history as the top-selling skin treatment of all time, despite its hefty price of fifty dollars a jar.

There had never been a cream with such an outspoken claim in its name. In Jan's opinion, the article correctly deduced that the Food and Drug Administration's surprising pronouncement the year before that sun exposure caused not only skin cancer but premature aging was the basis for Towers's brilliant marketing. The *Times*'s scientific correspondent, like a Sherlock Holmes, had put two and two together and concluded that a genius over at Louise Towers ("from her existing track record, probably the founder herself") had seen the potential in using sunscreen ingredients in a skin cream in order to advertise it not only as a sun protector, but as an anti-sun/anti-aging product.

The only question the writer had posed had been one Jan wanted answered himself: How had Louise Towers managed to produce such a cream so soon after the FDA's decision had been made public? "It has been suggested by Louise Towers's competitors that the company had prior knowledge of the momentous announcement made by the government agency."

Victor had made wild accusations in print about Louise's payoffs to government officials, but those assertions, on investigation, had in no way held up. All the same, Jan didn't doubt for a minute that the marketing idea had come from Louise. It sounded like her kind of original thinking, the kind of thinking she had seen exhibited so often by her reluctant mentor, the greatest of them all, Helena Rubinstein.

Jan sighed. The bird in the golden cage, as he referred to Louise in his mind, had once again produced a golden egg for her captor, the dreadful Benedict Towers.

He didn't begrudge her one molecule of her latest great success. However, because of Benedict, Jan was more fueled up than ever to beat the Louise Towers company at its own game.

Sitting at the shining ebony boardroom table, with an electrifying view of the Alps soaring away in the distance, Jan spoke articulately to

K. Averbach's twenty-two board members about the cosmetics business in America.

"No longer is it perhaps quite so 'inflation-proof and recession-resiliant' but it still has plenty of potential. This is perfectly exhibited by the astonishing, overwhelming consumer response to Louise Towers's Wrinkle Fighter."

He paused as a few heads nodded their assent, then went on, "This is a masterpiece of marketing where, in effect, Louise Towers—a 'non-beach' house, not in any way associated with sun oils or tanning lotions—has used sunscreen ingredients in a fairly uncomplicated moisturizer to exploit the FDA's surprising public warning about sun exposure causing premature aging. In fact, Louise Towers has used the FDA announcement as the perfect tool to increase its skin-care business." He had captured the interest of the hardheaded group listening to him, at least half of whom he knew considered the cosmetics business beneath their dignity to discuss. Luckily, Averbach's chairman wasn't one of them.

This was the overture Jan had composed coming over on the company plane. Now he led into his main composition, slightly raising his voice as he began to enthuse about a little-known company called Natasha Aesthetique.

"From my preliminary conversation with Charles Towers, it's obvious to me that it's not the right time yet to show our hand, but from the way they're going, I see this as an admirable vehicle for some of our long-range plans. Natasha has the same drive as her sister, Louise Towers. If anything, she has more of a missionary zeal, condemning much of what she sees in the States as hocus-pocus . . ."

"She's right," said a German member of the board.

"Yes, but she doesn't understand that the industry is in a straitjacket, tied up by the U.S. 1938 Cosmetic Act, which hasn't only never been repealed, but has never even been amended! Few people understand the double standards, that there's no money and too small a staff at the FDA to look at the cosmetics industry and tidy up the antiquated rules and regulations. We should remember, gentlemen, that frozen food, which is what most Americans live on, wasn't even invented in 1938."

One or two board members cleared their throats. They'd heard Jan on this subject before.

"So what is your proposal?"

"If Charles Towers is on target with his projections for the last half of this year and the first half of next year, I think we should discuss our interest in a limited participation, not initially a controlling one. When Charles Towers sees what an infusion of money can do—for advertising, for instance, which they cannot afford now, not to mention use of our research capabilities—then I think he may be prepared for us to take him over. I'm not sure he has his father's stomach for the endless cut-and-slash of business."

"So you will watch the situation closely and keep us informed." It was more a statement than a question, but Jan answered anyway.

"Of course." There were no opposing voices. Jan knew the company well enough to feel gratified. If he made a deal with Charles Towers and Natasha, despite the chagrin Louise would invariably feel, she would know she had only herself and her despicable husband to blame.

Marlene was the go-between. She didn't like the role, but she knew that Leonard had always had a soft spot for his nephew Charles. He'd been too ill for anyone to tell him of the widening rift between Benedict and Charles, let alone to tell him that Charles had actually started his own small cosmetics company with Natasha. But Marlene knew Leonard would have approved of her making sure Charles didn't lose touch with his sister's children.

So far, she hadn't been able to do much about Kick. Louise and Benedict wanted to know the boy's every movement, as if he were some kind of little prince, but they didn't keep such a close eye on Fiona.

Now that she was a vice-president of Louise Towers, the only thing Marlene asked of Charles was that he not bring Natasha along to any rendezvous with his niece—or bring her name up in conversation. She personally had nothing against Natasha, but she knew Natasha was the reason for the falling-out.

Usually Marlene had the jitters whenever she arranged a secret meeting. Today was different. Fiona and Charles were coming to tea at her home, but Louise and Benedict were safely away on the other side of the world, launching Wrinkle Fighter in Australia and New Zealand, where apparently women were fighting in the aisles to get the stuff.

Fiona arrived first, straight from school, her dark blond hair as usual falling into her eyes, the pockets of her navy jacket weighed down with some rubbish or other, probably candies. Marlene never knew how Fiona was going to behave. She had always been a moody child, but today Marlene was relieved to find she was bubbly and communicative.

"Guess what, Aunt Marly, I'm going with a group to Studio 54 on Friday night. It's supposed to be to-die-for, and Midgey knows Steve Rubell, so we're going into the deepest dens of iniquity ... the worst ... or the best, depending on which way you look at it." She threw herself down in an armchair, exposing a fair amount of thigh. "I'm famished."

Marlene didn't like the Studio 54 news at all, but there was nothing she could say or do that would stop Fiona. She'd even heard Benedict say she was, if anything, more headstrong than Suzanne had ever been. She felt she should express her disapproval, but all she said was "It's overrated."

Fiona shot her a suspicious glance. "I bet you've never been. It's not your scene." She started to giggle. "They don't just let in anybody. They have these . . . these . . . guards . . ."

"Hooligans!" Marlene interrupted. She felt a headache coming on. She hoped Charles wouldn't be late. "You're right, it's not my scene, and I don't think it's yours either, a girl of fifteen. You're under age. It's against the law; they probably won't let you in, and that will be a blessing."

Fiona rolled her eyes. "You can bet your life I don't look fifteen at night, Aunty darling. I'm nearly sixteen anyway." Luckily for Marlene, the doorbell rang and Fiona squealed with delight. "It's Charlie, darling Uncle Charlie. I can't wait to hear what he's cooking up with Natasha."

Marlene said reprovingly, "Now, Fiona, remember our rule," but the girl had gone skipping to the front door to throw her arms around her uncle's neck.

He blushed with delight, the way Marlene remembered he always did from embarrassment, the darling boy. She sighed more than once as Fiona monopolized the conversation, daring Charles to come with her to Studio 54, "to the deepest den of iniquity . . . you know where that is, don't you, Uncle Charles," she said in a butter-wouldn't-melt-in-her-mouth voice.

At six o'clock, the time Marlene decreed that a car had to take Fiona back to East Seventy-third Street, Tate was at the door. After yelps of protest, Fiona smothered Charles's face in kisses, saying slyly, as she zipped out the door, "Ve've got to stop meeting like this, Charles. Vot vill ze neighbors say?"

"Get out of here, you litle vixen."

There was a heavy silence when the door closed behind her. "Have you got time for a drink?" Marlene asked nervously, hoping he didn't. Even though Louise and Benedict were thousands of miles away, she was afraid the phone might ring and she'd reveal her treachery in some way.

Charles didn't seem in any hurry to leave. "I'd love one—scotch and water." As she went to the bar in the corner cupboard, he said solicitously, "I hear you're working hard for the company. Natasha always said you'd be a great training director, because you see every-thing and forget nothing."

Marlene forgot her own rule. "Did she say that?" She beamed with pleasure. "Well, yes, I do like that part of the business, but Louise ..." She hesitated, not sure how Charles would react to the name. He sat impassively watching her. "Louise hasn't made up her mind about me yet. I'm told I'm on the longest orientation program anyone has ever had." She laughed self-deprecatingly.

"But at least you're a vice-president—that's a good beginning." There was no hidden meaning in his words, no malice. As a Towers, he accepted that was the way it should be for members of the Towers family. Marlene wished others in the company understood that.

On her wrist was a trace of Bravado, the about-to-be-launched Louise Towers fragrance. She longed for Charles to sniff it, to find out his opinion, but of course it was out of the question. Instead she asked, "How is everything with you?" She wanted to know, yet she didn't wish to open up any avenues for a personal discussion.

Charles put his feet up on the coffee table, appearing totally relaxed. "Well, Aunt Marly, dear, I have to say professionally things are incredible. Natasha ..."

Involuntarily, Marlene put up a hand.

He understood at once. "Don't worry, I'm not going to embarrass you with a list of her—or our—achievements, but"—he grinned mischievously—"one of the things you have to learn is the difference in markets. You're class, we're mass—no competition. Do you think I'd ever have started a business to compete with my own family's?" He looked at her intently. "I've discussed it often enough with Dad. I hope one day he'll be proud that I managed to do something on my own. We may not see each other much anymore, but we're not enemies."

Marlene remained silent. She felt he was feeling her out. She wanted to agree with him, but from what she'd heard, she wasn't altogether sure how her brother-in-law regarded his only son. The only thing she did know for sure was that Louise loathed her sister.

Finally she said lamely, "It's too bad we can't all be together, like the old days."

"Do you think it would make life easier if ... if I were to regularize things?"

For a moment she didn't know what he meant. "Regularize?"

"Yes." Charles sounded unnaturally testy. "Straighten everything out. If we start now with the application, by next year Natasha can have her husband declared legally dead. If we were to marry, do you think the family would come around, would accept it?"

Marlene felt sick. What could she say? That Benedict would probably like to, but that Louise, for whatever deep reason of her own, never

would? "I don't know, Charles. I wish I knew, but I don't." Out of
nervousness, although she longed for him to go, she took his glass and
refilled it, asking, "Why hasn't Natasha divorced her husband?"

"You can't divorce a missing person, otherwise she'd have done it
long ago," Charles said defiantly. "I want to settle down, Aunt Marly,
give Natasha security, perhaps even have a child."

"A child!" She was appalled.

His face was reddening. "Why not? Women in their thirties have
children all the time. In fact, Natasha thought she was pregnant the
other day. We were both delighted."

"Charlie! How would that have regularized things?"

"Well, it turned out she wasn't, but it made us realize we wanted a
family. We want to stay together. Until this happened, neither of us
was sure. So much has happened—Suzanne's death and all the terrible
family trauma, my leaving the business and buying Aesthetique—we've
never really had time, or at least I haven't, to know whether we wanted
to . . . to be married or not."

"And now you're sure?" For the first time, Marlene began to wonder
if what Louise had said in the past was true—that Natasha was manipulative and Charles was weak.

Charles brushed her question aside. "I've promised her that once
we're married, if we can't have our own child, we'll adopt." He looked
at her beseechingly. "Can't you do anything, Aunt Marly, can't you
somehow get to the bottom of it with Louise? I know Natasha still suffers
terribly over their falling-out. She'd give anything to be reunited with
Louise. If there was a chance, I don't think she'd hesitate about selling
the business. Neither would I. Sometimes I hear her crying at night. She
says she's dreaming, but I know she's awake, going over and over in her
mind how everything changed so quickly, why Louise turned on her. She
never hears from her mother any more, never has any news about her
daughter. For all she knows, Kristina may be dead after all."

He looked so miserable, Marlene felt tears come to her eyes. At that
moment she would have done anything to help him, but she knew it
wouldn't last. Despite her many kindnesses, Louise still intimidated
her too much. Natasha was a forbidden subject, so was Natasha Aesthetique, and so, most days, was Charles himself, but nevertheless she
heard herself saying, "I'll try."

He obviously didn't believe her. All the lightheartedness he'd shown
during Fiona's visit was gone. He stood up and said in a flat voice,
"Yes, I know you will if you can. Well, we'll see what happens in the
next few months."

For a long while after he'd gone, Marlene paced back and forth, unable to pick up the new training manual she'd brought home to study. Should she summon up her courage and try to act as a mediator between Natasha and Louise?

There was no doubt in her mind that the quarrel wasn't between Benedict and Charles, though her brother-in-law had been terribly hurt when Charles left the company. No, she was sure that if a rapprochement could be reached between the sisters, father and son would fall into each other's arms.

Even if Natasha was the conniving, power-hungry, jealous woman some people around Louise said she was, it was obvious that Charles was serious about giving her the Towers name. In that case, wasn't it better for everybody if there was a civilized family relationship?

Peace, not war, that had been her Leonard's maxim about everything, whether dealing with household help, business negotiations, or national and international affairs. As had become her habit, before getting into bed, Marlene took out her five-year diary and started to write down as much as she could remember of her conversation with Charles.

Before she put out the light, she said her prayers. She thanked God that she was somehow still being guided by Leonard, because now she knew she had to do everything she could to bring about peace in the Towers family.

London, 1978

"IF IT MEANS the silly children will like you more, let them call you LouLou as much as they want, and if your besotted husband wants to call you LouLou, too, encourage it. What's in a name?"

Sitting beside Lady Diana Cooper, who was at the wheel of her little black Austin Mini, Louise decided it was too perilous to tell Her Ladyship she had totally misunderstood her at lunch over the use of nicknames. The English had a habit of polling you at mealtimes, when, trapped at the dining table, opinions and beliefs were sought about all kinds of peculiar things.

As if she cared about being called LouLou! Perhaps in an unguarded moment in the past she'd mentioned to Diana her difficulties with the children, and Diana was reacting to that. Yes, that was likely. Apart from Alexandra Sanford, she had no confidantes at home, but overseas there were a few, and Lady Diana was certainly one of them.

London was the last stop on a month-long trip she'd taken with Benedict, mostly a vacation to celebrate their silver wedding anniversary. Louise could hardly believe how she'd weathered twenty-five years. Given the choice by Benedict, she had chosen the trip over a huge party, which pleased him, too. Now that Towers Pharmaceuticals was a public company, although Benedict was still very much the boss, he seemed to have more time for himself.

In any case, she hated huge parties, having to go through an evening with a fixed smile on her face, celebrating in public, instead of in private, what she considered her most notable achievement—her lengthy marriage. So they'd taken the waters in Baden-Baden; bought a rundown lakeside spa to rehabilitate into a Louise Towers Institute in Tegernsee, on the edge of the Black Forest; looked for but not found the site for an extra plant for Towers Pharmaceuticals in

Germany; stayed with the Rainiers in Monaco (where Princess Grace had confided she was a Wrinkle Fighter addict); then gone on to Venice to stay in Peggy Guggenheim's treasure-filled palazzo on the Grand Canal, surrounded, as Benedict had told her, by the very best in modern art and sculpture.

He'd insisted she study and remember them all—Pollock, Klee, Picasso, Henry Moore. It hadn't been difficult. He'd been impressed that she now knew so much about modern art.

Today in London she'd dismissed her driver, saying it was such a lovely day she would walk back to the hotel, then she'd been inveigled by Diana into meeting her "skin guru." If only she'd resisted.

As the Austin hurtled into the maelstrom of Hyde Park Corner traffic, Louise held her breath, praying the lucky talisman that obviously hovered over the remarkable eighty-six-year-old woman would stay in place until they reached her guru in the Mews just off Hill Street.

Despite the hair-raising drive and two flights of steep stairs, as soon as she stepped inside Carla Crespia's Skin Sanctuary, as the celebrated London skin-care salon was called, Louise was glad she'd come. Carla, the guru—"a few years younger than me," Lady Diana had volunteered—was as wrinkled and shrunken as her illustrious patron was smooth and upright, but Louise was fascinated by the Crespia "laboratory" in full view, with hundreds of tiny vials lining the walls.

"Carla uses aromatherapy to cure and maintain the skin," Diana boomed proudly. "All of these"—she pointed a long finger at a wall of labeled bottles—"contain miracle lotions blended specifically from plant and flower extracts for each of Carla's customers."

"What exactly is aromatherapy?" Louise asked, looking directly at Carla and hoping that she, and not Diana, would answer.

"It is the application and sometimes the inhalation of prescribed essential oils, to—"

"Rejuvenate, in my case," said Lady Diana triumphantly.

"Yes, my lady." The guru had a strong foreign accent.

Louise, irritated, persevered with a wide smile. "Please tell me more."

"The application of certain essential oils helps achieve total relaxation, which is not inertia. The disappearance of muscular tension frees energy." Although Carla's voice was monotonous, Louise was intrigued. "It frees the passages and makes the patient's skin particularly receptive to the active ingredients. In certain conditions . . ."

Lady Diane squeaked her chair on the floor. Louise could see she was becoming bored. To her dismay, Diana said, "Time is moving on." She waved her watch under Louise's nose. "I am sure your beloved will be wondering where you are."

"Can I make an appointment? I would love to talk to you more about this. I should tell you I have a cosmetics company in . . ."

Carla interrupted her, her face expressionless. "I know who you are."

Louise had a premonition. "Where are you from?"

"From Prague. My grandnephew Juta got out with your sister, Natasha, in the 1968 uprising. He thinks very highly of her."

Louise's enthusiasm to know more about Carla's aromatherapy faded as quickly as it had come.

As Diana was enthusing about coincidences and the small size of the world, Louise couldn't wait to leave. She felt the guru's eyes on her as she walked down the stairs and out into the sunlight.

"You didn't make an appointment?"

"No, I have to check my calendar. I'm not sure how much longer Benedict can stay here. I may not have time."

"Well, you scarcely need her, m'dear. That Wrinkle Fighter has certainly been fighting on your behalf."

Although Louise had promised herself she would walk back to the hotel rather than risk the Austin Mini again, like a sleepwalker she got into the car for the short drive to Claridge's. She kissed Diana good-bye, but hardly knew what she said on leaving.

My grandnephew Juta got out with your sister, Natasha . . . He thinks very highly of her.

By the time she reached the suite, Louise couldn't control her sobs. Thank God, Benedict wasn't yet back from the office. She flung herself on the bed, her body heaving with conflict and pain. She gave in to the pent-up tears of years. It made no sense. She didn't know why, but on this afternoon, following a simple mention of her sister's name, she felt she had to release her sorrow or break down forever. She was red-eyed, barely composed, when Benedict came rushing in over an hour later.

He was angry. He never tried to hide his anger. "Have you been talking to anyone, *anyone*," he repeated, "on the Czech desk at State behind my back?"

She shivered. Of all days to hear this. Benedict pulled her violently to her feet. "What have you been up to?"

"I don't know what you're talking about. If you mean have I ever spoken to anyone on the Czech desk, yes, yes." The tears she'd shed, her wrenching reaction to Crespia's mention of Natasha, had left her empty, incapable, for the moment, of feeling anything. It was as if Benedict were shouting at another person.

"Have you been asking Lasker, Brian Lasker, to initiate a search for Pieter Mahler?" His fingers dug into her shoulders.

"Lasker?" She wasn't playing for time as over the years she'd tried to do when confronted with a Benedict inquisition. She really couldn't remember the young man's name, but of course she knew exactly whom Benedict was referring to.

"Yes, Lasker! L-A-S-K-E-R," he spelled out.

Louise could feel his hand shaking as his fingers now pushed her chin up, forcing her to look him in the eyes.

She stared back, cool, calm. "Yes, I think Lasker is the name of the young fellow I met a couple of years ago at a reception at the State Department. I have spoken to him. Why? Is there a law against it?"

Benedict released her. He paced up and down the grand sitting room as, over the years, she had seen him do so many times when he was agitated. "Behind my back ... behind my back ..." he muttered. "You know how embarrassing it has been for me to deal with your squalid family, to hear the curiosity in the voices of these pen-pushing, no-account hacks as they reported to me the comings and goings of an elderly hairdresser in Prague. All these years ..."

"What is all this about?"

There was no longer any quickening of her breath, no anticipation, as there had been in the past when Benedict was about to relay news from Czechoslovakia. It had all brought too much pain; she didn't want to hear anything more.

"Why did you seek help from someone else? Why didn't you tell me? Did you think I wasn't doing enough to find out ..."

"Find out what?"

"Whether Mahler was alive or dead!" he screamed.

"Well, which is he?"

As she asked the question, blood flushed into her face; subconsciously her brain was betraying her, showing Benedict how much she wanted to know the answer, when she didn't even realize it consciously herself.

Her husband stared at her for a long minute, then said icily, "Your secret source of investigation has paid off, Louise. There is a report on your desk in New York about a man severely injured during the uprising, who has recently recovered his memory, a man identified as Pieter Mahler. He is a bitter, resentful man, still incapacitated from gunshot wounds. There are two letters from him awaiting your return, letters sent on through our embassy, one to you, one to be delivered to your sister, his wife."

Benedict's voice rose. "They are not pleasant to read. They accuse you both of abandoning your family. He accuses you of leading your impressionable young sister into a capitalist life of plenty, leaving him to struggle to bring up their daughter with the help of an old, sick woman. He hates you for what you have done. He still holds out hope for Natasha, that when she receives the news of his survival she will be 'saved' from your corrupting influence. Amusing, isn't it?"

She hardly heard what he was saying now. Joy had replaced—what was the word Carla had used—*inertia*, that was it. She had been inert, but now feeling was coming back.

Pieter was alive. Natasha was not free.

Who knew how Natasha would feel when she learned the news? For over two years she had been inconsolable over Pieter. There was no doubt she had loved him very much, just as Louise had come to realize Charles had once loved his wife, Blythe. They had looked to each other for consolation. Louise wasn't aware how she looked, how clearly she showed how much the news that Pieter Mahler was still alive elated her.

As she went over to Benedict, he jumped to his feet. "Don't come near me. How happy you are, aren't you? How this news thrills you, to learn your sister's husband is so safely alive. Perhaps she will attempt to go back to Prague now. I can see it written all over your scheming face. And why does this fill you with such delight?"

"Benedict . . ."

"No, don't dare interrupt me. Why suddenly do you look as if the weight of the world has left your shoulders? Why? Why?" He was white, shaking with rage.

Alarmed, again she appealed, "Benedict, I . . ."

"Shut up! Suzanne tried to warn me, and I heard your wretched sister say it myself. All along you've wanted Charles, my son, the young Towers. You whore! Why else would you turn on the sister you spent years trying to rescue? Once I thought it was some kind of professional jealousy." He gave a harsh snort. "I closed my ears, my eyes, yet always there was something that nagged away at me."

Trembling, Louise tried to put a hand on his arm. He pulled away as if he'd been stung. "Don't touch me. Behind my back, all these years . . . I couldn't believe it when my office told me this Lasker fellow was trying to reach you with good news. Oh yes, good news for you, all right!"

"You're wrong, Benedict. Please listen to me."

"I'm through with listening. I believed you when you told me there was never anything between you and Feiner. What a fool I've been. No wonder he and Avery try to ruin us at every turn. Of course, Feiner was the lover you double-crossed when I came along."

"No, it's not true!" she cried. "And you're crazy to say Charles and I . . ."

He threw out his arm as if he wanted to hit her. "I don't blame Charles. If you'd been given half the chance . . . but Charles was only interested in his own age group. I've alienated my son because of you. Suzanne was right all along. No wonder he wanted out of Louise Towers. God knows how you must have tried to throw yourself at him, you wicked cunt. And I suspected my son, God forgive me, I allowed you to turn me against him and your sister. I allowed you to influence his rightful inheritance. But for you, he would never have left the company."

Years of suspicion, years of jealousy poured out. There was nothing Louise could do or say to stop him. The phone rang several times in the next few hours. Neither Benedict nor Louise picked it up. They had planned to go to the theater, but neither remembered.

They were in a no-man's-land where the present had ceased to exist and only the past was in the room, a past revealed by Benedict as full of her treachery, a past where he had suffered for over twenty years since she had first betrayed him, secretly taking birth-control pills to ensure that she did not conceive.

"Slut . . . whore . . . blind ambition . . . you've lived a lie from the beginning, pretending to love me. Suzanne was right; she warned me . . ." Again and again Benedict evoked the name of his dead daughter who had warned him about her from the start. Finally he sat bleakly in an armchair, waving her away as she tried to come near him. "Go away. Go phone your sister. Tell her the news you can't wait to share with her. Call my son. Say I've given up the fight. He can have you if he wants you, which I very much doubt. I'm too old for this. I don't want it. I'm sick of it and you."

She went into the bedroom, every part of her body aching, her head throbbing, reeling with what had overtaken her in the space of a few hours. She was bereft, unable to cry, lying on the bed, staring at the ceiling, waiting to hear the door in the next room slam as Benedict disappeared out of her life, but there was silence.

When the phone rang again, she jumped and put on the bedside light. "Yes?"

It was the hall porter. Their chauffeur was still waiting outside. Were there any instructions for him? Louise saw the clock on her bedside table. It was nearly midnight. He had been waiting outside to take them to the theater since seven o'clock, another life ago. "No, no, tell him to call my husband at the usual time in the morning."

The usual time in the morning. Was there any hope it could possibly be just another usual time? Was there anything she could say now that would make Benedict realize she hadn't been living a lie, that she admired and respected him, that she was proud of being his wife and had never wanted to be married to anyone else? That he had taught her how to love and be loved, that she had remained faithful to him for twenty-five years?

It was all true, but would she be lying when she said she also had never considered being unfaithful? Would she, that night in the office, have really allowed Charles to make love to her? She shuddered. She didn't dare think about it. The most important thing now was to convince Benedict she loved him and always only him.

She brushed her hair and teeth, took off her suit, undressed, and slipped on her negligee. This had been the worst day of her married life. She would never wear that suit again.

She nervously opened the sitting room door. Benedict was still sitting in the same chair. "Benedict," she said softly. His head was on his chest. "Benedict . . ." She was used to waking him gently and leading him to bed. Please, God, she prayed, let it be like the other times. Please, God, allow me to lead him into my arms.

She knelt before him. There was saliva coming out of his mouth. She tenderly put her hands on his shoulders, whispering, "Time for bed, darling . . ."

His body felt heavy. In the light shining through from the bedroom, his face looked strange, contorted. Terror surged through her. She switched on the lamp beside the chair and screamed. One eye was closed, the other half-open. Benedict wasn't asleep. He was unconscious.

With Claridge's help, it took less than an hour to get him to the London Clinic, where the doctors wouldn't allow her to stay by his side. Another three hours passed before it was confirmed that Benedict had had a heart attack, that he was in intensive care. "Please try to get some rest, Mrs. Towers. There is nothing you can do for the moment. We will be able to tell you more in the next twenty-four hours."

They were cool and clipped, voices of authority that brooked no opposition. "I would rather wait here," she said, as cool and clipped as they.

They shrugged their shoulders and left her in the empty waiting room. Just before six, desperate for help, she called Tim Nolan, who had been running Towers Pharmaceuticals in Britain for nearly thirty years. As he ran into the waiting room no more than forty minutes later, one of the doctors reappeared. He beckoned Louise to one side. "Your husband is responding well to treatment, but it is too early to tell how much damage has occurred."

"Is he conscious? Does he know what has happened? Can I see him?"

"He is exhibiting essential life signs. For the moment I am afraid there can be no visitors." He looked over to where Nolan was sitting. "Is that a member of the family? Someone who can take you home?"

Louise nodded impatiently. "A very close family friend. Does my husband know I am here?" The doctor hesitated imperceptibly before giving a curt nod. Louise guessed what it meant. Benedict knew and didn't want to see her.

She sank down on a bench and covered her face in her hands. She wanted Benedict to live, and she wanted to die. She was responsible for what had happened. She was a sick woman, sick in the head, but for the moment there was nothing to do except return to the hotel and, with the help of a strong sleeping pill, try to sink into oblivion for a few hours.

The next day Benedict's doctor, Arthur Priestley, flew over with New York's leading heart specialist, Isidore Rosenfeld, and in forty-eight hours Benedict was out of intensive care and resting in a private room. At last word came to the now busy waiting room where she had spent most of the past two days that she could visit her husband.

As she followed a nurse down the corridor, Louise felt increasingly nervous. Charles was on the way. Did Benedict know? Should she be the one to tell him?

Louise knew that Nolan had already been allowed to make a five-minute visit before her. He had to know something was wrong between them, but it didn't embarrass her. The majority of those running Towers Pharmaceuticals subsidaries around the world were longtime cronies of Benedict, used to following orders, used to shaping their opinions according to his, hot and cold, for and against.

He lay pale and drawn, a multitude of wires and tubes attached to his body, a monitor on one side of the high hospital bed showing the uneven beat of his heart. Louise's eyes filled with tears. He had taken her from obscurity and poverty and made her dreams come true, and she had repaid him with a restless, foolish heart.

"Benedict . . ."

"Yes, Louise, here is your broken man." His voice was little more than a whisper, but the words struck her as if he were still shouting, screaming. She would never forget them.

There was only one thing to say. "I love you, Benedict." Tears streamed down her face. "I've always loved you, and I have always been faithful."

"In thought, word, and deed." It wasn't a question. Whispered or not, it still sounded as if he were mocking her, but he allowed her to hold his hand and stroke it. The fire had gone out of him.

"Yes, in thought, word, and deed. I'm so sorry, my darling. I love you."

He nodded sleepily. "Yes, I believe you do. Your boyfriend is on the way—you know, Charles, my son—and if I don't get out of here anytime soon, I've asked for Kick to come, too." He looked at her for one frightening moment as if he didn't recognize her. "Kick, my other son, but I don't want anyone to frighten him yet," he rambled. "His studies mustn't be interrupted."

"Benedict, Charles is my stepson, not my boyfriend," she said softly. "Things are going to change. We're going to be one family again."

"That would be very nice." He spoke politely, as if to a stranger. His eyes were closing.

"Benedict, please know I love you."

He didn't hear her. His mouth hung slightly open. He was already asleep.

Charles called her at the hotel later that evening, and they arranged to go to the London Clinic together in the morning, though Louise told him over the phone that it was too tiring for Benedict to see more than one person at a time. It was true, but in any case there was no way she could sit in the same room with father and son at the moment.

As she dressed with particular care, scrutinizing her makeup, looking for signs of age that weren't there, Louise told herself it wasn't because she hadn't seen Charles for months. She didn't want to be excited, but she had to admit she was, excited but mostly apprehensive.

As part of her self-imposed, perpetual education process, she had recently been studying Jung. One paragraph told her what months with the psychiatrist had never done. "Fear of our erotic fate is quite understandable. For there is something unpredictable about it."

She yearned for the unpredictable. It was a long time, months since Benedict had been able to arouse her. If he knew, he never said so. Was it inevitable that even for the most experienced lover, as Benedict certainly was, the movements, the positions became perfunctory? He still wanted her—or wanted sex, not so often, but with a certain regularity. She never dreamed of refusing him, but did her passivity, her lack of pleasure, mean she was going back to the frigid state of her youth?

"Mr. Charles Towers is here."

"Send him up." She had said they would meet in the lobby, but now that the moment had come, she couldn't see him after so long in such a public place.

When the bell rang, all she could think about was seeing his dear, sweet face. Everything else was momentarily forgotten.

"Louise . . ."

There were tears in his eyes. She didn't stop to think why they were there. "Charlie, oh, Charlie." She flung her arms around his neck as if it were the most natural thing in the world. For one second he put his arms around her, then, just as she felt the fast beating of his heart and the slight bristle on his cheek, he stepped back.

As she began to say, "It's been too long," Charles asked anxiously, "How is he?"

It was still there, goddamn it, it was still there, the look, so like his father, yet unlike him, the look that proved how true were Jung's words. Unpredictably her knees had turned to jelly, and—another perfect phrase came to her mind—there was that "old elevator-climb of desire" zooming inside her body.

She turned away. For everyone's sake, she had to make peace now or never.

"He's longing to see you. The doctors say you'll be a great tonic."

"I can't wait to see him," Charles said nervously. "Is he . . . is he going to be all right?"

"He's going to have to change his life, according to Dr. Rosenfeld. Cut down on work, cut out cigars and brandy." Louise looked at the attractive man, bursting with health and vitality, standing before her. She didn't think. She burst out, "He needs you, Charlie, he needs you as never before. Can't you come back to us, to Towers?"

Charles frowned. To Louise's horror, he said curtly, "Don't give me any emotional blackmail, Louise. You know how involved I am. Dad and I have a lot to work out before I can even start to consider that. And in any case"—he gave her a hard, angry look—"how do I know if that's what Dad wants, or if it's what you want? You never give up, do you? Even at a time like this."

Charles had never used such a tone of voice to her, not even on that terrible night. If he wasn't directly antagonistic, there was certainly no warmth. All resolutions to ask nicely after Natasha vanished. She had been planning to tell him about Pieter, to suggest they get together to work out once and for all what was best for the families, personally and professionally.

If things went well, she'd had a plan to suggest that there might be a way to amalgamate the two businesses, Louise Towers and Natasha Aesthetique, to the financial advantage of everyone. But most of all she hoped there might be a way for the two of them, the "junior members of the family," finally—to use an English expression she particularly loved—to bury the hachet.

But she'd been fooling herself. She'd been right all along in believing that Natasha had influenced Charles against her. He would never have answered her that way before he left the company, the family.

Before she could say anything, the phone rang to say the car had arrived to take them to the clinic. She was relieved. As Benedict had directed her all her life, it was far better to remain silent when she was in danger of saying something she would later regret.

She had hoped to have dinner with Charles, to catch up, to start to mend fences, but she didn't see him leave the clinic, and there was no message from him when she returned, exhausted, to the hotel at the end of the day.

"Well, how did you find Charlie?" Benedict had asked, freshly shaved but still wan.

"He seems very well."

"And happy, he tells me. Very happy with his Czech, as I was once with mine." If Benedict was trying to hurt her, he was succeeding, but Louise told herself that at least it was a sign he was gaining strength.

It didn't take her long to realize Charles was going to great trouble to avoid seeing her again. They met in the corridors of the clinic and once in the waiting room, when the doctors were examining Benedict, but otherwise Charles made no attempt to see or talk to her.

"Where are you staying, Charles?"

"With friends."

"Have you no time for a quiet dinner?"

"No, I'm afraid not. As soon as Doc Priestly tells me Dad's on the mend, I have to go to Switzerland."

"Oh. On business?"

"Yes."

At the end of two weeks, Doctor Priestly made arrangements for Benedict to return to Claridge's with day and night nurses, and Charles left for Europe. After another week, as Benedict grew irritable, fretting out loud about his homesickness, his yearning for a good pastrami sandwich ("Forbidden," said Dr. Priestley) and for the company of Kick and Fiona, it was agreed he was now strong enough to fly home on the Towers company plane.

"At least something good came out of this," Benedict told Louise en route to the States, as he sat with his head resting on her shoulder.

"Yes, darling?" She hoped he was going to say something positive about their relationship.

"Charlie . . . dear Charlie . . ." his voice started to trail away as it often had in the past few weeks, as if he didn't have the strength to sustain his thought. "Yes, I think we recovered some lost ground. He's not a bad fella. Well, I don't need to tell *you* that." There was an edge to his voice, but not much. He leaned back against the seat and, with his eyes closed, said, "It's women who lead men astray, but perhaps Charlie has done all right for himself after all."

This was her moment to bridge the gap. She took it, although it made her want to vomit. "Yes, I think Charlie is very happy with Natasha. Perhaps we can all get together soon after all."

"Did you tell Charlie that Natasha's husband is still alive?"

"No. Did you?"

"No. Frankly, I had other things to think about," Benedict said grimly. He turned away from her and stared out into the stratosphere. "Thank God I made the decision to take Towers public when I did." It was as if he were talking to himself. "No one can say I didn't think ahead, didn't look after everyone in the family."

"You've always thought ahead."

"I've tried to, but you never know when you're going to be struck down. If I'd waited . . ." He turned to look at her, his expression strained. "If news had leaked out that I was ill, we'd never have received the price we did."

"But you didn't wait." She stroked his arm lovingly.

"But as you know, Louise Towers is totally ours, a family concern, just as the original pharmaceutical company was set up."

"Yes, that's wonderful, darling." What else was she to say? She'd learned more from reading *The Wall Street Journal* than from what he and Norris had told her about the restructuring of the Towers empire, the evaluation and setting aside of the Louise Towers assets for Benedict Towers to buy in order to keep the cosmetics division private.

She told herself now, as she had at the time, that Benedict had done it for her, recognizing all she had done to create the powerful, immensely successful cosmetics company. He had never told her so, but she had to look at it that way. It was, for her, the only proof that he considered her just as much a Towers as his adored grandchildren.

There was a small welcome-home family party arranged at East Seventy-third Street the weekend after their arrival. Kick came home on special leave from college; Marlene arrived early with Zoe, followed by Fiona and most of Benedict's cousins, old and young, their wives and children. The only ones who were not family members were the Norrises.

The big drawing room rang with reassuring phrases: "You're looking great, Benedict."

"We're so happy to have you back in New York, sir."

"Everything's great here, Benedict. Nothing to worry about now that you're back on your feet."

"Losing that weight suits you, Pappy. Now you can wear the new Ralph Lauren preppie look," Fiona cooed, snuggling up.

"Why are you wearing that godawful brown lipstick, Fi?" Benedict responded with a broad grin. "Is that the latest Louise Towers fashion?"

Fiona giggled, not a bit fazed. "It's a cheapo Max Factor. I'm on an economy drive."

"That'll be the day," said Kick. "What about that suede number you're wearing? I bet that's not cheapo."

"Get the facts straight, college boy. This is Ultrasuede from Halston, half the price of suede . . ."

Benedict listened, amused, as the bunch of teenage Towers prattled back and forth. When the decibel level started to climb, he wearily got to his feet to join Norris and his wife, Becky, chatting with his older cousins by the doors into the garden. Louise never took her eyes from him, but she knew he hated being fussed over. They had agreed that if he wanted to leave the party early, rather than break it up and alarm anyone, he would say he had to make an urgent telephone call. He was smoking a forbidden cigar to celebrate, but to Louise he looked very tired.

She beckoned to Banks, the butler who had come to them from London nearly four years before, to replace the faithful Thorpe on his retirement. "See if it's time for Mr. Towers's telephone call, Banks."

She watched as Banks approached, and thankfully saw Benedict excuse himself and lean on Banks's arm to walk toward the library.

As the doors closed behind him, Norris came over to her. "I'm worried about him, Louise. He seems to have no strength."

"He's got to take things very easy. I only hope I can make him remember that."

"I'll help you, Louise. You can depend on it. I'll come over every day and give him a report until he feels up to going to the office."

The next morning, Benedict didn't need to be persuaded to stay in bed. The trip home had exhausted him more than he realized. "Do you mind if I go to the office for a short while? I think I should just look in, but I won't stay long," Louise told him anxiously.

He gave her a strange, quizzical look. "You've got to catch up on your correspondence, haven't you?"

"If you mean the letters from Prague, yes, I do want to read them, but they mean nothing."

"When are you going to give your sister the good news? You've known for some weeks. Isn't it time you put her out of her misery? Not to mention your own."

She humored him, ignoring his sarcasm, straightening his pillows, putting the telephone nearer to his reach, tidying up the newspapers spread over the bed. "Don't worry. Natasha will be told as soon as I can get to it. She's waited ten years; she can wait a few hours longer."

As she bent to kiss him, he grabbed her face and kissed her hard on the mouth. "I don't trust you," he said, "but come back soon anyway."

In the car, she wished she hadn't left. She missed Benedict. She decided she would simply walk through the offices to reassure everyone that the boss was fine, read Pieter Mahler's letter, and then decide on the best way to tell Natasha the news. She felt uneasy, unnaturally nervous, perhaps because of having to contact her sister after so long, perhaps because of the strain of the weeks before. As the car stopped at a red light on Fifth Avenue, she decided that the easiest way for Natasha to receive the news was directly from Lasker at the State Department; then she would send Pieter's letter on with an accompanying note, explaining that she had authorized the extra search on behalf of both families. After Charles's cool treatment of her, she didn't know how she felt about him anymore; it was a mixture of love and hate.

The car phone rang as they approached the Towers Building. Her mind was miles away, thinking about her mother and Kristina in Prague and how the arrival of Pieter, apparently still wounded, must be affecting their lives.

"Mrs. Towers, Mrs. Towers . . ." Pebbler, the new young chauffeur they'd hired just before their trip to Europe, had pulled up to the curb. He was looking stricken. She snatched up the phone.

It was Banks, his voice low. "Mr. Towers has suffered another attack, ma'am. The ambulance is on the way."

They reached East Seventy-third Street as the ambulance was rounding the corner. By the time it reached New York Hospital, where a battalion of doctors and nurses were waiting, it was already too late. Benedict Towers had died at 10:05 A.M., from another massive heart attack. There was nothing anyone could have done to save him.

The mind played tricks. Louise wasn't aware of who was at the funeral, except for Kick and Fiona, who sat on either side of her, holding each hand—and Charles, holding Fiona's hand on the other side. But she did register that Madderlake had executed her instructions impeccably—to fill the side altars, large and small, with only unscented flowers, asters, dahlias, dusty-colored sedums, and fragile Japanese anemones in the colors Benedict had always loved best, especially orange, purple, and deep autumnal yellow. She would also always remember seeing a Fifth Avenue bus marooned in a sea of stretch limousines as, swept out with waves of mourners, she emerged from the church.

"Everyone was there," she would read, "with every world represented by its leaders, in politics, industry, the arts, medicine, journalism — every world." But she noticed none of them, and asked after only one name. "Was Natasha there?"

"Yes," Marlene told her nervously. "Natasha was there, two or three pews back from the front."

There would be memorial services in a month's time in Washington and New York and then in many of Towers's major markets overseas throughout the coming year. It was Louise who composed the memorandum with this information, printed on stark white paper, edged in black, and sent to thousands of people, longtime Towers employees, and friends and acquaintances throughout the world.

From the moment she had had to accept the impossible, she had moved like a robot, not collapsing as everyone waited for her to do, but instead overseeing all the details no one expected or wanted her to do.

"Have you seen her shed one tear?" Becky Norris asked her husband, who had shed a few for the old warhorse himself.

"No," he replied quietly. "Not outside. Inside I think she's crying all the time. I wish she would show it. I've felt for a long time — even last week, when we were all at Seventy-third Street — that she could very easily crack. Being married to Benedict Towers was no piece of cake, Becky."

"You should know. You were as good as married to him for much longer than Louise." Her tender smile took the sting out of her words. "Are the children helping? I thought she and Kick seemed to be getting on now. Not sure about Fiona."

"You're right. Kick has certainly warmed up to her. She's done everything in the world she could for them. Fiona's still a problem. I think she always will be. Thank God she's gone off on some fancy art-appreciation course with a bunch of girls from school."

"I'm sure that's a relief for Louise."

"I'm dreading Tuesday."

"Of course you are, but perhaps Louise knows already."

"She doesn't know. I tried to bring it up with Ben, that he should explain to her why he didn't want to leave control of the company in her hands. He certainly should have, but he always changed the subject. There was something that stopped him — I don't know what it was, but somehow he didn't trust her not to sell out if and when he died. I've never been able to fathom it out."

"In any case, surely she has been left a very rich woman? Company or no company, she'll have her hands full looking after her fortune — and, with her incredible looks, keeping away the fortune hunters."

Norris shook his head reprovingly. Women could be so hard. Even his own wife could shock him sometimes, but he didn't tell her so. All he said was, "The company means everything to her, and Benedict knew it. I never did understand his thought processes when it came to his family. Only Suzanne seemed to know how to handle him. He was never the same after she died."

Louise looked at her naked body reflected many times by the mirrored walls of her dressing room. She pinched her thigh hard, watching the flesh turn red. She was alive, though she felt dead. Every word, every gesture, every movement and step she took was an act of will. She was a producer producing each scene of her life, and in her head was the unforgiving, unrelenting voice of the director, who had directed her for most of her life. *Reveal nothing; don't let the world in; you'll make fewer mistakes that way.* It was Benedict's voice keeping her awake at night, keeping her going during the day. Nothing was real, not since the moment she had arrived at the hospital to sink down beside Benedict's lifeless body.

This Tuesday morning she had awakened, knowing that in a few hours she would be meeting with the executors of Benedict's will, both lawyers with the company for years, Gregory Phillips and, replacing Benedict's brother Leonard, Ashton Foxwell.

It would be the first of many meetings because Phillips had already intimated Benedict's will was complicated, involving not only the Louise Towers company, but also Kick and Fiona's trusts. She had asked Norris to be ready to come over to the house later, when she called, because she had plans of her own she wanted to relay in the presence of the lawyers.

Dear, faithful Norris, who year after year had sat by the door in the Towers boardroom while Benedict's relatives, not one of whom came close to measuring up to his stature, sat loftily around the grand boardroom table to give their stamp of approval to many of the sound ideas he had originated.

As she bathed, Louise thought about Benedict's actions in 1974. Had he known or suspected he had a heart problem when he'd made the surprising decision to take Towers Pharmaceuticals public, to safeguard its future, not to mention making fortunes for all the board members? Had he been warned about his health, when he'd paid out a fortune himself to keep Louise Towers assets private and safe for her? The doctors had assured her it wasn't so, that his two heart attacks and subsequent heart rupture had been, to quote Dr. Priestley, "acts of God."

How would she feel when, with a stroke of a pen, the company that bore her name and imprint finally became one hundred percent hers? She could remember every time Benedict had said the words "fifty-fifty." Over the years he'd said them often, beginning the day she'd opened the little shop on East Sixty-second Street.

He'd said them not so long ago, when, following Towers Pharmaceuticals' successful public offering, they'd celebrated her becoming president of the giant oak that Louise Towers had become, with factories institutes, and real estate in twelve different countries, millions of dollars in cash reserves, and more than twenty thousand employees all over the world.

Without thinking, Louise put on the same simple black suit she had worn to the funeral. As she went downstairs, she rehearsed in her mind what she intended to say.

"Mr. Phillips, although my husband told me that Mr. Norris, his most faithful lieutenant, was rewarded with advantageous stock options when Towers Pharmaceuticals went public, I now want to show my own appreciation of his devotion to Towers. I want you to find a way to give Mr. Norris equity in Louise Towers, as a measure of my regard for him and my confidence in the future. I want him to feel that he is part of the family. It is something I know my husband was unable to do because he was bound by constraints put upon him by his father. I want Mr. Norris to know, Mr. Phillips, that you and I are working to overcome those constraints." Whether it was feasible she didn't know, just as she didn't know so many things about the complicated maneuverings of Benedict's business dealings.

The exhaustion of the past few days was catching up with her. As she sat in the drawing room where, not even two weeks before, Banks had arranged such a charming welcome-home family party, Louise found herself dozing. She drank two cups of black coffee, something she usually tried to avoid, because it made her jumpy. She was jumpy enough. Strange that the thought of owning something that had been so much a part of her for so long should make her feel nervous. After all, she wasn't planning any radical changes.

At precisely ten-thirty, when Phillips and Foxwell arrived, she told Banks she would receive them in Benedict's library. It was more appropriate to sit in the place where Benedict had conducted so much business.

She shook their hands and indicated the chairs arranged around a table by the fireplace. They sat down. There was an awkward silence. To fill it, she heard herself say, "I've asked Norris to stand by at the office, to come over when I call him."

Phillips cocked his head curiously to one side. "Norris?" he repeated.

"Yes, I wanted to ask your advice. I know it's premature, but is it possible for me to reward Norris with equity in Louise Towers?" She certainly hadn't meant to mention it so soon, and she'd forgotten her little speech, but something about the lawyer's demeanor unnerved her.

They both looked startled, but she continued, "Although I know Norris was rewarded with advantageous stock options after the public offering of the parent company, I want to show him my own appreciation. I want to propose . . ."

"Mrs. Towers . . ." Phillips's voice was chilling.

"Yes?"

"If I may suggest it, we should discuss anything that does not immediately pertain to the reading of the will at some later date." He was opening a slim briefcase. He took out a letter and handed it to her. "Mr. Towers wanted you to read this before the reading of the will. It is my understanding that in this letter he explains the reasons for his directions regarding the Louise Towers company."

She opened the letter. Benedict's unruly handwriting filled two pages. *My beloved Ludmilla, whom I taught to become the perfect Louise, Louise Towers* . . . The words swam.

"I can't read this now." Her voice was so low, Phillips leaned forward to hear her. He impulsively covered her hand with his bony one. "It would be better if . . . please try."

She straightened up, folding the letter back into its envelope. "I will read it later. If this is an explanation for something concerning the company, I would sooner read it in private." Suddenly angry, she added, "I can't think why any explanation is needed. The company was set up in 1954 as a fifty-fifty arrangement. Over the years my husband assured me . . ."

Phillips coughed, a dry, interrupting sound. "As you know, the assets of Louise Towers were independently valued at one hundred thirty million dollars in 1974. Following certain adjustments and transfers to the pharmaceutical company, Mr. Towers paid the equivalent of one hundred eighteen million dollars to ensure that Louise Towers retained the close held standing enjoyed previously by the parent company."

Get on with it, her mind cried. If Benedict is dealing me a blow from the grave, give it to me now. I may not be able to take it, but let me find out *now!*

The will, a vellum document, was on the table in front of the lawyer. "Read the will, Mr. Phillips," she commanded.

" 'I, Benedict Charles Towers of the City, County, and State of New York, make, publish, and declare this as and to be my Will, and I revoke any and all of my prior wills and codicils.' "

Louise was used to Gregory Phillips's calm, unemotional voice. Again she had to struggle to shake her head clear of terrible fatigue; worse, along with the clouds caused by her sleepless nights now came nausea caused by a premonition as Phillips went through the usual introduction and explanations. " 'The words, "my residuary estate" mean "all the rest, residue, and remainder of my estate and property." As used in this will, the words "my wife" mean Louise Katrina Towers. As used in this will, the words "the foundation" mean the Benedict Towers Foundation. As used in this will, the words "the company" mean Louise Towers Incorporated.

" 'I give all my tangible personal property, excluding my art and sculpture collection to my wife if she survives me. (As already stipulated in foundation documents Anno 1951 and 1970, the art and sculpture collection shall on my death become the property of The Foundation. This in no way should include paintings already given to my wife, ownership of which are clearly documented.) If any blood relation of the Towers family shall request items of tangible personal property from my wife, I direct her to treat such a request fairly and with her usual good judgment.

" 'If my wife survives me: I bequeath her all my real estate and all the property over which I shall at my death have any general or special power of appointment or deposition with the exception of any and all real estate owned or leased by me in the name of the company . . .' "

Phillips paused and, without changing his voice, added, "Mrs. Towers, this is listed in detail for your later perusal." He continued on quickly, " '. . . and with the exception of my residence located at 5006 South Ocean Boulevard, Palm Beach, Florida (the "Tower of Health and Beauty").' " Phillips droned on, " 'I give my wife all of my right, title and interest in and to the house located at 3B East Seventy-third Street, New York, New York; I give my wife the house located at 500 Trellis Canyon, Bel Air, California; I give my wife the ranch property . . .' "

Louise heard a voice cry out, "Stop!" It had come from her, involuntarily. What the lawyers were telling her had begun to sink in.

"Don't read on. I want to know in plain language, not legal jargon, what you both already know. Who is the new owner of the Louise Towers company?"

Phillips and Foxwell exchanged glances, but again it was Phillips who took charge. "Are you sure you won't read the letter I was directed to give you first?" He was trying to be kind, but she didn't want kindness; she wasn't used to it, she told herself bitterly.

"Mr. Phillips, from what you have already read, it appears obvious that my understanding of the arrangement I had with my husband, the arrangement I trusted in all through the years, working to ensure the success of the company I founded and built, is . . ." She couldn't think of the word. Her reason was going. She felt she was going to faint. Phillips anxiously got to his feet. "Mrs. Towers . . ."

She gripped the arms of the chair. "I am perfectly all right. Fatigued, but able to withstand another blow, I think. Tell me—explain to me— what is behind all these 'exceptions' in real estate owned by the company." Out of nowhere a picture came to her mind of England's old Queen Mary, who never slouched, who always sat as if held up by the enormous choker she wore around her neck. Louise lifted her neck. She wasn't going to give anyone the satisfaction of seeing her collapse.

"Mrs. Towers, I really think I should continue reading the will, which is, of course, exceptionally favorable to you, particularly with regard to the percentage of Towers Pharmaceuticals shares. They alone represent almost ten million dollars and . . ."

"Mr. Phillips, must I really ask you again? Don't you understand what I am trying to establish?" Louise brought her face close to his, almost hissing, "The *company*, Mr. Phillips, what is going to happen to the Louise Towers company?"

Phillips sighed and looked at Foxwell, who shook his head in resignation. "Very well."

Elaborately, Phillips pushed the document aside and in simple phrases began to explain how Benedict had left the Louise Towers company. "In trust for Christopher Towers, who will inherit the controlling interest on his thirtieth birthday, provided he meets certain requirements, the main one being a minimum of five years working satisfactorily for the company prior to his thirtieth birthday. The same requirements are also demanded of his sister, Fiona, and cousin Zoe, both of whom can be asked to join the board from twenty-eight onward, depending on the board's assessment of their contribution to the company."

"The board? And who will be on that board when Kick reaches thirty in . . . what is it, twelve, thirteen years' time?"

Phillips looked embarrassed. "Well, that is something for you and Norris to decide. As Christopher is your legally adopted son, Mr. Towers, of course, knew you would always act in his best interests."

Louise stood up so quickly her chair rocked back and hit the wall. She knew she looked wild. She didn't care. She wanted to take the chair and the table and the will and heave them all through the library casement windows. "And what if young Christopher Towers wants to sell the company on his thirtieth birthday? Since it is a close held corporation, has he the right to do that?"

Phillips coughed to clear his throat. "As the controlling shareholder, yes, provided the majority of the board agrees, but Mr. Towers made it clear that he hoped that would not be the board's decision, and he stipulated clearly the company cannot be sold to a competitor, that it must be offered to a member of the family first."

"Does Norris know all this?"

"I'm not sure, Mrs. Towers."

"And the children?"

"No, absolutely not. If you will permit me to continue reading the will, you will learn that Mr. Towers left that to your discretion. As to the question whether Christopher should be told before his twenty-fifth birthday . . ." He picked up the will.

Louise swept her hand toward it as if to knock it out of his hand. "No, no, I don't want to hear any more. I am sure it is in the letter." She began to pace up and down the library, now agonizingly all too wide awake. "What about Charles? Why wasn't he chosen?" She laughed sardonically. "It would have made a good amalgamation, Louise Towers and Natasha Aesthetique!"

Phillips didn't answer.

"Well?" She stood with her hand on her hip, her dark eyes blazing, her black curtain of hair emphasizing the pallor of her face. Neither of the two men had ever seen Louise Towers exhibit such emotion. It left them tongue-tied.

Foxwell stuttered, "You will understand there . . . there was a certain amount of estrangement in the past, and pain on the part of . . . of . . . Mr. Towers. He was adamant that he wanted Mr. Charles Towers to have nothing to do with the Louise Towers company, but a codicil was added, giving Charles an additional bequest of Towers Pharmaceuticals shares. This was arranged while Mr. Towers was . . . just before his return to New York."

"When?"

Phillips turned the many pages of the will. He read out the date. It had been signed while Benedict was still recovering from his first heart attack at Claridge's.

"And"—she stumbled over the word—"Natasha?"

Phillips shook his head. "No, no. There are, of course, a number of bequests to longtime servants and friends of the company, to Mr. Norris, to Audrey Walson . . ."

"Who is she?"

Phillips again turned the pages of the will. " 'An annuity of twenty thousand dollars a year to my good and trusted friend Audrey Walson, compliance officer of the Food and Drug Administration.' "

It was a large annuity. What had the good and trusted Audrey done to deserve it? Louise didn't give it another thought. She had something much more important on her mind, but she felt calm enough to say with a note of finality, "Thank you, gentlemen. I think I must go upstairs and read my late husband's letter before getting a little rest."

As she walked out with them to the front hall, she was once again a robot with Benedict's voice in her head *Don't let them see what you're thinking.* I won't, I won't, she responded silently. Only when I get to my room can I shout out to the world how much I hate you.

Dry-eyed, she lay on the bed reading Benedict's last letter to her. As she'd expected, it never once addressed the truth behind his decision to leave the company to Kick.

> When you read this letter, I will be gone. You will be surrounded, I know, by wise and good friends and colleagues who know they have a duty to look after you and guide you for the rest of your life. But you and I know it's not enough.
>
> Without my support, I can't in good conscience put the whole weight of a major company on your beautiful shoulders. You have never had the financial responsibility of running Louise Towers; that unrelenting burden has quite rightly been in the able hands of Norris, under my direction. Now that you are alone, I cannot put you under extra duress. Instead of working harder, I want you to work less, to learn—as you already have learned so much—more about the world and its treasures, to travel unencumbered by business worries.
>
> Provided you do not entertain the idea of starting another business, you will have enough money to do whatever and go wherever you wish, to enjoy freedom from the demanding responsibilities connected with work.

What did that paragraph mean? Was there yet another shock in the will, another restrictive directive from the grave, giving her financial independence only provided she acted according to Benedict? She couldn't stop shivering as she read on:

> You can do as little or as much as you want for Louise Towers. I want to release you from that role, knowing at the same time I can count on you to guide our children by adoption, my Towers grandchildren by birth, to continue what you started . . .

She didn't leave the room for three days. She told Banks she was not to be disturbed. She could hardly eat, she was so full of hurt, humiliation, and anger. She drank only jasmine tea, cup after cup, which did nothing to soothe her.

She didn't return phone calls. She was not "at home" to any visitors. On the fourth day she skimmed through the long list of people who had been calling: Kick once; Marlene and Norris two or three times every day; Alexandra Sanford and her daughter, Harriet Davidson, every day. Even Alexandra's fifteen-year-old granddaughter Penelope, who was also Louise's goddaughter, had called once, though there was no call from Fiona or from Charles, but—Louise drew in her breath sharply—Natasha's name was on the list. Her sister, Natasha, had called twice.

Louise had no intention of returning her call, but Natasha's name got her out of bed. What irony! Because of her own husband's sudden death, she had not yet told her sister of Pieter's return to life.

On Saturday morning, Banks announced that Norris and his wife were downstairs and were very concerned about her. "Please, Madame, would you be good enough to speak to them on the internal telephone. I cannot reassure them myself, and they say they will not leave until they hear from you personally that you are not ill."

She harbored no grievance against Norris, even though he must have known what Benedict intended to do. "All right, Banks. Put Mr. Norris on." She knew her voice sounded weak, tinny. "Hello, thank you for coming by. I'm trying to be strong . . ."

"Come out to lunch with us, please. Everyone misses you so much."

"I can't, not today. Perhaps Monday."

"Promise?"

"I can't promise."

"I won't take no for an answer." Norris tried to sound stern. "I'll come to collect you on Monday at about noon. We have a lot to talk about, a lot to achieve."

He was right about that, but she repeated, "I can't promise."

As soon as she put the phone down, it rang again. "Madame, your sister, Mrs. Natasha Mahler, called earlier this morning. She requested that I ask you if you would possibly see her this afternoon. I told her it was unlikely, but she insisted."

"I can't see her," Louise said quickly.

"I asked for her telephone number, ma'am, but she said she could not be reached, that she would come by the house at about four-thirty or five o'clock when I could give her an answer."

"I don't think so, Banks."

"Will you accept any calls today, ma'am, from members of your family or close friends?"

"Perhaps, Banks." She felt terribly weary. Ten minutes hadn't passed before Banks called again. "A Mr. Feiner is calling you, Madame, a Mr. Jan Feiner, who says he is a very old friend of yours. He says he knows you will want to speak to him."

She hesitated, then realized how much she wanted to hear Jan's voice. It was like a lifeline thrown into the water.

"Lou ... Louise, oh, Louise, I've been calling every day at your office. I didn't want to call you at home. Louise, I'm so sorry, so sorry. He was a giant ..."

She didn't want to hear any eulogies, least of all from Jan. Surely he'd learned by now how much Benedict had loathed him.

"Jan ..." Could he hear the note of appeal in her voice. "Jan, I'm so happy to hear you, you don't know how happy I am."

"It's wonderful to hear your voice, but you sound so weak. Are you all right? Can we perhaps meet for tea or a drink?"

"Well, not yet, not right now. Perhaps in a little while, when I feel ..." Her voice trailed away. How did she have to feel? Wanted, admired, capable, someone with a future, not just a past.

"Hello, hello, are you there?" On the phone, Jan's Polish accent came through. She liked it; it warmed her to him all the more.

"Yes, I'm here. I'd love to meet you. I promise, soon," she said.

"I want to explain something to you, Louise, something that will shortly be in the papers. I want to tell you in person before you read it, then talk about you, your future ..."

If he was going to tell her he was getting married again, she wished him only the best. She'd made many mistakes, she knew that now, and one of the main ones had been to drop Jan from her life. It was amazing that he still sounded as if he was her friend.

"May I call you next week?"

"Of course you may."

When she put the phone down, she wished she'd agreed to see him over the weekend. Suddenly the room was too quiet, too empty, too devoid of life with Benedict. Benedict was right. After a lifetime of following his commands, she didn't know how to think for herself. She filled her bath with a new lily-of-the-valley-based Louise Towers bath product in an unusual gelike formula, and lay in it for a long, long time. She must have fallen asleep, because she woke up with her teeth chattering from the cold. By the time four o'clock came, she had changed her mind a dozen times about receiving Natasha.

She had also changed her mind several times about what to wear, but at least now she was out of her robe for the first time in days, dressed in a somber gray and black checked dress, her hair, which was in need of a haircut, tied back with a black velvet ribbon.

Would Natasha think she'd aged? And how would Natasha look? Although she'd seen her on television a few times, she hadn't seen her in person since the terrible night in the Park Avenue apartment, when she'd thrown a bottle of perfume at her, a bottle so appropriately named Revelation.

Now, in her own powerless situation, thinking about Natasha living with Charles and running her own business with him made her feel suicidal. Aesthetique is small, nothing in comparison to Louise Towers, she told herself, but it's theirs, to do with as they like.

She had decided she couldn't face the meeting when Banks rang to say Natasha had arrived. Instead of saying "I can't see her," she put the phone down without answering. She paced up and down. *See her*, said Benedict's voice.

Natasha was taller than she remembered, taller and much, much more stylish in a well-cut dark blue pinstriped suit with a soft matching cashmere stole draped around her shoulders. As Louise put her hand out, Natasha tried to embrace her. Louise drew back, unsure of how she felt, old emotions jostling new ones.

Natasha was carrying a bunch of orchids; it was a Czech custom to bring flowers to a house of mourning, as it was to bring them to a house of rejoicing. Was today to be both? Louise led the way to the library. "Tea?" she offered.

"Yes, please."

There was silence. Louise was a master of silence without feeling embarrassed, but then they both started to speak at once. Louise stopped, and Natasha continued. "I've wanted to see you so often, so much. It is a terrible thing that has happened between us. It is surely my fault. Will you forgive me?"

Louise gulped. For the first time since Benedict's death, she felt the onset of tears. They must not appear, must not. "I forgive you," she said with difficulty.

"Oh, Ludm—Louise, I know how you are suffering. You remember how I suffered, too." Natasha began speaking fast in Czech. "We, Charles and I, we want to return to the family, to be close to you, as the sister I am, as the brother Charles wants to be."

Louise wanted to drown her words, lose the meaning, the old emotions of anger and jealousy pushing through. She didn't want Charles as a brother, not now or ever, and if that meant she must lose her sister, it had to be.

She tried to control herself. Banks's arrival with the tea on a large silver tray helped. "I'll look after it, Banks," she said, and busied herself. "Lemon? Milk? Do try a piece of Mrs. Poole's chocolate cake . . ."

Natasha began again with her soulful condolences. Louise tried to stop her, but she was unstoppable. "Louise, perhaps we can work together again one day. We want to make up for all our years apart. This is the first time I am in your magnificent house. You do not know our apartment . . ."

Our apartment . . . we . . . us . . . Shut up, she wanted to scream, shut up. Why did it have to be you with Charles, and not me?

Natasha leaned forward in a confiding way. "Louise, you must spend time with us. You are the first person to know that . . . that I have applied for petition to obtain legal status as widow. It is likely"—her voice was proud—"is likely I can have a child." She corrected herself. "Am with child."

Louise's expression showed her horror. Natasha misunderstood it. "Don't worry, Louise, the doctor tell me I am very fit. I can still have a child." Her voice became mournful for a moment. "I never hear from Kristina or Mama. No news. I write, but they never answer me. No news. Do you hear from them?"

Louise clenched her hands; they were trembling uncontrollably. "Yes," she said coldly. "I have news. I received news the day Benedict died," she lied. "Natasha, I have to tell you, your petition is useless. You are not a widow. Pieter is alive. He was terribly wounded in Brno; he lost his memory; he is disabled, but alive and living back in Prague with Mama and Kristina."

Natasha sat looking at her in shocked disbelief, the color draining from her face. "Alive? Pieter? But are you sure?"

"Yes, I am sure. At the office is a letter for you from him. I have also received a letter. I have not yet read it myself. I was on my way to the office to read it. Benedict . . ." She stopped. For a second she'd almost thought of him as still alive. "Benedict told me it was a bitter letter, attacking me for leading you astray, influencing you with the good life into abandoning them all. Both letters arrived opened—I imagine by the government. I am told that in your letter Pieter holds out more hope for your eventual salvation when you are reunited. I am sorry not to have sent it to you, but you can understand why. I will see it is delivered to you today."

Natasha stood up, tears running down her cheeks. Slowly she said,

"Nothing has changed, has it, Louise? You are happy that Pieter is alive. I can see that what I thought before was true then and is true today." She looked anguished. "What is the truth, Louise? Explain it to me for once and ever. You are in love with Charles, is that it? But he is not in love with you. Can't you accept that? He loves me as a woman, you as sister."

Before, there had been screams, a bottle thrown, an ugly, terrifying scene. Now there was only the ticking of the library clock.

When Louise spoke, she felt removed, detached, although she knew she hated the young woman in front of her.

"Natasha, you have obviously learned nothing.. If you are determined to have this illegitimate child, perhaps you should take some time off and try to learn to grow up before the baby is born. From what I have been told about the letters from Pieter, he is determined to join you one day. Perhaps you should consider finding a hiding place now." She paused and added sarcastically, "Because it seems unlikely you would consider leaving the world of capitalism to rejoin your husband and daughter in Czechoslovakia."

Natasha carefully put her cup down. "I feel sorry for you, Louise," she said quietly. "It is you who have much to learn. I am very happy with Charles. We will have to deal with this new situation as best as we can. I don't know yet how, but"—she wrapped her stole high around her throat before turning to leave—"I will never hide away as you say, baby or no baby. I was going to give you what I thought might be good news for you to hear. Now I am not so sure any good news for Charles and me would be good news for you. I will tell you, all the same. We have just finalized plans for a very big company to invest in our company. It will be in the papers next week. A giant as big as Towers in Europe will support us in our expansion plans. It is called Averbach in Europe, K. Avery here in the U.S.A."

Jan

Los Angeles, 1982

FROM THE WINGS of the stage of the Hilton Hotel ballroom, Natasha surveyed the packed floor, filled to capacity with the people she called "our troops."

In a few minutes she would be addressing them at the company's largest ever sales meeting. She would be congratulating and handing out engraved watches to those she'd named "our heroes" in the company's new in-house newspaper. These were the salesmen and saleswomen of the year, who with grit, guile, and tenacity had "sold in" the Natasha products (they'd dropped the clumsy "Aesthetique" from the company's name) to the chain and drugstore buyers across the country—more often than not tight-fisted, self-important people who ruled their cosmetics counters like pompous potentates.

She nervously ticked off on her fingers the other groups she had to salute for their winning performances. Although after a heated discussion with Charles it had been decided that the salesmen had to come first, as far as she was concerned the success of the business really began and ended with the cosmetics counter girls (whom she insisted be called "Natasha cosmeticians"). Then there were the training directors and regional managers who had to inspire the salesmen to keep up the pressure and persuade the store buyers to use their wonderful displays to help "sell through" to the customers. As she had learned in her early Louise Towers days, the toughest part of the cosmetics business was that, in common with the book business, it wasn't enough to "sell in." If the products didn't "sell through," they were returned.

In the three years since K. Avery had started to pump in money for advertising, promotions, and extra sales and training staff, Natasha products were beginning to "sell through" in great numbers. It was the reason the big boss, Jan Feiner, had agreed to fund not only this fancy sales meeting in the first quarter, but the hugely expensive—and revolutionary—1982 TV and print ad campaign they were about to unveil. It was a campaign Natasha was sure would trigger a change in public perception of inexpensive drugstore skin care.

Below the microphone, center stage, was the main table, where Natasha could see Charles sitting, talking animatedly, at his happiest, surrounded by the cream of the crop of their female employees and chain drugstore cosmeticians.

Every one of them had doubled and in some cases tripled their Natasha sales in the last year. On Charles's right, Natasha could see the girl from Washington, D.C.'s People's drugstore, looking very pleased with herself. She had reason to be pleased. She'd sold through almost five thousand dollars worth of Natasha products in one month alone. Easy to do with Louise Towers's department store prices, not so easy with the money-saving prices of Natasha. "Money saving"—it would not be too long before that message was heard loud and clear, everywhere in the country. She couldn't wait to know Louise's reaction.

The lights were being lowered, and the orchestra struck a majestic chord. It was time for her to move into the spotlight. Once Natasha had been nervous about public speaking, especially about her accent and her English mistakes. Now she moved confidently to center stage, knowing her midnight blue velvet dress emphasized her small waist and showed off her flawless white skin, her glowing chestnut hair.

She concentrated, in the opening minutes, on projecting herself to the back of the room, now in darkness. Her troops were there too, perhaps unhappy they weren't up front, in the only reserved seating in the ballroom. "Talk first to them to include them, to make them happy, too," she'd been taught by one of New York's leading speech therapists, who had swiftly gauged her personality and knew it took her mind off herself to think of those struggling in the ranks, as she had once struggled. It always worked.

The applause was so deafening and sustained, she had to hold up her arms beseechingly again and again before she could speak. Charles marveled, as he always did, at how stunning Natasha looked with a professional makeup. In many ways he wished she was professionally made up more often, but it wasn't her style. After the miscarriage, when she'd finally acknowledged that she looked washed out, and not a good advertisement for a business about to have a new Swiss godfather with very deep pockets, ready to send them into the top cosmetics echelon, she'd started to wear blusher and more eye makeup. Today she literally radiated as she had in the old Project-TV days, wearing false lashes, smoky kohl around her eyes, and a vivid peony pink lipstick, while a contour stick emphasized her cleavage as well as her cheekbones.

"From coast to coast, belief in our Natasha products is growing, thanks to every one of *you* . . ." She paused after emphasizing *you*, as she had been taught to do by the speech therapist. ". . . in this room. Our customers are overjoyed to find they can buy reliable, effective skin care at such amazingly low prices, and because of *you*"—another pause—"customers are thirsting for the knowledge that *you*"—pause—"bring to them."

Charles nodded proudly as he heard her pronounce the word *thirsting* perfectly; she'd had great difficulty with the word, but typically had refused to ask public relations to think of another one, saying, "It's perfect." She'd even woken up practicing it. Now she was in her element, off and running. "The beauty-full, public-spirited idea we pioneered with local banks in the Southeast, making it possible for any depositor opening or adding to an account with fifty dollars or more, to receive a special package of Natasha Skincare Assets free at certain designated chains, has been such an overwhelming success that it will now be repeated in Florida and on the West Coast . . ."

He knew the presentation by heart. He started to daydream as Natasha began reading out the names of those receiving awards, asking them to come up on stage. Following this ceremony, the big screen would come down and he would join her on stage to show the troops their knock-'em-dead new TV ad campaign. How the Louise Towers people would fume when it began to roll out. Too bad. All's fair in love and war. Louise had certainly exhibited how she felt about that. Thinking about her still made him burn with rage.

If it hadn't been for Louise, they would be married by now. If Louise hadn't continued her own search, perhaps Pieter would never have been found, who knew? Lasker, the young man at the State Department had told both of them that they owed Pieter's reappearance in Prague entirely to Louise's persistence and covert placing of money in the right hands. Lasker had thought they'd be overcome with gratitude. Well, they hadn't been, although they hadn't shown how they really felt.

If it hadn't been for Louise, Charles was sure Natasha would not have miscarried, although Natasha refused to blame her sister. It had been her decision not to follow the lawyer's advice and seek a divorce from Pieter.

"Not now, I can't," she'd said after days of anguish. "My family thinks I abandoned them; that's why they don't answer my letters. If I divorce Pieter now, the moment I've learned he is still alive, they will never believe me; there will never be a chance of reconciling." For one startling moment she'd looked so fierce she'd reminded him of Louise. It was the only time he could remember that happening. "I want my daughter back, Charlie. I haven't given up hope. I'll never stop writing, trying. It has to happen one day."

He'd had to accept it. He didn't like it, but he accepted it. They had two separate apartments, although everyone close to them knew they lived together. Because of their association with K. Avery, they had both been too busy to sit down and really discuss a divorce again, as he felt they should after the initial shock of learning Pieter was still alive. Every so often he promised himself he'd bring the subject up, but he never did.

Debby Smithie, the feisty, five-foot-nothing young girl from People's Drug, was getting up now to receive the Cosmetician of the Year Award. What a wonderful day for the poor kid, Charles thought, noticing the scuffed heels of what were probably her best shoes, a piece of cotton hanging down from her badly cut, shiny velvet skirt. She'd sold a phenomenal amount of products—he was told it was a record for People's—but without the commission money, if Ms. Smithie earned more than a hundred dollars a week he'd be surprised. He wrote a note to remind himself to go and watch her in action behind the counter. If she was consistently as good as the figures indicated, there might be a spot in the company for her.

Natasha was bending down to embrace the girl. Natasha was so tall and Debby so short that the audience broke up in laughter, escalating into screams and cheers when Natasha lifted the girl up in her arms like some super Amazon.

Charles frowned. Natasha still liked to play the fool. It was a mistake. One of the reasons Louise had built such a huge empire was her aura of mystery, which attracted people to her—like a Medusa, he thought grimly.

Feiner's crazy chemist brother, Victor, had told him once that Jan Feiner had taught Louise everything she knew about skin care, that many of her early formulas she'd stolen from him, when they'd worked together at Rubinstein. He'd tried to bring it up with Jan, but he'd made it clear it was a subject he did not discuss. However, Charles knew that Helena Rubinstein, too, had used mystery, ruling her empire as an empress, not just as an employer. Louise must have learned from her how useful mystery was in the cosmetics business. Rubinstein would never have picked a salesgirl up in her arms to play the clown before her employees, and neither would Louise. Natasha had to learn some mystery of her own one day.

The giant screen was slowly descending behind Natasha. It was his cue. Charles bounded onto the stage to shake the hands of the award winners as they began to file back into the audience. Again the applause rang out. He grinned boyishly and put his hands over his ears.

Behind him, he knew, the lipstick-red handwritten Natasha logo would be appearing, followed by a picture of one of the best-known models in America, Lyric Masters. A respectful, anticipatory hush fell. "Friends, colleagues, troops, I don't need to tell you the name of the beautiful young woman behind me, the most famous face in America . . ." There were whistles, catcalls, and shouts of "Lyric! Lyric! Lyric!"

"If you're all very good, you will soon meet Lyric in person." As the whistles started again, Charles put up a commanding hand. "Natasha and I are proud to tell you that Lyric Masters has signed a contract to appear exclusively in our ads, and will be a spokesperson for Natasha Skincare, a first in the history of mass-market skin care." As the noise level began to grow, again he put up a silencing hand. "Pay attention to why this beautiful young woman has chosen Natasha products for her skin-care and beauty-care needs," he said sternly.

K. Avery had financed an extensive study to see if and by how much the use of a famous face was still helping to sell beauty products, but especially skin care. The study had proved it was certainly helping Estée Lauder and Revlon, and recently Lancôme had signed Ingrid Bergman's daughter, Isabella Rossellini, as its "face." But they were all department store lines, and as the study had pointed out, Louise Towers was in the top three without a "signature face," except occasionally her own.

The country's largest-selling cosmetics company, Cover Girl, in the same mass area of distribution as themselves, had started the whole idea of the famous face legally and exclusively bound with a product about twenty years ago when commercial television was in its infancy, but that was for *makeup*. Would it work for mass skin care, a much more difficult pitch because of the trust that had to be involved?

Natasha thought so, and Feiner had finally been sold on it because of the unique message the commercial also carried.

The screen came to life, showing Lyric walking down a leafy, sunlit lane, stopping to pick and smell a hedgerow flower. "I'm a natural girl," the voice-over said, light, lilting, "and I love natural beauty . . ." The camera started to rise to show for a few seconds the countryside surrounding her, before descending to show the same country scene from a window, a bathroom window. "When I'm indoors," the voice continued, "I like to bring that country-fresh feeling to my skin, too. I don't want heavy chemicals in my products, the kind you buy in fancy department stores, chemicals that push the prices up. I want the best, fresh skin-care ingredients from experts who know and care about giving the best value for money, the experts at Natasha Skincare."

A closeup of Lyric's apparently unmade-up face filled the screen. She looked incredibly beautiful, bewitching, but above all country-fresh. The camera went back to the country scene sparkling outside the window, before returning to her face as the commercial ended with the words spoken in another voice. "At Natasha we don't want you to pay more than you have to for your skin care. Why pay fifty-five dollars for this cream . . ." An elegant, pale hand produced a jar with its name just hidden, but a jar that any skin-care aficionado would recognize as Louise Towers's Wrinkle Fighter. ". . . when you can get Natasha's new age-fighting cream . . ." The same hand in close-up produced a pristine white jar with the name Preventage in bright emerald green letters on the label. ". . . Preventage, a remarkable skin treatment, for only nine-ninety-five. Why pay more? The best Natasha skin care is available at your local drugstore, at prices everyone can afford."

This time Charles let the applause, the foot-stamping, the cheers go on unrestrained for several minutes before approaching the microphone. "It gives Natasha and me great pride to introduce you to the perfect Natasha woman, Lyric Masters!"

Louise missed the first showings of the much-discussed, controversial Natasha commercial because she was on a cruise in the South Pacific with her old friend Alexandra Sanford and Alexandra's daughter, Harriet Davidson, son-in-law Henry Davidson, and the Davidsons' teenage daughter Penelope, named after Harriet's twin sister. She hadn't wanted to go, but Paunch, Alexandra's husband, had died the year before and both twins had pleaded with her "to help cheer up poor Mama."

It had probably been a plot, because as she'd soon found out Alexandra didn't need cheering up at all. Far from it. From Bora-Bora to Tahiti, Alexandra had flirted outrageously with the ship's officers and stayed up later than all of them. Louise had often thought that Alexandra and Paunch led separate lives, and the cruise to "help Mama recover" had confirmed it. Of course, she was so different from Alexandra anyway.

While Benedict was alive, Louise had sometimes longed to be alone, but it wasn't as she'd imagined it. It wasn't an oasis to retreat to; it was a prison, solitary confinement of the mind and spirit, whether one was surrounded by people on a cruise or not.

One day she'd woken up and found the world totally occupied by couples, everywhere she looked, in restaurants, at the theater, not to mention at the endless stream of benefit balls and dinners she was expected to attend as president of Louise Towers.

It was only in the lab that she came alive. She was spending too much time there, she knew that. However innovative and brilliant the end results of her labors were, her best contribution to the company came from her public appearances; she knew that, too, but she hadn't the energy or the interest to appear publicly for Louise Towers anymore, despite the increasing competition.

She was very much missed; Norris told her so, over and over again. The terrible thing was, she didn't care about that either. Why should she care, she asked herself. Although most of the world didn't know it, she was, after all, merely a caretaker for Kick. So it was, of course, she who needed the cheering up.

There was still something robotlike about what she said or did. On the cruise, Alexandra told her so, trying to break through to find out what was really troubling her. As Alexandra repeatedly told Harriet, "It isn't only the shock of her husband's death. There's something else, I know it."

Even though Louise usually cut her short, throughout the month afloat Alexandra had kept after her like a drill. "Don't you believe there aren't any men out there. Even at my ancient age, I'm not lacking, my dear. The important thing is to keep busy, to travel, not to look as if you're looking, and then real men pop out of the woodwork when you least expect them. When we get back, it's time I found you a walker or two."

"Walker?"

"Yes, a walker, my dear Louise." Alexandra had sounded as if she were humoring a dull child. "One of those perfectly harmless, amusing men who can squire you around ... like playing tennis with a pro. *Women's Wear* described them perfectly as 'asexual social gadflies,' but it's better than going out alone."

Then she'd hit a nerve. "Why don't you sell the company?" she'd asked. "You're still young—what are you, fifty, fifty-two? No wonder everyone loves your creams; you don't look a day over thirty-five ..."

It was because she knew now that Benedict hadn't wanted her to continue to work for Louise Towers, that she forced herself to keep involved, and to go to the lab every day while she was in New York. He hadn't wanted the company to be sold, either. He'd thought only of Kick and Fiona continuing to keep the Towers family name and fame alive.

One conversation had helped during the cheer-up cruise, with Henry

Davidson, Alexandra's outwardly languid but apparently razor-sharp lawyer son-in-law, who flew out to Papeete to join the cruise halfway through. Louise hardly knew him, but there was something about his cool, relaxed demeanor that made her feel she could trust him.

"Benedict's will . . . regarding my company . . . it was not what I expected." He'd come across her, leaning on the rail, staring bleakly at the receding waves just before dinner. He hadn't said a word, yet for some reason she'd begun to talk. She hadn't told him much, just enough to let him know that she was suffering, that there were unjust restrictions, that she had not, in fact, inherited the company she had devoted her life to, although everyone assumed she had, that it was locked up in trusts for Benedict's grandchildren, Kick and Fiona, who, when their parents were killed, she and Benedict had legally adopted.

"Please don't say anything, not even to Harriet. I don't know why I told you, but . . ." His stern look of reproof had shut her up.

"If you ever want to tell me more, call me. Perhaps there's something you can still do." Later, Henry Davidson had given her his direct line at the office.

The Natasha commercial first aired in February, but Louise didn't see it until March on her return. Norris had told her what to expect, and she'd read the clippings: "Natasha goes in punching . . . tries the comparison-shopping technique in impressive new TV campaign," John Ledes' highly influential Cosmetics World trumpeted.

"It doesn't take a genius to realize it's Louise Towers's Wrinkle Fighter that Natasha Skincare is taking on in brutal, thirty-second price-comparison TV spots . . ." the advertising column of *The New York Times* reported.

K. AVERY HELPS REAR ADOPTED BABY NATASHA WITH MULTIMILLION-DOLLAR AD CAMPAIGN, was the headline in *Advertising Age*.

While Marlene and the Louise Towers marketing and advertising staff watched her, Louise watched both the long and short versions of the Natasha Skincare TV ads over and over again in the company's screening room on the fortieth floor of the Towers Building.

She was as impassive as ever, although not missing a thing, Dougy Faseff, now a VP of creative marketing for the domestic division, thought he saw her tap her foot once or twice.

When Louise stood up, the lights in the screening room immediately went on. To everyone's surprise she was smiling. It wasn't, however, a pleasant smile.

"Well, what do you think, Lou . . . Louise?" Dee Possant, who everyone in marketing had once thought would defect to Natasha's camp, still sounded nervous whenever she used Louise's first name, although as a senior executive she'd long ago been told to do so.

Louise looked around the room. A few uncomfortable seconds passed before she spoke. Then, dramatically, she slowly unpeeled the pale gray doeskin gloves she was wearing. "I think it's time we took our gloves off, don't you? Time to go to work!" Her eyes rested on Dougy, but she was really speaking to herself.

As she'd looked at each frame of the cunningly clever commercial, so clearly disparaging of their company in particular, but of all expensive department-store skin-care brands in general, she'd felt a rush of fresh adrenaline through her body; she'd felt her frozen brain thawing; her feeling of not being needed or wanted vanishing; her misery at Benedict's dismissal from the grave receding; above all, her disdain and hate for Charles increasing. That a born member of the mighty Towers family should stoop to this!

"Where's Norris?"

"In Canada," someone volunteered.

"Socializing with Eatons," Dee added. "We've had some trouble with out-of-stock products . . . oh, nothing important." She let the sentence trail away.

Louise fixed her with an icy stare. "Everything's important, and don't let anyone forget it!" Her tone softened. "I know I haven't been much help to you these last couple of difficult years, but that's all going to change. It's a funny thing, but the trash I've just been watching was obviously the tonic the doctors have been telling me I needed. I have to tell you, I suddenly feel like a new woman."

Everyone came rushing around her. "Oh, Louise, that's wonderful," Marlene squeaked.

"When do we start our attack?" Dougy asked with relish.

"Right now, this goddamned second." Louise couldn't believe she'd actually said "goddamn," but to her relief the room rang with cheers.

"I'll go call Norris," Dee said excitedly.

"No, I'll call him." Louise rushed out of the room, excited, pink-cheeked. It was true. She did feel like a new woman. To the Henry Higgins tune from *My Fair Lady* she sang under her breath, "Just you wait, Charlie Towers, just you wait."

From then on, Louise dove back into the business, giving it her full attention, scheduling meetings with different department heads every day, crisscrossing the country as she hadn't done in years, visiting Louise Towers Institutes, giving pep talks to the Louise Towers beauty consultants, to Marlene's training sessions, studying international reports, often working until the early hours of the morning. She also made a few carefully orchestrated public appearances, at which she was relieved to discover that she hadn't lost her touch, that women still hung on every syllable and acted on every piece of product advice she gave, "buying up a storm," as even the august *Wall Street Journal* reported after running a short update on the company following her appearance at Saks.

The only thing she adamantly refused to do was be interviewed by the press. "I'm not ready, but when our salvos start hurting them . . ." She didn't need to explain to Norris that she was not talking about Lauder, Lancôme, or Revlon. ". . . then I'll have something to say, all right. When Kick leaves college next year and comes into the company, we'll have a press conference, but not now. I don't need it; the company doesn't need it." Norris had never been prouder of her. Here was the beautiful, fascinating woman with whom Benedict Towers had fallen in love.

One evening as Louise left the office late, at about ten-thirty, followed by her secretary carrying two bulging briefcases, a paparazzi photographer was waiting outside. The photograph appeared later that week in the city's newspapers. One caption read, "Louise Towers Back in the Saddle"; another read, "No More Time Off for the Working Millionairess."

"Mr. Jan Feiner, the president of K. Avery, is calling." A tiring but satisfying advertising budget meeting had just broken up the next day, and Louise was sipping her usual end-of-day jasmine tea.

"I am in a meeting. I will call him back."

And indeed she would enjoy calling him back, to tell him exactly what she thought of him. But what audacity the man had! As she sipped and rested before her next meeting, Louise realized she hadn't felt so well in years.

Her secretary knocked on the door and put her head in. "Mr. Feiner would very much like to meet with you. He is at your disposal."

Louise shook her head in wonderment. "He will have a long wait."

Feiner's office called every day for the next week. He could have gone on calling forever, as far as Louise was concerned, but Norris thought she ought to find out what he had on his mind. "He's a major player, and his investment in Natasha is paying off, whether we want to admit it or not. I mean, in terms of the Natasha business growing. Since you took your gloves off"—he looked at her with undisguised admiration—"Louise Towers is growing again, too. All the same, I'd like to know what he wants."

In fact, so did she. Where should they meet? Someplace where he would be at the greatest disadvantage, which was probably her own office. Yet she hated the idea that the man she'd once considered her friend, the man who was funding her sister's missiles against her, should invade the place where she now found the most happiness, where the top-level meetings were held, the "war room," as many of the Louise Towers executives were calling it.

In the end she decided that the more public the meeting place, the better. Let the papers have a heyday; let their imaginations run away and presume and predict that all kinds of negotiations were going on. Above all, she hoped it would make Charles and Natasha feel uneasy, whether they knew what the meeting was about or not.

She agreed to meet Jay Feiner for lunch in the grill room of The Four Seasons, which had begun to be known as the power place for lunch. As the car approached East Fifty-second Street, she didn't know how she felt. She should hate Jan as much as she now felt she hated Charles and certainly Natasha, but for some reason she knew she didn't hate him.

After all, she had turned Jan down in Paris, and following Benedict's death, she had refused to see him or speak with him when Natasha had told her the news he had obviously wanted to give her first. She had cold-shouldered him whenever she'd run into him at industry functions. Why was she seeing him now? Well, she would soon find out.

She was exactly on time, but, as she'd expected, he was waiting for her in the left-hand corner banquette, the one the restaurant reserved for the most important guests. She knew heads were turning as she approached. She was glad she was wearing a body-hugging, brilliant red suit from the hot new designer Azzedine Alaia. She knew she looked terrific; she felt even more terrific when she noted with one glance that Jan was nervous.

"You look simply sensational."

No thanks to you, she thought. She nodded with a slight smile.

"You don't know how happy I've been since you agreed to meet me."

She looked at him directly, noticing the slightest touch of gray at his hairline, more wrinkles, but glasses with a heavier frame, which gave him a more statesmanlike air.

"I don't think we should spend much time on niceties, Jan. I came because of your persistence and because we want to know what's on your mind." Her voice was cool, firm, but her dark eyes blazed.

Paul Kovi, one of the restaurant's two owners, came over to welcome Louise. She realized from the jovial exchange between Jan and Kovi that Jan must be a regular customer.

They ordered Perriers; Louise perused the menu while Jan talked.

"If only you'd let me see you after your husband died; if only you'd given me a chance to outline what I then had in mind . . ."

"My sister got there first," she said dryly.

"No, you're wrong. That was only a small part of the plan." He suddenly covered her glove-clad hand with his. She tried to move it. He wouldn't let her. "You know how I've always felt about you, Louise. Your husband knew. That's why I don't think I was ever really embittered, despite all he tried to do against me; it's why in all these years I never allowed myself to listen to Victor, to turn against you." He half laughed. "He did his best—you know Victor—but, well, it was impossible for me to think badly of you."

Again she tried to remove her hand, without success. "I would say you are certainly getting your revenge now. That should please your brother very much."

Jan didn't seem perturbed. "Revenge? What nonsense. I'm a businessman, Louise, just as you are a businesswoman. I have always wanted to work with you again, you know that. What I said in Paris is still true today, but after I heard from Towers's big guns"—he wrinkled his nose in a boyish way, again half laughing—"I'd had enough. I knew there was no point, so I switched my attention to another market, where there was the next best thing, your sister."

Rage gave her strength. She wrested her hand away. "I didn't come here to talk about Natasha and the conspiracy against my company."

"What conspiracy?"

"Please, Jan, spare me the innocent-bystander, nothing-to-do-with-me technique. You're acting like the owner of one of the trash papers, who says he has nothing to do with its contents. Why did the commercial use Wrinkle Fighter as an example of overcharging? Why not a Chanel or Lauder anti-aging product, both of which cost more than Wrinkle Fighter?"

"Good business," he said firmly. "Great publicity, although, as you very well know, the name has never been shown and Natasha has never admitted it is a Louise Towers product."

He stopped talking and looked at her with wonder. God, he would give anything to make love to her, to see her naked, to make her throb under his touch, to make her ache for him as, to his amazement, he found he was aching for her now. For a crazy couple of moments he fantasized about taking her to his new and spectacular apartment with the sweeping view of the river, to lay her down on the enormous rococo daybed by the window, and take her in the full light of day. Was it a futile dream? Could it ever happen?

"I can't believe how beautiful you are, Louise. Every man was looking at you as you came in; you have the figure of a girl of fifteen." He corrected himself, looking at the full curve of her breasts. "Eighteen."

Their food arrived, but neither of them ate very much. "Louise, here is an offical statement. Averbach wants to buy Louise Towers. They are willing to commit to a five-year program of major investment at every level, to build new plants in new markets, and, of course, we want you as president for as long as you want to be."

Hot tears came to her eyes. She blinked them back. She had suspected this was what it was all about, had both hoped for and dreaded hearing it. Jan saw the tears, but said nothing. "We want to build a tiered cosmetics business, with Natasha and other acquisitions in the growing mass marketplace, and Louise Towers as the main jewel in our crown of prestige brands." His voice softened. "It would be foolish to say it would be like old times. It will be new times, you and me together. I can't think of a more unbeatable team."

I want you to work less, learn more about the world's treasures . . . Unbidden, the words in Benedict's last letter to her came into her mind. Benedict hadn't even wanted her to remain at Louise Towers, and he had done everything in his power to prevent it, assuming that she would be too humiliated to continue, and at first he'd been right. But here was a man who had no jealousy, who had admired her and her work for years, yet she was powerless to take advantage of the great opportunity he was offering both her and the company.

He had mistaken her tears. "If you're wondering how everyone can work together, I assure you it can be worked out. Whatever your differences with your sister—and I know nothing about them whatsoever—Averbach believes in decentralization, except for financial controls. Natasha Skincare operates independently with its own senior management group, with an Avery budget review twice a year, and so do all our acquisitions. It would be the same with Louise Towers, and of course, in your case . . ."

"I can't do it, Jan." She had always been pale, but now she was paler.

"Why not, Louise? It's the perfect marriage," he pleaded. "Everything I told you in Paris is even more true today, now that Benedict is gone and Towers Pharmaceuticals is disinterested in the cosmetic business. Louise Towers is going to be in trouble with all the competition out there. Now is the time for us to scale the heights together with a solid program of investment."

Again she said, this time with the sadness audible in her voice, "I can't. It's not possible."

"What do you mean? Can we sit down with Norris, with the Louise Towers legal team, so I can explain more?"

"No," she said sharply. The shame of his ever learning what Benedict had done was sweeping over her. She had to get out of there before she broke down. She started to get up, but Jan pulled her fiercely down in the seat.

"Don't let the world see how much you hate me. At least have the decency not to humiliate me like that."

"Oh, Jan, I don't hate you. Far from it, despite Natasha . . . despite . . ."

"Despite what? Again and again I've shown you how I feel. What am I to think except that you don't care anything for me, never have and never will?" He swallowed down the remainder of his Perrier and then his coffee. She remained silent, knowing that if she attempted to speak she would sob.

"So that's the answer, is it? No interest? A declaration of war?" He tried to sound lighthearted, without success.

"Jan . . ." her voice broke. If he only knew, but she could never tell him the truth, it was too belittling. "Jan," she said again, "I wish we could be friends. I admire and like you more than I can say, but"—Again she had difficulty getting the words out—"circumstances are against us. I wish you only good things always."

He stood up and gave her a mocking little bow. "How gracious. I echo your sentiments, Mrs. Towers. I wish you only good things also."

Louise called Henry Davidson that afternoon, and met with him later in the week with a copy of the will. "I can't promise anything, but if there are any loopholes I will find them," he promised. She didn't pin her hopes on it. Over the years she had seen the thoroughness with which Benedict conducted his affairs. *Always look for the loopholes.* She'd heard him say it dozens of times as he'd tightened the screws to ensure that no loopholes existed.

She was so busy, so intent on putting Louise Towers far out in front, that she didn't spend a minute fretting. Marketing was urging her to counter the impact of Lyric Masters acting as a spokesperson for Natasha with a famous face of their own, but Louise didn't agree. "People copy us; we don't copy anyone," she said fiercely, dismissing a wall display of model candidates.

Instead she held a well-publicized search to find a new advertising campaign. Doyle, Dane & Bernbach won the contract with a big, bold-copy approach that stressed the number of breakthroughs the company had achieved, the number of skin doctors working with Louise Towers to help every one of their customers achieve smooth, glowing, ageless skin.

It seemed to work, as did the mini skin clinics Louise set up as special promotions in major stores across the country, which, backed by a massive public relations campaign led to coverage and interviews by local papers and TV stations, where Louise Towers's Personnel emphasized that hands-on, expert skin care was only available in department stores. "Drugstores are for drugs and toothpaste," was one line the Louise Towers training directors were told to get across to the beauty consultants, who would then pass *that* message on to their customers.

She was still searching for the big idea to deal a swift uppercut to Charles and Natasha. It wasn't because Natasha products threatened Louise Towers's sales.

As *Business Week* pointed out, despite the negative advertising approach Natasha Skincare had adopted, there was no real competition between the two companies because their customers, for the time being, were so different. In the long term, if there was a recession, the price differences could attract customers away from Louise Towers, exclusively in department stores, but right now, in the booming eighties, it wasn't happening. *Business Week* had no way of knowing that although Louise Towers's sales were increasing, Louise Towers herself had more personal reasons for her obsession with finding something to overshadow Natasha.

Out of the blue the following year she found it, while flying back from Paris on the Concorde after a lightning trip to the European institutes. As she moved the pages of the *Herald Tribune*, somehow she knocked over her neighbor's glass of wine.

"*Merde!*"

Louise turned to offer a cool apology, already irritated that, contrary to her office's instructions, in an overbooked plane someone had been seated beside her, though they had purchased two seats to prevent this. It was beneath her to make a scene, and now this!

Red wine dripped down onto an expensive-looking alpaca suit sleeve. She met two eyes as dark and as unfathomable as her own. She saw a vaguely familiar face, a face as disquieting, she told herself, as that of a young Marquis de Sade. "I do apologize."

"You shouldn't read such a bloody big paper on such a small plane, Mrs. Towers." The voice was almost too English, too perfect. There was also no mistaking the gently mocking note. Did she know him? Probably not. Her dark glasses didn't conceal her fame. On occasions like this, she missed Towers Pharmaceuticals' fleet of planes. She could use one occasionally and, because it was a public company, pay for the privilege, but she could no longer take it for granted.

As the stewardess came with soda water, "Another suit ruined," the young man said in a matter-of-fact voice.

"If you will give me your name and address, I will see that you are compensated." Louise took out a gold pencil.

"How typically thoughtful, Mrs. Towers. But I would rather give you a suit than have you give me one."

She looked at him quizzically, and then she remembered. He was Peruvian or Colombian or something South American—a dress designer, Destina something or something Destina, whom she'd heard about from one or two of her friends. In fact, Harriet had worn something of his on the cruise that she'd really admired. Vaguely she remembered he'd been hailed as a major new talent by WWD, and shortly afterwards he'd been invited to Paris to work for Dior, or was it Ricci?

There was something sinister about his looks, she decided, the way his eyebrows came together in a heavy black line over dark, somber eyes, his patrician nose and wide, cynical mouth. Then he smiled. It transformed him in the same way, she supposed, that Benedict had thought her smile transformed her. He had the whitest teeth, and a smile that was both sexy and sweet.

"Derek Destina." He put out his hand.

"Louise Towers." She shook his hand, then examined her palm in disgust. It was sticky with red wine.

"*Merde*," he said again, softly. He carefully dipped his napkin into the soda water and wiped the stickiness away.

Although she hated talking to strangers, Derek Destina was such an entertaining companion, for the rest of the journey she found herself listening, laughing, and responding to his gossip and wry descriptions of the differences between couture and ready-to-wear in Paris. "When David Hockney learned his paintings had inspired Marc Bohan's latest collection, Hockney had never heard of him. 'Who is he?' he asked. 'One of the leading couturiers in Paris,' he was told. Hockney's reply was a riot. 'I'll steal from anyone, too,' he said."

Before they landed, Destina showed her a notebook full of exquisite designs and swatches of exotic and colorful fabrics. "Why, they're extraordinary," she told him. "Who are they for?"

"Can you keep a secret?" Again came the movie-star smile.

"I can try—if I want to."

"Well, I'll tell you anyway. I've received an interesting proposal from Elizabeth Arden—you know they have the Fendi license for perfume, and Karl Lagerfeld's Chloe. Karl's lost thirty-seven pounds, by the way; his jowls have disappeared"—Destina shot her a sly glance—"along with other interesting parts of his anatomy."

He paused, hoping she would react, but she was expressionless. "Perhaps you don't know that Elizabeth Arden also has a reputation for discovering fashion designers. Years ago, Miss Arden herself discovered Oscar de la Renta." For the first time there was a note of respect in his voice. "She was the one who backed him when he first came from Santo Domingo. Well, now Elizabeth Arden is owned by this drug company, Lilly or Gardenia or whatever it's called, and for respectability they want to try a little patronage themselves. They're interested in backing my own line. This is the reason I am going to New York, to see what they have to offer."

Louise was amused at the thought of the giant Eli Lilly pharmaceutical company seeking respectability through an arrangement with Derek Destina. How out of touch creative people were, but from what she had just seen in his notebook, this Destina was certainly a creative talent.

"Do you need a lift?"

"I'd love one."

The Air France station manager was at the door of the Concorde to greet her and whisk her through immigration and customs. Destina followed behind like an obedient puppy. When they emerged into the terminal, there was a shout. "Derry, Derek, here, over here!"

Louise saw, at the back of the waiting crowd, a tall blond boy, waving hysterically. "It seems you are being met after all."

"Not at all," said Destina smoothly. "It's a young acquaintance of mine. He must be waiting for somebody else." Louise saw him wave casually to the boy, then he walked rapidly with her to her waiting limousine.

"I meant what I said," Destina said warmly, on their way into the city. "I would love to design a suit or something for you as a present."

"That's out of the question, but I would like to see your collection." Louise made up her mind. "If you're not satisfied with what Arden has to say, perhaps you would like to talk with us."

He smiled broadly. "I would like that very much. I don't think I want to become your competitor so soon after we've met." Again he shot her a sly glance. "I would much prefer working with a brilliant woman than for a bunch of faceless money men in a drug company."

His choice of words was not lost on her—"*with* a brilliant woman"; "*for* a bunch of money men"—but she gave him her card and said, "Hardly a competitor, but we may have something to interest you. Call me anyway."

Destina had briefly perused the pile of mail waiting for him—that day's New York papers, including *Women's Wear*—and showered before he heard the key turn in the door of his Central Park South apartment an hour or so later.

He looked approvingly in the mirror to see how his close-cropped dark hair, still wet from the shower, clung to his head, emphasizing its strong shape. "Roman," as Bernard, the obese, oaflike textile multimillionaire had described it at the exclusive all-male club off the Faubourg St.-Honoré.

"Yeah, Pontius Pilate," had replied one of the wiseguys from Seventh Avenue, who only came out of the closet in Paris, perhaps the reason he was insatiable and occasionally had to be roped in like a crazed steer.

In the white linen robe he had designed for himself, with the small gold crown over the right pocket, Destina sat down regally in the gilded armchair in the all-white bedroom overlooking Central Park. He picked up the phone but didn't dial as he heard the boy thunder through the apartment.

As the bedroom door was flung open, he quickly put down the receiver.

"Who are you calling? Only home a minute after weeks and weeks away and calling . . . who are you calling? I don't care." The voice was high, only just missing hysteria. "So I get a car like you tell me and wait with all the peasants and you waltz out with Madame Cunt and nod to me like as if I was a servant and . . ."

"Aren't you?" Cool, amused, his best Noël Coward voice.

"Aren't I what? Oh, very funny. A servant is it called now? Who is she, Madame Nose-in-the-Air? Someone who'd better watch out, that's for sure, if Mr. Fancy Destina fancies anything about her, especially her money, I would imagine. Who is she?" The boy was whining. Destina was already bored.

"None of your fucking business, pretty boy."

"I know who she is."

"Then why'd you ask, you pitiful worm?" He stood up and placed a commanding hand on the chairback. Without a trace of being sorry, he said, "I'm sorry, but as I've explained to you before, business is business, and Madame Cunt, as you so poetically describe her, is definitely future business. Now . . ." He paused and dramatically pointed to the bathroom. "Pleasure is pleasure. Wash your fucking nuts before you come near me, and scrub with Lysol every fucking orifice that's been near anyone else while I was away, you male whore."

The blond boy tossed his head, in the hope of appearing nonchalant. It looked petulant, but Destina was used to that. He estimated that the boy would probably interest him for another few months, but after that . . . well, there was always another "after that."

The boy came out of the bathroom in a white toweling robe. He looked like a choirboy, pink and white skin, pale hair stuck to a pink scalp. Destina stirred with desire. It was the pink of his skin and the fine, pale quality of his hair that had first attracted him. At that moment the boy looked no more than sixteen, seventeen. He said he was twenty, but he was probably lying.

As he sauntered over to where Destina was lounging on the pristine, linen-covered bed, he said, "I'm tired of being treated like . . ." Destina pulled him down so violently he heard the crack of his shin against the wooden base of the bed. He clamped a hand over his mouth, sliding the other hand beneath the toweling robe.

"Shut up," he said, smiling in a way Louise would certainly have thought more reminiscent of the Marquis de Sade than the smile she'd noted on the plane. "Shut up," he repeated. "I don't think we're remembering who we're talking to, are we?" The blond boy groaned as, beneath the robe, Destina began to move his hand.

"I don't think we're remembering who brings Pretty Boy his leather toys, his new boots from Paris, are we? Who allows him to work in his glamorous apartment, who allows him to valet for him and sometimes even wear some of his designer clothes?" With each statement, as Destina worked with experienced fingers, the boy's groans and whimpers increased and he began to claw at Destina's robe. "I don't think we remember who rescued him from the big boys in the leather-and-spike room at The Pit, do we? And now I come home to this ingratitude. I think we have to be taught a lesson, don't we?" Destina smiled down at the angelic, now sweating face. It was going to be a long and very enjoyable evening.

Louise had everything ready for Norris to study. If she could persuade him, putting the idea before the Louise Towers' directors would be just a formality. Dougy Faseff had been in his element, creating a board of Derek Destina's fashion achievements. He didn't know why Madame Towers wanted it, but it was his kind of project, and the board, now erected in her office, was impressive. No wonder she'd recognized Destina. He'd even won a coveted Coty Award, and Dougy had told her he'd had so much publicity in the last couple of years it had been difficult to know exactly what to feature.

On her desk she had information that would, she knew, interest Norris far more, facts and figures about other designer names in the fragrance and cosmetics business, names that contributed hugely to the profit picture. In buying Charles of the Ritz, for example, Squibb, a major competitor of Towers Pharmaceuticals, had found themselves the owner of the cosmetics rights to Yves Saint Laurent's great name, thanks to the foresight of the earlier chairman, Richard Salomon, who'd apparently snapped up the rights after seeing only Saint Laurent's second collection back in the sixties.

"We've been concentrating so much on building our skin-care business, I think we've lost sight of where our first big success came from," she told Norris earnestly as he perused Dougy's board.

He turned to smile at her. "Revelation?"

"Of course! It's still out there paying a lot of our bills, but none of our other fragrances, except Bravado, ever really came close. Of course, it has a lot to do with the fact that American women came so late to the wearing of fragrances. But now . . . well, I don't need to tell you what's happening. From this report, it seems that since Revlon launched Charlie . . ."

"When was that?"

Louise turned the pages of the report that marketing had so efficiently prepared. "Eleven years ago, in '72, when annual sales of fragrance were only around three hundred million dollars. It seems hard to believe." She wrinkled her nose in self-disgust. "I haven't been giving enough attention to this area. Fragrance sales, as you know, are now on the way to one-point-five billion dollars, and we're not getting anything like enough of the pie."

"Didn't Charlie Revson buy Norell's name for cosmetics? Norell was the first American designer scent, I can remember Becky telling me that. I tease her about the fact she still likes to wear it, but she has to be one of the few, because it's never gone anywhere."

Louise looked at him with admiration. Norris could still surprise her with his knowledge. "You're right. Revson was smart enough to launch what he called the first American designer scent. Becky's got good taste, Norell's good, but even when Revson was alive he never gave it much support."

Norris laughed. "Because it didn't have his own name on it. It wasn't until he used his own name that he spent the kind of bucks needed to make Charlie number one. Revlon's sure been lucky with that one."

Louise shook her head. "Not lucky, Norris. Revson never missed a trick. He saw what we missed, or rather didn't pay enough attention to, the reason for the fragrance revolution here, the reason behind its incredible growth, what Kick calls 'having the street smarts.'" She and Norris exchanged glances. They both thought the same thing. "Shall I ask him to . . ." she began as Norris said, "Let's get him in."

Kick had begun a year-long orientation program the month before, one that would take him into every department of the company. The following year, it was planned, he would spend with Louise Towers overseas. "Ask Kick Towers to come in for a few minutes. I think he's in the buying department with Talbot."

Thank God he doesn't look like a Towers, not like Benedict and, thank God again, not in any way like Charles, Louise thought as, after knocking politely, Kick came striding confidently into her office. Only Suzanne's dark blue eyes, the best feature in his thin face, reminded her of the past. It wasn't enough to disturb her.

"Hey, Kick, how's it going?"

"Fine, sir, just fine." Kick gave Norris the polished smile he felt was expected of him. He was, as he appeared, totally at ease.

"Do you know whose work this is? Are you familiar with the name?" Norris indicated the board.

"Sure, sir. That's Destina. Fiona's crazy about his things. He's doing a collection in Paris for . . ." Kick hesitated for a second. ". . . I think Lanvin, but I can check with the kids."

Louise knew Kick usually referred to Fiona's group of friends as "kids," though some were the same age as he, or older. Since Fiona and he now shared an apartment, she didn't know much about his life outside the office. "Do any of the 'kids,' as you call them, buy much fragrance?" Louise asked, then added casually, "What do your girl-friends wear?"

As Kick looked startled, Norris interjected, "A little market research, Kick. In-house stuff that often produces useful results. You'll get used to it in time."

"Well, yes, sure, they love the stuff." He looked embarrassed.

Again Norris reassured him. "Don't worry if they wear a competitor's brand. That's what we need to know."

"Well, they're into Halston, but that may be because they like his clothes. I can't stand the smell myself."

"Do they like musk oil?" Louise asked.

"Yeah, how did you know that? Penny Davidson—she's forever find-ing these places in the village where they brew up all these fancy oils. I'd say they're definitely into musk."

"Why do you think that is?"

"It's . . . well, it's earthy, sexy, I suppose. Penny told me some garbled tale about it coming from a deer's sex glands, but I guess it's more what people are about."

"Packaged?" asked Norris.

Kick looked confused. "I don't know what you . . ."

"How is it sold? By name brand? Labeled? Loose?"

"Oh, oh, I see. Well, Penny's gang goes in for buying these little brown refillable medicine bottles, but I have seen a perfume with a musk label," he said proudly.

Norris said dryly, "I bet you have. Sales of Jovan's Musk Oil are up to about fifty million dollars annually, and it's sold in fifty countries."

Impressed, Kick let out a cool whistle.

"Do you think your age group would be interested in a fragrance from someone like Destina?" Louise made her question sound perfunctory as she wandered over to the board, keeping her back to Kick as if she were only slightly interested in the reply. "Or is there any other designer name your crowd likes?"

"Calvin Klein and, yes, Ralph Lauren, but then he already sells smells."

"Scent, perfume, or fragrance, Kick," Norris remonstrated mildly. "Remember what business you're now in. No jokes at your own expense. I don't ever want to see you quoted the wrong way, so get used to using the right terminology."

Kick looked downcast but remained silent.

"And what about a Destina fragrance?" Louise asked again.

"I don't know," Kick said. "I think so, I mean I can't think why not. Everyone was wearing his biker look last fall. Why not a biker sm— scent?" He looked around the elegant office as if looking for a way out.

Louise took pity on him. "Okay, Kick. Thanks for your help."

When he'd gone, Norris said, "I don't think Kick and Fiona's group are representative, even of our best Louise Towers customers. However, he certainly gave this Destina guy top marks. I think we should have him in, find out what the bottom line is if we commit to backing his collection and also get the cosmetic and fragrance rights to his name. You say he's turned down the Arden offer?"

"Yes, apparently there were too many strings attached, too much 'supervision of his artistic talent,' and"—Louise attempted to roll her eyes as she'd seen Benedict do with such effectiveness—"above all, he couldn't stand the big man he was meant to report to, the one who controlled his budget at Lilly. Apparently he was invited to the head office in Indianapolis, and after the meeting he discovered that the top honcho's wife was giving a wine-and-cheese party in his honor around the hot tub they had just built for entertaining in their living room! It was all too much for his sensitive soul to take."

She laughed as she had when Destina told her the story with many malicious asides. Norris didn't laugh.

"I know where you're coming from, Louise." He sat down heavily, facing her across her marble desk. "I think it's an interesting idea, and certainly one we should explore. I also agree with you that there's no reason at all why we can't expand, as Arden did years ago. We're in a better position than they were then; we have the space already, in New York, Washington, and Los Angeles, to add a small, exclusive fashion and accessory area. All that's good, and so is the addition of a designer scent or even a line of scents, but"—he leaned forward to rest his arms on the desk—"I don't want to choose the wrong designer. As you know, beginning next year, I want to do less leading up to my eventual retirement in '85."

Louise closed her eyes. "Oh, please, Norris, let's not think about this now."

He gently thumped the table. "Louise, this is no surprise to you, but getting back to Destina, I don't want us saddled with a prima donna, however talented. It isn't worth it. That's all I have to say, but let's get him in and see what it's going to cost us and what the conservative R.O.I. can be."

Two months later, Destina called to tell Louise the latest piece of gossip. There had been few days when he hadn't called, although nothing as yet had been resolved between his lawyer and the lawyers acting for Louise Towers.

"This is gospel, Louise," he breathed into the phone. "Chanel has just signed Karl Lagerfeld to do their next collection. Is his influence going to be big, the clever boots! Arden lost no time, no time at all, planning another Lagerfeld perfume. We mustn't miss the boat, you know. If I can't work something out soon with your company, I've decided, re-luc-tant-ly, *c'est la vie*, that I must return to Paris and bid you a sad *au revoir*."

Louise wasn't fazed by what she was sure was his bravado. She agreed with Norris and the Louise Towers lawyers that Destina's demands were too high. Now she said coolly, "I'm amazed that Chanel would sign someone who already has an arrangement with another cosmetics house. After all, the name has only lived because of the success of the Chanel perfumes." *Touché*, she thought.

The next day Destina flew to Paris without telling her, returning at the weekend with a gift of a multicolored feathered cape, the reason, he said, for his impromptu trip. "It's the only place in the world where they still have seamstresses who know how to sew feathers."

Two weeks later, as Fiona arrived at the office to pick Kick up for lunch, Destina was in Louise's office to sign a five-year contract with Louise Towers, Incorporated, to produce a collection twice a year.

Norris wasn't one hundred percent pleased with the terms: a no-penalty exit clause for both parties after three years, a guaranteed increase in terms not less than fifteen percent if renewed for the two remaining years. Nevertheless, through sticking to his guns and not in any way being flustered by Destina's hotshot young lawyer's tactics, it was much more flexible than the terms Destina had originally demanded. Above all, there was no liability on their part if they didn't pick up their option to the rights to his name for a fragrance or cosmetics line. Already, he knew, Destina didn't like him. He'd have been worried if he had.

When Louise was told of Fiona's arrival at the office, she invited her and Kick into the Louise Towers boardroom for a celebratory glass of champagne following the signing.

"Destina, I'd like you to meet the future of the Louise Towers company, Fiona and Christopher—known as Kick—Towers, my adopted children, the grandchildren of my late husband, Benedict." How ironic it was that although she often used those words, few realized how literally true they were. She gave all of them one of her vivid smiles before turning to the young designer. "I should tell you now that young Kick here, probably without realizing it, influenced Norris and me to pursue what has just been finalized this morning. It was Kick who made us realize what a wide following you have among his generation."

The rich impressionable and probably incredibly innocent generation, Destina thought as he courteously shook the Towers children's hands. He liked the look of Kick, vulnerable, despite his just-out-of-rich-boys'-school veneer. He was probably just as easily led as his pretty boy back on Central Park South. Well, he wouldn't try anything with this one. He wasn't such a fool. He knew where the golden eggs lay, and he had no intention of cracking them.

Destina smiled sweetly as Norris toasted the company's bold new step into the world of fashion "with such an extraordinary talent as Derek Destina." He couldn't resist giving Kick a sidelong wink, though, as with his hands behind his back he gave Norris the finger. Bless the Kick boy. He was blushing; he was too precious.

Everything was precious, except for the old fart Norris, but *he* wasn't going to stand in Destina's way. Oh no, Destina's five-year plan was all worked out, thank you very much, and nothing and no one was going to stop him from becoming a major influence in both Louise Towers's business and personal life.

Washington, D.C., 1987

"THE BROTHERS FEINER," as the press often referred to Jan and Victor respectively, president and senior vice-president of research and development of K. Avery, strode purposefully into the annual medical conference being held at Washington's Academy of Sciences.

They were a few minutes early, but already the lecture hall was packed with eminent researchers, professors, doctors, dermatologists, medical reporters, and editors, most of whom they knew by sight. To Victor's fury, as they took their assigned places in the front row, Jan said softly, without looking at him, "I wish Louise were here today."

He could hardly believe his ears. Louise! On this day of days, how on earth could his brother be thinking of such a tramp, of the amoral, scheming bitch who had done everything in her power to destroy him? Victor was so angry that tears of self-pity came to his eyes. By the mention of her cursed name, Jan had spoiled everything for him. He scowled and was about to curse the woman to hell when the lights dimmed and a movie screen descended.

The brothers exchanged sharp glances. Victor had warned Jan there might be some showmanship exhibited at this usually most austere and serious of conferences. Jan had told him to stop daydreaming. As a slide of a famous painting was projected onto the screen, Victor felt vindicated. The celebrated professor of dermatology they had all come to hear was up to his usual nonconformist tricks.

The painting, which they had both seen many times in its home in the British Museum, was *The Fountain of Youth* by the German artist Lucas Cranach. There were a few titters from those in the audience who were unfamiliar with the scene of old, tired, sagging people waiting their turn to step into the fountain, to emerge on the other side revitalized, energetic, and, above all, young.

Jan leaned forward eagerly as the eminent doctor began to speak, using the plural as opposed to the singular to indicate that medical research was always a team effort. "We rarely give a lecture nowadays without showing this painting because it illustrates what we dermatologists regard as a holy educational mission, that the change of a lovely child into a wrinkled crone is not inevitable; that it is not the chronological passing of time that results in this unhappy situation, but that it is caused by exposure to the sun."

Although Jan had upset him, Victor began to relax as the lecture went on. Soon he would be joining the great dermatologist at the podium to receive his congratulations. He couldn't wait to see the looks of surprise on the faces of some he had seen in the audience, prestigious men of medicine who looked down their noses at him, men who had been quoted in the press as saying he wasn't of the same caliber as his baby brother, Jan.

Today, at last, his moment of triumph was going to come. In a few minutes the audience would hear from the great doctor that the drug he, Victor Feiner, had worked on for so many years of his life, the magical AC3, appeared to retard and even reverse the effects of premature aging from the sun. In treating acne patients with AC3 over a period of twelve years, this most famous of all the teaching dermatologists in the country had documented amazing and thoroughly desirable side effects from the regular use of their vitamin-A-acid drug. The doctor was talking about them now. ". . . skin became rosier, smoother, and younger looking, and brown spots disappeared. Following the opening of our Clinic for Aging Skin six years ago, my professional colleagues and I embarked on a formal study of scores of photo-aged or prematurely aged patients, treating them successfully with AC3."

Cranach's *Fountain of Youth* disappeared from the screen to be replaced by a series of remarkable before-and-after pictures, with the professor pointing with a lighted beam to some of the more visible results of skin improvement. As the lecture came to an end and the lights went up, Victor wondered if Jan could hear what he could hear, the nervous thumping of his heart as his name was called.

It had been Jan's idea that he should share the podium to talk about the early days of AC3, the dark and difficult days before its value had been fully appreciated, the first patent granted to Averbach for the treatment of acne, and now a new patent given to the professor for its use against photo-aging. Because he was talking to men who understood his language, the language of chemistry and physics, Victor's nervousness soon disappeared and he began to go into more and more detail.

"I wish to God he'd shut up," someone in the row behind Jan whispered. "We'll all be asleep in a minute."

Jan immediately stood up and started to applaud. Victor blinked, then turned to the famous man beside him and started to applaud, too. It was a few minutes before the audience would stop clapping to allow the professor to announce that K. Avery, the wholly owned subsidiary of the giant Swiss Averbach pharmaceutical company, had agreed to fund a new, multimillion-dollar clinical investigation "for AC3's new indication affecting the aging of the skin, the first investigation of its kind in the world."

There was a hush in the large hall as Jan went to shake the professor's hand. Everyone there realized the significance of the moment. If the studies proved conclusive, it could mean the beginning of the end of wrinkles, and possibly the long-awaited solution to meaningful "cosmeceuticals" for the skin, part drug, part cosmetic, passed and blessed by the FDA.

And which company stood to reap the greatest rewards from all of this? As news stories reported the next day, obviously it was K. Avery's Natasha, the declared enemy of Louise Towers.

Destina looked older on television, or perhaps it was because he was wearing his hair longer. Whatever the reason, someone other than Louise would have to tell him.

"So, instead of numerals, à la Chanel, you say you convinced Louise Towers to use initials, letters, the letters of your name for what will eventually be a small fragrance collection? Let's see, D-E-S-T . . ." Joan Lunden counted the letters on her fingers. "A seven-piece collection, right?" She looked as if she really cared about the answer.

"Yes." Destina picked up the gold and enamel bottle of fragrance and held it up to the camera so that the letter D was clearly visible. " 'D' first, of course, a fragrance that combines many unusual, subtle notes as surprising as my clothes exhibit with their mix of unexpected fabrics. If this is the success we expect it to be, 'E' will follow, and then, as you might guess, the especially sexy formula for the wondrous letter 'S.' I am working with the Louise Towers perfumers on both 'E' and 'S' now."

Despite the stream of lies coming so effortlessly from Destina's mouth, Louise found herself laughing at his audacity. The almost-too-perfect English accent she had noted when they'd first met on the plane was very effective on TV, as was the way he moved his body, as graceful as a ballet dancer, as dangerous as a matador. No one handled public relations better than Destina. Who else would have thought up the initial idea? It wasn't such a bad one, either, if no one had to count the cost. Because of Destina's extravagance and total disregard for the economics behind the creation and launching of a perfume, it had taken almost three years to produce "D."

"We're running out of time," Joan Lunden laughed happily as, with a graceful bow, Destina sprayed a little of his first fragrance onto her wrist. Louise switched off "Good Morning America" as Destina smiled his by-now-celebrated smile to say good-bye to the television audience.

Should she call Dee Possant and tell her not to have a nervous breakdown? That it was all Destina's fantasy? That "E" and "S" and "T" and whatever other initials followed had never been discussed in preliminary form, or budgeted for, let alone "worked on" with their perfumers? Probably, but even as she went to the phone, it rang.

"Mr. Christopher Towers is calling, ma'am." Banks was the only person she knew who always called Kick by his given name.

"Wasn't he wonderful?"

"Wonderful! But of course you know it's all fantasy. We haven't . . ."

"Oh, Louise, of course I know it, but it's not such a bad idea." Kick was roaring with laughter. "He's such a good liar, eh?"

Well, that settled it. She needn't call anyone in marketing. She was overreacting. If Kick wasn't concerned, she certainly needn't be. What a help Kick was turning out to be. She hoped her instincts about him were true—that he was beginning to like her as much as she was beginning to like and depend on him.

She rang for more coffee, suddenly depressed, a feeling not helped by the memo sitting on her desk, the long, detailed memo she had brought home from the office, from Jewelson, Louise Towers's chief financial officer, regarding Destina's latest "outrageous" expenses.

She agreed with Jewelson's use of the word. They were outrageous. Destina was now overspending his annual expense budget by one hundred fifty percent, and she was the only one who could tackle him about it and extract a promise that he'd "be good," a promise that in the past had only lasted for a few months, until something else stirred his "creative juices." As Jewelson had acerbically pointed out, the problem was aggravated by the fact that they had only recently renewed his contract for a further two years after many prima-donna scenes, the majority of which Jewelson, thank God, knew nothing about.

It had been one of darling Norris's last services to the company, before he retired, to sit Destina down, knowing how much he hated him, and somehow get through his unstable skull that he would be better off agreeing to the two-year extension with a twenty-percent increase in remuneration, as set out in his original contract, than a divorce with no guarantee that in increasingly difficult times anyone would pick up the rights to use his name in a fragrance.

As Louise had discovered, beneath his bluster and tantrums, Destina was capable of cool self-appraisal. When he learned from Norris how much he would have to pay the Louise Towers company for the rights to "D," he'd signed like a lamb in less than twenty-four hours. There hadn't been any other signs of lamblike behavior. In fact, now that Norris wasn't there, Louise sometimes wished Destina hadn't renewed, despite the financial success of his fashion collection selling in special areas of Louise Towers boutiques in major stores across the country, and now the perfume, already number one in New York and Los Angeles.

Was Destina developing an expensive drug habit? The idea had haunted her since Dougy Faseff had indicated it at the embarrassing, emotional meeting he had begged for a few days ago when Destina had been out of town, "wooing and wowing the Reagan coterie of ladies on the West Coast with his spectacularly successful first perfume 'D,'" as *Women's Wear* had feverishly reported.

Dougy was terrified of incurring Destina's displeasure, certain, as he'd sobbed to her at their meeting, that despite his long years of service to Louise Towers, Destina now had enough influence to get rid of him "just like that." Dougy had snapped his fingers and mimed dropping something disgusting into the wastepaper basket.

She'd tried to reassure him, but it hadn't been easy. The truth was that Destina did have influence, and as far as matters of creativity were concerned—packaging, advertising, and store promotions—he was usually right. When she thought he was wrong, he sulked for days and even occasionally did his famous disappearing act, usually out of the country, always returning with a fantastic excuse, bringing back some extraordinary artifact "we must copy as a container for the new night cream" or an ornament, bijou, or one-of-a-kind piece of clothing for her, like the famous feather cape he'd brought back from Paris in late '83, a few months before signing the contract with the company. His last gift to her had been particularly inspired, Powder Blue, a rare silky blue-gray Siamese kitten, looking at her now through fathomless eyes.

She looked down the list of Destina's most recent expenses, many of which were marked by Jewelson as having no backup receipts—the $1,200 limo expenses for March 23, the $3,050 for fabric and "misc." Without receipts, the company could refuse to reimburse him. It wasn't the scenes that would provoke that worried her. Did these sums really represent payments to drug dealers, as Dougy had tried to tell her in veiled terms? If Destina was on drugs, it hadn't drained away his energy; his work output was prodigious by anyone's standards.

Had his behavior changed? Did Destina still respect her as she believed he had in the beginning? Did he respect anyone? Probably not. He would ridicule Marlene publicly, almost to the point of reducing her to tears, then just as suddenly do or say something that made the poor woman believe he was Leonardo da Vinci.

She had reassured Dougy that he would never be fired as long as she was in charge. She hadn't used those words, they were too revealing, but that's what Dougy had taken them to mean, going away reassured and happy, because he believed, as everyone did, that she would be in charge for as long as she lived, and that even after her death, she'd make sure he and other long-timers like him were protected.

Only she, Norris, and the lawyers knew the clock was ticking inexorably toward the next decade, now only three years away, when, in 1991, Kick would reach his thirtieth birthday to become the all-powerful head of the Louise Towers company, able to dismiss anyone, including her!

Because the secret was held by so few, nothing had leaked out, so Kick still had no idea of what lay in store for him. The lawyers had agreed it was not necessary at present for him to be told, perhaps because they were aware, as was she, that no one was more influenced by Destina than naive, trusting Kick, just completing his fifth year in the company. Neither had he ever been told that Benedict had insisted he spend five years working in every department before he could be considered eligible for the top Louise Towers job. Well, when the time Benedict had decreed came, Kick would have been working for the company for almost ten years, learning on the job and, unlike Fiona, handling the business with ease and obvious pleasure.

"Just like Charles," Marlene had said once.

Louise knew her wince of pain had been obvious, as it had been on another occasion when her celebrated mask had deserted her. It was the day Henry Davidson had ruefully confessed that Benedict's will had no loopholes. "Ironclad," he'd said, for once also losing his own icy coolness. "Your husband didn't overlook one blasted thing."

How would Kick feel about her when the day came to tell him the news that on his thirtieth birthday he would be the big boss? Would he remember how she had guided him, helped him in his long apprenticeship? Would he still turn to her for advice, or would he put her out to pasture like a spent workhorse?

As always, when her thoughts strayed in this direction, Louise forced herself to work. There was a neatly typed list of telephone calls she had to return, including one from Fiona, confirming their lunch that day. Yes, there it was, on her list of appointments. It didn't make her feel any less depressed.

Nevertheless, she was pleasantly surprised at how slim and chic Fiona looked in a Bill Blass checked suit as she arrived at Le Cirque fifteen minutes late.

Just like her mother, Louise thought as, with no apology for her lateness, after a perfunctory kiss in the air, Fiona launched immediately into the reason for the lunch. "You read a few months ago about Avery funding this huge clinical investigation to support the new anti-aging discovery—the new claims for AC3 . . ."

As she spoke, Fiona flounced her head back. Louise felt chilled. On the side of Fiona's neck, usually covered by her hair, was an unmistakable love bite. Memories struck her like knives. She bent her head to look in her bag for her dark glasses. Fiona, so full of what she had to say, didn't notice. "As we keep hearing, Avery is pouring money into this new vision of the drug, but I happen to know from a very well-placed friend of mine that AC3 is very potent and liable to cause dangerous side effects if used without the proper guidance. Avery wants to present it as the wrinkle remover of all time, and then link Natasha products to its use." Fiona was steadily growing more excited. "We have to plan a course of action. We have to prove somehow that it can be dangerous. Otherwise Natasha will bury us."

"Who gave you this information?" Louise asked curtly.

"I'd rather not say."

"Then I'd rather not believe you."

Louise told Kick later that afternoon about their conversation. "Has Fiona discussed AC3 with you?"

"Yes, there's a lot of sense in what she says," Kick replied defensively. "Obviously it's in Avery's interest to push this anti-aging claim hard. Women will clamor for the drug all over the world, and by association it won't hurt Natasha products either."

"I don't think we should get involved in any way at all. It can only sound like sour grapes. I don't intend to have anything to do with 'planning a course of action.' It's going to take months, or maybe years, before the evidence is ready for the FDA. I'm frankly shocked that Fiona ever proposed such a thing."

"Louise doesn't want to get involved," Kick told Fiona when she wandered into his office at the end of the day. "You know what that means. There's nothing anyone can do to change her. In any case, it's too early yet to worry about it. Let's just wait and see."

Like a rebellious child, Fiona wrapped her arms around herself and rocked back and forth on the chair. "I'm tired of Louise making all the

decisions for this company, tired of hearing her say 'I don't intend . . .' "
Her exaggerated mimicry of Louise's accent made Kick laugh before
he could stop himself. "She's so out of date, with all her Czech skin
potions and lotions that take hours to apply and weeks to see results.
That's not what women are into now."

"What *are* they into?"

"Fast results. Skin peels, the kind of thing Natasha is selling like
hotcakes—off with the old skin, on with the new."

"Sounds like something out of Aladdin, show biz or something,"
Kick said laconically.

"The beauty biz *is* show biz or *should* be entertainment, fun, not
always this cleanse, tone, and nourish rubbish. Eddie says . . .'"

"Who's Eddie?"

Fiona grimaced at her brother. "A friend of mine—someone who
knows what's going on." She stared at him defiantly. "It's time we got
our act together, brother, and acted like Towers. It's time we had more
say in the Louise Towers scheme of things. Certainly *you* should be
making decisions. Let's plan a palace coup and take over the joint."

Although Fiona was laughing, there was a glint in her eye that Kick
recognized. It spelled trouble.

Dear Aunt Louise,

    The other day I was very lucky. I was waiting in line with my best
friend, Radka Maudrova, at the Circorama, the cinema in the round in
Julius Fucik Park, when we were approached by a lady from Obuk, the
state fashion consortium. She asked us to come for an audition at the
Dum Mody (house of fashion) and I am honored to tell you I was
chosen as a model. (Radka, alas, was considered too short.)

    Grandmama is happy. Papa is not. I am sending you a picture which
is a little dark and makes me look as if I have black hair and not its
real red because the flashbulb did not work, but you can see a little of
me on the runway . . .

Kristina heard a creak on the stairs and quickly pushed the letter
under her bed. Papa was spying on her more than ever these days. It
was bad enough, living with the knowledge that the walls could easily
have ears, but now even her own family allowed her no privacy.

She opened the door, but there was no one there. From below she
heard the familiar sound of two old voices quarreling and coughing,
as her grandmother, limping about the kitchen with an arthritic hip,
complained about forever having to feed three people when there was
only enough food for one, and her father snapped back, coughing as

he filled the room with billows of smoke from the unfiltered cigarette forever hanging from his mouth or in his hand.

How she hated being there, and yet how full of pity she was for the two people she knew loved her more than life itself. She had been hearing for almost nineteen of her twenty-one years that her mother had abandoned her, seduced by a life of plenty. She had been told, and she believed, that her mother had even turned against her own sister, Louise Towers, the woman who had first opened the door to let her mother escape to the land of the free.

Of course, she despised her mother, as did Grandmama and Papa, and wanted nothing to do with her, but at the same time Kristina had decided a long time ago that nothing would probably have happened to Natasha Mahler if, as she'd seen from a few photographs, her mother hadn't been pretty, very pretty.

Because of this, and because of the movie magazines she managed to get her hands on, Kristina knew that a lovely face and an even lovelier figure were the passports out of obscurity, poverty, and even Czechoslovakia.

Even in dreary Prague, a pretty woman had a better time than a plain one. If she accepted half the invitations she received, Kristina knew there could be more bread on the table, more peroxide in the pitiful, rundown room that passed for a hairdressing salon, and even more cigarettes for her invalid father.

But according to her grandmother she was every bit as "particular" as her famous Aunt Louise, once called Ludmilla, had been. Over the years she'd loved to listen to Grandmama tell stories about Aunt Ludmilla turning down counts and ambassadors and even a prince or two, until she fell in love with the handsome general who had liberated Prague from the Germans, the general who turned out to be the richest man in America!

Since the return of her father from Brno, Kristina had learned the hard way that it wasn't wise to let him see her looking "tarted up," as he called the wearing of lipstick. It was "asking for trouble," as he also often said. She didn't need Grandmama to explain that that meant "Don't worry your father; he's been through enough. Don't ever let him think you're going to follow in your mother's footsteps." If only there was half a chance! But Kristina accepted that there was none. Nowadays no one, not even her hero, Vaclav Havel, gave any optimistic forecast for freedom or even a better standard of living from the cursed Russians.

So she would become a model for Obuk and make the best of her life. Her mother had wanted to be a ballerina once, and the ballerina dolls still sat in dust on the shelf in the bedroom, once her mother's, now hers. Instead of dreaming, Kristina told herself, she would work to become the leading model in the country. She looked in the mirror, pretending she was still on the runway in the suit made of rough material that had made her skin itch. She needed to work on her posture, the Obuk trainer had told her, and when her father was out, she intended to carry books on her head up and down the stairs until it became second nature to stand tall.

"Kristinaaaaa . . ." Here came the call from Grandmama to say the watery potato soup was ready on the table. Now that she was going to be a top model, it hardly mattered that there was often not enough to eat; top models, Kristina knew, hardly ate a thing.

As she ran downstairs, she vowed she would finish her letter to Aunt Louise later that night. She would tell her, as she had done often before, that despite everything she knew she was luckier than most of her friends because she had such a wonderfully kind, loving aunt, one she could confide in, one who granted every wish that was possible, one who had taken the place long ago of the mother who'd left her behind.

"Have you seen this . . . and this . . . and this!" Victor, his face contorted with rage, threw a cascade of press clippings onto Jan's desk.

"Of course I've seen them, or similar ones," Jan replied with a calmness he didn't feel.

Victor stalked from one side of Jan's large office to the other, before crumpling down on the long sofa opposite the picture window through which the East River glittered in the summer sunlight.

"Disastrous side effects . . . swelling, peeling, lasting redness . . . woman whose skin was damaged by K. Avery's AC3 sues . . ."

When Jan didn't answer, Victor jumped to his feet to shuffle among the clippings again. He read aloud in a hysterical voice, "Listen to this from *The New York Times*. 'Playing with Fire'! How's that for a headline? What will our Swiss overlords say about that, eh?"

Although Jan didn't respond, his brother continued to read aloud. " 'The FDA Commissioner announced today that the continued irresponsible press and television coverage of AC3 as a wrinkle remover has turned the drug into a national craze, as women everywhere flock to anyone with a medical degree for a prescription, and use the drug without following the proper cautionary directions, thereby producing the most serious side effects. So far, there has been no comment from the makers of the drug, K. Avery, whose stock has more than tripled in value since the deluge of publicity surrounding AC3."

Victor howled, "This terrible press will put government approval back years." Again he agitatedly strode back and forth in front of Jan's desk. "Louise Towers is behind it; I can smell her cunning in every headline. It's typical of the kind of dirty tricks she knows how to employ."

"You're crazy. There is no evidence whatsoever linking Louise Towers to this. This whole situation has been gathering momentum since last year, when the Medical *journal* published some corroborating results of AC3's effectiveness on fine facial lines. I blame myself entirely for not seeing where that report might lead, that it could easily be interpreted as saying a youth cream was at hand. I shouldn't have had to be reminded that women will do anything to obtain a wrinkle remover."

Although Victor heard the misery in Jan's voice, he ignored it, banging his hand on Jan's desk. "It doesn't matter what I say, does it? You've never believed me, not even after all these years! You've always been blinded by that woman. I tell you, all those snide references to the way our stock has risen so dramatically on the strength of an untried drug, all those veiled accusations and blind items in the press, suggesting we've been running a brilliant but dangerous PR campaign with no thought of the consumer—this is the work of an enemy, a dangerous enemy, the same enemy we've faced for years. You know full well who I mean, the woman who stole your perfume, who sent you into Siberia, who has always tried to ruin you, the bitch who for some reason only known to God still manages to mesmerize you—Louise Towers!"

When Victor, on the verge of tears, finally left his office, Jan wearily called in Peter Taunton, his head of corporate relations, to work on a release of his own. Whether or not it was a cunningly orchestrated plot to discredit both AC3 and their company, he had badly misjudged the hue and cry throughout the country as women misused the potent drug and tried to remove their wrinkles overnight.

"That's the damnable pity, Pete. If a little is good, more must be better. That's what women have been thinking, squeezing it out like toothpaste, which is about ten times the proper amount. It's ironic that in the dosage for acne they follow the directions explicitly, but when it comes to wrinkles, they ignore what it says and just pour the stuff on."

To Jan's surprise, Taunton, who was usually quite circumspect, especially for a PR man, said, "I don't think these press attacks happened by accident."

"Have you been talking to my brother?"

"No, why?"

"All right. What do you mean?"

"I was over at Natasha, talking to Charlie Towers about something else, and he told me he was worried months ago about the digs and taunts his niece, Fiona Towers, had been making. It seems she kept bringing up our 'wonder drug'—her words—all under the guise of good humor, suggesting that Charlie shouldn't be too pleased yet with what 'the K. Avery folks had accomplished,' that somehow, sometime, a stick was going to be put in the AC3 wheel."

"Madame, a Mr. Feiner is on the telephone."

"Thank you, Banks." Louise sighed with pleasure that Jan was calling her. In the last few weeks, reading about the problems he was having with AC3, she'd wanted to call him herself, but hadn't had the courage. She picked up the phone expectantly, hoping he was going to ask to see her again, knowing she was going to say yes.

"Jan, how are you?"

"It isn't Jan. It's Victor Feiner, the brother who sees you for what you are, an evil, dangerous woman. Now you've gone too far—"

"Wait a minute! What on earth are you talking about?" Victor Feiner! She could hardly believe Victor Feiner was daring to call her, the man who, over the years, had never failed to show his hatred in vicious attacks in the press.

"I'm talking about the plot you dreamed up with your stepdaughter. I didn't need to be told that the silly little slut had been boasting to her uncle, Charles Towers, another man you tried to ruin, about your plans to wreck us."

Anger made her voice shake. "Plans? You are mistaken, Mr. Feiner, if . . ."

"Don't you 'Mr. Feiner' me. I'm warning you, I've had enough of your evil machinations against my brother. He may be fool enough not to see you for what you are, but I see you only too clearly." Victor was growing increasingly out of control. "This is my official warning, Madame High and Mighty, that I am going to get my revenge and put you back in the gutter where you came from. This is no idle . . ."

Louise quietly put the phone down. She thought she was calm, but her hands were trembling. A threat of revenge from Victor Feiner? All the loathing of years had been in his voice. She remembered the first time she'd met him, at the miserable lunch in London. He'd made it clear he didn't like her then, but threats of revenge? She had never heard so much hatred in a voice, not even in Benedict's at his angriest.

"Your stepdaughter boasting to her uncle, another man you tried to ruin, about your plans to wreck us." She had controlled her feelings

for so long she could now think about Charles without wanting to weep. She could also distance herself from both Natasha and Charles. At least she thought she could. Above all, she had to get to the bottom of what Victor meant.

As if her days weren't full of threats of a different kind. Only yesterday she'd read a confirmation that Steven Holt, "the most successful unauthorized biographer in the world," had received an advance of two million dollars to write the story of her life. There had been two or three second-rate biographies before, full of half-truths and whole lies, biographies that had died on the shelves. Holt was different. Of course, the usual warning not to cooperate had gone out to everyone from Louise Towers's public relations department, but as everyone well knew, Holt's reputation had been built not only on his writing skills, but on his ability to penetrate the most private of lives, the Agnellis, the Mellons, and—his most recent triumph—an astonishing book about the King of Spain that had sold millions of copies.

There was also the much closer to home threat from Destina, forever boasting of Hollywood offers if he didn't get his way, fueled recently by his jealousy of the fuss being made over a new Italian designer, Armani, who'd just had a huge success with his collection on the West Coast.

Still shaken, Louise went to her dressing room to get ready for what was already a momentous day, meeting with the lawyers and Kick in the boardroom, when he would learn the full details of his destiny, planned so carefully by his grandfather, her husband, Benedict Towers, the man who had betrayed her. She shivered at the thought of Steven Holt revealing to the world how much she had trusted and how little she had really known. She hated being late, but her energy had gone. She collapsed on her chaise longue, stroking Powder Blue's sleek coat, trying to compose herself.

Gregory Phillips and Ashley Foxwell, the two executors of Benedict's will, had set the date. "It's time," Phillips had told her the month before, with his usual about-to-go-to-the-guillotine expression. She'd been waiting for it. Somehow she'd thought she would be the one to tell them the date, but perhaps, as usual, Benedict had been right: women, he'd always said, whether they were aware of it or not, procrastinated over decisions they subconsciously didn't want to make.

Thank God, it had been agreed that because of Fiona's long record of absenteeism and her evident lack of interest in working full-time for the company, she would not be present at the meeting or the lunch that followed. It would be Kick's responsibility to discuss with his sister whether she wanted a future with Louise Towers or not.

On the way to the office, Louise tried to put Victor Feiner's accusations and threats out of her mind, but they kept intruding. Was it fate that Fiona who, working on another floor, using another bank of elevators, ran after her in the lobby?

Her face was flushed, excited, but her words chilled Louise. "Isn't it wonderful, all this terrible press AC3's getting?" The look on Louise's face stopped her. "Is something wrong?"

"Yes, there is something wrong, dreadfully wrong," Louise answered grimly. "Please call my office and make an appointment to see me this afternoon."

Fiona, looking furious, didn't answer, but flounced off to her elevator bank.

Again Louise's hands were trembling, not a good start to a day that she'd hoped—no, prayed—would not be emotional in any way. In the luxurious bathroom adjoining her office, she went to the truth-light mirror by the window, the one where over the years she'd personally tested so many Louise Towers products. Her skin was remarkably unlined; she'd never had a facelift, although *The National Enquirer* had run a fictitious "exposé" of her secret stay at one of Brazil's most famous cosmetic surgery hospitals.

How little of the truth the much-written-about truth-light mirror revealed. Her reflection showed what the world saw, a woman of a certain age, with smooth, beautiful, ivory-colored skin, dramatic dark eyes, and—the only real change in her appearance—an upsweep of dark chestnut hair, softened in color from her original jet black with highlights to hide the gray around her temples.

But how she looked and how she felt were two different things. Today she felt like the defenseless, vulnerable girl she'd been in her twenties in Switzerland, when she'd first been swept up by Benedict Towers's overwhelming hunger for her.

Lonely and afraid, Louise took a deep breath, squared her shoulders, and went out into the corridor toward the boardroom, where Phillips and Foxwell were already waiting. Kick came in, poised, happy. Had he already been told what the meeting was about? What did it matter if he had? She had to acknowledge that Kick worked hard for the company. He wasn't a genius, and if he hadn't been born a Towers, he probably would never have become chief executive officer, but he wouldn't let the company down, either.

When neither lawyer spoke, once seated at a small table near the window, Louise took the initiative. She looked intently at Kick as she said, "Your grandfather, Benedict Towers, gave me a rare opportunity in 1954 when he funded the beauty salon I wanted to open and the first Louise Towers Institute was born."

The lawyers looked at her apprehensively, wondering where this was going to lead. Louise put her hand briefly over Kick's. "Under Benedict Towers's guidance, from that little acorn, as you say in English, the Louise Towers oak has grown." She hadn't planned any of what she was saying, but it was coming easily. "Because, above all, your grandfather wanted, as I did and do, that oak to live on under the shelter of the Towers name, he set down a future plan for the company, one that Mr. Phillips will now read to you."

If Phillips was a kissing man, she was sure he would have kissed her. Instead he gave her one of his rare, shy smiles of approval and, turning the pages of the document she knew so well, began to read.

There was no doubt Kick hadn't known or even dreamed he was going to hear what Phillips read. His eyes filled with tears as the lawyer finished, ". . . providing he meets certain requirements, the main one being a minimum of five years working satisfactorily for the company prior to his thirtieth birthday."

Kick wiped his hand across his eyes and cleared his throat. He jumped up and hugged Louise before saying, "I am stunned. Do you realize that? Stunned! I never expected this and . . . and . . . I can only say I imagine in view of the five year requirement being fulfilled already . . . you . . . you decided to tell me this now"—he attempted a laugh—"because my report card's okay. Yes?"

"Yes," Foxwell answered, though Kick was looking searchingly at Louise. "As you have just heard, the same requirement was laid down by your grandfather for your sister, Fiona, and your cousin Zoe. In Fiona's case . . ." He turned to Louise.

She had no problem answering. "I think, Kick, you would agree with me that the jury's still out concerning Fiona's interest in working for the company. At the right moment, it's up to you now to explain to her what her prerogatives are, provided she fulfills her grandfather's expectations."

The lunch that followed was stiff but fortunately brief, with less talk about the eventual transfer of power and more about the FDA's new crackdown on cosmetics claims and K. Avery's problems with AC3.

After the lawyers left, Kick walked Louise back to her office. "I still can't take it in," he said. "I obviously have you to thank, Louise. I must say I never expected it, and I'll never forget it."

How far he was from the truth, but in a God-given moment in the boardroom she'd suddenly realized she had to make Kick believe it was just as much her idea as Benedict's; it was one way she hoped to safeguard her position.

She smiled the enigmatic smile he knew so well as she replied, "I know you won't let me down."

"Agents are the most important element in Hollywood," the sparrowlike man with the large nose and huge horn-rimmed glasses was saying within earshot to a group apparently awestruck by every word out of his mouth. Not missing anything, through half-closed eyes Destina saw the big-shot producer he'd hoped to meet here today purposefully approaching the sparrow.

He stretched hard, arms in the air, letting the muscles ripple, knowing that the producer, an experienced stud collector, would note his good figure, his velvet-smooth golden tan, and the parts of his anatomy best emphasized by his black bikini. He slipped on a matching cotton shirt, so fine it was almost transparent, and sauntered over to the circle surrounding the sparrow.

"He controls, oh, fifty percent of the stars, actors, directors, and writers, so you'd better be very, very nice to Mike Ovitz. I'm his idol, he says, so that makes him a nice guy already." There were appreciative titters and, just as the waves pounding below continually changed the pattern of sand on the Malibu beach, so, during the next forty minutes or so, did the pattern of groups change on the wide terrace. People came and went, and the sparrow's group splintered into two, then three, until Destina achieved exactly the pattern he wanted, sitting on one of the many turquoise-toweled chaise longues, this time cozily side by side with the producer, who, seen close up, was much hairier than he'd expected.

"I've heard about you from Jean-François. You're Derry Destina, aren't you? Very original, I've heard, even by swing-gang standards."

Destina smiled his most evil smile. "No one who really knows me would call me Derry. I was never called Derry, not even in the old days when, as Derek Destina, I was only known for my originality. I'm Destina now, known more for my"—he laughed, he hoped provocatively—"experience and knowledge."

The producer, who had had three box-office hits in a row, moved his bare foot the fraction needed to touch Destina's bare foot. "Yes, I see," he said, with a faint trace of a Midwestern twang. "Enough knowledge to paint your toenails. What shade is it, Louise Towers's Shy Sebum?"

There was an edge to the voice that irritated Destina, but he didn't let it show. "Touché," he said with a light laugh.

So the big-time producer thought he was some small-time cosmetics

company freak, did he? For an idle second he wondered if anyone in
La-la Land realized how much money could be made in the cosmetics
business, how much money he was making in bonuses with the block-
buster success of the "D" perfume?

As a soft Pacific breeze ruffled Destina's hair, imperceptibly the producer moved nearer and they leaned back together on the chaise
longue built for two. "I'm teasing you," the producer said in a little-
boy voice that didn't fool Destina for a minute. "I've seen your work.
It's interesting, talented. I guess you know I'm thinking of doing a
remake of *The Wizard of Ox.*"

Did he ever! Destina's mind raced. He'd never dreamed the producer would bring up so soon the one subject he most wanted to
discuss, the movie everyone was talking about, the movie that *Variety*
had recently claimed would give any designer associated with it the
kind of stature designers had had in Hollywood's heyday. If he was
chosen, this, added to his other claims to fame, could make him the
most famous designer in the world and he could live the kind of life
he longed to live, like Lagerfeld and St. Laurent with their palaces
and courts, not at the beck and call of an overrated *arriviste* like Madame Towers and her boring, suburban grandchildren. He suddenly,
badly wanted some snow.

The producer placed a hand covered in blond hairs on his knee.
"I'd like to talk to you about it sometime. When you can get away
from the lipsticks . . ."

A month had passed since Louise and the lawyers gave Kick the
incredible news that on his thirtieth birthday he would become the
boss and owner of the Louise Towers cosmetics company. It had taken
a while for the realization to sink in. He'd also had his hands full
dealing with Fiona, who'd impetuously followed a boyfriend to London, only to return brokenhearted when he'd apparently callously
dropped her, a situation not helped by the fact that Louise also suspected her of spreading stories to scuttle Avery's hopes for AC3.

Then there was the much more taxing problem of getting Destina
to renew his contract. If only it expired in 1991, when he would be
in complete charge. The lawyers had told him they were powerless to
help. With Norris gone, until 1991 Louise was the deciding voice, and
she'd made it clear that she had had enough of Destina's tantrums and
threats, that unless he agreed to her terms, she wasn't interested in
putting up with him anymore. Well, he didn't like Destina's attitude,
either, but he felt very differently.

In Kick's opinion there was no one in the world to match Destina's creativity, except perhaps Lagerfeld, and their competitors had him sewn up well into the twenty-first century. Didn't Louise, for God's sake, realize this?

Now, this evening, after Destina's latest row with Louise, he had to go himself to mend fences behind Louise's back, to plead and give the superstar his word that if he renewed his contract on Louise's terms now, he would be in a position in '91 to make it very much worth his while.

Kick looked in the mirror and brushed back his obstinate hair. He was dissatisfied with his appearance. No matter how much he worked out, he was still too thick around the middle. Destina had advised a new form of cosmetic nip-and-tucking called liposuction to remove his "love handles," but that wasn't for him. Not for the first time, he wished he had a fraction of Destina's seemingly effortless style. He made work so much fun, too. Somehow, during the next few hours, he had to make Destina realize not only how much he valued, admired, and wanted to emulate him, but that if he'd only be patient and wait until Kick was in the saddle . . .

The intercom phone rang to announce that the first problem he had to deal with was on her way up. Kick was shocked when he saw his sister. "Sis, you look . . ." He stopped himself. He never knew what to say to women. "Here, let me take your coat. I was just about to open a bottle of your favorite Domaine Ott. Okay?"

"No, I've given up drinking," Fiona said dramatically. She flung herself down on the sofa.

"Oh? That's an interesting development. What brought that on?"

"I'm sooo depressed, Kick."

Kick threw an arm around her shoulders. "He's not worth it, Fiona, there are plenty more where he came from." He turned her averted face toward him and said sternly, "Louise told me . . ." Fiona tried to squirm away from him, but Kick pulled her back. "Just listen. Louise received a call from Feiner's brother—Victor, I think his name is—one of the big R-and-D guys at Avery. Seems they knew each other back when. He apparently threatened her, accused her of fueling all their bad press, so she looked into what's been going on." Kick shook his head sorrowfully. "Sis, you really screwed up on this one. Louise knows about your little hints and tips to all those press vultures."

Fiona started to cry, but it didn't faze Kick. He was used to it.

"Listen to me, Fiona, I love you. I asked you to come over this afternoon because I'm going to give you a break. I'm going to treat you like a grownup."

As she bristled, he began to tell her in abbreviated form what he had learned from Louise and the lawyers, including the inescapable fact that everyone in the company was aware she had been less than an asset to Louise Towers since her arrival, four years before.

As Kick talked, color began to come back to Fiona's wan cheeks. She sat upright; she laughed at his self-deprecating remarks; she smiled and finally said, "Oh, Kick, this is so marvelous. Why didn't you tell me before? You mean you'll really be the big boss in two years, and if I behave myself I can join the board and get some equity and really"—she squealed with excitement—"make decisions?"

"Yes, but only if you behave and work your ass off instead of wasting your time with second-rate men, bloodsuckers who know a rich girl when they see one." He used his grandfather's term deliberately, and Fiona knew it. "The lawyers have given me the responsibility of deciding if and when any of that could happen, and, believe me"—he spoke slowly, emphatically, measuring every word—"much as I adore you, I don't want you in the company unless you show me with hard work that you mean to contribute."

Seeing her downcast expression, Kick got up and said with a slow smile, "Shall I open the Domaine Ott now?"

"Oh yes, yes. Kick." He knew that beseeching note well too, and wasn't moved by it.

"So what's the answer, Fi? Hard work or hard luck?"

"Kick, I promise I won't let you down. It's so different, working for ourselves."

"Well, that's one way to look at it."

As he poured the wine, Fiona took out her compact and applied fresh lipstick. "I look a mess," she said in a matter-of-fact voice, "but as sister of the president-elect, I promise you I'm going to do better. Why, I feel different already. There's nothing like access to power, nothing like realizing the yoke of Louise is finally on the wane. It's strange that Steven Holt would be interested in her when she's on the way out."

"Now, wait a minute. I didn't say anything about Louise leaving the company. To start with, the company needs her. Who's Holt? Is he the one who wants to write a book about Louise?" Before Fiona could answer, Kick said grimly, "I hope you're not talking to him?"

Fiona dismissed his question with a flip of her hand. "Nothing to be alarmed about. I met him at a cocktail party the other day, but everyone warned me he's dangerous." She shot Kick a mischievous look. "Good looking, though . . ."

"Fiona!"

"No, listen, darling, dearest brother . . ." Fiona crossed her legs coyly.

"Now, I have something to tell you, something that may surprise you. Did you know that K. Avery once and maybe even twice made Louise an offer that most people would have found impossible to refuse, a multi-multi-million-dollar offer?"

"A takeover?"

"Precisely," said Fiona in a crisp, businesslike voice. "Uncle Charles found out somehow, and when he asked Jan Feiner if it was true, he admitted it was, and what's more"—she paused for dramatic effect— "Uncle C. says Feiner is still interested, that he thinks marrying one of the most important prestige names in the cosmetics world with their incredibly successful mass-market Natasha business would be the most perfect match, both supported by their dynamite Swiss pharmaceutical R-and-D expertise. Makes sense to me, but why didn't Louise accept in the past?"

"Because she couldn't, because Granddad wanted the company to remain in Towers hands. That's why he left it in trust for me, for us."

"Yeah, I suppose you're right. Boy, how mad she must have been to find that out."

"I don't think so. She said it was as much her idea to put me in charge as Grandpa's."

Fiona laughed sardonically, but Kick ignored her. "If this is true, though, it's great to know for the future. It would never work while Louise was still around, because of her relationship with Natasha, but working with Natasha wouldn't bother me. It's funny, Fi, but recently, because of all this, I've had the urge to call Uncle Charles for his advice. Maybe, now that you've told me this, I will see him again." Kick leaned back, toying with his wine. "Multimillions, eh? I wonder if any management contracts came with it? I wouldn't mind that kind of money with, say, a ten- or even five-year guaranteed contract to help them run their first prestige cosmetics company. It sure sounds preferable to the kind of grind I see ahead for myself now."

"Oh, Kick, do see Uncle Charles. It would be so wonderful. The Towers getting together again . . ."

"I don't want to see Natasha, though. I'm not ready for that yet, with all the lying to Louise it would involve." Kick poured out more wine. "Remember, Fi, nothing can happen for two more years. We've got to sit tight for '90 and much of '91 first. By then, who knows if some other big conglomerate might not want to buy us—to add another multi to the multi, to give Avery some competition." Kick caught a glimpse of the time. "Oh God, Fiona, I told you I've got to go out. Sorry, puss, but I'm already late."

"A date?" she asked slyly.

"You could call it that. No, I wish it was. This is what I mean about the grind. I've got to try to woo Destina to sign on for at least another two years. Louise doesn't want to try anymore."

As Fiona gave an exaggerated shudder, he said, "Okay, so he's a pain in the you-know-what, but he's also one of the most talented guys around."

"It's the only thing I agree with Louise on. I can't stand him." Fiona gave another exaggerated shudder.

"Well, you're in the minority. He not only gives us endless wonderful publicity, the customers adore him and he can sell anything he puts his mind to. Even Dougy, who loathes him, grudgingly admits he's a genius."

"So what's the problem?"

"He wants a ton of money and much more of what he calls 'freedom.' "

On the way to Destina's new Park Avenue penthouse apartment, with its famous spiral staircase leading to an enclosed, all-weather roof garden, Kick savored the feeling of what was in store for him in '91. Once he could make all the decisions, perhaps he might consider an offer for a takeover. He knew there were certain clauses in his grandfather's will about selling, but the lawyers had intimated they were not cast in iron. It appeared that once he inherited, unless his decisions were deemed reckless by the board or unnecessarily undermining to the company's future, Louise Towers would be his, as the deciding voice, to do with as he wished. It was a heady thought.

Halfway through a bottle of Cristal champagne, trying to feel relaxed as he sat uncomfortably on Destina's enormous, velvet-covered daybed, Kick wondered whether he dared take Destina into his confidence, because he was getting nowhere. The designer alternately pranced and pouted, sat in majestic, remote silence, and leaned forward to hold Kick's hand and tell him how he admired him more than anyone in the world—except possibly a celebrated Hollywood producer who was offering him "the moon and the stars and the planet Earth to move to California to work for him on his next picture, *The Wizard of Oz*."

"You see, my dear Kick Christopher Towers"—Kick loved the very correct British way Destina enunciated every syllable—"it isn't that I don't feel I am appreciated. I know the remarkable lady who is both your stepgrandmother and adoptive mama—so complicated, your American arrangements—is de-light-ed with the success of my 'D' perfume, but nothing, ab-so-lute-ly not one thing, has been discussed about the follow-up 'E' perfume! Such a ridiculous lack of momentum. Then there are these vul-gar marketing people, who know ab-so-lute-ly nothing about fashion!"

Destina poured himself a glass of sparkling water from a Bristol-green glass decanter with a silver "Perrier" bracelet around its slender neck, and, without waiting for an answer, asked him sorrowfully, "Can you blame me for my frustration, dear Kick?"

He could not. On the contrary, he had to agree with everything Destina said. There wasn't one criticism that wasn't valid. Now, with his newly acquired knowledge about his future, Kick wanted to go back to the office and summon his secretary immediately to dictate crucial memos, right, left, and center, instructing marketing to tie Destina's fashion and beauty commitments together. Why hadn't it been done? Why hadn't Destina received the staff he'd been requesting for months?

After listening to him for the past hour, Kick realized it wasn't only the renewal of Destina's contract that had to be discussed, it was treating him in the way he should be treated, as an invaluable star.

As Kick, slowly becoming fuzzy-headed, vowed to call an emergency meeting, whether Louise liked it or not, a beautiful—it was the only word—black boy glided in with, first, a bowl of delicious-looking caviar and a plate of wafer-thin toast, exiting to return seconds later with a silver bowl heaped with what looked like the finest white talcum powder and an elaborate oriental stand holding several delicate spoons.

Destina smiled what Louise called his Marquis de Sade smile as he watched Kick look at the black boy as he sauntered out. "Good looking, isn't he? He's my latest houseboy, John-o—he wants to be a model. I might use him on the Coast."

"On the Coast?" Kick repeated plaintively. "I thought you told me you hadn't made a decision yet. That's why I came over to talk you into staying with us."

Destina leaned forward to pick up one of the exquisitely carved spoons and scoop some of the powder onto his wrist. "The moon and the stars . . ." He seemed to be talking to himself. He turned winsomely to Kick. "What is your pleasure, my friend? Pearls from the Caspian, or drops of pure snow from the Sargasso Sea?"

Snow? So the office gossip was true. Destina was into cocaine. Kick wasn't shocked. If anything, he was impressed that Destina obviously could handle it without its affecting his work.

He watched as Destina brought his hand to his nose to inhale deeply, closing his eyes, then opening them to fix them, dark, brilliant, on him. For a moment Kick was tempted. It would do no harm; he was sure it would be exciting, but, but . . . he was too anxious about his mission to get Destina to renew his contract on terms that Louise would accept.

As Destina scooped more of the powder onto his wrist and offered it to him, Kick shook his head. "Another time. Not tonight. How can I relax when you're talking about leaving us?"

"But I have received an offer, how do you say, that I really cannot refuse." This time Destina sang the words softly: "The moon, the stars, the planet Earth . . ."

It was the second time in a few hours Kick had heard the phrase "impossible to refuse." "Wait, Destina," he said impulsively, "please wait before you make up your mind. I can't tell you everything tonight, but if you agree to Louise's terms and sign a new contract now for another two years, I promise you will not regret it. I am prepared to give you a written guarantee that in two years I will be in a position to meet any offer you receive, moon, stars, Earth . . ." As he spoke, he realized with a foggy pang just how much he would miss Destina. He brought glamour and excitement into his life, and he was only just beginning to know him on a personal level. He couldn't bear the idea of letting him go.

Rain began to beat against the penthouse windows. Destina got up languidly to close heavy magenta curtains, shutting out the weather. He stood facing Kick with his arms crossed, proud, arrogant. "I don't know what you mean. Please explain."

"I can't, you must just trust me."

Destina stared at him as if he were a stranger. "Why should I?" Before Kick could answer, Destina was back beside him on the daybed. He stroked his shoulder. Kick wanted to draw back, but was afraid of offending him. "Trust me," he said again, weakly.

Destina continued to stroke him with a stronger and stronger hand. Finally he brought his mouth so close to Kick's ear. His breath tickled as he whispered, "I will let you know in the morning."

"Where's Destina?" Louise asked, although she already knew the answer. She wanted Kick to realize how irresponsible Destina had become, and how impossibly difficult to work with.

Why was Kick blushing? Louise's uneasiness grew as she saw him look around the conference table, as if expecting to find Destina sitting there. Was it because he knew the answer? Or was he embarrassed at Destina's absence, knowing, as everyone else there knew, that this was a "must attend" meeting to discuss the all-important twenty-fifth anniversary of the first Tower of Health and Beauty Spa?

Louise looked directly at Dougy, knowing he would be delighted to tell the senior group around the table what he had phoned to tell her earlier that morning.

"He was called away"—Dougy pursed his mouth derisively—"on affairs of state."

"Affairs of state?" Kick looked both hurt and bewildered. Louise was relieved. He obviously didn't know. "What does that mean?"

"Well," said Dougy, with a self-satisfied smirk, "I happen to know, although Mr. Destina didn't think he needed to explain himself. He's gone to help Hollywood prepare for a royal visit." Dougy raised his eyebrows. "Minor royalty, actually, but I happen to know, from my own contacts in La-la Land, that Mr. Destina is transforming a rather unattractive mansion in Beverly Hills into Oz."

Kick looked as if someone had punched him in the solar plexus. Dee Possant snarled, "Oz? What the hell does that mean?"

Louise rapped on the table once. It was all that was needed for everyone to pay attention. "I think it means Mr. Destina is not interested in our twenty-fifth anniversary, but that is why we are all here. Now, Dee, let me hear your plans for the store and institute tie-ins . . ."

The meeting lasted the rest of the afternoon, with no more mention of Destina's flagrant nonappearance. Only Kick made little contribution. Most of the time his thoughts were three thousand miles away. He had rarely felt so miserable, so betrayed. Although he'd extricated himself clumsily from Destina's embrace, he'd been sure that Destina liked him—a lot—and that their business relationship was now going to be strengthened by a personal friendship, yet all the time Destina must have known he wouldn't be at the all-important meeting, that he'd be flying out to do a favor for the Oz man, the moon, stars, and planet Earth producer.

If Destina didn't return anytime soon, should he follow him to the West Coast to see what it was he liked so much about Hollywood? After all, he could scarcely lose his job now. He was only treading water until 1991.

Kick caught Louise's eyes on him, watchful, critical. When, as usual, Louise cursorily dismissed the idea of unveiling a surprise celebrity or top model as a new face and spokesperson for the company at the anniversary celebrations, he spoke up with new-found authority. "I think you're making a mistake, Louise."

He was surprised at the firmness in his voice, and so, he could see, were the others around the table. No one answered Louise that way, least of all he, although he had been careful to use a respectful tone.

"It isn't a question of the importance of Lyric Masters to Natasha products or Isabella Rossellini to Lancôme. Top models are becoming the country's superstars. Today's young consumers are copying them, just as their mothers copied movie stars. To attract that young audience, we should seriously consider finding a superstar model for ourselves." He knew he was parroting Destina, even using the same words he'd heard him use, but then he agreed with him totally. They should find a new face, and if Louise didn't like it . . . well . . . In his depression he remembered what Fiona had told him the night before about K. Avery's offer to buy the company.

Louise answered smoothly. "I hear what you're saying, Kick. I just don't happen to agree with you. Women have never bought our products because a famous face says she uses them—although many famous faces have and do. We don't need that kind of secondhand patronage. Our authority in beauty has been built on the rock of performance, of visible results." To Kick's irritation, Louise showed the subject was closed by turning to Owen Rhylls, their new head of fragrance, lured away from Revlon. "Mr. Rhylls, we need a new fragrance for the anniversary."

Elation replaced his irritation. So there was going to be an "E" fragrance at last, the perfect peace offering to give Destina, the perfect reason for him to stay with the company, but Louise's next words horrified him. "Mr. Rhylls came to us with the promise of something extraordinary. He has been working with a new kind of essential oil, from the living flower." She smiled around the table. "You all know Louise Towers's business took off like a rocket with the introduction of Revelation, its first perfume. This will be Revelation number two—an intoxicating new kind of scent for our special celebration. Please, all of you, start thinking now of an appropriate name."

Just as Kick was about to ask, Dougy Faseff jumped in to confirm his worst fears. "So this is not to be the 'E' addition to Destina's fragrance collection?" He was laughing as he spoke.

Expressionless, Louise said, "No, I think we will allow Mr. Destina the pleasure of developing that for himself."

Kristina heard the news as, with thousands of other people, she was swept into Jungmannova Square. "Husak's out . . . Husak's resigned . . . Husak's disgraced . . . we're free . . . we're free . . . at last . . . at last!"

Holding tight to the hand of her best friend, Radka, Kristina sang with the rest of the crowd, lightheaded, drunk with happiness, oblivious of the light snow swirls decorating her hair like sparkling jewels. She'd been out with the crowds every day for more than three weeks, demonstrating, joining the general strike, blocking the streets as part of the human barricade, forcing first Milos Jakes, the hard-line Communist head of the Politburo, to resign, and now this, Husak out! If it was true—and Kristina was sure it had to be—it meant that with the advent of Gorbachev and *perestroika*, Papa had been right to be optimistic.

"Russian tanks will never again roll in to keep us down as they did in 1968," Papa had said, only this morning. It was the year Papa hated most of all, the year Natasha, his wife, her mother, had left them behind, and Husak had replaced Dubcek to rule over them with a harsher hand than anyone could remember since the Nazis.

There were tears in her eyes. There were tears in Radka's eyes, in everyone's eyes, though their mouths wore huge, wide smiles as they shouted their joy to the skies and church bells boomed, car horns screamed, and boats on the river hooted to celebrate the fact that their beloved country had at last achieved freedom, like the rest of Eastern Europe. Communist regimes had been collapsing like dominoes since the summer. It was as if a wicked witch had at last lifted her curse, thought Kristina.

Now she was marching in a line thirty, forty—who knew how many—abreast, moving toward Wenceslas Square, where a new song was being sung, "Havel . . . Havel . . . Havel . . ." Their gallant, gentle hero.

Kristina didn't get home for hours, and when she did her street was crowded, too, with people dancing the mazurka and beer and cigarettes being passed around as if it were Christmas, still two weeks away. Even her father was talking animatedly outside the house, not using his crutches or even holding on to anybody. As she rushed into the front hall, she almost collided with her grandmother coming out, a bright spot of color on both cheeks. "Oh, Kristina, Kristina . . ." she began to sob. "You have just missed your mother . . . no, no, I am sorry, I mean your Aunt Ludmilla . . . I mean Louise. She's coming home . . . she's coming home on the first plane that can get her here . . ."

But Louise didn't fly into Prague. She decided she had to arrive slowly, to drive with a Czech driver or someone who knew the country, to absorb the sights and sounds, to soak up her old country, to cushion the pain she expected to feel after an absence of over forty years. Was it going to be bearable? She didn't know. She only knew that since seeing on television what the American press was calling Czechoslovakia's "velvet revolution," nothing had mattered except returning home. She hadn't cared about Kick's petulance concerning her adamant stand on Destina; she hadn't even been upset by the news that Kick had gone to visit Destina for a weekend in Malibu, or by Fiona's arrogance and impertinence, suggesting she buy both of them out!

Nothing had mattered except to be reunited with her mother and

391 MY SISTER'S KEEPER

to persuade her to come back with her to America, so she could look
after her for the rest of her life. And if Pieter and Kristina wanted to
come, that was fine, too. She had no hidden agenda, she told herself.
This had nothing to do with trying to embarrass Natasha and Charles.
At last she felt she had gone far beyond all that.

As it was, it took until the first week of the new year before she was
able to cross the border into Czechoslovakia. There was a photograph
of Vaclav Havel above the immigration officer's door, but otherwise
nothing seemed to have changed since the day she would never forget
in 1968, when she'd waited in the rain for Natasha at the Austrian
frontier. The officials were still unsmiling and suspicious, and they
carried conspicuous guns. She was obviously expected, but one acne-
faced young soldier opened two of her bags, picking up, shaking, then
taking his time to return the gaily packaged parcels inside.

On the road to Prague, Louise froze as a long convoy of Russian
army vehicles, moving with tortoiselike slowness, forced her car over
to the side. The convoy took more than thirty minutes to pass.

"On their way back home to Lithuania or Azerbaijan, after twenty
years away," her driver told her. "A small fraction of the five Soviet
divisions 'guarding' Czechoslovakia for its own safety," he added
sarcastically.

Through the low, frost-covered hills they picked up speed, she looking for signs of her childhood as they crossed the Bohemian plateau,
where once she'd watched hops being picked for the original Pilsner
beer, Plzen; on through icy villages of granite cottages and pastel-
colored churches, until, waking from a doze, she recognized that they
were driving down one of the steep hills on the outskirts of Prague.

"Stop," she said in the center of the city. A thin sun was trying to
break through the clouds; the people looked cold, but the streets were
packed, the pavement cafés full. She wanted to sit in a café for a while,
to feel part of the crowd. "Sit with me," she said to the driver. He
understood.

There were surprising sights. Among the scurrying, drably dressed
housewives and overcoated businessmen were boy and girl punks with
their hair on end, rings through noses and ears, wearing the national
colors—red, white, and blue—in tie-dyed T-shirts and scraggly-looking
scarves. A group of Hare Krishna devotees passed by singing and
shivering in their saffron colored robes, followed by a tall, bald
man goose-stepping in military fatigues, with a stuffed goose strapped
to his back.

Louise looked questioningly at the driver, as people at tables around
them stood up and cheered.

"He cost the Czech people twenty-one lost years," the driver explained. "*Husa*, the Czech word for 'goose,' is the root of the name of the disgraced, just-displaced President Husak."

Louise stayed in the café, watching the passersby for almost an hour, then it was time to cross the river, to go home.

Had the house always been so small? She was so nervous that at first she thought she'd come to the wrong street. As she hesitated to knock on the splintered door, its paint almost peeled away, the wind blew it open. A familiar smell, a mixture of hair solutions, dyes, and meat cooking on a spit, overwhelmed her with grief. Tears poured down her face. She was once again the girl who had left this poor hovel as Milos's new wife, to join him in a new life in America.

In seconds, flying down the stairs, impossibly long legs in a micro-miniskirt, came a beautiful young girl with high, exotic cheekbones, large, almond-colored eyes, and red hair cascading around her shoulders. She was crying and laughing and shouting in Czech, "Oh, Aunty Ludmilla, Aunt Louise Towers, it is I, Kristina." At that exact moment Louise knew that Louise Towers, Incorporated, would have a new face after all—and who it was going to be.

"I'm sorry I'm late, Charles." Jan Feiner was only five minutes late for their now-regular lunch meeting, held every two months or so at The Four Seasons, but Charles knew how being unpunctual disturbed him. He only wished the rest of the world were the same. Especially Natasha, who was incapable of being on time for anything. He thought Feiner looked terrible.

"Problems?" Charles asked sympathetically, not expecting to learn what they were. The two men got on well, but they were not intimate friends and never would be.

To his surprise, Jan said immediately, "Yes, but not, for once, about AC3. My brother—he's not too well. He's been overworking but refuses to accept it. Well now, what shall we eat?"

The food at The Four Seasons was recognized as among the best in the country, but in common with other top businesspeople in the grill room, they ordered only one light course, grilled fish, with their Perriers. In thirty minutes Charles gave Jan an efficient update on their cash flow, their new accounts, and the overall climate in the cosmetics industry, in both "mass and class" as he described it. The last thirty minutes of their usual hour-long lunch was when Jan spearheaded new ideas and gave Charles anything he felt he ought to know about Averbach's reactions to the cosmetics business in general, and Natasha in particular.

Today, however, before Jan began to speak, Charles stuttered awkwardly, "Jan, er, I thought I ought to tell you . . . my sister's children, my niece and nephew, Kick and Fiona Towers—you know they lost their parents in an airplane crash some years ago—well, I haven't . . . since I left my father's company, for family reasons I haven't seen much of Kick, but for the sake of my sister, I've always tried to stay in touch with my niece . . ."

"What are you trying to tell me, Charles?" Jan sounded weary. The mention of the Towers name, following another outburst from Victor that morning, depressed him.

Charles cleared his throat. "They both asked to see me while . . . while Louise was away, seeing her family in Prague. They knew of your—of K. Avery's—onetime interest in Louise Towers."

"Yes, so?" Jan's tone was unencouraging, terse.

"It appears that my father did not, as everyone assumes, leave Louise Towers to Lou—to my stepmother. The controlling interest was left in trust for Kick to inherit on his thirtieth birthday, provided certain conditions were met, with some equity going to his sister and cousin." Charles looked embarrassed, but when Jan didn't speak, he went on, "I must say I was surprised to learn this. Kick told me it was also Louise's idea, but that strikes me as unlikely. It would, I think, have been natural for her to assume . . . er . . . in view of all she has done for the company, to expect that the company would be left to her."

I should say so, Jan thought grimly.

"In any case, the reason they came to see me was to . . . to test the waters to see if I could ascertain whether there might still be any interest in Avery acquiring Louise Towers. Kick read in the *Wall Street Journal* the other day the piece about Averbach still looking to acquire something in the prestige area." As Jan remained silent, Charles began to sound defensive. "Now that Unilever is so involved and Procter & Gamble is about to become a serious player, it was a natural question."

Jan's mind was whirling. No wonder Louise had dismissed his offer summarily; no wonder she had been so upset that day in this same restaurant. He didn't believe for one moment that it had also been Louise's wish to leave the company to the Towers children. How could it have been, when neither of the children had contributed anything to Louise Towers? It was ludicrous. He looked coolly at Charles, remembering the threats he'd received years before from Benedict Towers's strong-arm lawyers after his first proposal to Louise. So his assessment of her life had been right all along; she was and always had been a bird trapped in a golden cage—a golden Tower. What a monster Benedict Towers had been.

"And if there is still interest, what do these innovative Towers children have in mind?" Jan's tone was light, but he was seething. Despicable traitors, he thought, waiting until Louise was out of the country to approach her known enemy.

Charles laughed uneasily. "Well, I don't know. It appears they are restless. Kick is twenty-eight, so he can't take over for another two years, and they both feel there are certain things that need to be done in the company now, things I gather Louise is opposed to." The expression on Charles's face, as he mentioned Louise's name, told Jan all he needed to know about Charles's feelings toward her. Oh, Louise, my poor, isolated Louise-Ludmilla, he thought. Despite the money, the power, what a life you must have lived in the clutches of this dreadful family.

Charles fidgeted with his napkin. "Fiona, my niece, she's always been headstrong—like Suzanne, my sister. The kids were only about ten or eleven when she was killed with her husband."

"Yes, I remember."

"Fiona told me she'd suggested to Louise recently that she should consider selling out while there was still interest—to have an easier life, with all the increased competition, to take advantage of an offer they would both agree to."

"That must have gone down well." Jan lifted his eyebrows sardonically.

"You're right, but you don't know Fiona. When Louise dismissed her arbitrarily, Fiona pressed on, saying that if Louise was determined to remain in charge for the next two years, she should buy them out now, or they could make life difficult for her!"

"What?" Jan was outraged. What a viper the girl had to be.

"Well, I see the kids' point of view in a way," Charles said, ignoring the scornful expression on Jan's face. "When Kick inherits the company in a couple of years, there's nothing to stop him from kicking Louise out." When Jan scowled, he continued firmly, "I don't think he would, and of course there are the old board members to consider . . ."

"Whom Kick Towers could also dismiss with the help of new members of the board, his sister, and, you say, his cousin?"

"Well, yes, but again I am sure he wouldn't do that, if only for the sake of public relations. The point is, although it would put an intolerable strain on the company, if Louise wants to remain in charge with no opposition for the next two years, it is one option open to her."

"To buy them, the Towers children, out?" Jan couldn't believe what he was hearing. His estimation of Charles plummeted. "Could Louise, Mrs. Towers, afford it without incurring a huge debt? A debt at a time like this? Are you serious?"

Charles saw the look on Jan's face. He backtracked, but not much. "No, it would be foolish. Louise would never do it anyway, but she's got to face the fact that my father made this decision for the future of Louise Towers, a future where young members of the Towers family will be in charge. If there is still interest on K. Avery's part, I believe all Kick and Fiona were saying was that the deal should be made now, when there could be a contract in it for Louise, and they would not stand in the way."

"How very thoughtful," Jan murmured. He sometimes thought the Swiss were manipulative and oppressive, but in comparison to the Towers family, they were in the kindergarten class.

It was time for him to be manipulative, too. "So you get the impression that in two years Kick Towers will be open to an offer?"

"I get that impression, but I should tell you that Kick implied there may be obstacles in Benedict's will to prevent a sale to a competitor. He was not willing to look further into the matter until he knew for sure whether or not K. Avery still had an interest. The lawyers have told him they feel that once he is in charge, decisions can be made that cannot be made now. You can understand why."

Yes, I certainly can, Jan thought to himself. Oh, my poor Louise. "Let me think about it, Charles. Thank you for bringing it to my attention." He knew he would never feel the same again about Charles Towers.

On his return to the office, Jan called in Frank Gelb, his chief financial officer, who in the past had proved to be a good sleuth. "Find out all you can about the financial health of Louise Towers, the staff situation, et cetera. Let me have a report in a week—they may be a possible acquisition after all—and, Frank, keep this to yourself, just between you and me, eh?"

Unfortunately, Laurie Brockman, Frank Gelb's secretary, shared a fourth-floor walk-up apartment in the city with Amy Hitchcock, Victor Feiner's secretary. Laurie assumed that as usual the brother of the president knew everything going on in the company. The two secretaries enjoyed their privileged positions; work was the only interest they shared, and their jobs were the only interesting aspect of their lives.

The following Monday, as Amy poured Victor his second cup of coffee, she remarked innocently how cold her roommate had found the offices over the weekend, where she'd had to spend several hours typing up all the Louise Towers information.

Victor almost choked. "What information?"

"Oh, the report Mr. Jan has asked for—in case the company is for sale."

Amy shook her head as Victor jumped up and raced out, headed toward his brother's office, but Jan had left that morning for California. That night, refusing to take the tranquilizer his doctor had prescribed, Victor stayed up, trying to compose a letter of resignation, if Jan was in any way serious about proposing to buy Louise Towers. Elise, much as she agreed with her husband about Louise's evil nature, tried to dissuade him. "Why should we be the ones to suffer because of that woman?"

Finally, Victor threw down his pen. "You're right. It's no good. If I leave the company, there will be no one left to protect Jan." He threw his arms in the air. "But I have to do something. I have to find a way to keep that woman out of our lives forever. Oh God, please tell me what to do!"

New York, 1990

"THE BEST WAY to explain it is that I was never in love with my husband."

Penelope Davidson gulped with shock. Had she really heard Louise Towers say that? Did Louise realize what she had just said? Penelope hardly dared move, in case Louise should stop talking. What a tragedy it was that all this wonderful copy was going into her paper's obituary file.

After three months of taping Louise, Penelope was as much in awe of her as ever, perhaps more so. Louise was her godmother, the best friend of her own grandmother; they had spent vacations together; she'd even been one of the few people in the world to see Louise Towers without makeup—and she still looked incredibly beautiful! Nevertheless, despite all she had learned, every time they sat down to work together, Penny was overcome with a mixture of shyness and respect that inhibited her ability to respond.

"There is another kind of love, one that is vested in respect, admiration. He taught me everything ..." It was not surprising, Penny thought, that after admitting she had not really been in love with her late husband, Benedict Towers, Louise was now paying him a series of compliments to soften the shock.

"We were really exceptionally happy together, despite the difference in our ages ..." Louise paused, noting how Penny was hanging on every word. As she finished the sentence, "... despite the jealousy of his children," she saw Penelope push the tape recorder a little closer to her.

These sessions were very tiring, yet in another way they were cleansing. She was surprised that Penelope never questioned her about why she was telling her so much—much more than she had expected to get for the obituary file. Soon, very soon, she would give Penny the answer to the question she had never asked.

To scuttle Holt's book—which, so far, her PR people had told her, wasn't getting very far despite a suspicion that Fiona was talking to him—Louise had decided to write her own. As Penny sat there recording facts for her obituary, Louise was simultaneously recording herself, later listening to the tapes to trigger her memory, to decide what and what not to use.

She already had dozens of pages of extensive notes, and she had decided only in the last few days that Penny was so capable, she would give her the opportunity of a lifetime, to write the book she wanted written, one that would tell the truth about her life.

When Anne Marie came in to take away the coffee tray, Louise made another date to see Penny just before the anniversary gala, and then went up to her bedroom, followed by Powder Blue.

Every month so far in 1990 had taken an enormous toll. First there had been the emotional trauma of her reunion with her mother, then the ugly scenes with Pieter Mahler over Kristina's future. Knowing he could do nothing for his daughter, Mahler had nevertheless tried every inch of the way to block Kristina's path to a bright and, Louise was sure, very successful future.

"You stole away my wife. Now you want my daughter. Go away! Keep away! We don't need you, wicked woman!" But they *did* need her. It wasn't as if she hadn't offered him everything she'd offered Kristina: first-class travel to America, a new home, the best medical care. But just as her mother had dug her heels in and said now that her beloved country was free, she could never leave—and in any case she was much too old—so had Pieter, until Kristina had made up her own mind and turned up one day at the hotel in Prague with a small, battered suitcase, a passport, and a brave, enchanting smile.

As Anne Marie brushed her long, dark hair, Louise smiled at herself in the mirror, wrinkling her nose. It made her look a little bit like Kristina. What a wonderful day it was going to be when Kristina Mahler, her own flesh and blood, was unveiled as the New Face of Louise Towers. Louise knew Kristina regarded her as her mother, and she *should* have been her mother. Kristina had even volunteered that she didn't want to see Natasha, had no interest in even talking to her, and totally understood why, in order to make her appearance at the gala more meaningful, it was important to keep her arrival in the States secret until the day. The girl had a natural sense of theater.

If only her complaining father had kept to his original intention and not followed Kristina over. But Pieter Mahler had turned up a few days ago, using the ticket Louise had left behind for him, to ease her conscience, in case he changed his mind.

It had been one more problem for Louise Towers personnel to deal with, while she personally demanded that in exchange for his generous allowance, his U.S. sightseeing, and general looking after, he lay low until the gala anniversary, and did not contact Natasha, "the competition." What he did about Natasha after the anniversary, Louise didn't care. That was his problem—and Natasha's.

It was too bad that after only forty-eight hours, marketing had reported that Pieter's influence on his daughter Kristina was so unsettling that she was very unhappy. It would be in everyone's interest, marketing suggested, if Kristina didn't see her father until the gala anniversary. Of course, Louise had concurred entirely.

He had threatened and screamed at her yesterday when he couldn't find Kristina. Little did he know how many threats and screams she'd lived through in her lifetime. Oh, well, it wouldn't be long now, and then Mr. Mahler could make up his own mind what he wanted to do— hopefully to return to Prague and let his daughter live her own life.

Louise was humming as she slipped between the cool sheets and Anne Marie propped up the giant pillows so she could easily work on her notes and tapes in bed. She was humming "The Skater's Waltz" because only a few months ago she'd found her old music box and discovered she could play it without crying.

When Anne Marie left, Louise locked the door and, with Powder Blue curled up beside her, replayed the tape of the day's conversation with Penelope. Awkward though the girl was with her body language, Penelope's questions were first class, prodding her memory, leading her to articulate things she'd always felt but never clarified in her mind. "... and the jealousy of his children."

She frowned as the phone rang. After his last call about the anniversary plans, she had already told Banks not to interrupt her again unless absolutely necessary. "It's Mr. Feiner, ma'am. Mr. Jan Feiner."

She smiled. Dear Jan, what a real friend he had turned out to be, but she didn't feel up to discussing business or anything to do with what he had already told her about her stepchildren's avaricious plot to sell the company behind her back. "Tell Mr. Feiner I am not available now, but I am looking forward to meeting him tomorrow for dinner as he requested. Banks, please don't disturb me again unless it's an emergency. Thank you."

Jealousy . . . she'd just heard her voice on the tape talk about Benedict's children's jealousy. It had certainly been true of Suzanne, but then, who could blame her? It must have seemed inconceivable that her father could think of marrying someone who had not only been their servant, but who was only a couple of years older than she herself.

As for Charles, her feelings were still mixed up as far as he was concerned; perhaps they always would be. He had shown her in the most humiliating way that he felt nothing for her, though he must have realized, on that terrible night in his office, that he aroused her sexually to a point of near madness. For that, she was sure, Benedict had exacted his revenge by leaving the company she'd built to Kick.

Money and sex, sex and money—they were the two things in life that moved mountains, caused tragedies, toppled kings and kingdoms. She wasn't even angry as she would have been once over Kick's disloyalty. Saddened and disappointed, yes; frightened, yes; but she was too worried about him to be angry. What could she do to open Kick's eyes to the useless, feckless life in Destina's fast and dangerous lane, dominated, she knew for sure now, by drugs?

She didn't need to be told that Destina was her sworn enemy. She'd heard it from everybody after she hadn't renewed his contract. She'd heard it directly from him the day after she'd read in *Women's Wear Daily* that Destina hadn't been given the Oz designing job after all, that Hollywood hadn't opened its arms to him, either. He was searching around for work, desperate for money for a drug habit that was no longer such a guarded secret. There was gossip on Seventh Avenue, Dougy had told her, that he was in the clutches of drug dealers, up to his neck in debt. She shivered as she remembered Destina's voice over the phone, cajoling and lighthearted at first, quickly becoming bitter and impertinent when she'd told him she couldn't see any point in setting up a meeting.

Only Kick was too naive to see through him. Kick wanted money and power now, and didn't want to wait until he took over the company the following year, because of promises he'd made to the designer. Dougy had told her Kick had loaned Destina money in the hope that he'd return to Louise Towers when Kick became boss.

Kick was weak, easily led, and Louise blamed Fiona for urging him on. She could hear her now: "Phillips says the will directs that if Louise Towers is to be sold, it must be offered to a member of the family first!" So, with Kick's permission, this little, spoiled good-for-nothing had had the audacity to "offer" her the company she had built every step of the way, the company that bore her name—"offered" it to her to buy from them, the almighty Towers children. Or agree to a proposal from K. Avery.

Louise leaned back against the pillows. She would never forgive Benedict. Never! She would reveal his betrayal in her book; it would be a warning to every woman never to put her trust in a man, particularly a powerful man.

Powder Blue sat upright, tense, alert. With the tape still playing, Louise stroked his elegant back. "What is it, P.B.?"

She heard something. Steps on the stairs . . . strange steps. She sat forward, listening. "Anne Marie? What is it? Anne Marie, is that you?"

Someone tried to open the locked door. A man's voice threatened, "Open the door or we'll kill your bitch of a maid."

"Is it true, Anne Marie? Are you in danger?"

Even as her maid sobbed and screamed that there was a gun at her head, Louise heard a gunshot, but the maid continued to scream. She was icy cold; it was as if it was happening to another person . . . another person being threatened by . . . by whom? Both Helena Rubinstein and Estée Lauder had had their homes invaded and their lives threatened by dangerous, desperate men, thieves who'd had no motive but greed. Who was outside, waiting to harm her?

There were names in her head from the notes she had just read, names who had motives. Pieter Mahler, accustomed to violence, desperate to take Kristina back to Czechoslovakia, away from her. Destina, consumed with hate and crazy for money to sustain his drug habit. Victor Feiner, who had threatened revenge for ruining his brother. And the name on the tape that was still playing . . . Natasha. Natasha! Humiliated by her for twenty years. Did Natasha know, after all, that her daughter was soon going to provide her with the greatest humiliation of all?

Louise tried to set off the alarm. It was dead. The door was about to be forced. She walked to unlock it. She suddenly realized she deserved to die.

New York, 1991

THE WORLD WAS still, the kind of stillness that follows a great hurricane, when people tiptoe and move their bodies slowly, in case they might cause another breath of wind. My eyes were heavy, but then I think I had been crying for a long time. I hoped they were not red.

As I dared to try to open them, I was rewarded by the most heavenly sight, my family surrounding me like a mirage. It had to be a mirage because my mother was there, her cheeks wet with tears as they usually were. And beside her? Pieter. I could recognize Pieter Mahler with his daughter, Kristina, and . . . Natasha! I wanted to cry again, but there were no tears left. "Natasha . . ." I know I spoke her name loudly, with confidence, to show her that all along I had wanted to be her sister, but the sound came out as a whisper.

"Ludmilla! Ludmilla! Thank God, thank you, God, Aunty Ludmilla, Louise, Louise." My mother and sister and niece were speaking in Czech but saying the same thing.

"What has . . . has . . . been happening?"

And other members of my mirage came nearer, Charles and Kick and even Fiona, looking pale, sad, lost. It was Fiona who said, "You have been very ill . . . in a coma for months . . ." She was always the one who wanted to be first, to lead the way, the outspoken one. Perhaps it was meant to be; perhaps she, and not Kick, would be the one to lead. I didn't know exactly what it meant, but it meant something.

"A coma?" I tried to move my hand to brush away one more annoying tear, but I couldn't; it was as heavy as lead. It was attached, as Benedict's hand had been, to hospital paraphernalia.

"Am I going to die?" I didn't fear the answer because part of me thought I was dead, especially seeing all these people together around what I supposed was a hospital bed, people who hadn't been together in years and years, people who were my family.

"No, dear Louise, thank God, now at last we know you are going to live and be well and we are going to show you how much we . . . we love . . ." Kick was choking up. I couldn't believe it. "I'm so sorry, Louise, so sorry. Will you ever forgive me?"

I couldn't understand what I had to forgive him for, but I loved him and so I again tried to say with strength, "I always forgive you for everything, but what . . . is this forgiveness for?"

I was very tired, now but now I understood what he was telling me.

"Destina . . . for what he tried to do to you . . . you were right all along. I am so ashamed," Kick was saying.

"Destina!" I must have shown fear as I remembered the man in the mask—and a terrible, agonizing pain.

"Yes, Destina!" Again it was Fiona who answered. "I always told Kick never to trust him. Destina thought it would be a breeze to rob you on the afternoon when most of the staff were off and you were always known to go to the Bridge Club. He planned it and sent in two of his charming thug friends." Her voice was a mixture of loathing and excitement.

"Have they been caught?"

I didn't really care what the answer was; all I now wanted was to close my eyes again, but I knew I couldn't, because the family was depending on me to still stay awake, to show I was really still alive.

Exhausted though I was, I recognized that Fiona was in her element as the family spokesperson. "Oh yes, they've been caught, all right. Once the news hit the papers—the coverage has been incredible, nonstop worldwide—and the company announced a huge reward for any information, there were squealers coming out of the woodwork, longing to put Destina where he's always belonged as far as I'm concerned, behind bars. He's in jail now; he can't find anyone to put up the bail money."

A nurse was beside my bed, a nurse with a stern expression. "You have to leave now," she was saying to my family.

"Tomorrow, please tomorrow . . ." She was a pretty but very brisk nurse. When I grow stronger, I would like a more gentle nurse.

All the same, she reassured me, "Yes, of course, they can come back tomorrow."

Another memory from the terrible day came back. "Powder Blue?"

Kick and Fiona exchanged sorrowful glances, and I knew my memory was correct. "Murdered?"

They nodded, all of them, and again I remembered, before the world went black, the blood, blood from Powder Blue on the white sheet.

"Tomorrow ... we love you ... see you soon ... thank God ... thank God." A small burst of happiness warmed my body as I saw Kick hold Kristina's hand as they left the room. He was going to be all right. From somewhere I heard a sardonic voice say "The Czech invasion." Suzanne's voice.

When the room was empty I closed my eyes. The world was gone. I was alone, stricken with a terrible sense of loneliness and failure. Someone had come in. I didn't want to open my eyes, but the brisk nurse was saying she had to give me a pill. She cranked up the bed.

I opened my eyes, surprised to find it was already easier to do so. The nurse was standing on my right, with a paper cup and a pill. Something caught my eye on the high hospital bedside table. It was familiar, something wonderfully familiar. "Please .. ." I gestured toward it, and the nurse put down the paper cup and the pill and gave it to me.

It was a small bottle. I recognized it immediately—Revelation, in its original 1953 packaging. "Where ... how did this get here?"

"A very concerned gentleman left it with a get-well-soon message. Recently he has been coming to the hospital every day. Would you like to see him tomorrow?"

The pretty nurse was smiling as if she could read my mind. Perhaps she could. Jan.

"Yes," I shouted with confidence that came out in a whisper. At last I had a revelation of my own.